More Praise for *The Walls of Jericho*!

"Unexpected plot twists make *The Walls of Jericho* quite a read."

—*The Detroit Free Press*

"Jon Land has clearly landed amidst the top writers of political thrillers. *The Walls of Jericho* do not tumble because this fast-paced novel is as tense as they come, especially when compared with all the real incidents deterring peace efforts. The lead protagonists are charming as they represent the best from both cultures, and the support cast adds Middle East flavor to a great novel."

—*The Midwest Book Review*

"Land has managed, in *Jericho*, to get the feel of the land, of the hot and dusty alleyways of the current capital of the Palestinian entity, and to create believable Israelis and Arabs. . . . There are enough unexpected twists in the plot, which I will not give away here, to keep you turning pages until its finale."

—*The Jewish Voice*

"With intriguing characters, timely backdrop, and short, action-packed chapters, Land delivers more than just your average thriller. Fast, exciting, and even more important, believable, this is recommended for most collections."

—*Library Journal*

"Land's diabolically clever thriller is packed with emotion and suspense, offering larger-than-life heroes and a nightmarish glimpse of life in today's conflict-ridden Middle East. A highly entertaining thriller."

—*Booklist*

"Land obviously did his homework for *The Walls of Jericho* . . . it's like taking a peek behind the headlines. *The Walls of Jericho* is tightly written and the characters well-drawn. . . . Better make room on the bookshelf for this hard-hitting, well-written novel of intrigue and mystery. . . . A very good read."

—*The Daily Breeze*, Cape Coral, Florida

JON LAND

THE WALLS
OF JERICHO

TOR®

A TOM DOHERTY ASSOCIATES BOOK
NEW YORK

This is a work of fiction. All the characters and events portrayed in this book are either products of the author's imagination or are used fictitiously.

THE WALLS OF JERICHO

Copyright © 1997 by Jon Land

All rights reserved, including the right to reproduce this book, or portions thereof, in any form.

A Tor Book
Published by Tom Doherty Associates, Inc.
175 Fifth Avenue
New York, NY 10010

Tor® is a registered trademark of Tom Doherty Associates, Inc.

ISBN: 0-812-56456-1
Library of Congress Card Catalog Number: 96-27427

First edition: April 1997
First mass market edition: May 1998

Printed in the United States of America

0 9 8 7 6 5 4 3 2 1

For my teachers, grades 1–12.
Thanks for the foundation to build this
and all the others.

ACKNOWLEDGMENTS

THOSE WHO HAVE read these pages before will notice several names keep appearing. The book business, after all, is a team effort, and I am very fortunate to have a great and supportive team behind me, quarterbacked by a wondrous agent, Toni Mendez, who is backed up by the creative genius of Ann Maurer.

Natalia Aponte, my editor at Forge, and I have learned that there's no book problem so big we can't solve it over lunch. True to form, some of the best twists and turns in this one were hatched at a number of the West Side's finer establishments. Tom Doherty's entire Tor/Forge team led by Linda Quinton, Yolanda Rodriguez, and Jennifer Marcus, in fact, make publishing a personal affair rather than a distant one.

Speaking of personal, thanks along the way to resident geniuses Emery Pineo, John Signore, and Alvan Fisher, as well as Nancy and Moshe Aroche, Art and Martha Joukowsky, and David Onik.

And a final thanks to Blaine, Johnny, and Sal for taking a book off so I could write this one.

"Home is the place where, when you
 have to go there,
They have to take you in."

ROBERT FROST,
"The Death of the Hired Man"

DAY ONE

CHAPTER 1

WHAT DO YOU know about the murders, Inspector?"

Ben Kamal shifted stiffly in the chair set before the desk of Ghazi Sumaya, mayor of the ancient city of Jericho. "The same thing everyone else does," he said, still wondering what he was doing here.

"And what is that?" Sumaya asked him.

"Seven in the past year in the West Bank: three prior to the Israeli pullout, four after. The latest occurred here in Jericho ten days ago."

The mayor leaned forward, the massive desk dwarfing his small frame. "You would agree that we're facing a serial killer, then. Al-Diib, they call him."

"The Wolf . . . Because his victims have been savaged, mutilated beyond all recognition."

"The one you caught in America, they had a name for him, too, didn't they?"

"The Sandman." Ben nodded.

"Why?"

Ben lowered his gaze. "He killed entire families while they slept."

"Until you stopped him."

"Yes."

"That makes you something of an expert."

Ben raised his head again. Shafts of the early morning sun streamed through the open blinds, making him squint. Above him, a ceiling fan spun lazily, catching some of the stubborn light and splashing it across the portrait of Yasir Arafat that hung directly behind Sumaya's chair.

"I have experience, that's all," he said.

The mayor's deep-set eyes sought out Ben's compassionately. "Experience, Inspector, is exactly what we need. I spoke to President Arafat last night. He has been contacted by the Israelis. They want to assist us in the investigation."

Ben's eyes widened. "Assist us?"

"Their offer is genuine, I assure you. I've already conferred with a representative of their National Police this morning."

"Did you ask him what they have to gain?"

"Perhaps they have the same thing to lose: peace. And toward that end the Israelis want to send an officer to liaise with a Palestinian counterpart. Are you interested?"

"No, sir."

His response took the mayor off guard. "Perhaps you didn't understand my question. I was asking if you want to officially take over this investigation."

"I understood what you meant. I don't. I'm sorry."

"Perhaps it is I who should be sorry," Sumaya said, sounding genuinely hurt. "Sorry for standing behind you when everyone else was calling for your head.''

"Put me in charge of this investigation and they'll be calling for yours as well.''

"Some already are," Sumaya lamented, "more with each day.''

He rose and moved out from behind his desk. The mayor wore a suit in an olive shade only slightly lighter than Ben's green police uniform. He was a small man, but carried himself in a way that made him seem taller. Sumaya had been part of the Palestinian delegation that had forged the original Gaza-Jericho First option. He had gained a master's degree in France years before and returned to the West Bank to chronicle the times he instead found himself a part of. His dark, graying hair had begun to recede, adding to the air of authority that hung over him.

"We have a credibility problem here, Ben," he continued. "These murders have become a symbol for our inefficiency. They are giving the growing pains we are experiencing a worldwide forum that the enemies of peace are seizing upon.''

Sumaya walked to the window and drew the blinds shut, trapping the sun outside where it shone off the chiseled white stone structure of the Palestinian Authority headquarters on the outskirts of Jericho. His formal office was located downtown in Jericho's Municipal Building, but as a member of the Palestinian Council as well, he preferred using this one.

"The peace talks are scheduled to reconvene next week," the mayor explained. "Six months without dialogue and finally the new Israeli prime minister seems ready to negotiate the final stages of withdrawal from the West Bank." Sumaya tightened his stance, almost to attention. "Almost a year we've gone without an *'aamaliyya,* an operation, carried out against Israel, and to a great extent your work is the reason. You have helped teach us how to arrest our own, Inspector. Hamas is running scared. We've infiltrated their ranks, preempted their strikes, jailed their militants. So they have seized upon these murders to destroy the credibility with the people we have worked so hard at building!''

Sumaya stopped to settle himself down, but the agitation remained in his voice when he resumed. ''You understand what I'm getting at here? There can be *no peace without the support of the people,* and these murders have taken that support from us. The talks will collapse, if they ever get started now.''

''Which is where this Israeli liaison comes in.''

''Let's face facts here. The Israelis don't trust us any more than we trust them. What we have between us is a mutual nonunderstanding. Now, I have spoken to the President and we are of one mind on utilizing your skills and expertise.''

''I'm hardly the proper representative for our people, *sidi,*'' Ben offered.

''I understand your bitterness over the treatment you have received in recent weeks. The behavior of your fellow officers has been inexcusable, and I wish I could have done more to change it.''

''But I'll need their cooperation, along with that of witnesses, families of the victims too. If they read the newspapers, it is safe to assume that such cooperation will not be forthcoming, certainly not in the ten days we have left before the start of the peace talks.''

''But we must *try.* Make an effort, a point.''

''And if that effort fails, what point have we made? That we are just as inefficient working with the Israelis as we are working alone? Incompetent as well as weak? You're taking a very big risk here.''

''The bigger risk lies in doing nothing, Inspector. If al-Diib is still at large one week from Wednesday, there may be no peace talks, and everything the authority has tried to accomplish will collapse. We have nothing to lose.''

''And, of course, at this point neither do I.''

''I wouldn't have put it that way.'' Sumaya cleared his throat uneasily. ''You will have my complete cooperation, Ben.''

''And will I have Commander Shaath's, too?''

''I know you have had a problem with him, since . . . the incident.''

''The two of us had problems before. That only worsened things.''

''He resents foreigners, that's all.''

''I'm not a foreigner. I was born here just as he was.''

''But Shaath did not emigrate to America as a child.''

''That was my parents' choice. I made the decision to return.''

''As your father did before you. Did I ever tell you I knew him?''

''You mentioned it once.''

''He was a hero,'' Sumaya reflected softly. ''I remember meeting him in 1967, not long after he returned in the wake of the Six-Day War. He said I was too young to help, told me to wait for another time.'' His voice drifted. ''I suppose he knew even then it would come.''

''I was seven years old when he left. He never told me.''

"I wept the day he was killed. We all did. He was given a hero's funeral."

"My family didn't learn of it until weeks later. They wouldn't ship his body to America."

"And how do you think he'd feel about you returning too, following in his footsteps?"

"I think he'd tell me I made a mistake."

"Why?"

"Because he had something to return to."

"And you . . ."

"I thought I did."

The focus returned to Sumaya's expression, as if his point had been made. "But don't you see? You *have* now. This is your opportunity."

"I'd prefer not to take it."

Sumaya seemed miffed. "You understand I'm under considerable pressure here."

"Because of the murders . . ."

"The murders and your own peculiar status. I went out on a limb for you, Inspector. I kept you from being transferred." His deep-set eyes blazed into Ben's. "Or worse."

"I appreciate that."

"Then help me now," Sumaya implored. "The Israeli police liaison will be here at three o'clock this afternoon. What should I tell him?"

"That I need more time to think about it."

"There is no more time." The mayor started to shuffle back to his chair. "You see, Inspector, the body of another victim was found in Jericho this morning."

CHAPTER 2

"**D**ANIELLE!" THE VOICE repeated. "Danielle, can you hear me?"

So as not to attract attention, Danielle Barnea waited until she was far enough from the crowd in Haganah Square to respond quietly to Shin Bet commander Dov Levy's edgy call. "I'm right here. Still in position."

"What happened? Where were you?"

"Trying not to stand out."

"The truck just turned into the market, approaching the warehouse."

Danielle gazed across the street at the man beneath the Ottoman Clock Tower she'd been watching for an hour now.

"Atturi's standing still, checking the time I think," she reported. "Wait a minute, he's moving."

"Which way?"

"East. Yefet Street."

"Yes!" the commander's voice beamed. "We're finally going to nail this bastard!"

Danielle waited until Atturi had walked a safe distance ahead before following. He had done nothing thus far to indicate he suspected any surveillance, but she wasn't taking any chances.

She had been promoted to Shin Bet, the Israeli equivalent of the FBI, after becoming the youngest woman ever to attain the rank of chief inspector in Israel's National Police. Quite a bit of fanfare accompanied the promotion, not only because it represented another incredible stroke of career forture, but also because of the event that had sparked it.

She had actually been off duty when she recognized Ahmed Fatuk, wanted for more than a decade for acts of terrorism, walking into a bakery shop in Jerusalem. Knowing Fatuk would be long gone by the time she could summon backup, Danielle made her move on him alone when he emerged from the bakery. Pretending to retrieve the contents of a spilled purse from the sidewalk, she had stuck a gun in the back of his head when he passed by. Since Fatuk's arms were loaded down with bags, there was nothing he could do but give up. A week later he was interned in the Ansar 3 detention camp, awaiting a trial the Israeli justice system would take their time in scheduling. That same week found her transferred to Shin Bet.

In the years since Prime Minister Rabin's assassination, the agency had undergone wholesale changes and been forced to endure a purge through its ranks. As a result, high-level field positions that almost never opened up were suddenly available, and Shin Bet officials scoured the army and National Police, culling the best from their ranks.

They never bothered to ask Danielle if she wanted the job; no one *ever* turned down such a prestigious position, a career maker that could provide the ticket to anywhere she wanted to go. Career, though, was the problem. They hadn't asked Danielle if she wanted the job, and they hadn't asked her what had brought her to Jerusalem on the day she had arrested Ahmed Fatuk. Events had conspired to make her a hero, rendering it impossible for her to follow the new path she had finally decided to embark upon. Now that path would have to wait. Again.

The investigation of Ismail Atturi, an Israeli Arab suspected of being involved in smuggling goods into the West Bank and Gaza, was well underway by the time of Danielle's promotion to Shin Bet, though with little to show for it. Neither Shin Bet nor the National Police had been able to directly link Atturi to the operation. Thanks to an informant, though, they had learned of a shipment going out this day from a storehouse located in the famed flea market in the old city of Jaffa.

"The truck has backed up against one of the sidewalk stalls," Commander Levy reported. "I'll keep you advised."

Danielle followed Atturi, easy to spot in his cream-colored baggy linen pants and shirt, down Yefet Street and then left on Oley Tsiyon toward the center of the market. To blend with the many tourists in this part of town, she herself was dressed in casual clothes: a pair of lightweight slacks and an oversized blouse baggy enough to conceal the holster clipped to the inside of her pants. The nature of this assignment dictated that she carry her Beretta in that fashion, but the holster's designer must have cared little about the painful bite it made into the hip, to say nothing of the unsightly bulge she hoped her blouse was hiding.

She listened to the shouts of various salesmen pitching their wares from stands on the sidewalk, moving carts, or open-front shops adjacent to the flea market. The peddlers and shopkeepers strained their voices to have their boasts of bargains heard and heeded. Everyone other than tourists knew the quality of the merchandise was generally low, but the spirit of the merchants who battled for street space and customers was keen.

"I'm just entering the market," Danielle reported. "Suspect still in sight," she added, catching a strong whiff of freshly caught fish, the official welcome to Old Jaffa's flea market.

"Agent Tice should be coming into view any moment," Levy told her. "Fall back once he takes up pursuit."

Joshua Tice was a top Shin Bet field agent she had been lucky enough to be paired with in her first months with the organization. A no-nonsense, generally humorless man, he worked as many hours as they would let him and longed for nothing else. Was that what lay ahead for her ten years down the road? Considering that possibility always set Danielle trembling.

Up ahead, Atturi moved past an array of Oriental rugs draped over car roofs and hoods, ignoring the pleas of merchants to come over and admire the fine silk and wool. Following in his wake, Danielle gave the endless row of stalls no more than a fleeting glance, despite the boisterous salesmen hawking flashy, cheap jewelry. One attempted to loop a garish necklace over her neck when she passed, and it was all she could do to fend him off without causing a ruckus.

By then, Atturi was crossing the street toward the line of miniature warehouse-like buildings that specialized in ancient, rusted appliances. The incredibly high duties levied by the Israeli government on such merchandise when it was new created an extraordinary demand for recycled items such as televisions and refrigerators, often regardless of their condition.

The buildings housing them were no different. Old Jaffa was a city mired in its storied past, the ancient structures virtually untouched by redevelopment or renewal. Torn and tattered awnings flapped in the faint breeze above merchants negotiating every deal down to the last shekel. Windows peeked out from behind shutters more broken than whole. Most of the buildings were constructed of stone, smoked gray or black through the years and laced with a dusty, heated stench Danielle had never forgotten ever since her father had brought her to Old Jaffa for the first time as a child.

Danielle shifted her eyes from Atturi long enough to register a truck backed up through one of the warehouse fronts that looked as old as the merchandise around it. If their informant's information was correct, though, that truck was in the process of being loaded with stolen goods Atturi would be transporting into the West Bank. One of the strange dividends peace had brought. She noted the yellow Israeli license plates, undoubtedly forged, that allowed passage through the West Bank checkpoints without fear of detainment and potential seizure.

When Danielle glanced back at Atturi, she saw that Tice had cut in behind him sixty feet in front of her.

"All right, Agent Barnea," Commander Levy instructed her, his voice calmer, "back off and stay alert. Don't move until I give the order for the other teams to do the same."

"Roger," Danielle replied, keeping her eyes on Atturi as he cut a diagonal path across the busy street toward the warehouse in question. Tice lingered well behind him.

Tice had to stop when several cars snarled in the endless grind through the market refused to give ground, leaving him no room to cross the street. Danielle kept her pace steady, eyes sweeping the crowds until she locked on a group of four figures slicing forward, wearing jackets in spite of the sweltering heat. Too fast, too stiff, something clearly on their minds besides buying and bargains.

Joshua Tice never saw them; his attention was riveted on Atturi as the Arab approached the truck. But it was not Tice the men were after. They too headed for the truck, their eyes, Danielle was certain, fixed on Atturi. She felt her pulse quicken and fought to remain calm.

"Go Red," she said into her nearly invisible microphone, using the signal for imminent danger.

She couldn't see the other agents posted along the street, yet knew they were in motion even now, heading toward her position as relayed by Commander Levy.

Tice had brought a hand to his ear, slowing as he listened, eyes darting about in befuddlement.

Danielle continued to push through the crowd toward him, straining to maintain at least a partial glimpse of the jacketed figures. She caught three in her field of vision again, hands ducked inside their coats now. Still in motion. Taking their time.

Danielle shoved some bystanders aside and drew her Beretta nine-millimeter pistol. She caught sight of Tice holding a twin of her gun low by his hip forty feet from her. The jacketed figures were hidden from his view by the knotted crowd.

A man jostled Danielle from the back. A soccer ball ricocheted off her leg, bounced off a car fender, and rolled straight toward Atturi as a sliver of space appeared briefly in the crowd. She saw two of the jacketed men raising their own pistols. A third pulled a sawed-off shotgun from under his coat and leveled it straight at Atturi's back.

Tice turned and took a step sideways to kick the soccer ball aside, placing him directly between the shotgun's barrel and Atturi.

Danielle registered the boy chasing the ball about to cross that path as well. At that instant her instincts took over. She had raised the pistol in her hand and fired before she even knew her finger had moved. The sound reverberated inside her head, as she pulled the trigger again and again.

One of her bullets struck the shoulder of the man wielding the shotgun and spun him just as he fired, causing him to miss the boy, who had frozen in place. She was dimly aware of Tice twisting violently and clutching for his face, staggering—his gun useless. The next gunfire she heard belonged to two of the other jacketed men. Their twin fusillades slammed Ismail Atturi into his truck, spraying blood all over the hood and windshield, as Danielle launched herself through the now-panicked crowd.

She chanced a fresh series of shots at the jacketed men through an opening, angling herself to cover Tice, who was writhing on the pavement. She realized the boy in the soccer uniform was still in the line of fire too, and shoved him to the ground as she squeezed off fresh rounds toward Atturi's slayers.

The fourth man! What happened to the fourth man?

No sooner had Danielle realized she had lost track of him than the familiar click-clack of submachine gun fire made her twist to the right, hearing screams erupt on that side of her. The fourth man was trying to escape, firing wildly on the run, his bullets felling a pair of pedestrians who had ended up between Danielle and him. Before she could swing her Beretta on the assassin, three more of the Shin Bet team charged into the street firing, one mounting the hood of a car and another a merchant's cart to improve their aims. The fourth man managed to turn away, then simply keeled over, riddled with bullets. Danielle ejected her spent clip, reached into her pocket for a fresh one.

The roar of an engine made her whirl back toward the truck as she jammed the new magazine home. One of the two final gunmen writhed in pain on the pavement, while the other stumbled toward her. His left shoulder oozed blood through his jacket; a pistol trembled in his right hand.

"*Suka!*" he screamed at her, trying his best to steady the gun and fire.

Danielle dove behind a pair of cars for cover and heard the windows of the nearer one explode as she chambered a round. She peered cautiously over the fender of one car in time to see the big truck screech from its berth in the warehouse. A violent lurch carried it into the street, where it plowed through stalled traffic and crashed into the final gunman, tossing him aside.

Danielle noted insanely that its ancient wipers were struggling to wipe the contents of Ismail Atturi's skull from the windshield as the truck smashed through another pair of cars and slammed them into the one she was perched behind, pinning her in place.

The truck bore down on her like a dragon spewing hot, gasoline-scented breath. Danielle could do nothing but angle her barrel upward and fire. Glass spiderwebbed around the three neat holes she drilled on the driver's side of the windshield, blood splattered on the inside now as well as the out. At the last instant before it was upon her, the truck turned into a line of parked or abandoned cars, coming to a halt with its ancient horn blaring.

Danielle climbed out from the twisted steel around her and sprinted over to the truck behind four of the team members, led by Commander Levy. Another pair had rushed to Joshua Tice, one pressing a handkerchief against Tice's face, while the other fought to hold him still. Guns steadied on the truck's covered rear from all angles. Levy nodded to the man closest, who leaped up on the sill. In one swift motion he drew the burlap flap back and the team braced, ready to shoot.

"Refrigerators," Danielle heard the first one say. "Fucking refrigerators."

"What the fuck?" another blared, climbing into the rear of the truck.

He grabbed hold of one of the refrigerator doors and pulled. The latch resisted at first, then came free when he yanked harder.

A cache of automatic rifles, both American M16s and Israeli Galils, spilled outward, clacking against each other as they tumbled to the pavement.

"*Elloheem!*" one of the Shin Bet agents exclaimed. "Holy shit!"

The second agent's use of English made Danielle think of what the last gunman had screamed at her, the word *and* the language:

He had called her a bitch. In Russian.

CHAPTER 3

WHEN **B**EN **STEPPED** out of the Palestinian Authority building, Commander Omar Shaath, the district of Jericho's chief of police, was waiting behind the wheel of an ancient Peugeot. His thick fingers gripped the steering wheel so tightly they seemed about to split the leather.

Ben had no doubt Shaath could do just that. He was a bear of a man with thick black hair, a bushy mustache, and the trace of a beard where he had shaved just hours before. A black patch strung around his head covered the socket of an eye lost to an Israeli bullet years before during a protest. Unlike the vast majority of high-ranking police officials in the West Bank and Gaza, Shaath had not been recruited from the ranks of Palestinian guerrillas from other nations. Instead, he was a native of the West Bank city of Hebron and former Fatah activist who had been trained in Egypt specifically to take on this command position.

He didn't look over once as Ben got in and closed the door behind him.

"Good morning, Commander," Ben tried, after Shaath had lurched the Peugeot into traffic.

A grunt was all he got in return, not another sound from Shaath until they approached the Baladiya Square on Jaffa Street minutes later.

"The mayor is a fool for doing this."

"Reinstating me or agreeing to work with the Israelis?"

"Take your pick. He thinks you're better than the rest of us, thinks the Israelis are better too."

"He thinks I've had more experience, just as he thinks they have, and he's right."

"No one will work with you anymore. No one will *talk* to you or them. You have no chance."

"Thank you for your confidence, Commander."

"You've earned it."

Ben had been out on a supervisory patrol four months before, when the report of a man's body being found in a drainage ditch by children on their way to school came over the radio. He went straight to the scene and didn't need a medical examiner to tell him the victim had been tortured before being killed. The killers had used a knife to carve a single word onto the victim's forehead in his own dried blood:

Ameel . . . collaborator.

The victim turned out to be a cabdriver who drove the popular Jerusalem route and as such would have known many Israeli soldiers and checkpoint guards by name. It was often easy to confuse congeniality for collaboration. With their presence dwindling in the

West Bank, the rumor was that the Israelis were going all out to recruit an army of informants to be their eyes and ears. The cabdriver's killers had obviously wanted to make an example and a point, whether justified or not.

As was often the case, Ben probably would never have found these killers if a trio of Palestinian policemen hadn't gone around boasting about being responsible. Taking a small detachment along, he arrested them himself, picked them right off the street without consulting Shaath or the mayor. His investigation had confirmed that the cabdriver was not a collaborator at all and, even if he had been, the three policemen had violated every rule associated with their uniform. Like them, Ben had wanted to make a point.

And his, too, backfired.

Officers already suspicious and resentful of him had the excuse they needed to disregard his orders and training. Ben had come back to Palestine to help modernize a force wholly lacking in investigative technique and procedure, to help make detectives out of the best and the brightest the West Bank had to offer. Unfortunately, his own zeal had rendered him incapable of fulfilling that role.

Yielding to popular demand, and for what he insisted was Ben's own safety, the mayor ordered that his recommendations be passed down strictly in writing. All direct contact with the officers he had previously been charged with training was forbidden without authorization. Committed to building a new life here in Palestine, Ben had managed to convince himself it would all blow over, at least improve.

It hadn't improved, would never blow over. Shaath had gloated and was still gloating today as he snailed the car on, honking the horn to disperse the mounting crowd that had gathered down from the Baladiya near the Hisbe, or shopping district, where the smells of fresh produce would soon fill the air as merchants opened up shop for the day. Ben knew he would have to work fast, or risk having the entire crime scene compromised, if it hadn't been already.

At last the swell of people became too much to deal with and Shaath simply brought the car to a halt half a block from the alley where the latest body had been found.

"Go ahead, Inspector."

"You're not coming with me?"

"It's better I stay with the car. Besides, this is your case now, isn't it?"

Ben threw open the door and stepped out into the street, tightening his beret. His green police uniform and gun belt allowed for swift passage through the crowd. A few recognized him from the stories that had run in the newspapers. Some of these lifted a finger his way.

"Kha'in!" he heard aimed at him by voices rough in their hate. Ben was careful not to seek out their eyes for the confrontation it might provoke. He thought he recognized a familiar figure among the pedestrian clutter, but when he looked again it was gone, and he pushed on, making his way to the crime scene.

Luckily for Ben, the vast bulk of attention was riveted on the alley he was approaching. The body lay at its edge, the blood reaching out like tentacles toward the early morning sun striking Jaffa Street, visible as soon as he stepped from the crowd into the cordoned-off area.

The three police officers standing guard over the

scene went rigid when they saw him, offering no greeting even though he was a superior. Ben could tell from their attitudes that they had been forewarned of his coming, so he simply nodded as he moved past them toward a bulbous shape hovering over the corpse.

"Good morning, Duktur."

Bassim al-Shaer, Jericho's medical examiner, stood half in and half out of the alley, peering intently at the body. He looked up when Ben spoke with a mixture of shock and disdain.

"What are you doing here?"

"I've been assigned to the case."

The fat man's eyes rolled upward. "Then I'd better hurry. I'd hate to get hit by a bullet meant for you."

"It would take more than a bullet to make you hurry, Doctor."

Al-Shaer snickered and returned his attention to the corpse. He always looked to Ben as if he was wearing yesterday's clothes. Today a wrinkled khaki suit hung shapelessly over his huge frame. A thirty-five-millimeter camera dangled from a strap round his neck.

"How long have you been here?"

"Long enough," al-Shaer replied tersely. He steadied the camera in his hands, but made no effort to raise it.

"Long enough to determine the cause of death?"

The medical examiner spoke while resuming his mobile inspection of the body. "Stabbed. Lots of times." He brought the viewfinder to his eye, focused, and snapped off two shots.

"Al-Diib?"

The camera thumped against the fat man's chest.

He tried to stifle a belch born of bad tea or coffee, and failed. Then he backed off and angled himself for a fresh series of shots.

"See for yourself."

Ben turned his attention to the corpse, which lay twisted on its left side, one leg stretched out and the other folded up toward the buttocks. The right shoulder was propped up in the air, the right arm extended behind the dead man's back as if to scratch it. The victim's head flopped heavily atop a neck crimped enough to cast his dead stare upside down toward the other side of the alley.

That and the shadows spared Ben sight of the face until he leaned further over, closer to it. The sight made him suck in his breath. The victim's face had been shredded, mangled. One eye had been ripped from its socket and hung obscenely over the cheek. The other was covered by torn strips of flesh and dried blood.

Just like the other seven . . . This made five in the West Bank now in as many months, the most recent two in Jericho.

Ben straightened up.

"I'll want a detailed report on the condition of the face," he told al-Shaer.

The fat man chortled. "You can't see for yourself?" His expression fell into a scowl marked by slabs of excess flesh. "It's the Wolf, all right."

"I want to be sure of that before proceeding. That means comparisons with past victims to confirm we're dealing with the same killer here."

"Their faces were all shredded too. That's not proof enough for you? You haven't learned yet, have you? Tell you the truth, I wouldn't give a shit whether you ever do, but when it affects my job, I don't have a choice.''

"You're right: you don't.''

Al-Shaer squeezed the camera between flabby hands that almost swallowed it. "What are you doing here?''

"I told you; my case.''

"I meant *still*. I meant in Jericho, in Palestine.''

Ben kept his eyes on the body and his voice steady. "How long has he been dead?''

"Several hours. As many as eight, even nine, I would say. Since midnight, would be a fair estimate.''

"And you're certain death resulted from these . . . stab wounds.''

The medical examiner was shuffling around again, firing off shots with his camera. "As certain as I need to be at this stage.

"You've called for the Cleaners, I assume,'' Ben said, referring to the van used to transport bodies, called that since it had originally been used by a pair of brothers who cleaned rugs for a living. The van had been renovated into an ambulance but was still driven by the same brothers.

"On their way.'' Al-Shaer pulled the camera from his eye. "This is my second roll. You can never be too careful.''

"No.''

The medical examiner tilted his head toward the corpse. "He wasn't careful.''

"Any identification?''

"None,'' the medical examiner said, fighting off a cough. "As usual.''

"Who reported the body?''

"Anonymous. Figures, doesn't it?''

Al-Shaer finished the roll and let the camera fall to

his chest with a thump of finality. He had started to back away when Ben fastened a powerful grip on his elbow.

"You are not done yet, Doctor. There are samples that must be taken."

Al-Shaer looked down at the hand holding him in place and then up at the cold stare of Ben's blue eyes. "Samples?"

Ben's gaze shifted toward the crowd which continued to swell. "Before the scene is contaminated, starting with the gravel in this alley. Six different patches, cataloged according to grid."

Al-Shaer just looked at him, too shocked to be enraged.

"I also want everything back five meters in the alley and forward five meters into the street sifted."

"Sifted?"

"For foreign material, anything anomalous to the scene."

Al-Shaer tapped his head dramatically. "Of course! How could I have forgotten? Very important to find out where our faceless victim was before he came here to be killed."

"Not him necessarily."

"What? *Who*, then?"

"Al-Diib," Ben said.

CHAPTER 4

BY THE TIME Ben walked back to the edge of the crowd, a jeep carrying four more police officers had arrived, followed closely by the ambulance driven by the brothers who used to clean rugs. The crowd booed the arrivals and slapped the ambulance with their hands as it crept toward the alley.

Ben watched the scene, recalling the mayor's words about what the murders were doing to the climate in the streets. Clearly the people were lashing out at anything even remotely resembling authority. Ben had not been in Palestine for the *intifada,* but had heard the atmosphere then had been similarly tense. The prospects for violence always seemed strong now and that did not bode well for the prospects of a final peace being achieved.

The reinforcements had come none too soon, for the Hisbe's merchants were starting to prop up the shutters draped over their storefront displays of fruits and vegetables lining the street, the smells of fresh produce already drifting into the air. Others were opening retail establishments that featured hand-woven baskets, rugs, and a vast array of merchandise. A difficult situation was about to become even more complicated. In addition to the normal complement of shoppers, the curious would come, drawn by word of mouth toward a new attraction amid the usual fare.

Ben waited for the four new officers to disperse along the front of the crowd before addressing the three who'd already been here when he arrived. The yellow crime scene tape, its DO NOT CROSS! warning printed in English since it was the only version Ben could obtain, flapped in the breeze behind him.

"Who was first on the scene?" he asked.

"Me," said the one in the center, bearded and gaunt, his uniform a poor fit over his frame. "I was closest when the call came in."

"What's your name?"

"Moussa Salam."

"Did you see anyone in the area upon your arrival?"

"No one, sir."

"What about lights burning in any of the windows of the apartments along the street?"

"I . . . didn't notice."

"Think back. Try."

"I secured the alley. I didn't think to—"

"There were lights," the officer on Salam's right interrupted. He was a much older man whose hair showed flecks of gray and whose beard was mixed evenly between salt and pepper. "But I'm not sure from which buildings now."

"Why does it matter?" Salam challenged.

"If lights are on, then people are probably awake. One of them may have seen something that can help us."

"A long shot," noted the third officer Ben knew as Fakhar. Dark with very curly graying hair and a scruffy beard.

"A starting point," said Ben.

"At the time of the murder it would have been too dark for anyone gazing down or across the street to have seen anything clearly in the alley," Fakhar noted, a slight edge to his voice.

"You are correct, of course," Ben acknowledged. "But they may have seen something else, someone passing by, for instance."

"At such an hour? Why?" challenged Salam.

"A late night walk. Perhaps returning from a friend's home."

Fakhar was busy making notes on a small memo pad pulled from his lapel pocket. "Yes, Inspector," he said, and wedged the memo pad back in his pocket.

"We are not merely looking for the person who reported the crime. We are looking for *anyone* who might have seen *anything*. A car parked nearby. A figure they can describe moving too fast or slow, standing out. Anything amiss in the late night or early morning routine they have come to be used to."

A fourth officer sliced his way through the crowd toward them, an excited expression lighting over his features. He gazed quickly at the trio standing rigid in front of the alley and then looked at Ben, composing himself.

"I apologize for leaving my post, sir."

"And you are . . ."

"Officer Issa Tawil."

"And where were you?"

"Speaking with someone, *sidi*. A witness."

TAWIL WAS EASILY the youngest of the four officers, barely college age if he'd been American, with a beard that failed to obscure his boyish face.

"You know who I am, Issa?" Ben asked him, after they had slipped through the crowd and moved across Jaffa Street.

"I recognized you, *sidi*."

"You shouldn't address me in such a formal manner. It occurs to me that your brother officers will certainly frown on your sharing information with me, as it is. They would have wanted the opportunity to talk you out of it. That could cause a young man of limited tenure some problems."

Tawil smiled. "But a man of such limited tenure could not be expected to recognize you as anything but a superior officer."

Ben nodded, holding back a smile. He would have added Tawil's name to the list of potential detectives instantly, had it still been his list to make. "Now tell me about this witness."

"I was patrolling the back of the crowd just before you arrived when she yelled for me from her window."

"She . . ."

"An old woman. Terrible eyesight. She thought I had come to remove her garbage. Her apartment is just over here, off the street."

"*Off* the street?"

"Yes, sir. She could never have seen the alley, or anyone even close to it."

Ben stopped as they reached the other side of Jaffa Street. "Then what *did* she see?"

"Another witness."

CHAPTER 5

BEN WENT ALONE to the old woman's apartment, stopping at the head of the alley to turn and look back. He was standing diagonally across from the alley where the murder had taken place, between forty and forty-five yards away. At this distance he thought it might be possible to catch a clear view of a face caught in the moonlight. But the view deteriorated and then vanished altogether the further he ventured down the alley to where the old woman lived.

The entrance to Rula Middein's apartment was a rickety door lacking both a knob and a lock. Leaking bags of garbage lay strewn in the alley beneath it. Ben held his nose against the stench and cringed as his feet sloshed through some of the loosed remnants. The stairs to the doorway were rotting and he took them lightly, wishing for a railing. An inner stairway awaited him once inside, another door at its top. Wide open, as if he were expected.

"Ya halla! 'Ahlan wa sahlan!" a friendly voice called in welcome as his feet thumped noisily upon the plank floor outside the apartment. "Come in! Come in!"

Another few steps forward brought a luscious smell to his nose, a happy contrast to the one from the alley. Passing inside the apartment, he could hear a spoon clinking against the side of a bowl. A single wall and curtain separated the kitchen from the rest of the shabby but good-sized apartment. A square wooden table, ancient, rested directly before him. It looked to be too heavy for the flimsy floor supporting it. A dozen places had been set around the table.

Beyond what passed for the dining area lay a neat assembly of patched furniture. Ben ran his eyes over the pieces and could see how even the patches had deteriorated, evidence of aging hands struggling with the inevitability of decay. He saw a radio but no television. Another curtain separated this room from the old woman's bedroom. The two curtains were the only things in the apartment that matched.

The one leading to the kitchen parted and Rula Middein emerged balancing a spoon before her, free hand cradled beneath it to catch any spilled excess.

"Taste," she ordered, jabbing the spoon Ben's way. *"Il-kabab wilful."*

He opened his mouth and sampled the kebab and beans.

"Ajib!" he complimented. *"Ajib, haja."*

The old woman glistened at his use of such a reverent title. Her white hair hung in poorly combed clumps. She pulled the spoon away with a frail hand and sniffed the food herself, reveling in Ben's acceptance of her *madafah*, hospitality.

"More spices, you think?"

"No. It's perfect as is. Leave it."

The old woman beamed. "You can stay and eat with us maybe? I have many to feed," she said, gesturing to the already-set table. "But there is always extra. I should set an extra place?"

"Not tonight."

"Of course, you must eat with your own family. Forgive me. Families are good. You have children?"

"No," he told her, feeling a dull ache rise out of his stomach.

"A man like you *should*," she scolded. Rula Middein held the spoon like a baton, conducting life as it should still be. "I have many children, children and grandchildren." Again she gestured toward the table. "They will be here soon. For dinner. We always eat together. A family."

The sun found an angle through the blindless windows and only then did Ben notice the thick layer of dust coating all the plates. The silverware looked rusted, destroyed by the humid Jericho air.

"You will stay?" the old woman asked hopefully.

"Another time."

"Promise!"

"I promise."

Satisfied, Rula Middein retreated to the kitchen to finish the meal no one would be coming to eat. Ben trailed the old woman slowly, careful not to alarm her.

"Other police were here before. They couldn't stay either."

"They sent me, so we could talk."

"They ask questions."

"I know."

"You ask same ones?"

"Some."

The woman's shoulders slumped. She looked sad for the first time since Ben had entered the apartment. "Was bad thing happened last night."

"One of my men said you saw something, someone."

"I saw police at entrance to alley, shouted at them to come up. One did. Nice boy named Issa. I tell him to get rid of garbage. He says he'll try."

"So will I."

"You promise?"

"It will be gone by this afternoon."

The old woman went back to tending the ancient stove, seeming to lose interest in him.

"The young officer told me you saw someone last night."

She replied without turning from her pots. "See him every night. Asked officer to do something about that too."

"Who is it that you see?"

"Sleeps in alley."

"Tell me about him."

"*Al-sabi,* a beggar boy. Sometimes I see him during day at Baladiya. Stealing. Running. I want to invite him to dinner but . . ." She shrugged her boney shoulders. "He run away before I can. At night I don't go out."

"A wise decision. And this boy, he was in the alley last night?"

"Every night."

"Describe him."

"Dirty. Long hair hanging like pieces of rope. Don't see many with hair so long."

"His clothes?"

"Pale. Used to be white maybe."

"Both shirt and pants?"

"Match," she said, and then looked up at him with what little hope her eyes could still muster. "You help boy?"

"I'll be waiting for him tonight," Ben told Rula Middein. "When he comes back."

HE MET OFFICER Issa Tawil back on Jaffa Street.

"Well?"

"You did good work, Issa."

"Thank you, *sidi*."

"The old woman told me about the boy who sleeps in her alley. A resident of one of the refugee camps you think?"

"Almost certainly. The Einissultan camp would be my guess, based on the old woman's description of his clothes."

"An excellent deduction."

"Drawn from experience this time, Inspector," Tawil said, features sobering. "I grew up there."

"A difficult place for a child."

"Or an adult." The young officer's eyes met Ben's. "But you are no stranger to hardship either, Inspector." He hesitated, cleared his throat. "Commander Shaath sent a message while you were upstairs with the woman. He has returned to the office with another patrol and has left you the car."

"Very considerate of him . . ."

"Excuse me?"

"Nothing." Ben stopped, eager to change the subject. "Do you think the boy will return?"

"I wouldn't if I were him, not if he saw anything, but you never know. He has staked out the Hisbe as his territory. Finding another is not as simple as it may seem. You will wait for him tonight?"

"Yes."

"I would like to join you."

Ben was about to resist, then changed his mind. He could treat it like a training exercise, pretend like Rula Middein that things were still the way they belonged. "Say midnight, unless I find the boy before then."

"In the *camp*?"

"Yes."

"Let me, *sidi*. After all . . ." Tawil completed his thought with a shrug.

"This is something I must do, Issa."

"Even for the police the camps are not safe."

"Precisely why I must go there alone."

CHAPTER 6

WE WOULD LIKE to go over it again,"
one of the men in suits told the Shin Bet agents assembled in the center of Old Jaffa. "One more time."

His remarks were aimed at all of them, but Danielle
was uncomfortably certain that his stare lingered on
her the most. She, after all, had been the first to draw
and fire her weapon. In the suspicious minds of the
three men who had come to assess what had occurred
hours earlier and make an account, that made her the
easiest target to pin blame on. One civilian had been
killed and two seriously wounded in the shoot-out.
And the three men dispatched internally started with
the notion that Shin Bet had erred and worked from
there—another ramification of the Rabin assassination.

Danielle wasn't sure which branch of the government these men actually worked for. They existed in
a professional vacuum, summoned only when the possibility of a mishap existed and disappearing once sat-

isfied (though perhaps disappointed) that it didn't. They had become the government's personal terrorists, feared more than any enemy from outside the state, the word they passed down law even if the facts didn't always add up to that.

The Shin Bet agents stirred anxiously and returned to their original positions.

The area where the shoot-out had occurred had been cordoned off. The bodies had all been removed, replaced by lines of chalk or tape to simulate their positions. The Shin Bet team had already done its best to reenact the events of the gun battle a number of times. Two soldiers had been recruited to play the roles of Tice and Atturi, the only two involved here whose careers did not hang in the balance.

"Agent Barnea," one of the mystery men called to her, "if you don't mind."

Danielle took her place in the street. She knew she had acted properly and didn't care very much if the men found otherwise. In fact, she might welcome that, because she had been looking for a way out for a long time now.

She had completed her mandatory tour in the army looking forward to starting a family, becoming a wife and mother. But then her oldest brother was killed and a new resolve filled her. It was the desire for vengeance at first that helped her complete the rigorous training for the elite Sayaret at the top of her class. Once she began serving in this new and dangerous capacity, though, the desire for anything but cold precision vanished. The world of quick-strike commandos has no room for emotion, and she quickly came to embrace that as the therapy she needed most of all. There would be time for a family later.

When her years with the Sayaret ended in distinction, she was overwhelmed by the offers for her services. The National Police provided the best prospects, at least the easiest to abandon once she met the right man. But then her second brother was killed and she was promoted to *pakad*, or chief inspector. Her father had suffered a stroke around that same time, as much from sadness as the aftereffects of taking a sniper's bullet while on routine patrol in the West Bank. In a family rich in the tradition of service, she could not possibly give up her position only to raise a family now. She was afraid it would steal what little hope her father had left, having lost both his sons.

But he got worse instead of better, her decision to stay on with the police having no bearing on his prognosis. So on the day she had arrested Ahmed Fatuk she had actually come to Jerusalem to tell her father of her decision to resign. She had no boyfriend, never mind a fiance, but longed for a life apart from her career.

As soon as Danielle recognized Fatuk entering that bakery, she knew her desires were going to be delayed yet again. She'd stay on at Shin Bet for six months, a year at most. But it didn't take nearly that long for her father's condition to worsen to the level of virtual incoherence. She could do whatever she desired now, tell him whatever she wanted and he would accept her words with a proud smile, never to be in position again to know any better.

Not only could Danielle not lie to him, though, she also could not stray from the path she knew made him most proud. To do so seemed like the ultimate disrespect. She would wait until his inevitable, and merciful, passing came and then . . .

Then would she find herself feeling she must be faithful to his memory? Or was this day, this shoot-out, the signal that it was time to live the life she had been trying to retreat to for years now?

"What did you do at this point?" one of the suited men asked, breaking her trance.

"I drew my gun."

"You said before you called an alert first," another pointed out.

"Yes, that's right. I'm sorry."

"You drew your gun before you saw any of these men draw theirs."

"They were wearing jackets."

"And you determined they were armed instead of cold, is that right?" the second resumed.

"*I* was right."

"We are not here to determine right and wrong," noted the first.

"We are here to determine if the course of action you precipitated was proper in consideration of the numerous bystanders in the area," added the second.

Danielle heard footsteps and saw Commander Dov Levy draw up even with her. "The course of action *we* precipitated and *I* approved *saved* lives."

The leader of the suits took exception to that. "You were instructed to wait aside until we are ready for you, Commander."

"I need to speak with Agent Barnea."

"When we are finished with her, Commander."

"*Now,*" Levy insisted.

He dragged Danielle away without waiting for the suited leader to respond.

"Thank you," Danielle said, relieved.

"Don't thank me yet," Levy said somberly. "I've

had a call from National Headquarters. You're wanted there.''

In spite of herself, Danielle felt her stomach sink at what that might mean. ''You think . . .''

''I don't think anything, and you shouldn't either. Wait until you hear what they want.''

They looked at each other for a long moment.

''Do you think I made a mistake today?'' Danielle asked Levy finally.

''You saved Agent Tice's life and the lives of at least a dozen civilians.''

''Not according to them,'' she said, gesturing toward the suits, who were waiting impatiently to continue with yet another reenactment.

''You did your job. They are doing theirs.''

Danielle wished she could feel glad, wished she could see this as an opportunity to slide quietly into a life that would allow for a family of her own at last. But not in disgrace. Not on the terms of three bureaucrats paid to find fault where none existed.

''You'd better get going,'' Levy said, extracting a set of keys from his pocket and tilting his gaze briefly on the three suited figures. ''These are to one of our friends' cars. I'm sure they'll understand the urgency.''

Danielle smiled. ''I'll bring it back when I'm done.''

Levy frowned, gazed at the soldiers and sawhorses blocking off this section of the street. ''You know where to find us.''

CHAPTER 7

BEFORE HEADING TO Jericho's lone refugee camp, Ben edged the Peugeot Shaath had left him along Jaffa Street, honking the horn to clear a path to the alley where Rula Middein lived. He eased the transmission into reverse and backed up over the sidewalk in a cautious series of starts and stops while pedestrians did their best to ignore him. He continued backing as far into the alley as possible, then climbed out and popped open the car's trunk.

It took twenty minutes to empty the alley of the greatest part of the garbage littered beneath the old woman's window. Once out of the town center, he would dump it at the first available opportunity.

"Perhaps you missed your true calling," a voice called out, and Ben looked up to see a man he recognized leaning on a cane just in front of the car.

He slammed the trunk and moved around to the driver's door. "I thought I spotted you in the crowd,

Jabral. I suppose I have you to thank for the chants of *kha'in*."

"You are many things, Inspector, but a traitor is not one of them. Besides, I like to keep a low profile."

"Then stay right there while I pull out; that should make you low enough to please anyone."

The man smiled briefly and limped over to where Ben stood, his cane clacking ahead of him. "I was hoping we could talk."

"You know the one thing the Palestinians have in common with the Americans, Jabral? The media is full of shit. Thanks for making me feel at home."

Ben climbed into the car and closed the door. Zaid Jabral moved to the open window and rested a hand over the edge for support.

"Tell me something, Ben. Did I misstate any fact? Did I print anything other than the truth?"

"The truth came from only one side."

"You wouldn't give me your side, so I was left with what I had heard. You know what they say."

"What do they say?"

"That you were only invited to return because you are the son of the great Jafir Kamal. I did a story on him once."

"One of the few distinctions I share with my father. And I wasn't invited; I came on my own."

"Perhaps you should have waited for a war, like your father," Jabral said cynically.

"I did."

"You gave up your homeland and built a new life, only to abandon it so you could return and live in his shadow." Jabral looked pleased with his own revelation. "Would have made for an interesting angle, don't you think?"

"Perhaps, if you hadn't elected to devote so much space to branding me an enemy of my own people."

"I have an obligation to inquire, to inform, to—"

"Teach?" Ben interjected and watched Jabral stiffen at the word. "That would be logical since you were a teacher long before you became the top editor at *Al-Quds.* You were also one of the men I most admired. The great Zaid Jabral, a true architect of change. I followed your efforts, from the States, to make the West Bank curriculum more contemporary when independence was still a dream."

"Because true independence, my dear Ben, can come only through education."

"Did you tell that to the *shabab,* the children of the *intifada*?"

"What hypocrites! There was so much complaining when the Israelis closed our schools. Then we retaliate by closing them *ourselves* in order to protest!"

"For days, not years. And you continued your classes in spite of them," Ben said, and Jabral shrugged.

It was here that the story of Zaid Jabral became a mixture of fact and legend. What was known for sure was that he was giving a test to his twelfth graders when a number of dissident students appeared to roust them out into the streets. Jabral refused to let his students go until they completed their tests, much to the displeasure of the *shabab* leaders, becoming the first teacher to make a stand against them.

From this point the story grew murky; there were two totally disparate versions of the beating that had left Jabral a cripple. Popular thought had it that, upon exiting the building, he was attacked by the very *shabab* leaders he had disdained. His hip was shattered and surgery came too late to give him back his mobility. The second version, preferred from a propaganda standpoint, claimed that the beating occurred when Jabral stood up to the Israelis in another incident entirely, that he ended up as one of many held under the parameters of ''administrative detention'': incarcerated for months without being charged, and tortured in pursuit of a confession. Jabral hadn't confessed to anything, this version went, and had paid for his stubbornness with his hip.

Ben had never asked him which version was correct, continuing to hold the newspaper man in high esteem until two months earlier, when *Al-Quds* had helped make Ben an outcast, branding him a traitor by breaking the story of his arrest of the three Palestinian police officers.

''You know, Jabral,'' he said now, ''something I never asked you: why did you do it?''

''Because that cabdriver was an *ameel*, a collaborator.''

''*Suspected* collaborator, you mean, and only by the three police officers who decided to practice their own brand of justice on a fellow Palestinian.''

''He was a Palestinian only in name.''

''The same name shared by his wife and five children. Why don't you do a story on them?''

''And the three officers, they did not have families who will miss them too? Thanks to you, they were sentenced to life in prison by a tribunal of three high-ranking officers. A closed-door military proceeding. No appeals permitted.''

''Should I feel sorry for them?''

Jabral shook his head. ''Strange that an American should embrace such a nondemocratic process.''

"We are not ready for a wholly democratic process here yet."

"Nor are we ready for you, Inspector. You should have stuck to being a detective, to showing the Authority's trainees how it is supposed to be done."

"Funny, that's what I thought I was doing."

"I'm talking about nuts and bolts, casework."

"Look the other way, then . . ."

"Or not look at all."

"Difficult not to see a man's balls stuck in his mouth. The cabdriver was still alive when they cut them off, you know. I don't think I ever read anything about that in your paper."

"Because I don't want my paper to go the way of your career in Palestine. You made yourself a pariah."

"With a little assistance from you."

Jabral's features seemed to relax. "Maybe that's why I'm here now."

"To make amends? Extend an olive branch?"

"I'd take it if I were you. Now that you're in charge of the case, you can use all the help you can get."

"Word travels fast."

"For one who knows how to listen."

"The mayor had his reasons. What are yours, Jabral?"

"There's a madman on the loose. Isn't that enough?"

"Only if you have a vested interest in the peace process succeeding."

Jabral looked down. "We've all had enough of the alternative."

Ben regarded him curiously. "You never returned to the classroom."

"I elected to follow other pursuits."

"They wouldn't let you back in the schools, would they? You went too far, even for your own people; you scared them. Too much risk, too much liability. Much easier to cut their losses and send you on your way." Ben watched Jabral grit his teeth, not finished yet. "The same forces that oppose peace ended your teaching career because you stood up to them, and you think I might be able to bring them down for you. That's what your olive branch is about."

Jabral didn't bother denying it. "I can't bring them down with my newspaper—none of us who grew up here can bring them down."

"Because you're afraid of being labeled a collaborator, ending up with your balls stuck in your mouth like the cabdriver?"

"No, because I'm afraid of the Palestinian police who will shut down our offices and confiscate an entire day's printing if I say something that disturbs Arafat or our"—he cleared his throat—"elected representatives."

"The Palestinian Protective Security Service has nothing to do with the police, Jabral, and you know it."

"Of course. Your police wait until a crime has been committed before you arrest the wrong man, while the Security Service arrests an innocent man before he has done anything wrong." Jabral nodded, pleased with his own analysis. "You would be wise to watch out for them too, Ben."

"Why would they bother with someone who's already been labeled a traitor? Then again, that's why you suddenly want to work with me, isn't it, Jabral? I'm the one with nothing to lose, and all of a sudden everyone has a use for me."

"The Israelis included," Jabral said without missing a beat.

"Really?"

"According to my source, they requested you."

That remark caught Ben off guard, and Jabral pounced on his sudden uncertainty like a hunter.

"You didn't suspect as much when Sumaya reinstated you? You really are naive, aren't you, Benny?"

"Why me?"

"I'm afraid you'll have to ask the Israelis. In the meantime, feel free to call upon me if I can be of any assistance."

With that, Jabral turned and started off.

"The Israelis are your source, aren't they?"

Jabral kept walking.

"*Aren't* they, Jabral?"

"Ask *them*."

"I'm asking *you*."

Jabral looked back over his shoulder at Kamal. "You're asking for trouble."

He had barely finished his sentence when a plate glass window just down the street exploded. A chair flew through it, followed by a man, who hit the sidewalk with a thud.

"And," the newspaper editor resumed, "it appears that you've got it."

CHAPTER 8

BEN REACHED THE man who'd been thrown through the glass just ahead of two fellow police officers running to the scene, their hands pressed against the butts of their pistols. A fresh crowd began to cluster like ants, shifting its attention from the alley where the corpse was just being hauled away by the Cleaners. Ben helped the man to his feet and dragged him aside.

"Who are you?"

The man wore a white apron, splattered with grease. Fresh blood dotted both his cheeks and stained his chin.

"The chef, that's all! I am the chef!"

"What's going on in there?"

"He's mad!"

"Who?"

"I don't know. He eats here a lot. Something went wrong. It wasn't the food."

A table sailed through the window, taking another hefty chunk of glass with it. The two police officers hovering nearby drew their guns and started for the door.

Ben cut in front of them, holding them back. "Let me try first," he said.

His colleagues looked at each other. One snickered.

"Give me a few minutes. If he throws me through the window, take over." Ben turned to the chef. "Is there a back door?"

"Locked."

"You have the key?"

The chef fished through his pockets. "Here."

Ben took the key and darted behind the building. Passing through the door, he found himself in a storeroom neatly stacked with boxes and cans. He could hear the sound of more plates and glasses exploding in the front of the restaurant and quickly located the door leading that way. A short L-shaped hall lay ahead and he crept down it into the kitchen, toward the smell of food burning and the sizzling sound of something left too long on the grill.

"Who would like me to cook them breakfast? Come on, I'm only trying to make friends!" a shrill voice boomed from the dining area beyond.

Ben slid past the serving counter and reached a curtain that led straight into the dining room.

"Hey!"

He heard more glass breaking, followed by the sound of something being slammed.

"I said, *get away from that door!*"

Ben slipped through the curtain and sat down at a table set back from the others that rimmed the room in a semicircle. Between these tables and the front door, a massive man lumbered across the floor, brandishing a club. He was at least as big as Shaath, probably bigger, and had muscle where the commander had long before gone to fat. His shirt was ripped, his hair uncombed, and even from this distance Ben could smell the alcohol.

"Don't move!" the giant screamed at a gaunt man standing behind an ancient cash register. "You had your chance to be fair."

Another man near the restaurant's front had risen from his chair when the huge man's stare froze him.

"Sit the fuck back down!"

He did as he was told instantly, and the huge man's eyes continued to sweep across the room. They passed right over Ben, then lurched back to his police uniform, bulging.

"What the *fuck* are you doing here?" Club raised overhead, a single lunge brought him within striking distance.

Ben made sure the big man could see his hands poised on the tabletop. "I heard you offer to make breakfast. I thought I'd take you up on it."

"I don't like cops."

"Neither have I lately."

"Nothing but trouble."

"I'm living proof of that."

The big man didn't seem sure how to respond. "What's your problem?"

"I made the mistake of arresting some men because they were guilty."

"I'm not guilty."

"Do you have your identification with you?"

The big man shrugged and produced the card from his pocket. The regulation was a holdover from the

Israeli occupation, meant to facilitate matters for the Palestinian police. But the huge task of replacing the IDs had yet to be undertaken, leaving residents of the West Bank with the same cards carried under Israeli control.

Ben examined the card, saw the big man's name was Yousef Shifa, and spotted the familiar triangles in each of the four corners, indicating he had served time in an Israeli prison. Ben wondered how long the incarceration had taken him from his family.

"What happened here, Yousef?" Ben asked. "The chef told me outside it had nothing to do with food."

"Good food."

"Then why'd you throw him through the window?"

"They called him out when I didn't have any money. Wouldn't give me credit. I promised I'd pay as soon as I was back on my feet, but they wouldn't listen."

Ben looked to the man behind the cash register. "May I have Mr. Shifa's bill please?"

The owner handed it across the counter and Ben counted out the proper amount of dinars from his wallet, adding a hefty tip.

"There's also the damage he's done to consider," the owner said.

"Which he will pay you for, once he has a job. Now, I know you could have him arrested and thrown in jail. But this man, I can tell you, has a family that needs him, and he'll never be able to pay you back from inside a prison."

"And how are you so sure he's going to get a job?"

"Because I'm going to get him one."

"You're *what*?"

"You *are*?" Yousef Shifa beamed.

Ben looked up at him. "We are looking for someone at police headquarters. It doesn't pay much and the work is rather menial, but it's a job, my friend, and it will allow you to walk out of here today with me."

"No jail?"

Ben rose and fixed his eyes on the owner. "Thanks to the kindness and good grace of this man, no. I think I will recommend this place to my colleagues, maybe post a few notices inside headquarters. What do you think, eh? Might give business a little boost."

Ben moved toward Yousef Shifa. Even hunched dumbly over, he still appeared huge. Ben took the club from Shifa's hand and let it clamor to the floor. He put his arm on the big man's shoulder and steered him for the door.

"Now let's see about that job."

Shifa stiffened, not quite ready to go. "How did you know I had a family?"

"Because," Ben said, "it was obvious you had something to lose."

CHAPTER 9

COME IN, PAKAD," a voice called to Danielle from just inside an office on the sixth floor of Israel's National Headquarters.

Danielle recognized the voice of Commissioner, or Rav Nitzav, Hershel Giott, intrigued that he had used her former rank as a chief inspector from when she had worked under him with the National Police.

The headquarters for Shin Bet was located at National Headquarters in Jerusalem as well, in this inappropriately plain, six-story beige building fashioned out of limestone and dominated by neat rows of utterly symmetrical windows. A flag tower had been built directly in the center and the massive black macadam parking lot seemed ever ready to swallow the entire structure because the lot was never more than half full.

Although Danielle had been transferred to Shin Bet some months ago, it was her former superior who had summoned her to National Headquarters in the message relayed by Dov Levy. She could not account for this and, in view of the morning's events, approached the meeting with extreme trepidation.

Entering Giott's office, Danielle instantly noticed that a prominent director of Shin Bet was seated in a chair on the left side of Giott's desk. Though Commander Moshe Baruch was in charge of her department, this was the first time they had actually met, and she sensed the circumstances were not favorable. Baruch was a gaunt rail of a man whose beard disguised the rest of his thin face. He had a reputation for chewing up any in his department who did not measure up to his standards of performance and spitting them out when there was nothing left but gristle. Some who were summoned to his office, it was rumored, were never seen again, their careers ended, literally, at the door, and Danielle couldn't help but wonder if hers too was about to end here in Giott's office. That might have been what she wanted, though on her own terms; not in a disgrace that would haunt her for years to come.

"Sit down, Pakad," the *rav nitzav* instructed.

Physically, he was the antithesis of Baruch: small and frail with an ever-present frown and a yarmulke riding his crown whenever he was in the midst of a difficult case, as if that were the only time he needed God. Strangely, Danielle had never seen him without his yarmulke and that, she supposed, was the essence of his work. Giott was as low-key as Baruch was harddriving. Amazing the two men coexisted at National Headquarters, managing their interdependent organizations as well as they appeared to. In fact, the relationship between Shin Bet and the National Police remained strong. Jurisdictional disputes were rare and cooperative ventures commonplace.

"We have reviewed what transpired this morning," Giott said when she was seated, "and have found the events to be most regrettable."

Danielle felt her stomach sink. Here it comes: dismissal, disgrace. She would walk out this door having been stripped of the rank that had so long imprisoned her, only to miss it desperately.

"That said," he continued, "while your performance cannot be considered exemplary, your actions almost undoubtedly saved the life of at least one fellow officer."

"Agent Tice's wounds were only superficial," Baruch reported in a voice that seemed too deep for his thin frame. "He will encounter some vision problems for a while but is expected to make a complete recovery."

Danielle breathed a sigh of relief.

"However," Giott picked up somberly, "this leaves us with a rather serious dilemma."

Uh-oh, Danielle thought, *here it comes . . .*

"Agent Tice was about to start a new assignment for us." Giott exchanged a quick glance with Baruch. "An assignment coordinated jointly through the commander's and my offices. Agent Tice had volunteered for this assignment. It was to start this afternoon and cannot be pushed back. So we find ourselves in need of a replacement."

"We would like you to take Agent Tice's place," Baruch added flatly. "Your record of commendations indicates you are more than capable of handling the job."

"Thank you, sir."

"Don't thank us yet, Pakad," Giott warned. "Tice was our only volunteer for a reason: we have decided to offer our assistance to the Palestinians in a joint operation aimed at catching the serial killer who's been terrorizing the West Bank for months."

Danielle looked from one man to the other. She wondered if she were being tested, if they were waiting for a response.

"The Wolf," Baruch elaborated before she could make one, and Danielle realized this wasn't a test at all. "He struck again last night for a second time in Jericho. You can appreciate our dilemma under the circumstances, I'm sure."

"But I cannot appreciate offering to help the Palestinians."

"The offer has been extended in the name of peace, Pakad," Giott told her. "The order to make it came from the Prime Minister himself. If you have a problem with your assignment, perhaps you should take it up with him."

Danielle tried to keep her expression blank. The chair seemed suddenly very stiff, the buttons pressing into her flesh.

"I must respectfully decline," was all she said.

Her present and former superiors looked at each other before Baruch spoke.

"You misunderstand, Barnea. We were not offering you a choice."

"You must *understand,* sir. My brothers, *my father . . .*"

Giott nodded. "All heroes to the State. How is your father, Pakad?"

"Failing."

"Unfortunate."

"My younger brother's death quickened the process. My father was just recovering from his wounds when it happened. The stroke followed."

"We *do* understand," Giott told her.

"But that does nothing to solve our problem," Baruch said, rising. "We need someone good, who can think on their feet without the advantage of preparation Tice had. You certainly proved yourself capable of that this morning."

Danielle accepted the compliment grudgingly, considering the entire matter in the flea market hardly finished.

"What about the guns?" she asked.

"Guns?" Giott wondered.

"The rifles found hidden in the refrigerators."

"The contents of the late Ismail Atturi's truck are not your concern," Baruch said firmly.

But Danielle couldn't dismiss the thought of Atturi delivering weapons with such firepower into the West Bank to be distributed like newspapers. Apparently, whoever dispatched the gunmen had found his intentions equally problematic.

"The four gunmen," she continued, "have they been identified yet?"

"They carried no identification on their persons," Baruch informed her, settling back in his seat.

"They were Russian."

The two men looked at each other again.

"Interesting conclusion, Pakad."

"One of them screamed something at me. In Russian."

"You're certain you heard correctly?" Baruch asked her.

"He called me *suka,* a bitch. It's a word I've come to know in many languages."

"We will certainly add that to the report, Pakad," Giott promised nonchalantly, and scribbled a quick note on a pad resting before him.

"I was just wondering why they would have attacked Atturi. Four well-armed men sent to kill a single man who is known to travel unarmed?"

"It would be better, Barnea, if you—"

"It's just that I'm wondering if they were trying to make a point," Danielle said, interrupting Baruch and regretting it instantly, though still not able to stop herself. "I wonder if what happened this morning has deeper roots than we think. It's an angle I've been considering. Perhaps I'd be of better service to you following it up."

Now it was Giott who rose. "Pakad," he began, while Baruch fumed quietly over the disrespect shown him, "we understand your reluctance to take on this assignment. But you must understand the difficult position we are in. Another, less compassionate eye might have seen and judged your actions this morning differently. You are no longer in the army, no longer a member of an elite force that does not have to account for its actions. On the contrary, since the assassination our people have come under increasing scrutiny. We must account for every shell fired and heroism can often be interpreted as recklessness, which cannot be tolerated by either myself or Commander Baruch."

"I understand," Danielle said, relenting as she grasped the intent in her former superior's words.

"Very well," Giott nodded, satisfied, as he sat back down. "You are due in Jericho at three o'clock. Let us move on to the briefing . . . ."

CHAPTER 10

THE GUARDS CLUSTERED along the front of the refugee camp didn't look happy to see Ben. The captain in charge wasn't on the premises, and his underlings claimed tempers were running too high within for them to serve as Ben's escort.

Jericho's Einissultan refugee camp was located on the outskirts of the town itself, at the very edge of the oasis that sits amid the vast desert plain. To the south lay a grove of orange trees, to the north rolling hills of desolation. An abandoned Israeli military encampment could be seen from the camp's entrance to the east. Ironically, the last time the encampment had been open, the refugee camp had been closed. But even limited self-rule in the West Bank had brought a flood of exiles back from Jordan and there was simply nowhere else to put so many more of the displaced Palestinians, necessitating the reopening of this and several other camps throughout the West Bank.

Ben had fully intended to proceed through the camp on his own in search of the young witness, until a young woman latched onto him just beyond the gate.

"What you come here for, cop, eh?" she asked, appointing herself camp spokesman. She slapped him on the arm. "There been a crime committed? Somebody file a report?" Another slap, harder. "Shit, I almost forgot. How can we call in a report when the camp has no phones? We can't even walk outside to use one since they're locking us in regular now—*our own people*, not the Israelis."

Ben tried to get ahead of her and failed. She poked at his holster and he swiveled his hip away.

"Why don't you tell me what you're doing here?" the young woman continued. "Maybe I help you."

She couldn't have been more than twenty-five. Her clothes and face were both clean. Her hair smelled of soap. In another place under different circumstances she might have been considered quite beautiful. Here, though, there was no beauty; hate blanketed the premises as hopelessness choked it off a little at a time.

Ben slowed his pace, not wanting to stop altogether because of the crowds beginning to cluster along the dirt street's edges. "Why don't we start with your name?"

"Why don't we start with what you're doing here? Investigating something, I hope. Maybe the conditions. File a report. Believe me, cop, it's a crime."

She was right about that much. The squalor these displaced people lived in turned Ben's stomach. The stench of unwashed bodies and raw sewage grew stronger the further he advanced into the camp. These were the people who had given birth to the *intifada*, the ones who celebrated the hardest when autonomy came. Now they felt betrayed, and this sense made them even more dangerous than before because they had no one left to turn to. In fact, conditions in the camps had been better under Israeli control. The Israelis may have lacked conscience and compassion, but they at least had resources.

"I'm looking for someone," Ben told the young woman.

She put her hands on her hips. "Aren't we all?"

"A boy."

"To question or to fuck?"

Ben swung toward her, but held his tongue.

"Why so surprised, cop? You think you'd be the first official to leave here in the company of a kid or a woman? Who can we complain to? Maybe that's why you bastards keep us locked up!"

"You ever leave here with such an official?"

"They never seem to choose me."

"I can't imagine why."

She stepped in front of him and halted. "What is it you want?"

"I want you to help me find this boy."

"What's he done? You gonna arrest him?"

"He hasn't done anything. He may have witnessed a murder."

"What's he look like?"

"Frail. Long hair hanging just past his shoulders. Standard-issue clothes," Ben finished, trying to recall all Rula Middein had said while she finished cooking dinner for the family that never came to eat it.

The young woman's laugh was real this time. "Should be easy to spot a boy looks like that. They're all playing soccer now in our wonderful field. We call it Arafat Stadium, a testament to his devotion for his people.''

She led the way to the right. They passed another grouping of the stained canvas tents and ramshackle huts and shanties, some missing chunks of their ceilings or walls. The dominant color was a faded, soiled oatmeal. There was no order to the construction, homes squeezed in wherever they could be, leaving narrow single-lane roads so vehicles could pass over the gravel and grime.

''The boy I'm looking for has been sleeping in the streets around the Baladiya,'' Ben told the young woman.

''Then he eats better than he would on the inside.''

''Could he come and go as easily as that?''

''The sneaky ones get away with it. Sometimes they come back, sometimes they don't. Sometimes they leave with men like you, sometimes they just leave.''

They had reached the soccer field, a filthy, muddy, uneven patch of land. Given the obvious lack of water, the mud confused Ben until the breeze blew the stink toward him. This was the leaching field where all the raw sewage ended up when the pumps were operating. In spite of that, the children had appropriated it since it was the only open stretch of land in the camp.

He stopped where the ground turned to ooze and studied the boys gazing at him suspiciously. There were literally dozens who fit the description of the boy from Rula Middein's alley, all of them looking discomfited by his presence.

''You said a witness,'' the young woman said suddenly.

''Yes.''

''Plenty of them here who could be a witness. Tell

me what you want them to say and I will arrange it.''

Ben turned toward her. ''It doesn't work that way.''

''It does in here.''

Ben swung on his heels and started to retrace his own filthy trail. He had been foolish to come to the camp, wasting time better spent on rehashing the case-work on the previous murders, at least the one in Jericho ten days before. Two killings in a row in the same location. Al-Diib seemed to be deviating from his own pattern.

He was glad for the thoughts since they distracted him from the squalor around him. When he came in sight of the gate, he thought he might be able to exit without further incident. Then, before he could reach it, the young woman caught up with him again, planting herself in his path.

''This is our world, cop. What you expect when you walked in? You want us to bow and kiss your feet? You figure you deserve that for all you've done for us? Even God doesn't bother about the crime that goes on in here. It's a good thing there's nothing to steal, eh?''

Crowds were milling on either side of the main drag leading back to the gate Ben knew he had to pass through in order to leave. The mutters and whispers grew from a hum to a buzz in his ears. He didn't stop, didn't hesitate, just kept walking at a steady pace. The young woman continued to badger him, feeding the ire of the crowd. Ben fought back the urge to shove her aside, afraid the crowd was waiting for any reason at all to pounce on him.

''Come on, cop! Why you so quiet?'' she taunted. Maybe she wanted him to strike her, was disappointed that he hadn't.

The crowd turned ugly anyway.

The first stone grazed his temple, felt like a hard slap to his head.

Ben kept walking.

The second stone caught him in the back of his head and sent a brief flash exploding before his eyes. Two in rapid succession struck his forehead and cheek. Warm blood leaked from both wounds.

"Come on, cop!" the young woman taunted. "Use your gun. Shoot us!"

Ben kept his hand plainly away from his holster. The urge to launch a mad dash for the gate rose in him, but he fought it down.

He kept walking, the young woman silent before him now, watching his face.

Some of the mutters, the whispers, had gained cadence and risen into chants. The stones that connected were accompanied by applause and cheers now. Ben's nose took a big one and he felt his eyes water. He stumbled slightly, then quickly regained his footing.

The front gate was still a hundred feet away and Ben feared he wasn't going to make it. He could see the guards poised unsurely just inside, frozen, afraid for their own lives if they intervened. Or maybe they were just waiting for Ben to summon them in a desperate cry that would bring the crowd down upon him and leave him humiliated once the guards came to his rescue.

Ben knew enough not to do that. The refugees might take him anyway, but at least they would be denied a certain satisfaction. Dirty, frustrated, and angry bodies reached down for larger stones, the pelting a game turning very serious. The next rock drew blood that trickled down his neck. A thud forced him one way, a whack shook him the other.

Ben righted himself and kept walking. He fought against the temptation to draw his gun and use it to clear a path for himself to the gate.

Instead, a strange calm came over him and he realized with detachment that he didn't care if he died here. In that irrational moment, death seemed preferable to both the past, which gave him a pain worse than the rocks, and the future, which gave him nothing at all. He knew the stones were still hitting him, but he didn't feel them anymore. The people lined up on either side of him were disappearing, the tunnel between them all he could see.

Then, incredibly and inexplicably, the rocks and stones stopped pelting him. Maybe the refugees had realized there was no sense in killing one whose lot seemed as bad as their own. The gate, a moment before so impossibly far away, was now before him. One of the guards was opening it with a trembling hand. The young woman whirled in front of Ben as he started to pass through, grasped him at both elbows, and spoke very quietly.

"You a fool, cop. Brave, but a fool. The boy you seek calls himself Radji. He ran away after hitting one of the guards with a rock."

"How long ago?"

"A month. Maybe two. I haven't seen him since then."

"Where was he from, originally I mean?"

"Same place we all are, cop: nowhere."

Ben slipped through the gate and one of the guards slammed it closed, leaving him and the young woman on opposite sides. She hung her hands through the links.

"How do you know him?" Ben asked her. "How can you be sure the boy I'm looking for is this Radji?"

"Because he's my brother."

CHAPTER 11

HE'S HAVING ONE of his better days,'' the nurse said, leading Danielle toward her father's room in the convalescent home. ''Lucid, smiling, his mind drifting, but only briefly.''

They reached the door and Danielle thanked the woman for her help. It was always a chore to prepare herself properly before entering. No matter how many times she visited, usually every day, the shock of seeing her father like this did not dissipate. She could not overcome her memories of the strong and strident Israeli war hero who glistened with pride at the accomplishments of his daughter. The fact that she had no husband and was childless, unheard of for an Israeli woman of thirty-two, had meant nothing to him in the face of her vast accomplishments in service to Israel.

Danielle took a final deep breath and entered the room wearing a smile like an ill-fitting coat.

''Hello, father,'' she greeted, striding to his bed and

kissing him lightly, feeling the drool and spittle against her cheek.

He sat up and brought the notebook computer from the night table to his lap. The machine had served as his voice since a paralyzing stroke had left him without the ability to speak Danielle positioned herself so she could see the screen.

IT'S GOOD TO SEE YOU, DAUGHTER.

"I need to talk to you about something. You're the only one I can share this with."

I'M LISTENING, he typed, looking attentive.

"I have been given an assignment . . ."

FOR THE ARMY?, he typed before she could finish.

"No, I'm not in the army anymore, father. I'm with Shin Bet." He eyed her quizzically. "They are sending me to the West Bank, to Jericho."

He seemed to shudder, though it was hard to tell.

"I'm to assist the Palestinian authorities there in pursuit of a killer. It's to be a joint effort, the first ever between our peoples."

He typed fast, eyes glowing alert. SOME HISTORY IS BETTER LEFT UNMADE! And he tapped the keyboard to further emphasize his point.

"I agree, but I was not given a choice." She elected not to burden her father with all of that morning's events, and chance losing him in the confusion. "If I do not accept the assignment, I risk demotion. From the field certainly, perhaps from service altogether."

BASTARDS, he typed.

"They feel this is a great opportunity."

What was left of Shim Barnea's expression turned suspicious. THEY NEVER DO ANYTHING BECAUSE IT IS A GREAT OPPORTUNITY. THEY ALWAYS HAVE SOMETHING MORE THEY ARE AFTER. I KNOW.

Danielle started to speak, but he kept typing:

I WAS ONE OF THEM.

He typed another line and Danielle found herself staring at the stern look in his usually blank eyes before reading it:

DON'T TRUST THEM.

''I could resign,'' she said, half hoping her father would agree that was her only choice.

YOU'D NEVER . . .

But then his eyes wavered, the life starting to flicker from them, the blank darkness not far behind. He seemed to catch himself briefly.

STOP REGRETTIN AOIHOIWIIWW

His shaky hands grabbed for the screen in frustration, able to make nothing but gibberish now. Danielle pried them away gently, grateful for the alert moments she had been given today and feeling reassured that these visits she paid him were truly worthwhile since they provided the chance for her father to use his mind. Taken so for granted until it's gone. Like life itself.

And today it had been sharp, one especially clear thought of her father's lingering in Danielle's mind as she fed him his lunch minutes later:

DON'T TRUST THEM.

CHAPTER 12

I AM SUPPOSED to lend you my fullest cooperation,'' Bassim al-Shaer said with little enthusiasm, holding the door open for Ben. ''The mayor called me personally.''

''Appealed to your compassionate side, did he?''

''Only if I ever want to practice real medicine again. Speaking of which,'' al-Shaer added, an edge of pleasure creeping into his voice, ''what happened to your face?''

''I ran into some stones in a refugee camp.''

''I could bandage it for you.''

''Stick to the dead, Doctor.''

Al-Shaer snickered. ''I'm a patient man, Benny.''

Jericho's bulbous medical examiner locked the entry door behind him and drew the blind down over it.

''Come,'' he said, beckoning. Al-Shaer was still wearing the wrinkled khaki-colored pants from the morning, but his jacket was off and he had rolled up the sleeves of his shirt. He reeked of stale sweat, cigarette smoke, and the many chemicals he spent his life around.

The medical examiner's office, temporary as many things were in Jericho, was located in the rear of a storefront veterinary clinic. In addition to an examination room converted into a pathologist's lab, there was a tiny windowless office that had once been a storage closet. The lab was only large enough for two gurneys to fit inside comfortably. Cold storage for the remains was a slightly renovated meat freezer obtained from Jordan.

Al-Shaer led him down a short, dark corridor toward the lab. Ben could have found it on his own by following the stench of formaldehyde. Inside the windowless room, fluorescent lights blazed off age-stained walls. An empty gurney had been shoved into a corner, leaving a single one occupying the center covered by a white plastic sheet. A bloody body apron hung from a peg on the far wall. Al-Shaer made no move to put it on. Only when he closed the door did Ben recall he was in one of the very few air-conditioned buildings in all of Jericho, aside from the plush hotels and inns on Jericho's eastern side within distant view of the Jordan River.

In the veterinary clinic occupying the building's front, Ben could hear dogs barking.

"The findings I am about to share with you came up in the preliminary. I haven't gotten much farther than that. I doubt I have to. Almost identical to the first body they brought me ten days ago."

"Pretend it's the first. Start from the beginning."

Al-Shaer grasped the sheet but made no move to expose the body beneath it. Instead he lit up a cigarette and puffed away. "Seventeen separate stab wounds, of which any of eleven could have proven fatal. The seventeen wounds, and this I can tell, were made by a single knife."

"What kind of knife?"

"A very sharp one."

"Thank you."

Al-Shaer smiled, pleased with himself. He leaned against the gurney. "The truth is, I don't know. What I do know is that the same blade that made the puncture wounds was also used to perform the mutilation on the face, abdomen, and genitals."

"Genitals?"

"I'm getting to that. The blade was as sharp as a razor, but sliced in a pattern and width altogether inconsistent with any razor in existence."

"How so?"

The medical examiner wedged the half-smoked cigarette into the side of his mouth and reached behind the corpse's head for a tray table where instruments were soaking in an alcohol-rich bath. The blood drawn from them had turned the solution pinkish. Al-Shaer pulled a scalpel from within the froth. Ben noticed he hadn't bothered to don latex gloves.

"The edge on this is comparable to that of a straight razor," he explained, words slightly muffled by the cigarette dangling from his mouth. "Notice the thinness. The weapon of mutilation was considerably thicker than this but equally as sharp. And the cuts it made flow in *both* directions."

"A double-edged weapon."

Al-Shaer nodded. "There may be something else as well. In the last killing, I found traces of an oil-based substance coating the stab wounds."

"I don't remember reading about that in your report."

Al-Shaer tensed a little and ashes dropped from his cigarette, fluttering to the floor. "I didn't mention the oil in my official report, because I was unable to identify it and therefore assumed it was just some kind of lubricant the killer used to make his work faster and easier."

"*What* kind of lubricant?"

"A mystery."

"One of many." Ben turned back to the gurney. "Is it present in the wounds on this victim?"

"Haven't gotten that far yet. But I did review the autopsy reports on the other victims. Nothing mentioned about any oil or lubricant being found in the wounds. Though I doubt my counterparts bothered to check for it," al-Shaer added with a smirk.

"What else can you tell me about the manner of this victim's death?"

"It was violent."

"I got that point already."

"Very well." Al-Shaer spoke without benefit of notes. "Severe body trauma, aeroembolism, cadaveric spasm, exsanguination—that's blood loss."

"I know what it is."

"Cutting of the throat is the primary cause of death, though. It caused the sudden exit of air from the lungs—"

"Aeroembolism," Ben said, before al-Shaer had a chance to explain.

"Yes. With such a wound, death is almost always instantaneous. But, make no mistake about it, he suffered plenty before then. Did I show you his hands?"

"No."

"They're all sliced up. He tried to fight back, but he lost too much blood from the initial wounds too quickly to have enough strength to make a stand."

"Any skin fibers under the nails?"

"I'm afraid not. Happy now?"

Ben nodded, surprised at the expertise of al-Shaer's work. He knew the fat man had practiced medicine for many years in the occupied territories, but had been imprisoned by the Israelis following allegations he had performed surgery in a drunken state and lost several patients as a result. He had been released shortly before control of Jericho was turned over to the Palestinians, and had fallen conveniently into this role. Mayor Sumaya had promised to grant al-Shaer a medical license, now that they were required in Palestine, if he did a good job. No time frame had been stipulated but, as far as Ben could tell, the only alcohol in evidence today was of the antiseptic variety.

"What else?" Ben asked him.

"Several interesting things," the medical examiner said. He dropped the stub of his cigarette to the floor and ground it out under his shoe. Drawing back the sheet, he revealed a portion of the torso that had escaped mutilation. He traced his finger down a white splotch of skin he had previously swabbed clean. "Can you see these small scars here?"

Ben peered around al-Shaer. "No."

"Three of them; here, here, and the third through the navel," the fat man said, jabbing at the flesh to punctuate each word. "They indicate the victim had his gallbladder removed under a process called laparoscopy."

"Doubtful a Palestinian would have had access to such a procedure."

"Not in the territories, for certain. And it's doubtful a Palestinian would have had his gallbladder out at all. We are used to living with pain and discomfort."

"What is the average age of a person undergoing such a procedure?"

"Normally thirty-five and over. If the condition is chronic, occasionally even younger. The gallbladder is one of those organs you can live without."

"But the odds point to the fact that our victim is at least thirty-five."

"Somewhere between that and forty would be my best guess. And his medical history doesn't stop at gallbladder surgery." Al-Shaer waddled to the head of the gurney, was about to expose the face, but then thought better of it. "I'll spare you on this one. You wouldn't know what you were looking at anyway."

"Which is?"

"His teeth. They're capped, almost every one of them. Brilliant job. I don't have to tell you that Palestinians are lucky if we can get a filling."

"What else can you tell me?"

"Just supposition from this point."

"Please."

"The victim was very well muscled, very strong, with all the indicators of someone who trained to use his body. An athlete perhaps, or a soldier."

"Height and weight?"

"A little over six feet, a hundred and eighty-five pounds."

"And in spite of that and his conditioning he was overpowered."

"Tells you something about al-Diib, doesn't it?"

Ben gazed at the shape covered by the sheet. "Any guesses as to the victim's real nationality?"

"What little remained of his skin tone and texture indicates Semitic dominance but Western breeding. European, an American perhaps. I'd say Israeli, except . . ."

"Except what?"

"He's not circumcized. If he was, well, Israeli might have been my first choice."

Al-Shaer's point was well taken, and Ben tried to consider the ramifications of his conclusions. Identification of the body—the first step in any investigation—now promised to be extremely complicated. No longer could he rely on missing-persons reports or even the supposition that the victim was a resident of Jericho. But why would a foreigner, and a non-Arab at that, be walking the town's streets after midnight?

"I'm presuming you've cataloged the victim's personal effects."

"Of course."

"I would like to see his shoes."

Al-Shaer looked perplexed, and sighed in annoyance as he fished a plastic bag containing the victim's shoes from a large metal storage closet. He thrust them forward without comment, then tried not to watch as Ben carefully removed the shoes from the bag and turned them soles up.

Ben pulled a penknife from his pocket and scratched its blade across the sole of the victim's right shoe, careful to collect the debris on a strip of paper towel beneath it. Almost all of this debris was common road dirt and dust. But it came away quickly, revealing the black sole beneath it.

"I should have thought of this before," Ben muttered.

"Thought of *what*?"

"Of course, I didn't know he was a foreigner," Ben continued, rambling. "It seemed an obvious assumption that he had walked to Jaffa Street from wherever."

"And he didn't?"

"Test the dirt on the underside of this shoe and you will find it to be identical with the samples I asked you to take from the area of Jaffa Street where the body was found. Only, as you can see, there isn't much of it, which means the victim didn't walk very far before he was killed." Here Ben went to work on the second sole, a similarly small pile erected next to the first. "He was either dropped off or parked his car and *then* traveled the short distance to his meeting on foot."

"Meeting? Who said anything about a meeting?"

"We have a foreigner walking in Jericho after midnight. You think he was out for a casual stroll? Crossed the border and didn't know it? No, he was in Jericho for a purpose, a purpose that was interrupted by al-Diib. Either that or the Wolf was who he came here to meet."

Al-Shaer made sure Ben could see him snickering. "Should I be writing all this down?"

"No, it's my concern. Yours is finding the knife al-Diib used on his victims."

Al-Shaer chuckled. "You think he was considerate enough to drop it off somewhere in the area?"

"With the wounds of two victims to compare now, he might as well have. I am going to send you as many knives as I can find, Doctor. I want you to test all of them."

"Test?"

"Measure the precise specifications of the wounds

they leave. See if you can come up with a match for the one al-Diib used."

"That lubricant might make it harder to identify."

"We're only looking for a starting point here."

"And what exactly am I supposed to test these knives on?"

"A side of beef would do, even a slab of fish if it's firm enough."

Al-Shaer almost smiled at him. "A body would do better. You wouldn't be available, would you, Inspector?"

"That depends on whether or not I solve this case."

CHAPTER 13

   BEN HAD ONE more stop he wanted to make before returning to the Palestinian Authority building to meet his Israeli liaison. He drove over to the eastern edge of Jericho toward the expensive villas that looked out over palm trees and banana groves, the Jordan River visible as a thin white streak amid the desert's reach beyond. Some of the villas had been abandoned and remained derelict, lost to swarming vines and undergrowth, their owners still not having returned to rescue them. Ben had vague recollections of playing in the area as a child and remembered asking his father if they could live in one of these lovely homes.

His father had always said *someday*.

Those memories had been rekindled years later just after his mother's death. A trip to the attic had turned up a collection of letters to his father written over the course of the nearly five years he had spent in the

States before returning to Palestine. They were letters from a woman named Dalia Mikhail, love letters with a return address that was somehow familiar.

That address turned out to be the villa where his father had taken Ben to play, using the opportunity, no doubt, to visit a mistress whose letters Ben crunched in his fist as he read them. He felt betrayed, might have thought his father's entire return to Jericho had been a lie too, if he hadn't been assassinated.

Ben kept those letters, smoothed out once again, and reread them occasionally in the years that followed. He wondered if his mother had any idea of what had gone on, if that partially explained why she had not put up a greater fight when Jafir Kamal told her he was leaving. Ben had often thought about writing Dalia Mikhail himself to learn what the letters could not tell him. But he never did. She remained a specter, a shadow to him until his own return to Jericho.

He had had no idea what to expect or what exactly he intended to say, so he couldn't really say he was surprised when she opened the door, took one look at him, and said, "I've been expecting you."

She had known he was back, having followed all the publicity made of his return and the role he was to play in helping to train a Palestinian detective force in the West Bank. Despite his misgivings, Ben found himself almost immediately entranced by her. In her sixties now, he judged, she was still elegant, with fine features and a slim body. A Palestinian Christian, her letters indicated she had always opposed the Fundamentalists. She was not afraid to have Israeli friends visit her and never hesitated to visit them.

First out of wonder, then curiosity and perhaps, finally, loneliness, Ben had become friends with Dalia

Mikhail. They met frequently, sharing meals and memories. While sitting on her terrace, Ben could remember playing on the lovely stretch of land beneath her villa, throwing stones and imagining they might reach the Jordan, while he waited for his father who said he had business to attend to.

I played with Daddy, he would answer when his mother asked him what he'd done that day, and it seemed to him that he had.

Dalia Mikhail's two-story villa had lost none of its charm since those days, furnished with perfectly stated period pieces and art treasures of museum quality, from innumerable periods and cultures. Each piece had a story to go along with it. Ben had heard many of them, but he never tired of hearing more.

None of the furniture in any of the villa's rooms matched in terms of style or period. The overwhelming sense was of pale, cool colors set off by dark floors and a few dark wood chests. Contrast made for character, and the symmetry existed in the wondrous mind of the person who had done the arranging.

Dalia Mikhail was content to live alone with her art. She kept her distance from the rest of the world, using a personal computer tied into the Internet as a buffer zone for companionship when the international phone lines worked. Beyond that, the world stopped at the windows and upon her two decks. There was nothing to beckon her. Her world was inside. Dalia Mikhail, in many ways, was Rula Middein who had accepted the fact that the family was never coming to dinner.

The only exception was the relentless campaign she waged against the current Palestinian administration through weekly letters to the editor in the various Palestinian dailies. They were seldom published anymore and her requests to pay for advertising space to print them were summarily denied. Still she kept writing, and Ben found himself turning to the editorial page first now on the chance that her efforts had proven successful.

Today Ben followed her into the living room, which reminded him in some ways of the home he had left in the States. Her television had been tucked into a tall armoire that rested against the near wall. The wires from the roof-mounted satellite dish had been fished invisibly through walls and floor, so as not to disturb the room's mood. Directly opposite the armoire on the far wall, just to the side of the sliding glass doors that opened onto the villa's first floor deck, was her computer. The villa's many windows were covered with light-colored blinds made of natural fibers especially woven to keep the fierce sunlight from destroying Dalia's treasures during the hottest and brightest times of the day.

Ben took his customary chair. Dalia sat down opposite him on the couch.

"You see *Al-Quds* this morning?"

"Not yet."

"Don't bother. Another of my letters gone to waste. They refuse to print anything relating to the troubles in the refugee camps."

Ben rubbed one of the wounds he suffered at the camp late that morning. "I learned of them first-hand just a few hours ago."

"Is that what you came to me about?" Dalia asked.

"Why must there always be something I come to you about? Can't I come just to visit?"

"You could, but you don't. You always come when there's something on your mind."

He conceded the point, head tilting guiltily. "Just a case I'm working on."

"Al-Diib?"

"How did you know?" Ben managed, taken aback.

"It was only a matter of time before they asked you for help."

"There's more: I'm to be working with an Israeli counterpart."

That seemed to satisfy her. "Becoming part of history like your father?"

"Reluctantly."

"You think it was any different for him?"

"I thought it came easier, more naturally."

"He was just a better actor than you are, Ben: he even fooled himself." She bounced up enthusiastically from the couch. "I almost forgot. I want to show you something, my latest *amanah* . . . "

She moved to the armoire and opened its doors gently, removing a miniature ebony chest that looked Chinese to Ben's untrained eye.

"Ming Dynasty," she explained, cradling it lovingly. "Very rare."

"And exquisite."

"Take it," Dalia said, and Ben lifted it from her hands like he was holding a baby.

"It's called a Buddha chest. The legend is that if you store your secrets inside, Buddha himself will make sure they end up in the right place."

"Interesting."

"And practical. The Orientals are always practical. We Palestinians could learn something from them." Ben was ready to give the chest back, but she liked it where it was. "You might learn something from them too, Ben. Any secrets you want to store away inside?"

"I'm scared," he confessed, saying what he should have said in the mayor's office that morning.

"Of failing? Of losing this opportunity to regain your good standing?"

"No, of succeeding. Of being the one to catch this monster, just like the last one."

Dalia's expression sank, saddened. "I'm sorry. I was being trivial."

Ben rose and handed the chest back to her. "It's all right. The problem's mine, and I've got to get past it. You'd think I would be glad for a chance to go after another of these monsters."

"Not after what the first one did."

"*Because* of what the first one did." His voice fell after that. "But it's the last thing I want, going through that again. They scare me, Dalia, because they're not people as we know them. They operate on a whole different plane. I looked into the Sandman's eyes after . . ."

He sharpened his voice. "I don't know what was in them, but it wasn't human. I don't know if I can stand to see that sight again, face another monster. I went through the motions this morning, did my job, but the truth is, a big part of me *wants to fail.* I don't want to be the one to catch al-Diib, because I can't pay the price for succeeding again." Ben tried for a smile, didn't even come close. "I've got nothing left to pay with."

Dalia moved to the armoire and returned the Buddha chest to its place.

"Tell me about the Israeli you'll be working with," she said, closing the doors.

"I'm meeting him at three. That's all I know."

"Let's see if I can find out a little more," she offered, seating herself before her computer.

Dalia used E-mail to contact a friend who worked as a records clerk at Israel's National Headquarters. When he came on line, she stated her request and then sat back to wait for his response.

Outside, a mild breeze was blowing in from Jordan, providing the villa all the air-conditioning it needed. In the late afternoon hours that view, encompassing the mountains, valley, and outer reaches of the oasis on which Jericho lies amid an otherwise barren valley, is as magnificent as any on earth.

"Ah," Dalia said finally, a reply appearing on her screen, "he's in a talkative mood today and—Wait a minute . . . Most interesting."

"What is it?" Ben asked.

She turned toward him. "Come have a look for yourself."

"At what?"

"Your new partner."

CHAPTER 14

BEN WAS ALREADY twenty minutes late for the meeting with his Israeli liaison when he reached the Palestinian Authority building. He mounted the stairs quickly, struggling to collect his breath as he neared Mayor Sumaya's office on the third floor. The door was partly open. He knocked anyway.

"Come in," Sumaya's voice called back.

"Sir," Ben greeted, entering.

"Ah, Inspector. We've been waiting for you." The mayor rose at his appearance. Commander Shaath, seated directly in front of the desk, did not. "There's someone I'd like you to meet . . ."

Ben's eyes followed the mayor's slightly awkward gaze to the right and watched a ravishing, dark-haired woman rise from one of the twin chairs perched there.

"This is Chief Inspector Danielle Barnea of the Israeli National Police," Sumaya announced.

They met halfway across the floor and shook hands. Danielle's grip was firm and warm. She had small hands for her size, but carried plenty of strength within them. Ben felt calluses at the base of her fingers.

"I look forward to working with you," he said, hoping his lack of enthusiasm didn't show through.

"The feeling is mutual, Inspector." But Ben could tell her own reluctance matched his.

The fact that the Israeli liaison was a woman came as no surprise, since Dalia Mikhail had uncovered that fact for him mere minutes before. With no picture sent to her screen, what Dalia could not uncover was Danielle Barnea's beauty. Ben let his eyes linger after Danielle's had turned away. She was wearing a plain skirt and blouse colored an almost military olive green. She had an athlete's build, that of someone who was used to working out. Her dark brown hair tumbled easily over her shoulders.

"Chief Inspector Barnea was a last-minute replacement," the mayor continued to Ben, seizing back control of the situation. "As such, she may need additional time to acquaint herself with the case."

"That won't be necessary," Danielle said surely. "And I'd like to get started immediately, if you don't mind."

"Not at all," the mayor agreed. "Inspector Kamal?"

Ben turned his gaze briefly on Sumaya. "I'm sure I can fill in any gaps in the chief inspector's knowledge."

"And just how long have you been assigned to the case?" she asked him.

"Since this morning," Ben answered before the mayor could chime in.

"It would seem you suffer from gaps of your own."

"Not so far as the most recent victim is concerned, and right now that is our primary concern."

Danielle swung back to Sumaya. "I was expecting to be paired with someone with more intimate knowledge of this investigation as a whole."

"Until this morning," Ben countered, "there was no investigation as you would understand it. That's why the mayor asked me to step in."

"After five murders?"

"Eight now, counting the three Israeli authorities failed to investigate thoroughly and tie together."

Sumaya rose. "Well then," he said, as Ben and Danielle stood staring at each other, "I don't suppose there's any more to be accomplished in this office."

In the hallway, after they had taken their leave, Danielle moved ahead of Ben and stopped at the top of the staircase. They stood there frozen as if each was waiting for the other to take the first step down.

"We should go to my office at police headquarters," Ben told her. "Review the case, get to know each other better."

Danielle Barnea took his remark as a challenge. "Bayan Kamal. Born 1960 in Ramallah. Son of the hero Jafir Kamal. Emigrated to America in 1965 to join relatives in Dearborn, Michigan. Father returned to the West Bank alone in 1967 and was assassinated in 1968." Danielle sought out Ben's eyes at that. "After a brilliant high school career, you attended the University of Michigan, graduating in the top third of your class. One year of law school followed by enrollment in police academy. Again graduated in top third of class and accepted job in Detroit police department.

Married same year to an American woman. Two children. Was that a problem for you?''

"Having children?''

"Marrying an American.''

"I am an American.''

"I meant when you came back here. It would have been a problem for an Israeli.''

"There were too many other problems for people to worry about that,'' Ben told her.

Danielle moved on. "I'll skip ahead in your file to the point where you were assigned to head a task force investigating a series of brutal family slayings by a serial killer known as the Sandman. Shot and killed said killer when you found him—''

"That's enough,'' Ben said.

"You don't want me to finish?''

"Let's skip to more recent history,'' said Ben. "I came back here just over a year ago hoping to put my life back together. Teach detectives who didn't even qualify as novices what a crime scene was and how to secure it.''

"Maybe the Authority should build a police academy.''

"We have two, actually: one here in Jericho and the other in Gaza. I've lectured in both. Anything else?''

"Why do they call you Ben?''

"It's not in your file?''

"I wouldn't have asked if it was.''

"After we moved to America, the kids in school couldn't pronounce my real name, so I became Ben. When I moved back, the name stuck. Now, quid pro quo, what do you say?'' Ben feigned clearing his throat, ever so thankful now for Dalia Mikhail's computer. "Danielle Barnea, born in Jerusalem 1962. Enters the army in the Engineer Corps in 1980, but requests transfer to Special Operations division of the Israeli Defense Forces following completion of her mandatory service two years later, just after the first of two brothers dies in the Lebanon incursion of 1982. Becomes first woman ever given full commission in the Sayaret. Seventeen active missions. Rank upon retirement from duty at age of thirty, lieutenant—"

"Actually," Danielle interrupted in a steely voice, "I was commissioned a captain on my last day."

"—Completes accelerated police training course and joins National Police with rank of *sgan mefakeah*—did I pronounce that right?"

"Close enough."

"Or deputy inspector. Eighteen months later becomes the youngest woman ever to be promoted to *pakad*, or chief inspector, the same year a second brother was—"

"I think we can move on now."

"Not quite. I was just coming to the part of your file that details your transfer to Shin Bet, effective three months ago following your arrest of the alleged terrorist Ahmed Fatuk."

"Not alleged. Fatuk masterminded the suicide bombings of two city buses."

"I heard he had moved in with his Christian wife in Jerusalem well before they took place."

"We had evidence."

"You have no proof."

Danielle took a deep breath. "You've made your point."

"As you've made yours."

"Then let's go to your office, Inspector, and I'll tell you what I know about the Wolf."

*   *   *

WHAT WOULD YOUR mayor think if he knew I was from Shin Bet?'' she asked when they were outside the building.

"Anything you want him to, so long as you say favorable things about him to your superiors.''

"We've come a long way, Palestinians caring what Israelis think about them.''

"The mayor is smart enough to know who the real enemies are.''

"And the big man, the one who looked like an ape and sat silently in the chair the whole time I was in the office?''

"Commander Shaath. He's not smart at all.''

"He wouldn't shake my hand.''

"Something else you and I have in common. Why try to hide your true position from us?''

"Because the involvement of Shin Bet implies a more vested interest on the part of my government. We wanted to keep this cooperative venture on a civilian level.''

"But it's not, it can't be. Everything about this is government, politics. Yours, mine. The whole world is watching this cooperative venture of ours, and if it blows up, it won't be civilians like you and me who pay.''

"That's why both sides are so determined to make it succeed.'' She looked at him with that same knowing stare. "Something I get the impression you don't care too much about.''

"I like to remain detached,'' Ben said.

"Were you detached when you went after the Sandman?''

Ben felt a slight surge of static roll up his spine. "It was something I learned afterward."

"I understand."

"Do you?"

"I know your file, you know mine. Ask yourself."

"Different."

"Loss—always the same."

"We do have certain things in common then, don't we, Pakad?"

"Circumstances, not politics."

"Politics *are* circumstances."

They lapsed into silence, strangers sharing the same sidewalk and nothing more.

"We should stick to the matter at hand," Danielle said finally.

"Fine, then. What can you tell me about the three killings that took place while the West Bank was still under Israeli control?" Ben asked her.

"Unfortunately, the first two murders were not followed up on satisfactorily. We can only be sure of the two that came after Shin Bet's involvement."

"That makes *four* before the pullout, Pakad. Nine total now, instead of eight."

"The first occurred in the Muslim quarter of Jerusalem, not the West Bank."

Ben let the remark pass. "And the two locations that followed Shin Bet's taking an interest?"

"Ramallah and Bethlehem."

"I grew up in Ramallah," Ben remarked. "I'll have to show you my childhood home sometime."

"I imagine there's nothing to stop you from returning to it now."

Ben gave her a long look before moving on. "In

any event, Jericho's the first place al-Diib's repeated himself.''

''I can tell you that the cases we investigated prior to the pullout were virtually identical to the ones you're facing here.''

''You didn't hand over the files?''

''No one asked for them.''

''You could have offered.''

''We didn't think you'd want our help.''

''Or, maybe, you didn't want to give it.''

''We didn't have a lot of reason to.''

''Because the victims were Palestinians?''

''Because we were certain you would read something else into such an offer.''

''And have we, Pakad?''

''I'll let you know tomorrow, Inspector.''

''Of course, since you couldn't catch the killer after four confirmed murders, why should we even want your help?''

''The Wolf was no more visible under our tenure than yours.''

''But he leaves at least one trademark behind, doesn't he? Tell me about the areas of your victims' mutilations, Pakad.''

''Faces and genitalia. The Wolf is someone who enjoys his work, who always makes sure he has enough time to finish what he starts. When soldiers found the first one in East Jerusalem, they were not certain initially whether the victim was male or female, there'd been so much cutting.''

''And the others?''

''Not as bad.''

''Our victims have all been bad.''

''I know.''

"Did he empty the pockets of the victims you investigated as well, Pakad?"

"Yes. Why do you think he does that?"

"To throw us off the track, perhaps; make us think robbery was the true motive. Or it could be just a ritual for him, souvenirs to collect and remind him of the kill. Neatly cataloged and displayed so he can relive the event in his mind. Monsters do things like that."

"What did the Sandman collect?"

"The clothes his victims were wearing when he killed them. We didn't release that information to the press until after"—Ben felt a shudder rise through him—"he was dead. Otherwise we would have had an entire city sleeping in the nude."

"Or not sleeping at all."

"That's what it finally came to: the entire routine of a city altered. It's fightening the damage a single man can do."

"Why are you so certain it's a man in this case?"

"Physical strength. In both attacks here in Jericho, the victim was badly overpowered. Make no mistake about it, Pakad; he's big, strong, and male."

"And ritualistic."

"As most serial killers tend to be."

"But our killer doesn't fit all the norms, does he? To begin with, his victims come from both sexes. That is most unusual."

"Was there any evidence of sexual activity in the victims Shin Bet investigated?"

"No evidence of semen anywhere on the scene in our cases," Danielle reported. "Also no indication of penetration, either vaginally or rectally. Are we saying, then, that sex is not important to the killer we're after?"

"The mutilation of the genitalia in both male and female victims would seem to indicate something like that. But someone either asexual or androgynous would still tend to prey on one sex, not both."

"Of course, all we know is there was no evidence of sexual culmination on the scene. That does not mean it did not follow in the Wolf's natural order of things once he returned home. Like clothes for the Sandman."

Ben remained calm. "That could be."

"Do you think he could be incapable of *any* sexual response? Say, if he too were mutilated, like the cab-driver whose murder you investigated."

"The motivation in that case was considerably different."

"I wasn't talking about the case; I was talking about what surviving such a mutilation might do to a man."

It was something Ben had failed to consider. He should have, of course. Maybe he had missed it on purpose.

"If we could generate a list of men maimed in such a way," Danielle continued, "we'd have something to start with."

"Then we'd better start with your files, Pakad, because the odds are the maiming came as a result of Israeli torture, most likely at your Ansar 3 detention camp."

Ben expected Danielle to bristle at his comment. Instead, she showed no reaction at all.

"If that were the case, Inspector, perhaps you could tell me why he's killing Palestinians instead of Jews."

"Torture can do strange things to a man, Pakad."

"And just assuming his wounds occurred at *Palestinian* hands . . ."

"Then treatment may have been obtained at one of the hospitals or clinics your army allowed to remain open during the occupation. I'll run some checks. I'd ask you to do the same with your Ansar 3 records, but I imagine there would be too many to sort through. So the only thing we have for sure to help us at this point are the victims. Uncover how he found them, or why he chose them, and we find him."

Danielle loosened slightly. "If you're looking for common denominators, our computers have already failed to find any worthwhile to us."

"Perhaps because they did not have all the information they needed. Testimony of witnesses and family members, for example. It is doubtful such people would have felt comfortable talking to Israelis. And a computer cannot visit the scenes of the killings like we can. A computer cannot weigh information that the original investigators may have missed."

"With that in mind, I'd like to review your files of the five victims found since the pullout. I have mine in the car."

Ben led her toward the parking lot. "Then let's get started."

CHAPTER 15

"You're early," Ben greeted Officer Tawil as he approached the car Ben had parked in the dark shadows of Jaffa Street at eleven o'clock that night.

"So are you, *sidi*."

"Couldn't sleep."

"No sign of the boy yet, I assume," Tawil said, as he climbed into the passenger seat of the Peugeot. He took another look at Ben. "No uniform?"

"Didn't see the need, so I chose comfort over function. Besides, I doubt we'll be arresting anyone."

"What happened to your face? I was right, wasn't I, Inspector? I hope you made the man who did that pay."

"There were too many."

"All of them, then," Tawil said, and Ben could hear the hate building in his voice.

"Who should I have made pay, Issa?" he asked knowingly.

Tawil lowered his eyes. "My parents were executed when I was ten because they were suspected of being collaborators. Their killers made me watch."

"And were your parents collaborators?"

"No more than the cabdriver those police officers killed was. They begged for medicine I needed, antibiotics, and when the United Nations administrators couldn't help, they turned to the Israelis. That was their crime. If they had let me go without medicine, they would have lived. Since they received the antibiotics, they had to die." Tawil looked up again. The rage had narrowed his eyes into angry slits. They looked watery. "Your father came back and tried to make a difference. He stood up to the Israelis on behalf of people like my parents."

"It wasn't the Israelis who murdered them, Issa."

"But they murdered your father, *sidi*."

THE PALESTINIANS HAD inherited the old police station in the Baladiya after the Israelis relinquished control of Jericho. The limestone building sat perpendicular to the Municipal Building on the square, easily distinguishable by the open veranda that lay before its entrance. The cells were located in the basement and the three stories above were neatly laid out with offices and conference rooms, the detective branch taking up the bulk of the first floor.

That afternoon, Danielle had followed Ben back there and joined him in his windowless office off by itself in the rear where they reviewed the case files together until she took her leave just before six o'clock. None of the Israeli autopsy reports mentioned anything about an oily substance found within the wounds of the victims, and he had neglected to ask her if any retesting were possible to see if the results might jibe with Dr. al-Shaer's. He was jotting down a note to himself, when a knock came on his door just before it creaked open.

"I was hoping I would find you in," greeted Major Nabril al-Asi, head of the Palestinian Protective Security Service. "Can you spare a few minutes?"

Ben shifted uneasily, not sure what to make of this on top of everything else that had happened today. Since the PSS's offices were located in the Palestinian Authority building, al-Asi must have made a special trip over here, and that alone was cause for concern. The Palestinian Protective Security Service was generally regarded as Yasir Arafat's secret police, and had inherited many of the roles left vacant by the Israeli withdrawal. Their primary charge was to keep opposition groups in check, but to accomplish this al-Asi had expanded his mandate considerably. From often unlawful detainments and seizures to baseless arrests and extended incarcerations, al-Asi did his job at the expense of driving a rift between his service and the people it was supposed to be protecting.

Al-Asi preferred tailored Western suits, which his official "civilian" status allowed him to don daily. Ben had heard Israeli contacts obtained the suits for him in Tel Aviv, the same contacts al-Asi often exchanged information with. Every time Israeli commandos captured or killed a wanted terrorist, rumors flew through the streets that al-Asi had done everything but pull the triggers. Still no one crossed him, because his power was broadly defined and he had to justify his actions only to Arafat. He kept a low profile, and all Palestinians avoided his Security Service personnel at all costs. Including Ben.

"I'm busy," he said.

Al-Asi was already closing the door behind him. "This won't take long." He sat down in the single chair set before Ben's desk and began tugging at the salt-and-pepper mustache that made him look a little like Omar Sharif. "A name has come across my desk I would like your input on."

"I'm sure there's nothing I can add to any of your investigations."

"Dalia Mikhail."

Ben stiffened.

"I believe you are acquainted with her and that it is something of, well, a family tradition."

"What do you want?"

"I told you."

"She writes letters to the editor—lots of them. She's got a way with words and a good wit. Have those become parts of your domain now?"

"When they are inciteful and inflammatory, absolutely, Inspector. I was hoping you could be more illuminating about Ms. Mikhail."

"You want to know how many times my father slept with her?"

"We are more concerned about who she could be sleeping with now."

"I've never seen her bedroom."

"I have pictures if you're interested," al-Asi said sharply.

Ben curled his fingers into half-fists. "What is this about?"

"A routine investigation."

"Ruining someone's life is never routine."

Al-Asi's gaze turned suspicious. "You expect us to find something?"

"Don't you always?"

"Only when it's there, Inspector, and that happens all too often, unfortunately."

"You're wasting your time with Dalia Mikhail."

"She's totally innocent, then?"

"No, she's guilty of expressing herself and speaking out on injustices in the West Bank. Worried you're going to be the subject of a letter, Major?"

Al-Asi stood up. "I already was, Inspector. The newspapers apparently lost the copy."

He took his leave, leaving Ben drained and ready to call it a day.

Upon returning to his homeland last year, he had been assigned a modest one-bedroom apartment with a single bath. On a scale of one to five, where a villa like Dalia Mikhail's would be a one and the Einissultan refugee camp a five, his home was a clear three. It had running water that worked except during the frequent shortages, electricity, and even ceiling fans that made the oppressive heat tolerable. Ben had purchased the fans on the thriving black market, the only available source for many expensive items. Televisions, VCRs, even prized air conditioners were available, although he was certain his apartment lacked the voltage to run all of them at once. The closest thing to air-conditioning he had was the bag of ice he had placed over his throbbing head after sprawling on the couch first thing when he got home.

He awoke suddenly at ten p.m., lurched upward certain he had overslept. As always, his sleep had been deep, dreamless, and utterly disorienting. He never awoke refreshed and cared nothing for his lack of dreams, since there was little they had brought him for years now other than the blank face and cat's eyes of the Sandman coming toward him as he had that last night.

He had been working on the Sandman for six months, during which time four entire families were slaughtered in the greater Detroit area while they slept. The case left him precious little time to be with his wife and own children: Tyler, who was seven, and Ryan, who was five. He was the point man on the investigation, the detective whom both the press and the public took their frustrations and fear out on.

Ben had returned home that night confident that they had finally accumulated a list of suitable suspects, ready to take the investigation in another direction the next day. Dead tired, he left his car in the driveway and started up the walk.

Halfway to the steps he saw the front door was cracked open.

That was the first time he felt the now-familiar electricity dancing through him, in shuddering jolts that felt like shock waves sliding up his spine. He remembered how hard it had been to breathe as he drew his Glock nine-millimeter pistol and charged up the stairs, screaming his wife's name.

He smelled the blood when he reached the top, just before a blur whirled at him in the darkness. He recognized Jenny's nightgown, torn and bloodied, and that made him hesitate until he saw the knife. The Sandman held it overhead as he charged, and Ben opened up on him with the Glock. Instinct fueled his shots, but rage kept them coming. It seemed to take forever, the longest four or five seconds in Ben's life.

His first bullet obliterated the Sandman's chin and part of his right jaw, left sinew and bone hanging where a face used to be. Two more and then a third blew chasms in his chest, one direct to the heart which caused a spurt of blood that splattered the walls.

The Sandman kept coming.

The monster still had the strength to start a thrust of his knife downward before Ben's last hollowpoint bullet blew away the top of his skull. The Glock's slide had locked into place when the Sandman finally keeled over and fell at Ben's feet.

There was no sense of triumph, just an over-whelming fear that settled like bile in the pit of his stomach before he surged into one son's room and then the other. He would never forget the sights that greeted him there; the dreams, when they came, would make sure of that, too. He entered his own bedroom last to find his wife's naked body lying facedown, looking as though someone had sprayed it onto the sheets.

Ben was not surprised when the Sandman turned out to be a locksmith. The fact that none of the vic-tims' homes had shown signs of forcible entry kept him clinging to that theory, even after a careful check of all area locksmiths turned up nothing. The Sandman had only apprenticed in a shop as a boy, and that had been years before; his name turned up among several others only the previous day after Ben expanded the search. Never forgot the trade, though; stayed sharp with lots of practice.

The Sandman must have known the police were get-ting close. That accounted for his paying a visit to Ben's family; upping the stakes in search of a new challenge. Ben could almost imagine how much he'd enjoyed it, the danger involved, the chance that a cop with fourteen hollowpoint slugs could be returning any moment. And yet only the fact that the Sandman was into his bizarre ritual of wearing his victims' clothing shifted the odds in Ben's favor.

In the end, there was nothing special about the killer. No abusive childhood, no traumatic experience as an adolescent. No previous indication that he was capable of such unthinkable acts. He was, simply, a monster.

The tragedy of Ben's heroism took him beyond celebrity to virtually mythic stature. He slid through the press conferences and interviews in a trance, accepted condolences and congratulations in the same handshakes. When the handshakes stopped, he was left only to his own thoughts and pain. He took a leave of absence from the force and then accepted a disability pension which left him with nothing but time on his hands—too much of it, since sleep was so difficult for him—and the temptation to use his Glock one last time.

Then peace, at least a form of it, had come to the Middle East. The Palestinians were to be granted their shot at autonomy, the whole load of civil services about to be thrust into their eager but ill-prepared hands. A ten-thousand-member national police force, recruited from former guerrilla fighters out of Lebanon, Jordan, Egypt, Iraq, Libya, and other Arab countries, was hastily trained and equipped. But that number had proven barely enough to handle the Gaza Strip, never mind the considerably more populated and infinitely more urban West Bank. Add to this the fact that little thought had been given to the requisites of an actual *functioning* investigatory detective force.

Crimes during the occupation had seldom been followed up except for the obvious, so there was no precedent to draw upon. Accordingly, the last-minute formation of a detective bureau had opened the door for Ben Kamal to return home.

He plunged into the effort and left his other self far enough behind to be able to sleep again, though he still rarely dreamed. The transition had been surprisingly easy for him at first. After all, he spoke the language, understood the customs, and, most importantly, felt he had a reason to live again.

While Palestinian Authority officials had welcomed him with open arms for the services he was providing, however, the people had treated him with suspicion and trepidation from the start. Ben tried not to let this bother him. Give it time, he told himself. After all, Palestinians had every reason to be suspicious by nature. But ten months had seen little change as he busied himself with providing on-the-job training in such areas as crime-scene preservation and investigation by the numbers.

The case of the murdered cabdriver affected him on a personal level and became one of those he elected to pursue himself. He thought that by catching the poor man's killers he could change the way the people of his homeland perceived him. But when the trail indisputably led to the arrest of three fellow police officers, the uneasiness about him turned into ostracism and even danger.

What am I doing here?

Ben had asked himself the same question so many times of late, most recently as he stepped from the shower following his nap that night, the grime and stink of the refugee camp scrubbed away. Toweling himself dry, he peered into the small wall mirror. Everything about him looked worn and weary. His eyes were drawn and bloodshot. The lines beside his mouth had deepened. Moving to Jericho meant a barber instead of a hair stylist and he kept his hair too short as a result, further exaggerating the furrows in his forehead.

What am I doing here?

Standing there, looking at himself while the mist cleared, he found he had no answer and probably would have left if he had somewhere else to go. But he was fresh out of homelands. The Sandman had chased him from one and now al-Diib threatened to chase him from another. Logic might have indicated that pursuit of this second monster was *exactly* what he needed most to banish the ghosts left by the first. But logic was nothing compared to fear, and Ben found the mere possibility of a second confrontation terrifying. Catch this man and he'd have to run the risk of facing him. The best strategy to pursue was to simply go through the motions.

But first Shaath and then al-Shaer had aggravated Ben and forced him to look for clues when he had no interest in finding them, needing to prove something. Then Danielle Barnea had appeared on the scene to challenge him further. Ben found himself *wanting* to outdo her, to make a stand for his people. Zaid Jabral from the *Al-Quds* newspaper had said he had only been selected because the Israelis had insisted. The *Israelis* had chosen him. An American must have made them feel safer, any other Palestinian was not good enough for them. Solve the case himself and see what they thought of that, because he was just as Palestinian as anyone in the department.

Ben broke off his thoughts and turned toward Tawil in the front seat, then fixed his gaze back out through the windshield. It had begun to rain; the intensity of the sudden downpour made it hard for Ben to see out through the glass.

Outside, a shape was approaching the car.

Ben turned to Tawil, who seemed not to notice it. The windows were misting up and he swiped a sleeve against the inside of the glass to clear his view.

The shape was still coming, but the rain prevented him from seeing it clearly, so Ben leaned his head out the driver's side window, feeling the torrents drench him as he peered ahead.

The shape was that of a naked woman, coming through the downpour, not wet at all. Ben drew a sleeve across his eyes to wipe the dripping water from them.

He froze, felt something cold and sharp grab his insides.

The shape was his wife, Jenny, naked as she'd been after the Sandman had finished with her, the rain washing the blood from her knife wounds only to have more run out after it.

Ben couldn't move, cried out for Tawil, but the young officer did not acknowledge him from the passenger seat. He just sat there dumbly, as Ben's naked wife came close enough to the car for him to see the neat slice across her throat, her eyes refusing to close. Groping out with a single hand, maybe for the nightgown the Sandman had stripped off her.

"Jenny," Ben muttered, feeling a scream starting to build behind his lips. *"Jenny!"*

But it wasn't Jenny anymore; it was Danielle Barnea, just as dead and reaching for him through the open window, her hand grasping his shoulder when the scream finally emerged.

CHAPTER 16

I DIDN'T MEAN to startle you, Inspector,"
Tawil apologized, pulling his hand away as Ben came
awake.

"Oh. Sorry." Ben felt totally disoriented, the street
a maze of opaque nothingness through the windshield
before him.

"I think you were having a nightmare."

"How . . . long was I out?"

"A few minutes."

Ben checked his watch. "More like an hour." He
noted the rain was mirage, just as the figure of Jenny
had been.

Tawil shrugged. "Haven't seen a soul. Quiet night."

"No kid?"

"No kid." He shifted toward the door on the passenger side. "I need to take a piss."

"Glad to cover for you," Ben tried to joke. He
cleared his throat.

Tawil climbed out and walked around the car to Ben's open window. "You sure you're all right, *sidi*?"

"Just tired."

"This isn't going anywhere. We should call it a night."

"We'll discuss it when you get back."

Ben ran his hands over his face, tried to squeeze the life back into himself. He sighed loudly and massaged his eyelids. Realizing how stiff he felt, he climbed out of the car and stretched, then leaned against the door as he breathed deeply.

A shuffling sound turned his attention up the street. He saw the shape of a woman clinging to the shadows, scampering with her eyes darting behind her as if to check for a pursuer.

Ben moved away from the car, suddenly alert, wondering if it might be al-Diib she was fleeing, just as the woman's eyes found him fearfully.

"Help me," she mouthed, and Ben started her way, drawing his gun.

He passed the alley where al-Diib had struck the night before. The little of the yellow crime-scene tape that had survived the day flapped luminously in the breeze. He drew closer to the woman, peering beyond her into the night toward whoever she might have been fleeing.

"It's all right," he started. "I'm a—"

Ben felt the presence of someone coming up behind him in time to duck just as a powerful arm tried for a grasp around his throat. His hands snapped backward and closed on a thick head of hair, yanking as he dropped to one knee and letting his gun go flying.

The frame of a large man carried up and over him, slamming down hard on the road surface; then instantly the man tried to right himself. Ben saw he had a knife and kicked it from his hand before the man could straighten up, wondering how close the blade had come to his throat a moment before. The knife clanged against the pavement and bounced. The man was scampering sideways to retrieve it when Tawil's voice froze him.

"Don't move!"

The young officer stood slightly off to the left, his nine-millimeter pistol aimed directly for the man, whose hand quivered within reach of his blade.

"Touch it and I will shoot!"

Ben started forward warily. "That's all right, Issa. I have everything under control."

In one sudden, swift motion, he grabbed the man by the lapels and propelled him backward until his shoulders slammed against the nearest storefront's shuttered exterior. Ben's head ached with rage. He could feel his anger simmering over, was only vaguely conscious of the assailant's skull ping-ponging off the shutter.

A pair of surprisingly powerful hands grasped his shoulders from behind, held them.

"Let him go, *sidi*," said Tawil.

Ben released his grip. The man slumped down. A thin trail of blood followed him. The shutter showed a series of cracks down its center.

"*Zaiyel mara! Zaiyel mara!*" the woman ranted, shouting the worst of all Arab insults, enough to make Tawil start forward with his gun rising purposefully.

Ben cut in front of him, while she scraped across

the dirt-strewn street with her boot, searching for the discarded knife probably.

"It's over here," Ben said, lifting up his shoe to reveal the knife beneath it.

The woman stormed toward him. "I spit on you, cop!"

She tried, but the spittle fell short.

"Issa," Ben spoke, calm again, "I believe we have captured a prostitute here. Would you care to quote her the punishment for her crime?"

"In the time of my grandfather, the first offense was punishable by the slicing off of a nipple. The second by the loss of the entire breast."

The woman spat again.

"But we've become far more civilized in recent months, have we not?"

"We have indeed, Inspector. I believe the punishment now is a mere twenty years in jail. Mandatory."

"I'm not a whore!" the woman ranted.

"With this scam you and your friend are working, you might as well be." Ben drew closer. "A man was killed here last night, sliced up with a knife." His foot rattled the discarded blade across the pavement. "Wouldn't be too hard for Officer Tawil and me to make a case against you and your friend. Who would argue? Who would believe otherwise? Easiest solution. And the most convenient. The penalty for that is—"

"All right!" she relented. "What do you want to know?"

"You were seen on this street last night," Ben lied. "You must have seen something. I want to know what it was."

"No, not me!" Her voice lowered. "Someone else."

"Someone else pulling this same scam? Who?"

She took a deep breath. "Shanzi. She was the one. I heard her talking tonight, in Ramallah."

"Where can I find her tomorrow?"

"Same place as me: the Jalazon refugee camp."

"The one under curfew?"

"There are ways to get around that."

"I think you'd better head back there now," Ben ordered. He heard a moan and saw her accomplice struggling to rise. "And take your friend with you."

She took a few steps and started to kneel.

"Leave the knife," he told her.

Tawil moved between Ben and the woman. "You were very lucky tonight. Praise Allah for His blessing and make sure we never see you on this street again."

She hoisted her accomplice to his feet and dragged him off, glaring back hatefully.

"A long day, Inspector," Tawil commented when they were gone.

"But well worth it, my young friend," Ben replied. "We have two potential witnesses now, which is two more than any of these murders has ever had before."

BEN RETURNED TO his apartment feeling far more optimistic than he had when he set out earlier in the evening. First thing tomorrow—actually, *this*—morning he would pay a visit to the Jalazon refugee camp in search of the woman who claimed to have been on Jaffa Street around the time of the murder.

And he would also have to look into Major Nabril al Asi's investigation of Dalia Mikhail. Anytime the

Protective Security Service got involved in something, it was serious. Maybe Ben could convince her to forego her letter writing for a while, at least temper her words enough to get al-Asi to back off. The major's visit to Ben early that evening may have actually been a warning, cloaked in the language of a threat al-Asi was more comfortable with.

Ben eased his key into the door and pushed it open. As he started for the stairs, he noticed the light was out in the lobby and felt his way through the darkness.

The thump of a misplaced footstep sounded. Ben sensed movement in time to twist, and the move saved his skull from the full impact of the club. The blow, though glancing, spun him toward the wall, where a pair of hands grabbed him at the shoulders and slammed him face-first into the plaster.

His forehead hit first, sizzling stars exploding before his eyes. Ben lashed his arms backward, yanking himself from the grasp. It closed on him again, this time from the front, and something that felt like steel rammed into his stomach. He doubled over, gasping but still flailing with his hands until an arm closed over his windpipe and hot breath found his ear.

"You're going to die."

CHAPTER 17

"EASY!" A NEW voice ordered. "We need him alive! Bring him outside! Quick!"

Ben felt himself dragged across the floor, out through the door. A van screeched to a halt at the curbside, its rear doors thrown open. He was hoisted through, stretched out horizontally, his face held against a musty, dank carpet. The van sagged as several more men pulled themselves inside. Ben heard the rear doors slam and then a hand slap against the cab to signal the driver.

"Go!" The same voice.

The van tore away, tires screaming against the pavement. One set of arms jerked him upward while another fastened a hood over his face.

"Now?" from a new voice.

"Wait till we're out of town," returned the one he recognized. Authoritative, slightly nasal.

Ben shifted.

"Tie his hands!" The voice was well known to him now, obviously belonged to the leader.

He could feel someone shifting toward him, grasping his hands and clumsily bringing them together as the van bobbed across Jericho's decaying streets. Thin rope bound his wrists together, the knot digging into his flesh.

The first miles passed in silence. He could feel the road settle and then begin to climb as they headed up from the valley in which Jericho was contained. Ben knew better than to speak first. This kind of brazen act was right up Hamas's alley, but with the enemies he had made in the West Bank it could have been anyone.

"Check behind us," the voice of the leader ordered. "Anything?"

"Clear."

A pair of hands closed on Ben's lapels and snapped him forward.

"You know who we are?" the leader shot at him, close enough for Ben to feel his breath through the hood.

"No."

"Take a guess, you American shit."

"Hamas."

"Very good. You should never have come to our country. You don't belong here. Consider yourself exiled, either dead or alive—your choice."

Ben felt himself thrust backward and the back of his hooded head slammed against the cab wall.

"Well?" the voice taunted. "Which is it, dead or alive?"

"You tell me," Ben managed.

"I will tell you what you have to do to live. You

have to talk to us. You have to tell the truth. You have to give us what we want.''

''In that order?''

A backhand spun his face to the left. ''I don't like you already. Don't give me reason to like you even less. The man who was found murdered yesterday morning, where are his personal effects? Identification, papers . . .''

''There weren't any.''

Another backhand slashed across Ben's right cheek. ''Liar! We want them, American. They are your passport to staying alive. I will ask you again. What have you done with the papers he was carrying?''

''Why do you care?''

The leader pounced on Ben and jammed a forearm beneath his throat, leaving him just enough air to breathe. ''It is not your business why I care. Your business is what I want, and that is answers.''

The van took a bump hard. Ben felt his bound arms jostled upward, wrists forced against the knot binding them.

He could feel the knot giving, coming apart, and rotated his hands together, continuing the process.

''The man was found with no papers or identification on his person,'' he said through a mouth that had filled with the taste of his own blood, ''just like the previous victims. Don't you read the papers on the days you don't blow up school buses?''

Ben expected to be hit again, welcomed the strike for the further distraction it would provide, but what he got instead was a laugh.

''They did not tell me you were this bold, American.''

''People have been known to misjudge me.''

"It would not bother you terribly if I killed you, would it?"

"Not really."

"Too bad," the leader said, and Ben heard the distinctive clack of a pistol slide being snapped backward just as his hands came free.

Ben threw himself forward into the space where he judged the leader to be, arms thrust out before him. Impact came fast, forcing both men back toward the van's rear doors. Ben could hear and feel the desperate shifting about him, as the rest of the Hamas soldiers scrambled to join in the struggle. They might draw their guns, but with their leader and Ben so close together, they could not even think of firing them.

Ben managed to fasten a hand onto the wrist of the leader's gun hand. He jerked it upward and the pistol sent a round exploding through the van, the sound ear-numbing. Then he drew the leader toward him and smashed his forehead into the man's nose. He felt the bone give under the pressure and projected himself over the body, tearing free of the hands groping for him as the van careened around another corner. Ben never actually felt for the latch holding the rear doors closed; he simply crashed into the doors and happened to knock them open with his shoulder.

The doors blew backward into the night and Ben tumbled out of the van. He braced himself for the fall, but impact against the road was nonetheless stunning. He hit the pavement and rolled, desperately worried about losing consciousness. He came to a stop at the side of the road, tore his hood off, and turned back to look at the van which was spinning to a halt at least a hundred yards beyond him. Men began spilling out, firing their pistols clumsily in his direction.

Ben climbed to his feet and stumbled, the nearby mountains of Judah casting long moonlit shadows across him. Had the van reached the barren and desolate land beyond them, he would have found himself with no viable cover.

As it was, Ben surged into some brush off the shoulder. The gunshots continued to trace his flight, none close enough to cause concern as the darkness of the trees shielded him. He was not sure how many men were in pursuit; four at least, five maybe.

One of his ankles began to throb and stiffen, and he found himself using the overhanging branches to help pull himself on. He ducked low amid the thickest foliage, as footsteps crunched the underbrush behind him, growing louder. He crossed over the crest of a hill and lost his footing yet again, tumbling into a prickery thicket on the periphery of a sprawling grove of orange trees that shifted in the wind like a single canopy.

Ben felt stinging pain on his arms and face where he'd been scratched. He was able to drag himself into a hollow formed by a nearby nest of bushes just as footsteps plunged down the hill in his wake. With the night serving as camouflage, the men from Hamas rushed right past his hollow for the grove of orange trees beyond.

Ben waited until he had recovered his breath before emerging. He busied himself with trying to get his bearings; he was several miles down Jaffa Road, the main route linking Jericho to the rest of the West Bank.

He had leaned over to retie his shoe when he heard the crack of a branch snapping in a grove just before him. Stilling even his breath, Ben realized the terrorists must have left one of their number behind on the chance that he had doubled back in an attempt to elude them. Whatever the case, this man stood between him and any chance at escape. And he couldn't delay here much longer, not with the others from Hamas sure to return once they found they'd lost the trail.

Ben swallowed hard and crouched lower, feeling about the ground for a branch or log. Instead, he located a rock partially buried in the ground. Extracting it took little effort. The rock felt light in his grasp, but weighed easily enough to serve his deadly purpose.

He still couldn't see the Hamas man poised a mere ten feet before him and had only the single crack of that branch to provide any clue to the man's position. Ben rose into a hunched stance and crept forward, holding the rock at waist level. The night breeze ruffled some thick brush directly before him, revealing the man he sought. As he fixed his gaze, the man turned slowly and stared almost directly at him. Ben felt his heart skip a beat and prepared himself to make the desperate lunge that now seemed inevitable.

But the terrorist swung back around heedlessly. Ben paused long enough to resteady his breath before continuing. He straightened from his haunch and drew to within arm's distance, the man just on the other side of the thick brush. Ben brought the rock overhead and started it downward as he surged through the thicket. He knew it was happening fast, yet the whole act seemed to unfold in slow motion, every move exaggerated right up to the point he slammed the rock down on the terrorist's skull.

It sounded like an egg cracking, only much louder. Ben felt his own breath leave him as the Hamas man simply crumpled. He'd expected a grunt, a moan, a muffled rasp—something. But there was no sound at all until the soft thud of the body hitting the ground.

Ben rushed up the hill, retracing his earlier steps back to the road. He determined the safest strategy to pursue at this point was to cling to the cover of the woods adjacent to that road, staying out of sight in case the terrorists widened their search for him. He had started walking back toward Jericho when a car screeched around a curve before him, its headlights catching him in the last instant before he dove into the brush.

DAY TWO

CHAPTER 18

THE CAR CONTINUED on harmlessly, and Ben vowed to keep himself closer to the cover promised by the trees and brush. By the time he approached the scattered lights and buildings of Jericho, camouflaged in foliage, he had gotten his bearings. He finally arrived at his apartment just before sunrise, drenched in sweat, his limp much more pronounced.

He lay down, exhausted, but sleep refused to come. After a long hour he abandoned the attempt and jumped into the shower instead. By then it was late enough to try phoning al-Shaer at the medical examiner's office. When there was no answer, a fresh dose of foreboding struck him and he headed straight over.

The door was open when he arrived and, as he drew closer, Ben saw why: it had been shattered in the area of the latch, kicked in, by the look of things. He looked up to see Doctor Bassim al-Shaer lumbering down the hall with broom in hand.

"When did this happen?"

"Sometime late last night. You want more specific than that you'll have to ask the residents who slept here," he said, cocking his stare backward toward the storage room. "Of course, there's one less to interrogate now."

"Yesterday's victim . . ."

"Very intuitive." Al-Shaer stopped his sweeping long enough to give Ben a closer look. "Your face hasn't healed very well."

"I suffered a setback."

"Last night also, of course."

"You lifted the corpse's fingerprints. Please tell me you did."

"Certainly. And whoever ransacked the place took all the cards."

Ben felt his whole body sag.

"Relax, Inspector. Fortunately, our friends didn't understand my filing system. *That* fingerprint card is still here."

Ben breathed a sigh of relief. "What about the tests I asked you to perform with knives? Without the body . . ."

"I took pictures and precise measurements of the wounds."

"And the oil you mentioned from the wounds on the first Jericho victim?"

Al-Shaer shook his head with genuine regret. "Sorry. I didn't get that far. Put the tests off on the most recent victim until today. They would be difficult even if I still *had* the body. Come, I'd better show you . . ."

*　　*　　*

NOT ABLE TO distinguish which were the belongings of the corpse they were interested in, the intruders had emptied al-Shaer's entire supply closet and left most of its contents spilled and scattered on the floor. When these personal effects had not yielded the information they sought, Ben figured they had kidnapped him in the hope that he could provide it.

"There are still some blood and tissue samples from the wounds of yesterday's victim I can use to see if the same type of oil was present as on the first victim I autopsied," al-Shaer offered.

"That's something, anyway."

"And the knives," al-Shaer reminded, newly determined thanks to the state of his office. He was taking this personally now. "As soon as I receive them . . ."

"I have assigned an officer to that task already," Ben said, referring to Tawil. "He will be delivering them to you late this afternoon."

Al-Shaer smirked, his jowls quivering. "Tell him not to forget the side of beef."

Ben took the fingerprint card off al-Shaer's hands, hoping it would yield the identity of the most recent corpse.

It was just past nine a.m. when he reached the old police building, still an hour to go before his meeting with Danielle. His head was pounding, and he dry-swallowed a pair of aspirin as he approached his office, realizing the door was open just before he saw the shadow of a man cast on the wall of the cramped, windowless room. He smelled pungent cigar smoke and noticed it drifting into the hall.

"Excuse me?" Ben said from the doorway.

The smoker swung away from an inspection of the wall map of the West Bank divided into colored grids according to the level of Israeli troop withdrawal. When Danielle Barnea was here yesterday, Ben had inserted pushpins denoting the locations of all al-Diib's killings, which the smoker had seemed to be studying.

"May I help you?" Ben continued.

"Hope so," the man said, dragging the cigar reluctantly from his mouth.

At first Ben thought he was fat, but the way the man held himself made him realize his bulk was anything but. Knobs and sinewy bands of muscle were barely contained within his suit jacket. The man's impeccable posture made his suit resemble a uniform, even though his shirt was unbuttoned at the collar, partly revealing a chest shaped like a keg. He had a square face and flat jawline. His hair was brush-cut almost to the level of a standard military crew.

"And maybe I can help you, too," the stranger finished.

"I don't believe I've had the pleasure," Ben said.

"Colonel Frank Brickland," the stranger announced, extending his hand.

"Inspector Ben Kamal." And Ben felt the hand swallow his in a grasp strong enough to let him know that the fate of his fingers hung in the balance.

"I know." Frank Brickland wedged the cigar back into his mouth. "That's why I'm here."

"What exactly is it I can do for you?"

"Help me find my son. He's missing."

"You've come a long way to file the report."

"Because he may have been here, or was. That body you discovered yesterday, I think it was him."

* * *

THE TWO MEN moved outside and sat down atop a backless stone bench in the shade facing the square, Brickland doing so as precisely as he seemed to do everything.

"My friends call me Brick. Some of my enemies, too. They call you Ben around here, I'm told."

"I find my friends and enemies very hard to tell apart these days, Colonel."

Brickland rested his hands on his knees. "Not just here. And it's only 'mister' now."

"Not from where I sit."

"Yeah, like they say, you can take the man out of the army, but you can't take the army out of the man. I'm six months retired out of Fort Bragg, North Carolina, in the good ole U.S. of A. Fifth Special Forces Group. A victim of cutbacks and consolidation. Two of our groups are being deactivated. I went because I raised a stink."

"Giving you time to travel to all the world's most popular vacation spots."

"I told you what brought me to this shithole, and a couple hours in-country's all I need to question any man's sanity who stays when he's got a choice."

"Who said I had a choice?"

"Who said I was talking about you? Maybe you're not the only one who got totally fucked for doing his job."

"Something you can relate to."

"Damn straight. So let's keep this one American to another, short and sweet. I'm here because the specs on that body you turned up yesterday match my kid's."

"Just how did you come by the report detailing them?"

"Shit, hoss, information's a commodity like anything else. You know where to buy, it's there for you to purchase. Store's always open. Clerks are eager to do business. And the market's networked. I let the right people know what I was looking for, what to watch out for. I got a call last night."

Doctor al-Shaer had only filed his report late yesterday, Kamal calculated. Stiff as he looked, Colonel Frank Brickland moved like lightning.

"Obviously," Ben said, "you did not come from the States after you got that call."

"Nope. I was in Cairo by way of Beirut and Amman. Tripoli was going to be next on my list."

"Visiting all the Mideast tourist traps, I see."

Brickland's expression turned into something between a smile and a smirk. "Yeah, all those places where you're apt to find bullets instead of beaches."

"What makes you think your son was the man we found murdered yesterday?"

"Tough being a father, you know," Brickland said. "Almost as tough as being a son when your father's a major asshole like me. My kid ain't smart enough to realize that, so he wants to follow in Dad's footsteps. Special Forces Group Five, a goddamn fucking legacy. Desert Storm instead of Nam. Hey, the bastard got to win anyway! Spent the whole war zeroing mobile scud launchers and assorted other installations."

"Zeroing?"

"It goes like this, hoss. All that high-tech hardware we got cruising the skies is useless until someone tells them where to aim at. In Desert Storm, SF troops had laser sights rigged straight into the missiles' targeting systems. Point, signal, aim, shoot. End of fucking story."

"Different than your role in Vietnam, I suppose."

"In a big way. Everything there was up-close and personal. We carried a killing knife instead of a laser beam, and the only thing we sighted was the next Gook commander in our cross hairs. That was the problem."

"What do you mean?"

"Daddy's footsteps, remember? Kid didn't get to fill them all. Yeah, he got enough of a taste of the up-close personal stuff over there to want a full helping. Too quiet these last few years, though, to fill his plate."

"You're saying he came *here*?"

"Walked away from the SF when it was time to re-up and signed on with the Israeli Defense Force. Easy logistics since my ex-wife is Jewish. They welcomed him with open arms, gave him a chance to practice the up-close and personal stuff in the countries I been trailing him through." Colonel Frank Brickland's eyes seemed to tear up, however briefly. "Yeah, he ended up in the old man's footsteps, let me tell you, maybe a size or two bigger. Then he disappeared."

"Israelis can't help you?"

"Information commodity doesn't trade as freely over there. I dug around and found out what I could, hit a stone wall going back maybe three months. Nobody knows shit from that point, or the people that do ain't talking."

Ben considered the prospects. "Which brings us to the body found yesterday morning."

"Think about it, hoss. He goes undercover. Maybe he's on to something, something big. And somebody snuffs him to keep it in the family."

"We are proceeding on the premise that the body

we discovered yesterday was the victim of a serial killer responsible for several other murders in the West Bank.''

Brickland frowned. Even his cheeks looked muscled. ''Yeah, the Wolf. I read that in the report, noticed your pushpins on the wall too.''

''The report didn't impress you, obviously.''

''As a cover; killer of my kid creating an alibi for himself.''

''You don't find that farfetched?''

Brickland stood up and turned away. He rested his hands on his hips and took a deep breath. Ben could see the muscles rippling beneath his shirt. Brickland turned around slowly, a frighteningly calm look drawn over his face.

''You never served, Benny, but you're living in a fucking war zone now, and you volunteered for it. You got yourself stuck deep in enemy territory and you're still holding the fort even after everybody and his brother has *you* zeroed. You got any idea why you're still alive?''

''My father was a hero. Some say they let me live out of respect.''

''Respect's got nothing to do with it. It's fear. You're alive 'cause they're scared of you, scared of what you'll do to them if they fuck up. That's what holds people back: fear of what happens if they don't get it right. You showed 'em what you're made of when you arrested three of your own, and they want no part of you. I'd take that as a compliment.''

''If you say so.''

''Thing is, even though you never been one, I got to figure you know what it's like to be a soldier, so I want you to consider something. The average soldier compared to someone in Special-Ops is like comparing a school kid to a college graduate. That's what my son was and that's the kind of people he got himself mixed up with in Israel, if I'm reading this right. And people like you, no offense intended, can't even imagine how these kind of people operate. What they know, how they manipulate others with that knowledge. It's not so much that they follow a plan that makes them different, Benny, it's that they've got one.''

"Assuming all this could be true—''

"You damn well better assume that!''

"—then what exactly do you want from me?''

"If that turns out to be my son you found yesterday, you're way out of your league. That being the case, you want to stay alive you better have somebody who knows how to play at this level right alongside. You keep me briefed on your investigation and I'll watch your back. We can start with a visit to the medical examiner's office. Let me take a look at the body.''

"We've got a problem there.''

BEN WAS VAGUE about the kidnapping and his escape the night before, only slightly more specific when it came to the condition in which he had found al-Shaer's office earlier that morning.

"Shitty day you had yesterday,'' Brickland noted stoically when he had finished. "Beat up, tortured, stoned, and shot at. What are you going to do today?''

"Ask questions. Hope the answers lead somewhere.''

"You got those fingerprints back in your office?''

"I was just about to send them along through the proper channels."

"Be nice if you could make a copy beforehand."

Ben said nothing.

"I'd like to know if that body was my son's, soldier."

"And if the prints don't match his?"

Brickland looked at him harshly. "You're telling me this guy wasn't a native, maybe even came from the States like us. What do you think the chances of your 'channels' getting his prints run through Washington or Interpol anytime soon?"

"Not very good."

"So give me a shot. What do you have to lose?"

"Did your son ever have his appendix out?"

"No, it was his gallbladder. I sent him a card from wherever the fuck I was at the time." He tilted his head with a cocky sneer. "Nice try, though."

Ben stood up noncommittally, realizing Brickland was actually an inch or two shorter than he; it just seemed as though he should be taller.

"Give me some time to think about it," he told Brickland.

"I'll be waiting."

Ben watched him start to move away. "You're a long way from home, Colonel."

"We both are, Benny."

CHAPTER 19

BEN CALLED ZAID Jabral, editor of the *Al-Quds* newspaper, as soon as he returned to his office.

"Ready to take me up on my offer to make amends?" Jabral said from Jerusalem, sounding as though he was glad to hear from Ben.

"Perhaps I only wanted to see if it was genuine."

"Go ahead."

"I need some information on a man, an American . . ."

Ben described to Jabral his brief encounter with Frank Brickland. Jabral promised to see what he could do, suggested Ben call him back later in the day.

No sooner had he hung up the phone than Danielle Barnea was escorted into his office at precisely ten o'clock. He rose as she came through the door.

"I trust you're ready to get started," she said, no greetings exchanged. "I reviewed the files again last night. Some questions arose. I'd like to see the body."

Ben took a deep breath. "You can't. It's gone."

"Gone?"

"Someone stole it last night."

"Another mystery?"

"Not really: Hamas."

"And how can you be so sure?"

"Because they kidnapped me when the body didn't yield the answers they wanted."

"They obviously thought you would have those answers."

"They asked about personal effects, papers—anything recovered from the corpse."

"And you told them . . ."

"The truth. The corpse had no personal effects, papers, or anything else when we found it."

"Why would they care?"

"I never got the chance to ask them."

"Few survive such encounters with your Hamas."

"They're not 'mine,' Pakad."

"In any event," Danielle resumed, without missing a beat, "I'll have to settle for the next best thing: the murder scene itself."

THE ONLY REMAINING indication that something had occurred in the alley where the murder had taken place were several dirty yellow strips of the crime-scene tape clinging doggedly to their original spots.

At Danielle's request, Ben reviewed every aspect of the case while she performed her own methodical check of the alley. He filled her in on the steps he had ordered his men to take and the conclusions that

formed the basis for his strategy. She listened attentively, asking an occasional question, seeming content
to merely accept items drawn from his official report.
When he had finished, Danielle stepped off distances,
sifted her hands through gravel, inspected areas of the
alley.

"So much blood," she noted, imagining the way it
had been the previous morning. "The killer should
have been covered in it himself, under the circumstances."

"He may have been. We have no way of being
sure."

"Did you check the street for additional drops?"

"Yes, and found nothing. We also typed a dozen
blood samples taken randomly from the scene. They
all came from the victim."

Danielle accepted that like input into a computer.
She moved back into the sun and squinted her eyes
against its jetting rays. At ninety feet below sea level,
the town of Jericho held heat like an oven.

"Vulnerabilty and isolation," Danielle said finally.
"All victims were killed alone and in the dark, usually
fairly close to their homes. Unusual, don't you think?"

"Practical, more likely. Maybe al-Diib stakes out
their homes instead of stalking them. Kills them when
they return or follows them when they leave."

"But no one ever notices."

"Or admits they do."

"What about the first of the two Jericho murders?"

"Eleven days ago. Friends dropped a girl named
Leila Khalil off in front of her house. No one ever saw
her alive again."

"The Wolf was lying in wait, then."

"As he always is. He must stalk them until he has

their routines—their very lives—committed to memory."

"But how does he get away?"

"Walking a long distance would be out of the question," Ben said.

"Especially since not all the victims were killed within walking distance of their homes."

"Someone who knows how to blend in, then, someone who doesn't stand out."

"Maybe he's a cop," Danielle surmised.

"Cops stand out here. Believe me."

"Granted. So if the Wolf's following his victims, how does he know when to park the car or have the taxi deposit him? And how does he get back to it without ever drawing any attention to himself, or leaving any trail of blood?"

"Again, he would have to be able to blend in."

"Blood *never* blends in."

"That is, if any witness has the opportunity to *see* it. I've been thinking about his vehicle, Pakad. We've never had one identified or even spotted anywhere close to a crime scene. But he has to get there somehow, doesn't he?"

Danielle rose, brushing the grime of the alley off her hands and skirt. "Why don't we take a look at another one of the crime scenes? Let's go and see exactly what the killer saw."

"Not yet, Pakad. We need to stop at a refugee camp first."

"And what are we looking for, Inspector?"

"A witness."

* * *

BEN BRIEFED HER on the varied events of the previous night during the one-hour drive to the Jalazon refugee camp outside Ramallah where the woman named Shanzi supposedly lived. They arrived to find the whole camp still under curfew after a series of protests several days before had ended in a particularly violent fashion. There were rumors of several shootings as recently as yesterday, and Ben sensed a pall even thicker than the stifling air hanging over the camp.

The only people in evidence at Jalazon were those belonging to the security force. They functioned like a militia, their training similar to, but not nearly as complete as that of the Palestinian police force. They had taken over security in the camps from the Israelis and were often accused of even more brutal behavior.

Upon entering Jalazon, the first thing Ben noticed were the ominous guard towers the Israelis had built in each corner. Though abandoned, they had not been dismantled and that seemed to symbolize how little things had changed for the residents.

"Good morning, Inspector," a captain named Fawandi greeted Ben, after he had been escorted into his tin box of an office; Danielle remained discreetly outside the camp by mutual consent. "What can I do for you?"

At least here, unlike his experience at the Einissultan camp yesterday, he had a name to go on. "I am looking for a woman who is a resident here."

"Her name?"

"Most recently, as far as I know, Shanzi."

"Last or first?"

"Only."

Captain Fawandi scanned his registration book,

every item handwritten, the idea of computers in Jalazon and the other camps only a dream at this point. "We have no one by that name I can find."

"She is among several women running late-night robbery scams."

"Wait a minute," Fawandi said, and went to a file folder resting on the top of his desk. He ruffled through a few pages. "Yes, I thought I remembered her . . ."

"What?"

The captain's eyes looked up emotionlessly. "She was shot yesterday during the protest. Killed."

Ben felt like he'd been kicked in the gut. "I wouldn't have thought her the type to join the protest."

"She was a bystander. Stray bullet got her in the skull." Fawandi shrugged. "It happens."

"Rather too frequently."

"Look, officer—"

"Inspector."

"*Inspector.*" Fawandi lowered his voice. "Is there anything else?"

"I want her body transferred to the medical examiner's office in Jericho. I will send a car."

"You don't have jurisdiction here."

"This is still the West Bank, Captain, and I am the chief investigating officer."

"I wasn't aware you were investigating this woman's death."

"I believe it could be connected to others I *am* investigating."

"All the same, there is nothing in the articles to say that camp militia must comply with requests from civilian authorities."

Ben sat down on a rickety chair poised before Fawandi's desk and made himself look comfortable. "Do you know why I'm here?"

"Not really."

"You heard about the murder committed two nights ago on Jaffa Street in Jericho near the Hisbe?"

"Of course. Everyone has. Another of al-Diib's victims."

"I'm here because official opinion is that al-Diib comes from one of the camps, and I've only got a week left to deliver the mayor a suspect. I could bring in anyone, fabricate a whole case, and the authorities would buy it with a wink. Do you like your job, Captain Fawandi?"

"Do not threaten me, Inspector."

Ben leaned forward and lowered his voice. "I've heard it told that many of the goods intended for your residents end up being sold on the black market. Now there's a subject that would make for an interesting investigation. Or, better yet, a newspaper story. I know an editor who'd be most interested."

Fawandi's expression didn't change. He simply fixed his gaze ahead and drummed his fingers against his desk, the only sound in the tin room while Ben waited.

"I will get the body ready to transport," Fawandi said finally.

BEN FOUND DANIELLE standing outside the camp gate being eyed lasciviously by a complement of guards.

"I should have told them you were a Jew," Ben said, glad to be driving off.

"They asked. I told them I was your sex slave and that you beat me regularly."

"That explains the looks I got on my way out," Ben said. He spent the next few minutes updating her on what he had learned inside the camp.

"Do you expect an autopsy will turn up anything?" Danielle asked him after he finished.

"I don't like the coincidence of one of our only two likely witnesses to Sunday night's murder dying accidently. Too convenient."

"That's the American in you again. The Palestinian side would *embrace* the convenience."

"And which side did the Israelis request to work with?"

She didn't bother denying it. "The one who can better serve our interests, of course."

"Our interests are the same, Pakad: solving this case before the peace talks reconvene a week from tomorrow."

"Then come with me."

CHAPTER 20

JERUSALEM WAS THE only part of Israel Ben had ever been to before, but his memories did not do it justice. Built on a hilltop, the walled city of legend is itself overlooked by taller hills. From the higher peaks nearby, Mount Scopus and the Mount of Olives, the church spires, bell towers, golden domes, and minarets that compose the city's skyline are breathtaking.

It was not the sights, though, that Ben remembered most about Jerusalem; it was the sounds. The ubiquitous yet pleasing chime of church bells, the muezzins' precisely timed calls to the faithful, and the constant murmur of prayer at the Western Wall. He knew of the latest security precautions, but nothing could quell the fervor and devotion so many cultures brought with them to the Wall.

The first of the Wolf's known victims, a twenty-six-year-old woman named Najwa Halevy, had been found in the Muslim Quarter of the Old City. According to Danielle's file, though, she lived in East Jerusalem. She had stopped in briefly to visit her parents in the Muslim Quarter. Her body was found four or five hours later, dumped in an abandoned cistern within sight of Damascus Gate.

"A guard just happened to peer down the well on his rounds," Danielle reported when they reached it.

On her advice they had driven back to Jericho after leaving the Jalazon refugee camp so Ben could change his clothes before making the twenty-four-mile trip to Jerusalem. Although regulations demanded he wear his police uniform when on duty in the West Bank, the same did not hold true for assignments elsewhere. And on this assignment the last thing he wanted to do was draw attention to himself and risk any distractions from the subject at hand.

"Her wounds," Danielle continued, "as the case file indicates, were almost identical to those of your victim found in the alley off Jaffa Street. And the others."

Ben felt the gravel crunching underfoot as he moved about the scene. The fact that there were no residences in the immediate vicinity made it seemingly a much better place for a murderer to choose.

"She told her parents she was on her way to meet someone?" he asked.

"She told them she was on her way home, back to East Jerusalem."

"And she was killed at almost the same time of night as our latest victim." Ben turned back toward Danielle. "Did her parents know if she was carrying identification at the time she left their house?"

"A small handbag in which she kept everything," Danielle replied. "It could have been stolen after the fact, of course. Her body went undiscovered for as many as five hours, after all.''

''Could have been, but I don't think so. For al-Diib, destroying his victims' faces isn't enough: he wants to strip away all essence of their identities. That means taking everything on their persons that could tell us who they are.''

''Leaving them with nothing, so to speak.''

''Probably because that's what he feels he has, Pakad. He steals what's left of their identities in order to get back the one he himself has lost.''

''Could that tie in with the possibility of him having suffered some sort of genital mutilation?''

''The inability to bear children would certainly constitute an even deeper loss of identity. But inability caused by more basic sexual dysfunction wouldn't explain the time he spends mutilating them so horribly post mortem.'' Ben stopped, thinking of something. ''In the cases investigated by Shin Bet, do you recall which part of the bodies he mutilated first?''

''The face. In all cases.''

''So his victims wouldn't be able to look at him,'' Ben concluded. ''Meaning that the root of his crimes lies as much in humiliation and embarrassment as rage. A very dangerous combination, Pakad.''

''That further supports our theory that he himself was mutilated, either by accident, birth, or torture.''

''Only torture could create a monster like this.''

''Then we can focus our search for suspects on the year or so before the murders began,'' Danielle suggested.

''The problem is, we don't really know for sure when the murders began, do we? We can't be sure how many victims there really were before Shin Bet got interested. During the occupation the Israelis conducted virtually no investigations of crimes against Palestinians, as you know. That means we really have no idea how long our killer has been operating or how many victims he's claimed.''

"True," Danielle conceded. ''But up until this most recent murder in Jericho, there have always been significant gaps between the killings. Why the change in his pattern?''

''I don't know. It could be there have been more killings, at least attempts.''

"Which we have no record of.''

"Because it's doubtful they were reported. Or, if they were, the cases went neglected. First, by the Israelis, who didn't care. Then by the Palestinian Authority, who couldn't do anything even if they did.''

''Hard words.''

"Justified, believe me.''

"And yet you're still here.''

''I'm not exactly overflowing with options. I didn't have to burn my bridges; they collapsed on their own.''

"Then we're back where we started. Are you doing anything about compiling lists from clinics that may have treated wounds like the ones we believe the Wolf suffered?''

"The records at your Ansar 3 detention camp, Pakad, are far more likely to yield us our man.''

"I called the authorities there. They weren't very cooperative. Claimed such mutilations never took place there, and hung up on me. My superiors have agreed to see what they can do to help, but I wouldn't count on anything.''

"I never do.''

*   *   *

THE DRIVE BACK into the West Bank passed in uneasy silence. Although cities like Ramallah and Nablus had been transferred to Palestinian control, the negotiated agreements for limited self-rule had been very vague as to the specific parameters of a complete Israeli withdrawal. And, for her part, Israel continued to insist that security for the 120 Israeli settlements still in the West Bank remain the top priority.

Ben noted that most of the vehicles and people they passed were Israelis moving out of those settlements that had either been sacrificed to the cause of peace, or rendered impossible to defend under the new conditions. Over 130,000 Israeli settlers were estimated to be living in the West Bank, of which 5,000 were being displaced.

"I guess they know what it feels like now," Ben said, regretting his words instantly.

Danielle's response, though, was eerily calm. "We are used to wandering. Having a homeland is relatively new to us."

"And to us, as well. Not quite there yet, but we're getting closer."

She looked at him suddenly. "Why did you come back?"

"Don't you remember my file?"

"But you had thought about it before, hadn't you?"

Ben shrugged, not bothering to deny it.

"Maybe you discussed it with your wife. Maybe you didn't, because you knew she would never go along with it, that it wouldn't be fair to your sons."

"And it wouldn't have been."

"Would you have left them?"

"What makes you ask that?"

"Your father left you and your mother."

"I think he would have returned to America," Ben said, trying to sound sure.

"Why did he leave Ramallah in the first place?"

"He saw the writing on the wall, was frustrated by the fact that no one would listen."

"He saw the Six-Day War? Occupation through the territories?"

"That was the one thing he did *not* see. If he had, we never would have left. That, I'm certain of. He came back to rectify his mistake, then tried too hard and paid for it with his life."

"You think we killed him."

"That's what everyone thinks. He was a leader, a disruptive influence. He would have caused problems for you eventually. Some say it would have been he, and not Arafat, who eventually became leader of our people."

Danielle waited a long moment before responding. "Would you like me to find out?"

Ben snickered. "I doubt you'd find mention of his assassination in any file."

"Not written anyway."

Ben looked at her closely. "Your father was shot too, wasn't he?"

"A sniper's bullet caught him in the head while he was making rounds two years ago. They called his recovery a miracle. Then he suffered a stroke. No miracle this time."

"The sniper . . ."

"Never caught. No group bothered to claim credit for it. After all, it was just a single man and he had the nerve not to die."

"I'm sorry."

A sad smile crossed Danielle's face. "He was like your father, Ben. He also tried to make a difference. Do you know what the *gush emunim* are?"

"Private armies from the settlements that terrorized West Bank villages, often while the Israeli army looked on."

"My father took a stand against them. He recruited a platoon of soldiers who were as disgusted by their actions as he was and arrested the *gush emunim* whenever he could catch them. Not surprisingly, the charges never stuck, but at least he could live with himself."

"Your father was only one man. Think of the thousands who were involved in the administrative detentions, the torture, the terrorizing of our young, the closing of our schools. You tried to deaden us, make us numb and scared. But it didn't work out that way because too many of us already had nothing to lose. You wanted drones and instead you got the *intifada*."

Danielle looked at him defiantly. "Strange hearing such criticism from someone who spent the entire occupation, as well as the *intifada,* in America."

"And America has seen its share of tyranny as well. The internment of the Japanese in World War Two, McCarthyism. Forcing others to live in fear—that seems to be the credo of free-world democracies."

"That's the point!" she insisted. "The Red Scare, the horror of Pearl Harbor and the war that followed. People were frightened by the times. Even though in retrospect the choices they made seemed so wrong, at the time they were the only choices they had. That's the way it has always been for us."

"Black and white. No gray."

"But plenty of red. Let's not forget that, Ben," she

countered, using his first name without thinking about it.

"No, let's not. But let's not underestimate the power of fear, either. We are a people who has lived in fear so long that we know no other way to live. If it wasn't the Jordanians and then you, it was our own people, and they were the worst because they scared us the most."

"Like those three police officers you arrested."

"Not terrorists but, yes, exactly like them because they relied on fear. You think they tortured and killed that cabdriver for justice? They did it to set an example for anyone who dares turn to the Israelis for anything, because they don't want any Palestinian to realize he has somewhere else to turn. Did you know what happened when Israel refused to install air raid sirens in the West Bank during the Gulf War? It was *Israelis* in the West Bank who phoned their Palestinian friends to alert them when Scud missiles were flying. The Palestinians would then go into the streets and blow whistles, not as loud as your sirens but just as effective. Have you ever heard of Zaid Jabral?"

Danielle nodded. "His newspaper wasn't very flattering in its reporting about you."

"But he told me a story once, about one of the times the Israelis came and shut down all our schools. An elaborate house-to-house system of replacement classrooms was enacted, either by grade or sometimes by subject. After all that, the people still needed books if the classes were to work." Ben turned back to her. "It was the Israeli soldiers on patrol who unlocked the schools so they could go in and get them. Men like your father."

"But what do we do about those who leave us no

choice in how we deal with the rest? You saw my file, too, Inspector. You read about my brothers.''

''More tragedy,'' Ben frowned.

''Very bad for my family, since my father's brothers are both dead and none of them had sons. You know what this means? The family line dies and, worse, it dies with my father. And even on his less lucid days he knows that.''

''It's a terrible thing to lose your family, Pakad.''

''It's a fate all too familiar in Israel. That is why we must have peace.'' She looked once more down into the valley. ''Whatever it costs.''

''Not all lost families are casualties of war.''

''Yes, they are, Ben,'' Danielle said with as much compassion as she could muster. ''Just *different kinds* of wars. The war that took your family, the war that took mine.''

''Did you ever think of quitting?''

The question took her aback. ''No more than you,'' she lied.

''What makes you think I haven't, Pakad?''

''Because what would you be left with?''

Ben looked away from the settlement's slow death. ''I suppose we have more in common that I realized.''

''Then let's go,'' she called to him, ''and make it worthwhile.

THE FIRST VICTIM Shin Bet had formally investigated had been found in Ramallah by an Israeli patrol on a mountain road just before dawn over a year before. A man named Abu Bakkar, a local merchant over forty years of age, the oldest of any of the victims. As Ben and Danielle made their way through the last town before coming to Ramallah, young children tossed rocks at their car from school playgrounds, screaming with glee each time one connected.

Inured to this sort of harassment, Danielle didn't so much as flinch behind the wheel.

In most of the other cases, it was at least conceivable that the victims had been innocently en route to a friend's house or some late-night establishment. But in this case, the hillside offered no doors to knock on or establishments to visit. Abu Bakkar had simply come up here for a walk, something he did on a regular basis, according to investigators.

"The wounds were the same again," Danielle reported, the open case file in her hand, battling the wind as she led Ben along the hillside. "Mutilation too. In this case, apparently, the Wolf severed the jugular vein, resulting in an arterial spray that showered both the trees and the ground in the vicinity where the body was found."

"The killer couldn't possibly have escaped being bloodied in this instance."

"Exactly."

"Yet he walked away, returned to his vehicle. The problem of blood again; it must have been all over him, all over his vehicle. Still, not once in all the months and all the killings has anyone seen him."

"Perhaps he wears something over his clothes," Danielle theorized. "Strips it off when he's finished. Stuffs it in the same pack he carries the knife in."

Ben wondered if al-Shaer had gotten to work yet on the collection of knives he had sent over. "You were never able to identify the type of knife used in the killings either."

"No, but the autopsy reports indicate wounds identical in radius and degree of penetration to those your medical examiner found.''

"What about the lubricant he found coating the wounds of the first Jericho victim?''

"My people are checking if any samples were preserved they can still test.''

The final stop for the day was Bethlehem, and here conditions made it impossible for them to reach the murder site behind a Greek Orthodox church in Manger Square. The Palestinian force now responsible for security was having trouble quelling the third major disturbance in as many days, leaving them no choice but to close Bethlehem off. The Israelis resorting to the same tactic in the past had been met by cries of protest. Now similar cries fell on similarly deaf ears.

Danielle pulled off near the roadblock where they'd been turned away, still close enough to the town center and Bethlehem's ancient streets for her and Ben to catch glimpses of the protesters clashing with Palestinian security personnel outfitted in full riot gear.

"Anything special about this one?'' Ben asked, as the muffled clacking of gunfire echoed through the hills.

Danielle consulted her file. "She was the youngest, only eighteen.''

"The one who snuck out to be alone with her boyfriend.''

"Yes.''

"Any chance he—''

"No. He found the body. No one's that great an actor.''

"The first victim in Jericho, Leila Khalil, followed a similar pattern.''

Danielle nodded, recalling the file. "The Khalil girl

never got inside the house after she was dropped off by a group of friends.''

''According to their statements, none of them saw anything that can help us.''

Ben reached into the backseat for the files piled there, and flipped to the one on Leila Khalil.

''A boy she was quite close to was driving. According to his statement, he went straight home afterward. 'I left the car in the street and went to bed,' he says.''

Danielle's mind veered in a different direction. ''Interesting, isn't it?''

''What?''

''That all of the victims were killed outside, often in public places. Makes it even more mystifying how our killer gets away. How no one ever notices him, even though he must be bloodied. Any ideas?''

''Short of his really being a wolf, Pakad, not a one.''

IT WAS FIVE o'clock before they reached the old police building in Jericho.

''I'd better be getting back to Jerusalem,'' Danielle said. ''I need to follow up on the leads we've come up with today.''

''They're not much.''

''It's only the first day. We may get a break once the latest victim from Jericho is identified. If your medical examiner was correct in his assumption that the victim was not Palestinian—''

''Which he is.''

''—then our killer may have broken his pattern as well as shortened the lag between killings. We should start on that track tomorrow.'' She continued to stand next to him on the granite steps, not ready to leave. ''One of the oldest places in the world, Jericho. So much tradition, so many legends. Like the walls Joshua toppled with trumpets when he took the city.'' She paused and turned to look at him. The breeze blew some stray strands of hair onto her face and she brushed them off before resuming. ''They're coming down again, you know. Maybe that's what the two of us working together means.''

''Too bad it took murder to do it,'' said Ben.

BEN PHONED ZAID Jabral as soon as he was inside his office.

''It's Kamal,'' Ben announced in greeting. ''You find anything on Brickland?''

''I'm having trouble accessing his file. Are you certain you gave the right name?''

Ben spelled it for him again, just to make sure he had it right. ''Colonel in the United States Special Forces until six months ago, when he retired.''

He heard Jabral sigh. ''Until six months ago is correct, but not because he retired. Colonel Franklin Brickland's career ended in a helicopter crash, Inspector. He's dead.''

CHAPTER 21

AS SOON AS his conversation with Jabral had ended, Ben drove out to the home of the first victim found in Jericho, Leila Khalil. According to her file, she had been killed just a few days short of her twenty-second birthday; her body was found in the weed-riddled garden of an abandoned, dilapidated house not far down the street.

If the windows had been open in her home at the time, her family might have been able to hear her screams.

The girl had lived with her parents on a residential street lined with trees away from the gas stations and shops that clutter the commercial district of Jericho. The Khalil home was set comfortably back and lay partially hidden by dense, ten-foot-high shrubs. Large olive trees shaded the front yard and a picnic table was set on a terrace. The home was typical of those Jericho had been known for when the town had served as the winter home for wealthy and prestigious Palestinians, a respite from the harsh winds and chilling temperatures in the less temperate areas west of the Jordan Rift Valley, where a difference of twenty miles can mean a thirty-degree temperature change.

Like the villas further to the east, some of the homes in the area showed evidence of abandonment and neglect. Properties like the one where Leilah Khalil had been found were choked off by a wild, rampant growth of vegetation, the houses decaying.

Ben parked in front of the Khalil home and headed up the front walk, imagining that he was retracing the last steps of Leila Khalil's life. He rapped lightly on the door. A few seconds later it opened just wide enough for a woman in black to see him.

"Mrs. Khalil?"

The woman nodded her veiled head.

"I am Inspector Bayan Kamal of the Palestinian Authority. I would like to speak to you about your daughter."

The woman shook her head slowly.

"I believe the investigation into her . . . passing was not handled as well as it might have been. I would like to offer my help to correct that error, to bring justice to your home and your family."

She shook her head again, seemed ready to close the door when another woman's voice sifted through it.

"She is not interested in speaking to you."

A woman in her early twenties appeared in the doorway, between Ben and Mrs. Khalil.

"I am—"

"I know who you are, Inspector. I have read all about you."

"Then you have the advantage of me."

"I am Amal. Sister and daughter."

"The file said nothing about a sister."

"That's because I wasn't here. I came home for the funeral . . . and the mourning period."

Ben could barely see Amal through the shadows, but her beauty was evident even so. Her face was a perfect oval tightened by sorrow, her skin stunningly bronzed. And, unlike her mother, she was not wearing the traditional Palestinian *mandila*, or headdress. Auburn hair framed her face.

"May I come in?"

"Against the rules."

"Why?"

"Because you're a foreigner."

"You don't know me as well as you think you do."

Amal made no move to open the door all the way. "Yes, I do."

"Then you should know I am quite capable of bringing the man who killed your sister to justice."

"Our justice is in the eyes of God. A Palestinian would know that."

Ben knew arguing was pointless. "You said you came home."

"From Jordan. I live there. I didn't change my visa after the border was opened. It took me an extra day."

"I'm sorry."

"No, you're not."

"For your sister's death, I am. If your mother can't speak to me, then let me talk to your father."

Amal closed the door part of the way. "There's nothing he or any of us can say that would help you."

"Why are you afraid?"

She left the door open a crack. "We cannot cooperate with you."

"Then the murderer of your sister remains free."

"Not in the eyes of God."

"What about your eyes, Amal?"

Ben wished he could have seen if they registered any emotion. Hoping he'd get the chance, he continued before she could close the door.

"Either of your parents may know or have seen something that is very important without them realizing. I will come back and speak to all of you again another time. Please accept my condolences."

She snorted. "Forgive me if I don't."

BEN WAS WALKING back to his car when a Volvo sedan pulled alongside him, the rear passenger side door easing open.

"Give you a lift, Inspector?" offered Major Nabril al-Asi.

Ben kept walking. "My car's just up here."

"I know. Get in anyway."

Ben knew he had no choice and climbed in next to al-Asi. "Nice suit. Christian Dior?"

"No. Henry Grethel. I have an Armani coming any day. Let me know if you're ever interested."

"Only if the Authority changes our uniform."

"You won't be in uniform forever, Inspector."

"Or tomorrow, if some people had their way."

That drew a brief smile from the head of the Protective Security Service. "You must be careful of the company you keep, Inspector."

"If you're speaking of my Israeli liaison . . ."

"I was speaking of the American you met with ear-

lier today. Now, I'm not going to ask you who he is;
you have the right to do your job any way you choose,
just as I have the same right to do mine. Speaking of
which, I was hoping you had had time to reconsider.''

''Reconsider what?''

''The subject of our last discussion: Dalia Mikhail.
It would be a great help if you could answer some
questions about her.''

''I've told you everything I intend to.''

''Nothing . . .''

''And that was probably too much.''

Al-Asi leaned a little closer to him. ''We're running
our own detainment camps now, you know. Picked up
what knowledge and supplies we could from the Israelis, but we haven't quite gotten to human rights yet.
A woman Dalia Mikhail's age, well, let's just say such
a camp is not the place I'd want a friend of mine
spending the rest of her life.''

''What do you want from me?''

''I told you: answers to a few simple questions.''
Al-Asi paused. ''Maybe something more tangible
later.''

''Why are you even bothering with her?''

''Routine, just like I said.''

''What if I get her to stop writing the editorials, to
back off her inflammatory challenges to the Authority?''

Al-Asi reached across Ben and thrust open the door.
''If you change your mind, I think you know where
my office is.''

BEN'S PHONE WAS ringing when he got back
to his desk in the old police building. He rushed in
and snatched it up quickly.

"Where the fuck have you been this whole day?" the voice of medical examiner Bassim al-Shaer roared. "I've been calling and calling, for hours."

Ben rummaged about the top of his desk. "There's no message here."

"I didn't leave one, just kept hanging up when they told me you were out. Goddamn it! You drop something in my lap and just *forget* about it?"

The dead woman from the Jalazon refugee camp, Ben remembered: Shanzi. "It's just that I'm not used to such wondrous service."

"The body arrived just after one o'clock. Took me all of five minutes to make the determination."

"That she was shot."

"She was shot, all right," al-Shaer acknowledged. "But that's not what killed her. This girl was strangled to death hours *before* someone put a bullet in her skull."

CHAPTER 22

YOU CERTAINLY EARNED your salary today, Pakad," Rav Nitzav Hershell Giott said after Danielle had completed her summary of the day, settling back in a desk chair that threatened to engulf him. "It seems we made a wise choice in selecting the American to be your liaison."

"He's Palestinian as well," she reminded him.

"All the more reason to be leery of trusting him," cautioned Moshe Baruch of Shin Bet, "never mind wasting your time reviewing the individual crime scenes."

She looked at her superior, confused. "I thought that was what I was supposed to do."

"Waste your time?" Baruch challenged.

"Catch a killer."

Baruch sat there fuming, unable to respond before Giott beat him to it.

"It is unfortunate you were put in this position on such short notice."

"In fact, I had none."

"We had no choice if we wanted to preserve the operation."

"You mean, *joint* operation, don't you?" she asked Giott.

As she watched Giott and Baruch glance at each other, her father's warning on his laptop screen flashed through her mind:

DON'T TRUST THEM.

"Of course it is a joint operation," Giott conceded. "But each side has different priorities."

"Ours," Baruch picked up, "is to stay updated on how much the Palestinians know, what they have learned."

"How much do *we* know, sir?"

"Not enough to do us any good, I'm afraid. Why don't you tell us about your counterpart?"

She shrugged. "He's persistent and clever, reaches conclusions even though he probably would rather not."

"What do you mean?" Giott asked her.

"I think he would prefer not to catch this killer."

"That would be fine by us," Baruch said without hesitation.

Danielle looked at him, baffled. "But I thought the purpose of this joint venture was to—"

"You thought wrong. The purpose of this venture is to protect ourselves."

"Against what?"

"The possibility of the killer's identity coming back to haunt us."

"An *Israeli?* You think the killer is an Israeli?"

The two men looked at each other again, maddening in their silent exchange of information.

"We think," Giott began, "the *government* thinks, that we would suffer greatly in the eyes of the world if the killer turned out to be one of us."

"Then you chose the wrong man to be my counterpart because, according to our case files, he's already figured out more than we have."

"More?" Giott raised.

"He is following some leads that never occurred to us to check. Or that we didn't bother to check."

"Don't be ridiculous, Pakad."

"He has the advantage of knowing what he is facing from our case files, Rav Nitzav. Beyond that, the state of the bodies discovered in Jericho was far fresher."

Baruch rose. "Make no mistake about the reason we sent you to Jericho, Pakad. You are to monitor and assist in this investigation every step of the way, toward determining whether we have anything to worry about."

"And if the evidence points toward an Israeli suspect?"

"Then you are to squash it, Pakad," Giott ordered softly but firmly, leaving no room for question. "Using whatever means are necessary."

CHAPTER 23

AL-SHAER'S OFFICE STILL showed the effects of the break-in when Ben arrived. The only visible difference was a vast collection of knives lined up neatly atop the laboratory's largest counter.

"Your officer delivered these this afternoon," al-Shaer explained. "The side of beef is hanging in the cold locker. Oh, and he left a message for you. Apparently I'm not the only one who's had trouble tracking you down."

"What was the message?"

"He said to tell you there was a lead he needed to follow up."

"He didn't say what?"

"Do I look like your secretary? It was something about a car. I didn't write it down."

"A car?"

"That's what he said. Now, if you'll accompany me . . ."

Ben followed al-Shaer into the lab where the prostitute Shanzi's body lay covered by a sheet up to her face. That face looked sad and puzzled, eyes turned upward as if to look at the blackened wound just above the center of her forehead.

Al-Shaer patted his pockets in a search for cigarettes. When the search turned up nothing, he lifted a half-smoked stub from a specimen jar he was using as an ashtray and lit it.

"This one was easy," the fat man reported, puffing away contentedly. "Let me show you."

Ben noticed that al-Shaer donned gloves this time before proceeding, smoke still rising from the cigarette wedged in his mouth. He tilted the corpse's head upward and lifted her eyelids so Ben could get a good look.

"Notice the lines of broken capillaries and red splotches of hemorrhage? Clear evidence of death due to asphyxiation."

"Then she was shot so the killers might cover their tracks."

"They must not have realized that the fact she was dead already meant there would be no pooling of blood in the wound," al-Shaer said, holding the corpse's head up for Ben to see. "Or perhaps they did not expect a true professional to take an interest."

"Professional enough to estimate the time of death?"

"Between eleven a.m and two p.m. yesterday."

Ben nodded. Reports from the camp claimed Shanzi had been shot dead between four and four-thirty. Clearly, someone had first silenced her and then tried to conceal the truth about her killing. Any number of people could have known she was a potential witness to the latest murder by al-Diib; after all, even the woman who had accosted Ben last night had heard Shanzi boast about being on Jaffa Street the night of the murder. The real question was why anyone would bother silencing her, even if she did know something. Ben could pass her death off as coincidence. There were numerous other potential explanations for why she had been shot after being strangled, most notably a simple random murderer trying to cover his tracks.

But what if it wasn't?

Ben shifted his imagination into park. The one thing here that remained grounded in absolute reality was the existence of a second witness: the boy identified only as Radji. Shanzi's fate made it all the more imperative that Ben somehow locate him. A daunting task to say the least, and one he was ill-suited to undertake without a decent night's sleep.

Admitting to himself how tired he still felt, Ben left his official reports to file another time and headed straight home, leaving al-Shaer sorting through the specimen jar for another stub worth lighting. He arrived just after dark, opening the door to his apartment building with considerably more caution than he had the night before.

"Bad idea to trust the Israelis, Benny," said a voice as he stepped in, and Ben felt the breath wedge tight in his throat.

A familiar shape emerged from the shadows. "If it isn't Colonel Frank Brickland," Ben said. "What are you today, Colonel? Retired . . . or dead?"

The throaty laugh Brickland let out in response surprised Ben. "Did some checking up on me, eh, hoss?"

"That's right."

"Congratulations. I gave you a little test. You passed."

"Send me to the top of the class after you tell me what the hell you mean."

"Look, Benny, I need men who can think, not just listen. If you had bought into everything I said without checking further, I would figure you'd probably buy into whatever *anybody* said. If you hadn't checked things out, you never would have seen me again."

"And me thinking you wanted to help me . . ."

"Get used to it, hoss, because I'm the only one who can guide you through this brave new, fucked-up world."

Ben looked Brickland over. "Why does your file list you as having died six months ago?"

"You're an enterprising man, Benny. Why don't you tell me?"

"Because you never retired—"

"Very good."

"—but they wanted people to think you were out."

"Man like me, being dead's the only way people would buy that one."

"You still haven't answered my question."

Brickland's granite jaw unbent a little. "Tough times these, hoss. Hot spots popping up all over the world like summer bug bites on the back of a hound. U.S. can't enter them all officially, but we can go in secretly and try to head off any more Haitis and Somalias. American blood's been spilled in too many places where we didn't understand what the fuck we were doing there, pissing away plenty of tax dollars while we get ourshelves shit on. Me and my cohorts, we're the U.S.'s version of a kind of preemptive savings plan. Lives and dollars, Benny, spared because we went in first.''

"But that's not what brought you to Jericho."

"You know what brought me to Jericho."

"I know what you told me."

"And it's the truth. You're the only man who can help me on this one, hoss. What you don't know or believe is that I'm also the only one who can help you."

"Lucky me."

Brickland pursed his lips and frowned. "I know about the real cause of that woman's death, Benny."

Somehow Ben wasn't surprised. "You really are a remarkable man, Colonel."

"I just use what's available to me. Good lesson for you. Here's another: don't trust the Israelis."

"Why?"

"My kid was sleeping with them, and look what happened to him. They've got too much tied up in this investigation, too much to lose."

"Like all the rest of us."

"Some more than others. I'm going to give you some advice, hoss: forget about this whole case now, drop it like somebody handed it to you hot off the stove."

"And then who would be here to help you, Colonel?"

Brickland's soft smile acknowledged he'd been taken. "I'm pretty good at taking care of myself."

"So am I."

"I'm starting to get that feeling. Problem is, this time the deck is stacked against you. You can't win. They want you to fail, they're rooting for you to fail so they'll have someone to blame. Trouble is, you might succeed.''

''Why is that a problem?''

''Because if the killer's an Arab, he'll be made a martyr. And if he's not an Arab, well, use your imagination.''

''I'm not permitted to over here.''

''Then use mine.''

''I could have used *you* a couple of nights ago.''

''Main reason why I thought I'd stake your place out, 'case the fucks decided to come back.'' Brickland paused. ''Also, figured I could pick up those fingerprint records you promised me.''

''Funny, I don't remember that.''

''Expect the channels you sent them through to tell you the truth, if they tell you anything at all?''

Ben removed an envelope from his jacket, but stopped short of handing it over. ''Why should I expect anything different from you?''

''If it's my son, you'll know.''

''And if it's not, will you tell me anyway?''

''Shit, you want me to help dig your grave for you, just get me a shovel.''

Ben held out the envelope to Brickland. ''Some in Jericho would say I've already got one foot in it.''

''I been there, hoss,'' Brickland said knowingly, tucking the envelope inside his coat. ''And it's the second foot that counts.''

BEN WAS SOUND asleep when the phone rang, how many times he wasn't sure before he groped for it in the dark.

''Hello?'' he managed, still groggy.

"The mayor told me to call you." Shaath's voice, never tired, always the same no matter the hour.

"So you called me."

"There's been another murder. You are to report to the scene immediately."

Ben snapped upright, fumbling first for the lamp and then the pen and pad he kept on his night table. "Where?"

He started scrawling, stopped halfway through the address, no reason to go on.

The receiver trembled in his hand as Shaath continued speaking. The cold grasp of terror found his insides in the same spot it had that night he had walked into his house and knew the Sandman was upstairs.

Ben let the phone drop and threw on some clothes before rushing from his apartment. He didn't stop until he was in his car and screeching back into a nightmare he knew all too well.

C H A P T E R   2 4

DANIELLE SAT UP on the couch, not sleeping. Sleep had been eluding her a lot lately, especially since her second brother died.

She knew the United States had employed a "second son" rule during the Vietnam War which stated that the surviving son of a family having a KIA was automatically exempted from the draft and service. While Israel employed no such provision, the unwritten law had surviving sons given much less risky assignments. Usually this meant clerking, motor-pool work, maybe a short posting in Haifa or Elat.

Her brother David had felt he owed his country more than that. Their father, the general, begged to differ and they arrived at a compromise where David would be assigned to a security detail in Tel Aviv. He was on duty when a car bomb went off in a crowded outdoor market ten months before. Back then, Danielle was still with the National Police and had been the first ranking officer on the scene, having no idea her brother had been one of the victims.

Television doesn't show the true effects of a bomb blast; television *can't* show it. The bombs Hamas was putting together these days quite literally blew people apart. Danielle had been on the scene for an hour before a captain approached and asked if she had seen Lieutenant David Barnea. She looked at the blood, bone fragments, and stray limbs littering a street that would have to be repaved to hide the memories and, suddenly, she knew.

What she remembered most, strangely, were the sounds. First the lingering shrieks of terror and pain from the wounded, followed by the incessant wail of sirens, and, finally, the worst of all: silence. The bystanders held back at a secure distance not making a sound. Officials like her going about their grim business without exchanging a word. The silence was terrifying, for it told the clearest story of all.

Danielle insisted on telling their father herself, and remained convinced to this day that the news had been the cause of the stroke that had left him a voiceless cripple. She had lost an entire family to war, including her mother, who had never recovered from the death of her first son and died quietly like an old woman at the age of fifty-two. Danielle had told Ben that Israel needed peace at any cost, and became more convinced of that with each passing day. War doesn't work against an enemy who lives in the shadows, refusing to show itself. An enemy who claims its casualties from civilians and hides behind martyrdom. With peace, these martyrs would lose their calling cards, and the reluctance among Israelis and Palestinians to interact would slowly be vanquished. Future generations would not suffer from the curse hers and Ben's had.

Danielle had intended to go straight home following her meeting with Giott and Baruch, but found herself heading toward the convalescent home instead. It was another one of life's cruel tortures, never knowing what she was going to find when she entered her father's room. He seldom had two good days in a row and she could only hope this would be one of the rare exceptions.

The nurses and attendants called him "General," and even on the bad days that seemed to keep him calm. She wondered if the bad days weren't actually preferable, since they left him with less frustration over how much the stroke had taken from him after one war or another had taken everything else. Danielle entered his room and breathed a sigh of relief at the sight of a newspaper open on his lap. Closer to the bed, her heart sank, realizing the newspaper was upside down.

Nonetheless, he perked up when he saw her and smiled slightly.

"Hello, Father."

He looked weak today, so Danielle brought the notebook computer—his voice—from the night table and took away the newspaper to create a space for it.

"I was hoping we could talk." She more than just regarded it that way; she actually could *hear* his voice as he typed.

The prospect pleased him and his unsteady fingers fought with each key.

THE WEST BANK?

She smiled, ever so thankful he was not only responsive, but also remembered their discussion of yesterday.

"Different than I thought it would be."

HOW?

"Hope. I felt it in the people I saw. They have it now. The way they looked at me, I could see it in their eyes."

THE CASE?

"Challenging. There's a monster out there," she said, using Ben's term. "What he's done . . . It cuts across race, culture. Serves as an equalizer. We've got to catch him, but I don't know if we can."

His eyes drifted briefly, then sharpened again as he typed, THE PALESTINIAN?

Danielle knew he was referring to Ben, her investigative counterpart. "Intuitive. A superb detective for any part of the world. I went there expecting to hate him, *wanting* to hate him. I couldn't."

Her father's face asked the question this time.

"Because he was no happier with this assigment than I am. Because he understands about loss as much as we do. Because he wants peace. Because he's American, too." She paused. "He knows about monsters. I think I can learn something from him."

YOUR SUPERIORS.

Danielle noticed there was no punctuation mark this time and wondered if that was significant. "They haven't told me everything."

THEY NEVER DO.

"It seems I wasn't sent to help catch the Wolf. I was sent to make sure resolution of the case doesn't lead to any embarrassment."

THEY'RE SCARED.

"Of what?"

CONTROL. ALWA—Her father's fingers rebelled against him and he clutched them tight against his chest in frustration.

"They're afraid the killer's an Israeli," Danielle said. "They're worried how that would look in the eyes of the world. They want me to make sure it never comes out if that turns out to be true."

THEY ONLY FEAR WHAT THEY KNOW. His eyes were blazing now, the most alert she'd seen them since the stroke, willing the strength back into his failing fingers.

"I don't understand."

WHY YOU?

"I told you yesterday: I replaced a man who was wounded."

He shook his head demonstratively, leaving Danielle to wipe the spittle leaking from the corners of his mouth as he typed:

NO!!!

"I was there when the man whose place I took was shot."

Her father was breathing hard now, fighting with every key to depress, starting to lose.

ALWAYS U, was the best he could manage.

"I don't understand."

Danielle knew she was losing him, but one question remained to be asked.

"Did you ever hear of a man named Jafir Kamal?"

Her father's eyes flashed briefly back to life, providing her answer.

"His son is the Palestinian I've been paired with." She took a deep breath. "I need to know if we killed him."

The old man's eyes widened.

"Please. Tell me."

He managed to shake his head before it sank back to the pillow. His eyes had grown blank, his expression hollow. She stroked his face lightly. His skin felt so dry and lifeless. She stayed until he slipped off to sleep, even though he had ceased to recognize or respond to her.

But it had not been his revelation about the death of Jafir Kamal that had kept Danielle from sleep that night. Her father had known both Giott and Baruch during his years of service. Their names meant nothing to him anymore, but he understood their positions. It would have been easy to pass off his rantings and conclusions as the work of a mind at war with itself. She found she couldn't, though, because he was clearly in command of his thoughts, two lucid days strung back to back thanks to a purpose he had suddenly found:

To warn her.

What was really going on here? What was it her superiors weren't telling her?

She was pondering those questions yet again in the early hours of the morning when the phone rang.

CHAPTER 25

BASED ON THE level of activity outside
Dalia Mikhail's townhouse, Ben knew he was at least
an hour behind the first arrivals, maybe more. Even
the Cleaners had arrived ahead of him, waiting groggily in their van-turned-ambulance for al-Shaer to
summon them.

Ben approached the front door in a daze, feeling a
different kind of trepidation entirely than that he had
felt on his first trip up this walk upon returning to the
West Bank. He felt the grief as quick, jarring stabs of
static, fired by anger this time and not fear or remem-
brance.

The front door was open and no one was bothering
to guard it. Commander Shaath stood in the living
room, talking to a few officers in low, rumbling tones.
Shaath noted Ben's arrival and lumbered toward him.

"Why wasn't I called earlier?" Ben shot at the big
man.

"The first officers on the scene were not aware of your newfound importance."

"You were."

"I called you as soon as al-Shaer made his initial report."

"After the mayor ordered you to."

"What's the difference?"

"A contaminated crime scene, for one thing. A dozen officers traipsing around, obliterating footprints and who knows what else." Ben gazed at the commander's monstrous hands. "And where are your gloves?"

"I left them at home."

"I'm talking about the latex variety. You called me from the victim's phone, didn't you?"

"It was the closest."

"And you didn't wear gloves even when you touched it?"

"I didn't think the killer would have stopped to use the phone."

"No, you didn't think." Ben felt his mouth going dry, heart hammering at his chest. His vision sharpened. He saw Shaath, saw himself clawing the big man's eyes out, didn't know how he held himself back.

"Where is she?"

"Terrace."

Ben started past him, Shaath following with his words.

"Several of us know she was your father's whore."

Ben turned back around and was about to repond to Shaath's insult when he saw Major Nabril al-Asi enter the villa, flanked by a quartet of Protective Security Service personnel. Al-Asi was dressed in the same

Henry Grethel suit Ben had seen him wearing early that evening outside the Khalil home, but no tie.

Al-Asi and Shaath exchanged polite nods before the major continued on for the terrace.

Ben blocked his way.

"Is there a problem, Inspector?" al-Asi asked, as the men around him tensed.

"This is a crime scene."

"That's why I'm here." He tried to peer through the glass doors over Ben's shoulder. "I guess we can safely assume Ms. Mikhail won't be writing any more editorials. Now, if you don't mind . . ."

Ben didn't budge. "I do. This is my case."

"I merely wanted to—"

"You can do whatever you want, *after* I've had a chance to inspect the crime scene. We can call the mayor if that's a problem."

"I do not report to the mayor, Inspector," al-Asi returned, as if feeling belittled.

"Then you can tell whoever you do report to that a good woman was murdered tonight. Tell them I'm going to catch the killer, so long as no one gets in my way or interferes with my work."

"Fine. As soon as my men complete their check of the premises."

"See if they can find the addresses of the periodicals Dalia Mikhail contributed to for me: I'm sure those publications would be interested in hearing about a high-ranking Palestinian official trying to sabotage the peace process by interfering with the joint effort to capture al-Diib."

Al-Asi started to bristle, then simply smiled. "I suppose my men can wait."

"Outside, please."

"Very well," al-Asi said calmly. "If we find anything that belonged to your father, where would you like it sent, Inspector?"

Ben smiled back instead of taking the bait, then continued to the terrace. He could tell as soon as he neared the glass doors that things were even worse than he had feared. A half dozen officers were hovering near al-Shaer as the medical examiner went through his routine with the body. They all quieted as he approached, informed by Shaath no doubt that Inspector Kamal was well acquainted with the victim.

Dalia's body had already been covered by a sheet, but the blood was everywhere on the terrace, staining the wood dark in huge, aimless patterns. The professional in him knew he should pull back the sheet, see for himself. But the man in him wanted to remember her as she was, cling to the last living connection to his father.

"It was al-Diib again," al-Shaer said, fingering the camera dangling even with his chest. "I can say that much for sure."

The medical examiner fished a pack of cigarettes from his pocket.

"She didn't let anyone smoke in her house," Ben warned.

Al-Shaer left the pack unopened. "I don't think she's in any position to mind now."

"I am. Now get these men out of here," Ben ordered, afraid of the tone he would use if he did so himself.

Al-Shaer signaled the officers to take their leave and they did, muttering to each other.

"What were they doing out here?" Ben demanded.

"A number of things," the medical examiner replied, returning the cigarettes to his pocket. "I was utilizing their services."

"They weren't wearing gloves. Their shoes were uncovered. They contaminated the crime scene."

"Do you really believe it would have yielded any more clues than the others?"

"We'll never know now, will we?"

"He never entered the house. Climbed onto the terrace from the ground below and must have lured her out here."

"Or waited. She came out here every night. He would have known that."

"No witnesses, as usual. No one heard or saw a thing. A neighbor called to report the terrace door open. He thought a robbery might be in progress."

"How long ago was that?"

The fat man consulted his notes. "Two hours ago. A police detail responded thirty minutes later."

"They're improving."

"She died quickly, if that's any comfort to you."

"It's not."

"It's the first time al-Diib has killed on the premises of his victim." Al-Shaer closed his notebook. "And he was much quicker about things this time. I can tell that from the cuts and from the relative lack of mutilation. Just token really, like he was in a hurry."

"Afraid of being seen probably."

"Then why bother with this woman in the first place?"

The Cleaners approached the open glass doors, but al-Shaer held a hand up to keep them back.

"You knew her, didn't you?"

"Everyone else seems to know the answer to that, Doctor."

"I've heard the rumors. I thought I'd ask."

"Yes, I knew her, and that may very well explain the reason for al-Diib's taking such a risk."

"What?"

"To get to me."

"*You?*"

"He's afraid, but he can't come at me directly." Ben stiffened. "They never do."

"As I see it—"

"Your priorities, Doctor, are to measure the size of the dead woman's wounds and determine if that oily substance was present within them."

"Stay back!" al-Shaer ordered the Cleaners when they started forward again. He lowered his voice. "You've heard things about me, too, I suppose. How I drank too much and killed a few patients."

"I've heard the rumors," Ben conceded, nodding. "I should have asked."

"Nobody ever does. The truth is that I was a *hakeemna* for my village and held in the highest esteem everywhere else, believe it or not. It was I who initiated the blood-donor programs in Nablus, Ramallah, and Hebron. The procedures I dictated for identification and contact are still used today."

"What happened?"

Al-Shaer's voice grew distant. His eyes drifted away from Ben's. "There were two of them, a young girl and an elderly man. The young girl had taken an Israeli bullet that ricocheted off a building. They came and got me out of a restaurant. She was half dead by the time I reached her. We got her to my office. There was little I could do, but I tried anyway. A mistake as it turned out: when she died, I was issued a warning by the local Israeli military commander. He claims he had proof I was drinking.''

''I'm surprised he cared.''

''He cared about finding a reason to yank another physician out of the West Bank.'' Al-Shaer swallowed hard. ''The episode with the elderly man happened later that same week. I hadn't been drinking at all when they brought him to my office; feverish, blood pressure sky rocketing. It didn't take more than a quick examination to determine his appendix had burst. He had minutes to live, no time to get him to a hospital, so I operated on the spot. And I saved him! I saved him, Inspector!'' Al-Shaer's features fell as quickly as they had risen. ''But he died of a heart attack before we could get him to the clinic. A soldier reported seeing me drinking in my office earlier in the day: a diet soda, that was all, but not according to him. I was arrested and sent to the Ansar 3 detention camp in the Negev.''

Ben looked at him in silence.

''I'm telling you this,'' al-Shaer continued, ''because I want you to understand that loss is something quite well known in this part of the world. You might say it's what holds us together as a people. Get used to it.''

''Believe me, I am.''

Al-Shaer shrugged and finally signaled the Cleaners to proceed. They emerged through the glass doors and laid a stretcher next to Dalia Mikhail. They lifted her onto it carelessly and hoisted the stretcher up and out, as the medical examiner looked on, fingering his pack of cigarettes longingly.

Al-Shaer's eyes shifted suddenly and Ben followed them to the living room beyond to see Danielle Barnea making her way through, escorted by an officer on either side. Pretending as though they weren't there. Stopping to let the brothers carry Dalia on by.

"I came as soon as I heard," she said, stopping at the doorway. "I offered to have a full forensics team accompany me, but was refused permission."

"Doctor al-Shaer can handle things as well as they can," Ben said, his eyes on the fat man, seeing him in an entirely different light. "Just don't lose the body this time."

Al-Shaer allowed himself a small smile and walked through the apartment, cigarette already dangling from his mouth when he reached the door.

"Come on out, Pakad. The crime scene's already been corrupted beyond repair."

Danielle stayed where she was. "You knew her, didn't you?"

"Shaath tell you that?"

She shook her head. "He didn't have to." She cleared her throat. "Three killings in Jericho now, ten total, and he deviated from many of his established patterns to boot. Strange."

Ben looked up from the splotchy outline on the deck that had been Dalia Mikhail. "Not strange at all."

"You think he did this to get to you?"

"I'm sure of it."

"This isn't the Sandman."

"No, it's al-Diib, and he's repeating the pattern. The Sandman came at me when I was getting close. The Wolf is doing the same, going after someone— the only person—I cared about, because I must be getting close again."

"You think he'd go through all that just to scare you off?"

''I was already scared.'' Ben's entire expression, his very demeanor, seemed to change as Danielle stood there watching. ''I'm not anymore.''

He turned away from her toward the lush foliage to the east that rustled softly in the night breeze, questions of entry, fingerprints, and potential physical evidence very far from his mind. He saw himself climbing a staircase, the Sandman struggling to fit his wife's nightgown over his clothes, having to tear it to manage. Hitting him at home.

Al-Diib trying the same thing. In for a big surprise.

I'm going to kill you, you bastard. This time, I'm going to kill you. . . .

DAY THREE

CHAPTER 26

BEN LINGERED IN the apartment for the rest of the night, if for no other reason than to keep al-Asi's team stewing outside. Danielle insisted on staying with him, until another officer delivered a message from Officer Tawil that it was urgent Inspector Kamal meet him in the Baladiya, saying he had made a potential breakthrough in the case. Ben had forgotten what Tawil was following up. There'd been some messages, notes, nothing he could remember now.

"We'll take my car," Ben suggested to Danielle, watching the Protective Security Service men heading for the villa before he even had the door closed.

Ten minutes later, Ben pulled to a halt on Jaffa Street slightly up from the Hisbe, four blocks from the alley where the victim had been found.

"Good morning, Inspector," Officer Issa Tawil greeted Ben somberly when he emerged from the car. "I'm told you had a very difficult night."

"Left me very cranky, and very impatient, Tawil. Now tell me about this breakthrough."

Before he could begin, the young officer's eyes widened at the sight of Danielle emerging from the passenger side. "You have not had the opportunity yet to meet Pakad Danielle Barnea of the Israeli National Police."

Danielle nodded at Tawil and Ben was struck by the way the morning sun caught her face so that it looked as though a master artist had applied her flesh tones with perfectly measured strokes. Apparently Tawil noticed it too, his stare lingering uncomfortably.

"Chief Inspector Barnea and I are working together to catch al-Diib. She is to be afforded all respect due any other superior officer," Ben told him. "Our interests are identical. We will be holding nothing back. Now tell me the reason for dragging us here."

Tawil cleared his throat, refocused his thinking. "It's about a car, Inspector."

"As I recall, I assigned you to check hotels and inns in search of a missing guest who might have been our unidentified victim."

"I completed that task last night, Inspector. No such place reports any missing guest."

"Then tell me about this car."

"I got to thinking about your comments concerning the victim's shoes, how they only had a thin layer of dust affixed to their soles, matching only the samples from Jaffa Street."

"So?"

"So your conclusion was, he couldn't have walked very far before he was murdered. Then how did he get to the area he was killed in? No buses run at this hour. We checked the taxi services and found nothing. That meant he either drove or was dropped off, and since there were no abandoned cars in the vicinity, we ruled out driving himself.''

"That much I recall, Tawil.''

The young officer looked at Danielle, then back at Ben. ''Please follow me.''

He led the way down a through street that ran off Jaffa and connected with another main avenue on the other side. He stopped at a narrow two-story white stone house squeezed between two others halfway down, one of the few on the street with a driveway.

"I got to thinking where the victim might have left his car if he did drive,'' Tawil continued. ''I asked all the residents in the immediate vicinity who had private parking places or driveways.'' He looked at the home in front of them. ''The man who lives here has already gone to work, but I have his statement. He told me a man knocked on his door late Sunday night and paid him fifty American dollars to let him leave his car in this driveway for a while.''

"Did he describe the man?'' Ben asked excitedly.

Tawil shrugged. ''It was night. He has bad eyes. He remembers brown hair, dark eyes. Relatively tall, six feet anyway, with a firm build.''

Ben looked at Danielle. ''Consistent with the autopsy report.''

"The resident was much more specific about the car, Inspector: a yellow or cream-colored BMW.''

"What about the license plates?''

Another shrug. ''He never looked.''

"Did he say for how long the car's owner intended to leave his vehicle?''

"Not long. An hour at most. The man agreed, of course, took the money, and went to bed.''

Ben paced about the driveway, as if the uneven gravel surface might tell him something. "So our victim parks here, not wanting his car to be noticed. He walks toward his meeting, intending to be back after only an hour, you said. What happened when he didn't come back at all?"

"When the man living here woke up early the next morning, the car was still in his driveway. When he returned from work that afternoon, it had not been moved. He waited until the next morning, when he had it towed by a local shop."

"He didn't call the police."

"He did, but we did not respond."

"But you've found the car, haven't you?" Ben questioned, feeling a glimmer of hope rise inside him.

Tawil's features sank a little. "I thought I had. That was to be my surprise this morning, taking you to the station where it was being stored. Only they lost it."

"*Lost* it?"

"It was stolen from one of their bays."

"Damn." Ben thought of the prostitute's murder and now of the equally convenient theft of what might have been the murder victim's car.

"It was not a professional job, Inspector," Tawil added, as if reading his mind. "Glass was broken everywhere, the lock hacked open, not picked. I think it was amateurs, kids probably, trying to make a fast buck at the Mabara."

"Cemetery?" Danielle raised her eyebrows as she translated the word into English.

"In this case, a square in the slums of Nablus where black market goods are sold," Ben explained. "Called that because it borders an ancient graveyard. But don't let the name fool you. The Mabara has been very profitable since the gradual end to the occupation has reduced the flow of expensive items to the West Bank.''

''I would have thought just the opposite would happen.''

''So did everyone else. But our currency has little value and distributors don't see it being worth their time and effort. That has opened the door for a lively black market to fill the gap. The merchants of the Mabara offer items not always available before, but at a ridiculous cost. Color televisions, VCRs, even air conditioners . . .''

''And cars,'' Tawil added.

''Most everything there has been stolen. You can forget about unopened boxes and manufacturer's warranties, Pakad,'' Ben continued. ''In the Mabara you pay your money and hope for the best.''

''You think this car might be there now?'' she asked.

''An expensive item like that often takes considerable time to move,'' Tawil responded with a hopeful shrug.

Danielle looked at both of them. ''Then what are we waiting for?''

YOU CAN SEE it now,'' Ben said, pointing through the chalky windshield for Danielle's benefit. Their drive had taken them west along dusty roads to Nablus. ''Just up ahead.''

Of all the West Bank towns and settlements, Nablus was by the far the most commercial. The Mabara, the square where the black marketeers had set up shop, was squeezed amid rubble from run-down, rat-infested buildings on the edge of the ancient cemetery.

The setup in those spaces from which the rubble had been pushed aside looked to Danielle similar to that of the flea market in Old Jaffa, albeit lacking the colorful merchants and artistically arranged merchandise. Here, those with enough money bought from stacks of boxes or chose their wares from open crates. She could see the VCRs and color televisions, the air conditioners all of Jericho longed for. This was where Ben had bought the fans for his apartment, albeit not in uniform.

Most of the electronics equipment came from Israel, and there were rumors that Israeli merchants were the Mabara's largest suppliers. Deals were cut every day, profits shared on a reasonably equal basis. Peace, it seemed, was working out much better for the black marketeers than for the people at large. Danielle wondered if Ismail Atturi's refrigerators had been headed here, maybe even his guns.

Ben parked in the street and climbed out ahead of Tawil and Danielle. He could feel Tawil draw even with him and stand cautiously alert. Danielle hung slightly back, taking in the surroundings. The trio moved forward as one, through the array of difficult negotiations that dropped to a hush when they passed by. Quiet, caustic murmurs followed them like hungry dogs.

"Go away!"

"What do you want here?"

"We aren't hurting anyone."

"Mind your own fucking business!"

The remarks grew bolder as they drew deeper into somebody else's world. Ben was glad no one was selling guns—or carrying them, so far as he could see. Since the Authority had backed up its insistence that

Palestinians not be allowed to own guns with stiff penalties for violators, both supply and demand had dropped considerably.

The available cars were squeezed together behind a jagged cap rock wall. A pair of men looked to be doing the selling. There weren't many takers. The few men and women who'd ventured behind the wall were clearly browsing.

"What do you want?" a short, fat salesman asked Ben in an accusing voice.

"Maybe I'm here to buy," he said, scanning the assortment of cars. "You have specials for cops?"

"You serious?"

"I'm here, aren't I?"

The fat salesman seemed to relax a little, embarrassed by his earlier apparent indiscretion. "So you are. A man must have his transportation, and I have some very good models to choose from." He leered at Danielle. "Or something for the young lady perhaps?"

Ben felt Tawil touch his shoulder gently. He turned and followed the line of his finger to a mustard-colored BMW on the far right. The salesman fell in behind them as they started toward it.

"A wise choice!" he beamed. "An excellent choice!"

They found the doors unlocked and opened the front ones. Ben checked the center console, Tawil the glove compartment. Danielle lingered behind them to watch for any misplaced motion on the other side of the wall.

"Empty," Tawil reported.

"Here, too," Ben followed.

"Of course!" the salesman said, clapping his hands

lightly. "You think I would sell you a car that had not been thoroughly cleaned?"

Ben straightened up. "I think we'll take this one off your hands."

"Splendid!" The salesman's features sank just a little. "But we haven't discussed the price yet."

"Doesn't matter."

"Of course! Of course, it doesn't!"

"You see, we're going to do you a favor. We're going to take it off your hands, and we're not going to arrest you. A fair bargain, don't you think?"

"What is this bull—"

Ben lashed a hand out and grasped the salesman's fleshy throat before he could complete the word. "We don't want to be swearing in front of a woman now, do we? See, this car belonged to a man who was murdered Sunday night. Since it is in your possession, I can only assume you were involved."

"But—"

"Worth a tidy sum, I should expect. Enough to keep you in hard currency for your next thousand meals if you watch your diet. I don't know why, but if you get me the keys now I am going to forget how I came by this car. This really is your lucky day." Ben removed his hand from the man's throat.

The salesman was waving his arms concedingly, starting to move away. "A moment, just a moment!"

He hurried toward the open space in the center of the batch of cars where the other salesman was waiting. Ben kept his eyes on him the whole time, unsnapped the restraint on his pistol.

"Inspector," Tawil called from the front seat where he had leaned in on an almost impossible angle. "I think . . . I found . . . something. Yes," he finished, and wormed his way back through the passenger door.

Ben's eyes signaled Danielle to take over the watch, while he turned toward Tawil and accepted something he was holding out.

"It was squeezed between the console and the driver's seat."

"A valet parking ticket," Ben noted, and then he held it out toward Danielle. "From the Hilton in Tel Aviv, Pakad. Now what do you make of that?"

CHAPTER 27

THEY LEFT TAWIL to drive the BMW back to Jericho, and headed for Tel Aviv. Back in Jericho, they exchanged Ben's car for Danielle's, since his orange Palestinian police license plates did not allow for passage into any part of Israel other than Jerusalem.

She decided to tell him what she had learned from her father the night before after they cleared the final Israeli checkpoint.

"There's something you need to know."

He turned slowly and looked at her, the urgency clear in her tone.

"We didn't kill your father, Ben."

His expression was utterly blank, no response beyond that.

"Not the government, anyway," Danielle continued.

"I know," Ben said finally. "I think I always have."

"How?"

"A sniper's bullet would have been the Israeli method, not a clumsy ambush."

"Like the Palestinian bullet that destroyed my father?" Danielle challenged. "A man like your father, on the other hand, would have had much more value to us as a prisoner, even back then. We like to make examples, not martyrs."

Ben felt a heaviness in his throat. "I appreciate you looking into things for me."

"I did it for both of us."

The drive to Tel Aviv from Jericho took ninety minutes in normal traffic and, despite his excitement over a major break in the case, Ben found himself lapsing into uneasy silence the last stretch of the way. He had never been to Tel Aviv before, never been so deep into the heart of Israel. Jerusalem was different. Jerusalem was the world's city, whether the Israelis wanted to believe it or not. The only Palestinians found in Tel Aviv were the ones still lucky enough to hold down jobs, a rigorous undertaking since recent security precautions required them to be at checkpoints between three and three-thirty in the morning to be assured of passage through by six.

If Ben hadn't known better, he would have thought he was back in the United States. That's what Tel Aviv looked like to him, an American city. Danielle swooped her car around the Hilton entrance and left it in a no-parking zone beneath the overhang. She flashed her ID badge to an approaching attendant and then led Ben into the lobby. He could barely keep up with her, instantly aware of the stares drawn by his Palestinian police uniform, although he had left his gun locked in the trunk of the car.

Danielle marched straight to the registration desk and showed the ID badge again. A female clerk fetched the assistant manager for her.

"What can I do for you, Pakad?"

She slid the parking ticket, encased in clear plastic, across the marble counter. "My partner and I," she made a point of saying, "would like to know the name of the man who rented this car. Please do not remove the ticket from the bag."

The assistant manager grabbed it by the edges, as if afraid of disturbing the contents. He slid over to a computer, typed in some commands, waited, then typed in some more.

"The guest's name is Harvey Fayles from New York City. He was scheduled to stay with us Sunday and Monday nights with a Tuesday checkout. We have no record of that checkout, and the car rental agency has reported the car missing. Have you found it?"

"Yes, and it is now in police custody," Danielle answered, not bothering to add that the BMW was in *Palestinian* police custody. "You can tell the agency it will be missing a little longer."

"Has something happened to Mr. Fayles?"

"We're not sure. We found only the car. We would like his address, credit card number, any other information you can give us."

The assistant manager wrote the information down carefully on a slip of Hilton stationery and handed it across the desk. Danielle accepted it, keeping her eyes on the man.

"You will find out for us if anyone remembers seeing Mr. Fayles during the time he was here. A maid, perhaps, or someone in the bar. Maybe the parking valet who delivered his car.''

The assistant manager was writing it all down. ''Of course.''

''And we will want to know what time he picked up his car on Sunday night. We will want to know that immediately.''

''I'll get right on it, Pakad.''

The man disappeared into a back office. Ben slipped over next to Danielle and looked at the information on Harvey Fayles the assistant manager had given her.

''Can I see that for a moment?''

She slid the Hilton memo sheet in front of him. He read the address and snatched up the paper.

''Let's make a phone call,'' Ben said, and then led the way to a bank of phones tucked into an alcove within sight of the front desk.

''Hello,'' Ben greeted when the line was answered. ''Mr. Harvey Fayles, please . . . Yes, I see. I'm sorry. When? . . . He was so young—how old did you say? . . . I'm sorry to have bothered you . . . We were friends, you see. Again, I am sorry.'' He replaced the receiver.

''I heard a woman's voice,'' Danielle remarked.

''Mr. Fayles's wife.''

''Did she already know? It sounded like she already knew.''

''About her husband's death? She certainly did. You see, she was at the funeral—six years ago.''

HOW DID YOU know?'' Danielle asked, after the information had sunk in.

"I know New York City fairly well, from a stint I did with their Crime Scene Unit. That address the manager gave us is in a black neighborhood. The murder victim was Caucasian."

"You're saying that he must have assumed Fayles's identity. That's why you asked the wife about his age."

"Forty-two. Definitely within my medical examiner's estimate for the victim. It's a common practice, you know, easy to pull off in the United States. Find someone about your age who is dead and report to the appropriate hall of records to say you need a copy of your birth certificate, actually theirs. Simple as that, you can become someone else."

"I'm well acquainted with the procedure," Danielle continued, as they made their way through the lobby. "And usually, to avoid complications, the subject chooses someone who died as an infant instead."

"But this man didn't care about developing a superior alias, because he must not have planned on staying Harvey Fayles very long."

"A throwaway identity, then. Use a few times and then discard."

"So if al-Diib's latest murder victim isn't Harvey Fayles, who is he?"

ACCORDING TO THE assistant manager, the mustard-color BMW had been delivered for the last time at ten p.m. Sunday to a man meeting a description similar to the one given by the Jericho resident who had rented out his driveway somewhere around two hours later. The passage of time couldn't have been more perfect. Since the man calling himself Harvey

Fayles had driven to the West Bank, with luck there would be a record of his car passing through at least one of the Israeli checkpoints.

Danielle next made arrangements to inspect the room the man calling himself Harvey Fayles had been staying in. A security guard accompanied her and Ben upstairs and took up a post in the hallway after letting them inside. The large room was located on the hotel's concierge level and overlooked the pool. The bed was made and no personal belongings were in plain view. A suitcase and a tote bag lay in the closet, a pair of suits hanging above them. A toilet kit with its articles neatly packed rested on the bathroom counter. Danielle checked its contents, while Ben fished through the tote bag and then laid the suitcase across the bed.

"Mouthwash, toothpaste, aftershave," she said, emerging from the bathroom just as he was finishing. "In other words, nothing."

"Nothing here either," Ben said, the suitcase still open before him.

"We should check the room for fingerprints. See if they match those of the victim. I'll see to it."

Ben nodded, though he didn't see the need. In his mind they had found the man they were looking for. He checked the suitcase's inner compartments and found them empty, while Danielle busied herself with the drawers of a large bureau. As she opened the second, Ben watched her eyes widen in expectation. Her hand reached in delicately and emerged holding a torn and tattered envelope. She regarded it briefly and then held it out to him.

"Have a look at this."

The envelope's stamps were already canceled. The

top had been clumsily torn open and the flap was missing altogether. Ben studied the typewritten address:

Max Peacock
1100 AMsterdam Avenue
New York, NY 93097

"You think this Max Peacock is an associate of Harvey Fayles?" Danielle asked him.

"Either that or it's another one of Fayles's fake identities."

"If only we knew what had been inside."

Ben eased it into his right jacket pocket. "I have some police acquaintances in New York. At the very least, we'll be able to get a full report on that address."

"I thought you knew New York."

"Not that part of Amsterdam Avenue, I don't."

"How long will it take for them to get back to you?"

"Long enough for me to find that boy I think witnessed the killing."

CHAPTER 28

BEN HAD BEEN hoping Radji's sister would be at the gate of the Einissultan refugee camp in Jericho to greet him again, but he wasn't that lucky. The unrest in Jalazon and some of the other camps had led to a clamping down here too, in the form of an increased presence of Palestinian paramilitary militiamen patrolling along the makeshift avenues. Danielle had dropped him back in Jericho, then returned to Tel Aviv to follow up the Harvey Fayles lead as far as it went.

"How can I be of service?" the camp commander asked, after Ben had been escorted to his office.

"I was here on Monday."

The camp commander looked more closely at him, focusing on his uniform. "Oh, yes. The policeman who entered against the advice of my guards. Please accept my apologies, officer . . ."

"Inspector."

"You see, Monday was a difficult day. Things had already begun to simmer in Jalazon, Balata, Tukarem . . ."

"I visited Jalazon yesterday."

"Then you understand why my men were frightened. I suspended their patrols and kept them on the perimeter. I only wish I had been here when the . . . incident involving you occurred."

"It was nothing."

"If there's a way I can make it up to you, Inspector."

"Help me today."

"Anything I can do, please."

"There was a young woman who helped me, shielded me in the end. I don't know her name, but I need to speak with her again. If you could help me find her."

"An easy task, Inspector. I know the woman you are speaking of; everyone here does. Some forms regarding her just crossed my desk yesterday."

"Forms?"

"I'm afraid she was beaten rather badly. She's in the infirmary. Please allow me to take you there."

THE CAMP INFIRMARY was a corrugated tin hotbox laid out like a barracks. Ben heard the moans as soon as the commander parted the canvas entry flap and led him inside. He walked ahead of Ben between the twin rows of narrow cots layered with bodies roasting in the heat. The air hung thick and motionless, and Ben found himself feeling slightly light-headed in the midst of the oppressive temperature and rank smells.

He waited while the commander spoke to one of the

attendants on duty and watched her point out a bed further down the endless row on the left. The commander waved Ben forward.

"She regained consciousness late last night, and has been improving steadily today. The prognosis is favorable."

"What's her name?"

"Zahira is the one she gave us."

Ben continued on past him. The floor was moist, causing his shoes to squeak against it. The light in the tin infirmary came only from scattered bulbs dangling from the ceiling, hanging motionless, their beams as dead as the air. He stopped before the cot the commander had indicated.

Zahira's face was purple and swollen. One eye was closed, the other a mere slit. Her nose had been flattened, what remained of it covered by a bandage. She was breathing noisily and Ben could see some of her front teeth were missing. Her lips were raw flesh, pulp. She opened her good eye and recognized Ben. He thought she tried to smile, the effort quickly giving way to a grimace.

Ben came closer, brushing against a wooden clipboard that hung from the end of her cot.

"Hello, cop," she muttered.

"Who did this to you?"

She tried to wet what remained of her lips with her tongue. "Does it matter?"

"Then why was it done?"

Zahira said nothing.

"It was me, wasn't it?"

If she could have, she might have shrugged. "They didn't take too kindly to me helping you."

"They . . ."

"Actually, it was a he. Worse thing was, I let him see that it hurt, so he enjoyed it even more."

"Who?"

"I want a cigarette."

"I don't smoke."

"It figures." She grimaced, squeezing back the pain.

Ben crouched down beside her. One of her hands, looking anomalously young and clean, dangled weightlessly from the bed and he took it in both of his. "We need to talk again."

She tried to laugh. "Haven't caused enough damage yet, cop?"

"Your brother's life is in danger."

"It comes with being Palestinian."

"Another witness is already dead, maybe because of what she saw. I found her too late. I don't want to make the same mistake with Radji."

"Why are they killing witnesses?"

"I don't know. Not yet."

"You going to save my brother from them?"

"I'm going to try."

He felt her hand squeeze one of his. "If I say I witnessed the murder, would you save me?"

"Zahira—"

"Tell me what you want me to say. Tell me what I was supposed to have seen, who you want to have done it. Just promise you'll get me out of this place."

"This was my fault . . ."

"Would have happened anyway." She dry-swallowed air. "I don't do what the ones who run this camp want me to."

"The one who did this, he is one of them?"

"Head of the local assholes association. I'd spit on him if I could move my lips."

"I'm going to make sure you get better care."

"Doesn't matter. Soon as I'm out he'll do it again. Just for fun."

"Tell me where I can find your brother, Zahira. Tell me where I can find Radji."

The half eye he could see drifted upward, tearing. "I told him to watch his mouth, to behave. I told him the outside was even worse. He wouldn't listen, wasn't even sorry when they threw him out."

"Where would he have gone?"

"Where all the young *musharedeen* go: Jerusalem, the Slave Market. See what they can steal in the day, sell in the night. I've been there, cop. You won't like it."

"How will I know him, recognize him?"

"They all look alike. But Radji has a front tooth missing. The left one. Courtesy of the guards."

Ben started to stand up. Zahira clung to his hand. "You'll come back?"

"When you're better."

"He'll get the rest of my teeth next time."

Ben stroked her forehead. "No, he won't."

He backed off slowly. Zahira's hand hung outstretched in the air for a time. Then it flopped back to the bed and he hoped she had fallen asleep.

The commander was waiting for him at the nurse's station.

"You know who did this, don't you?" Ben accused.

"In this place, Inspector, it is better not to make trouble."

"It looks like someone has already done that."

"This is not your affair."

"She lies there now because of me." He moved so close their chests were almost touching. "You know who did this to her, *don't* you?"

The commander nodded.

"Take me to him. Take me to him now."

"Your authority ends at the gate, Inspector."

Ben snatched off his badge and yanked his gun from its holster. He held both out for the commander to take.

"Not anymore."

THE GROUP OF men were playing some sort of dice game, tossing a pair onto the ground and shouting for their numbers, when Ben approached.

"Ayad," he called to the biggest of the group, striding right through the center of their game.

The most feared man in the refugee camp stood up and glared at Ben, snarling at the sight of his uniform.

Ben kept coming. Their eyes had not even met when he smashed Ayad in the jaw with his fist. Ayad flew into the spectators gathered behind him, tried to push himself back upward.

"I want you to know what it feels like."

And Ben hit him again. Blood exploded from his nose, as Ben slammed a kick into the big man's ribs. Ayad stumbled, breath sputtering.

"You beat up young girls who can't fight back." Ben pushed him to the ground and shoved his face in the dirt. "Well, I can fight back." He threw him forward. "Come on, try me."

Ayad struggled back to his feet, wobbling. He lumbered forward and cocked a huge hand behind him. Ben saw the punch coming and easily ducked under it, crashing an elbow into the big man's kidney. Ayad screamed and lashed another wild blow outward. Ben hit him with a right and then a left, his frustrations spilling over, all bottled up inside since reaching Dalia Mikhail's home that morning—hell, maybe since the night the Sandman paid his visit. To Ben, Ayad was the Sandman and al-Diib rolled into one.

"Is this what happens when someone stands up to you?"

Ben hit Ayad so hard this time his hand went numb.

"Is this what happens when it's not a young girl who takes you on?"

Ayad's hands sank to his knees, before Ben could hit him again. He spat out some teeth.

Ben grabbed him by the hair and yanked, keeping him from collapsing. "Arresting you would be too kind. I should kill you. But I don't think I will. Know why? Because then there would be no one to look after the young woman's needs when she is well again. There would be no one to make sure she has everything she requires. You'll do that, won't you, Ayad?" Still grasping the thick, dark hair, he nodded the big man's head up and down. "I thought so. A true gentleman. I knew you had it in you." He moved his face closer to Ayad's, lowered his voice to a whisper. "Don't fuck with Zahira again. If you do, I'll come back. If you do, I'll kill you."

Ben pitched him down face first and walked away. He had forgotten the presence of the crowd. Today, none of them reached down for stones to throw at him. They stood immobile as he passed by en route to the commander, who was waiting just beyond the crowd that had formed, ready to give his badge and gun back to him.

CHAPTER 29

HOW WELL DO you know this place?''
Ben asked Danielle as their car approached Jerusalem's Slave Market.

"Every Israeli police officer knows it," she replied,
"although we would prefer not to."

"Tell me."

"You'll see for yourself."

They had met an hour earlier at nine p.m. at a
checkpoint station near the midpoint between Jericho
and Jerusalem. Danielle noticed instantly the new
wounds Ben had added to his collection. In addition
to the bruises on his face, now his hands were skinned
and swollen. He could barely close his right into a fist
and the knuckles on his left continued to throb. It
hadn't been until well after departing the refugee camp
that he even realized they hurt.

"How will you explain those to your superiors?"
she had asked him.

"I'll tell them my sex slave needed an extra beating," Ben had replied, actually feeling himself smile.

"You look much too good for that to be the case."

They drove together in her car, Ben having found a ride to the checkpoint. Once again he would be entering Israel in civilian clothes. In the Slave Market all cops were hated, no matter what their nationality.

"Learn anything more about the BMW our murder victim rented?" Ben asked her as soon as they were on their way.

"Unfortunately, our checkpoints are more concerned with who's coming out of the West Bank than who's going in. No log from that evening mentions anything about a yellow BMW. The real question is what brought him to Jericho in the first place."

"The answer to which won't explain why the Wolf broke his pattern for choosing his victims. Serial killers almost never do that, Pakad."

"This one did."

Ben thought about that briefly. "Which means we could be facing a killer who's evolving, altering his methods slightly to give himself new challenges."

"Meaning we haven't challenged him enough."

"Make no mistake about it, these monsters are fierce competitors. I've learned that the hard way— twice now. They thrive off being hunted as they are hunting themselves. They like being threatened at the same time they resent it. If al-Diib did not perceive that threat to be great enough, he may have purposely exposed himself to greater risk."

"Making it easier for us in the process?"

"And more rewarding for him."

* * *

WE'RE ALMOST THERE," Danielle announced twenty minutes later. "We'll drive along the Slave Market before we walk. It will help you to grasp what we're dealing with."

The Slave Market was a collection of streets running off a main avenue called Taifa. It was hard for Ben to tell what Taifa had been before; the boarded-up buildings and long-shuttered storefronts gave little witness. The streets were paved with cobblestone, mere alleys barely wide enough to accommodate a single car.

As Ben gazed out through the windows he found he did know the Slave Market, after all: not here, but in other cities where it went by other names. Every city had a place where for a price virtually anything could be had. Fetishes of all sorts were provided for. Drugs were available. Prostitutes battled homeless children and refugees for customers cruising the streets. Everything had its price. Money went a long way.

Few of the street lamps in the area functioned, casting the entire scene in an uncertain dull haze from the headlights of cars and the glow emanating from the buildings enclosing it.

"The police don't patrol this place very often," Danielle explained. "What's the sense?"

Young people, some looking fairly respectable in fashionable jeans and jerseys, gathered in groups on corners sharing cigarettes or marijuana joints. Liquor was freely passed around. Women showcased themselves for all who passed. A portable stereo was playing somewhere close and one group of young men and women had turned the cobblestone street into a dance floor.

"How would someone like Radji have gotten here?" Ben wondered.

"Because he's Palestinian, you mean? It's not hard to sneak out of the West Bank alone or in small groups, especially for children. In Tel Aviv, most of Jerusalem too, authorities would stop them and ask for papers, identification. Here, no one bothers."

She eased the car beyond the center of the Slave Market and parked.

"You'll want to carry your gun this time," she advised.

"Against your regulations, Pakad."

"I'm countermanding them, Inspector. Bring it."

Ben wedged a pistol in his belt under his loose shirt and followed her out of the car.

"It's strange," Danielle said as they walked, "but this is one of the few places where Jews and Palestinians mix socially, the children anyway. The Palestinians bring with them what the Jews want to buy—hashish, mostly, very pure and strong, perhaps ten times as potent as marijuana. They are very enterprising. They can earn more here in a night than their parents can in a month. It keeps them coming back, taking the risk of having us throw them in jail."

"And do you?"

"We have no choice."

"Sad."

"The saddest thing of all is that rarely does anyone come looking for them."

"Probably because they're scared to approach the Israelis."

"No, the families of these kids, for the most part, just don't care."

Around the corner, they came upon a group of Palestinian boys, who scattered instantly. A pair of teenage girls strutted toward them. Ben blocked their path.

"We're looking for a boy," he said. "A Palestinian named Radji."

The girls looked at each other. The taller one spoke. "There are lots of Radjis here."

"This one would be twelve, thirteen maybe. Long knotty hair. Missing a front tooth."

Again the two girls exchanged a glance. "Lots of them," the taller one said impatiently. "Take your pick."

And so it went. Ben and Danielle traversed the streets again and again, trying to blend with the scenery as much as possible. As time passed, the smell of drugs grew stronger in the heavy air and the sounds more hushed. Children of high school age weaved awkwardly from sidewalk to sidewalk. Others sat on the curbs, alone, heads bobbing up and down. Cars with their lights dimmed criss-crossed the streets looking for another kind of ware. The occasional slamming of a door indicated they had found it.

Ben watched as an old two-door, dark-colored BMW came to a stop in the center of the Slave Market. Only one of its brake lights worked. On the street, a teenage girl with long hair leaned her head in through the open passenger side window. As she flirted with the man behind the wheel, a throng of boys rushed the window, sticking their hands toward the driver. Their clothes bagged on their bodies, fashionably unkempt except for the grime that coated them.

"Money!" Ben heard one of them demand, as he drew closer. "Give us money, please. Whatever you can spare so we can eat." The voice, young but bold, was laced by a slight lisp.

"Fuck you!" the boy blared as the BMW's driver's side window started up. He darted to the front of the car and slammed its hood with his palms when the driver tried to edge it on. Ben gave him a long look. The boy's head bounced as he slammed the hood again, preventing the driver from pulling away. Long, unkempt hair flew haphazardly. A small rucksack nearly slipped from the boy's shoulder as he retreated a few paces. The boy turned enough for Ben to catch a glimpse of his face in the shadowy shroud cast by the BMW's headlights.

He was missing his left front tooth.

"That's him," Ben announced.

Danielle followed his eyes, looked back at Ben. "You're sure?"

"I'm sure. That's Radji."

Even from this distance, the boy's resemblance to his sister, Zahira, was unmistakable. Ben started forward, moving steadily but not hurrying, in the hope Radji wouldn't notice his approach.

The BMW lurched forward, stopped, then lurched again as the beggar boys darted in and out of its way, knocking on the car's windows and punching its fender. Radji remained boldly at the hood, backpedaling only fast enough to keep from getting run over.

Ben picked up his pace. He glanced behind him to find Danielle following tensely a few yards back and noticed an old dark Mercedes turn onto the street, picking up speed as it drew closer to the BMW. It slid past him and Ben assumed its driver was just another potential customer for what the Slave Market had to offer. He heard its brakes squeal and watched as all four of its windows started opening simultaneously.

"*Ben!*" he heard Danielle scream behind him.

He was in motion even before he heard her or saw the first weapons appear from inside the car. He had his gun out and was starting to cut across the street toward Radji when gunfire opened up from inside the Mercedes. The back window of the BMW exploded under the initial fusillade. Its tires spun madly, and the car careened into an abandoned row of fruit and vegetable stands, the street erupting in panic.

Ben and Danielle fired on the darkened Mercedes. In response, its occupants shifted their aim from the fleeing boys toward Ben and Danielle. Ben dove to the sidewalk beneath a barrage and rolled to confuse their aim. He caught a glimpse of Danielle running along the other side of the Mercedes spraying it with fire, her bullets like soft *pops* in the night.

"The boy!" she screamed, diving behind the crumpled remains of a pushcart for cover as the men in the Mercedes turned the bulk of their fire on her. "*Get the boy!*"

Ben lunged to his feet and spotted the group of Palestinian boys swinging into one of the Slave Market's alleyways up ahead. He began to run, exchanging a fresh clip for his spent one, the only spare he carried. There was a screech behind him and he turned in time to see the Mercedes bearing down. It clipped a street sign and was snapping at his heels when Ben threw himself behind a grouping of trash cans that looked and smelled as if they hadn't been emptied in a month.

The car continued to plow on toward the alley down which the boys had fled.

"Go! Go!" Danielle screamed, stopping to steady her aim before unleashing another barrage toward the Mercedes's back window. "That way!" she directed, gesturing at another alley near Ben's refuge behind the trash cans. "Cut him off!"

Ben scrambled to his feet. More rounds from her gun thundered toward the Mercedes. Spent shells danced on the cobblestones below.

Ben charged on past the hidden youths, who had sought cover nearby.

"Back!" he screamed at those in his way. "Keep back!"

As he neared the other end of the alley, a group of figures surged down the adjacent main street. He thought he recognized Radji's flapping hair bringing up the rear at the same time as he caught the distinctive hum of the Mercedes's engine.

With no time to think, he lunged out into the street paralleling the main avenue of the Slave Market. The Mercedes was coming at him dead on, one of its headlights shattered, the other winking on and off. He punched out half his remaining bullets and watched jagged holes appear in the windshield. The Mercedes wavered and skidded toward a row of abandoned industrial buildings. The driver spun the wheel wildly at the last, so the car merely sideswiped them, drawing a huge shower of sparks. It kept on going until it came to the next side street, where it swung left.

Had the boy gone that way? Ben hadn't seen, didn't know. He turned and took up the chase blindly.

Danielle reached him, didn't stop.

"I'm going after them!" she screamed back, running almost as fast as the Mercedes was moving before she disappeared down the side street in its wake.

Ben brushed against the rough exterior of one of the street's decaying buildings. His breath came in gasps, his chest on fire. Figures dipped and darted their way along the street in all directions, the children of the Slave Market still fighting to escape the chaos.

Suddenly a shape dashed out from a bulge in the crowd and sped down an alley a block away: a boy with long wild hair whipping across his face and a rucksack flapping from his shoulders.

Ben charged after him, aware the alley must spill out onto a normal avenue like the others. Considering Radji's head start, if he lost the boy here, he would lose him for good.

Ben spun into the alley, ignoring his body's plea for air and the hot pulsing of his heart. Ahead he could see the other end of the alley was blocked. He slowed as the boy reached it and watched him, after briefly considering his options, swing around and charge back.

Ben pressed his shoulders tight against a building, crouching beneath the cover of a rusted pile of old metal. He heard the boy's footsteps pounding toward him and lunged out just as they were ready to pass. He actually collided with Radji, who bounced off him and slammed into a building. The boy spun and tried to spurt by him, but Ben managed to grab him by the scruff of the neck.

"Let me go, you fuck! Let me go!"

The boy's long, tangled hair whiplashed from side to side.

"Let me go!"

Ben noticed a tooth was missing from the boy's scared but feisty face. He was kicking at Ben now, scratching and screaming:

"You fuck!"

It was Radji, all right.

CHAPTER 30

BEN YANKED THE boy away and held him fast at arm's length. Radji tried to bite his hands.

Ben jerked him hard when the teeth found flesh. "Hold it! I'm here to help you!"

"Bullshit!" The boy made a snatch for the pistol wedged once again inside Ben's belt. Ben knocked his hand aside and twisted to place the gun out of reach.

Both turned as footsteps clacked their way, Ben dropping a hand toward the butt of his pistol.

"Don't shoot," said Danielle calmly, sidestepping to survey all of the area around her.

"I found their car," she reported. "Abandoned. Blood. No bodies." Another gaze about. "They're on foot now. Could be anywhere."

Ben noticed her left arm was hanging limp by her side. Then he saw the neat patch of blood widening on her sleeve.

"You're hurt."

"Just a graze." Her eyes fell on Radji. "Is this the kid? Radji?"

"How do you know my name?" the boy demanded.

"I told her," said Ben.

"And how did you know it?"

"Your sister, Zahira, told me."

That softened the boy a little. "You know Zahira?"

"I saw her today."

"How is she?"

"Not good. Someone beat her up."

"Shit."

"It was my fault. I came asking about you."

"We need to get back to my car," Danielle said impatiently, backing up against them. "Quickly, before the men from the Mercedes come looking."

"I'll get it," Ben said. And, before she could protest, "You're in no condition to put up a fight if you run into them, or to drive. Let me have the keys."

She passed them over reluctantly.

Ben headed off without comment, pistol held out and ready before him. He swung right at the head of the alley and covered the four blocks to Danielle's parked car pressed against the dark shadows of the street's buildings. He covered the last stretch in a sprint and lunged behind the wheel, slamming the door behind him. Fumbling the keys, he managed to wedge the proper one home and turn it. The engine roared to life. He swung the wheel hard and gave it gas. The car screeched around, mounted a curb, and then steadied itself as Ben headed back to pick up Danielle and Radji.

She pushed the boy into the backseat, tucked his head low, and climbed in beside him. "Stay down."

Ben drove off, holding his pistol pinned against the

steering wheel in his right hand until he was sure they were not being followed.

"You need to get that arm taken care of," he told Danielle.

She leaned stiffly back in the seat and didn't bother to argue.

"The National Police building is five minutes from here," she said, conceding. "I'll direct you."

"Are you both cops?" Radji asked, drawing the logical conclusion.

"Yes," they said together.

"Am I under arrest?"

"You are under our protection," Ben told him.

"I don't need your protection."

Ben screeched into a right and then a quick left. "You did tonight."

"From the men with guns back there," Danielle added.

"They could have been shooting at anybody. Maybe they were shooting at you!" the boy insisted.

"They drove right by us. They came to kill you, and I think you know why," Ben told him.

"You think so?" Radji spat out.

"Because of what you saw Sunday night in Jericho. Because you witnessed a murder and they don't want you telling anyone about it."

"What if I didn't see anything?"

"They think you did."

"Why?"

"Same reason I do: you were there."

"Who says I was there? Who says I saw anything? If I didn't see anything, they'll leave me alone. You'll all leave me alone!"

"Too late for that now. They've already tried to kill you once. They'll try again."

"And what's to stop them?"

Ben looked at Danielle. "Us."

"What's your name?" Radji asked.

"Ben."

"That's not Palestinian."

"It's really Bayan. Everyone calls me Ben."

"You think you can protect me?"

"Yes."

"Bullshit! You don't even shoot good."

"Few do in real life."

The boy turned his hand into a gun. "Bang, bang! There's nothing to it."

"There is if someone in front of you is trying to do the same thing."

"Are you really Palestinian?"

"Yes."

Radji eyed Ben warily. "You don't sound like the rest of us."

"I was . . . away, for a while."

"No one ever goes away."

"I got lucky."

Ben thought he saw the boy's eyes dart toward the door latch. "How do I know you're not in on this with them? Find out if I know anything before you kill me."

"Because if I were one of them I wouldn't care what you know. I'd only want to make sure you didn't share it with anyone else."

"So I won't." Radji thought for a while. "Take me back to the camp. They'll never find me there, never even think to look probably."

"You were thrown out for hitting a guard with a

rock. They won't take you back. You know that."

"A cop like you can't pull strings?"

"Not in that place."

"Can't shoot, can't pull strings . . . What good are you?"

The kid was trying for bravado. Inside, though, Ben knew he was terrified. What little he had that was important to him was gone. Ben thought of Zahira lying in her infirmary bed. Brother and sister, two of a kind.

"I am going to take you to someone who will protect you," Ben said.

"Shoots better than you, I hope."

"He doesn't have to."

"Why?"

"You'll see."

THEY DROPPED DANIELLE off at the National Police building before heading back to the West Bank in her car. Radji remained quiet the whole drive east and actually nodded off a few times; even slept through one of two frustrating delays at Israeli checkpoints where the pass Danielle had provided did little to smooth their passage into and through the West Bank.

"Who did you say lives here?" Radji asked, when Ben at last pulled the car to a halt before a modest home on the outskirts of Jericho.

It was just after two a.m., and Ben and the boy stood in front of the small house nestled comfortably among others like it on the crowded street.

"A friend of mine."

As Ben started up the walk with Radji in tow, the door opened and the huge shape of Yousef Shifa emerged, ducking under the lintel. Shifa looked even bigger and more menacing than he had two days before in the restaurant he had single-handedly commandeered.

"Hello, Yousef."

"Right on time, Inspector."

Ben smiled. He had never been more glad to see anyone in his life. "I can't thank you enough for this."

"The call about the job came this morning. I start tomorrow. I am much in your debt."

"You can consider it paid in full."

The huge man looked at Radji before responding. "Your friends are welcome in my home any time, Inspector, no matter the circumstances."

"I wasn't sure you had room."

"Five kids inside already. What's another?"

"I will speak with the personnel department, Yousef. You will not be starting your job at police headquarters tomorrow. You will be working for me first, making sure this boy is protected at all times."

Radji looked from Ben to the giant. "He's no good at shooting."

"I," said Shifa, smiling at the boy who barely reached his massive chest, "don't have to worry about that."

THERE WAS A single message on his answering machine when Ben returned to his apartment. He pressed the Play button nonchalantly, starting to unbutton his shirt.

"Inspector Kamal, it's Tawil. I'm on Jaffa Street, near the Hisbe. You must come as soon as you return.

I will wait for you by the alley where the murder took place." There was a pause, then, "I think I know— *Oh my God . . .* "

Ben went cold when the sound of what could only be gunfire came over the line. He heard glass shattering over the tape, was halfway back to the door when the message finally wound to a close.

CHAPTER 31

BEN PULLED HIS car to a halt on Jaffa Street beyond the main square close to the Hisbe minutes later to find the area in utter chaos. Not surprisingly, Commander Shaath had taken personal charge. The big man was issuing orders from behind a makeshift barricade formed of two cars and three jeeps which closed off the crime scene.

Shaath watched him approach, not bothering to disguise the smirk of satisfaction on his features. "First your father's whore, now the young officer you corrupted. Maybe I should be arresting you."

In that instant Ben wanted more than anything to do to Shaath what he had done to the refugee camp strongman Ayad. Liked picturing the commander on his knees counting the number of teeth he had left. Instead, Ben took a deep breath and simply tried to walk past him.

Shaath blocked his path.

"How long ago did this happen?" Ben asked him. "Why don't you tell me how you learned of it?"

"A message from Tawil on my answering machine requested that I meet him here."

Shaath gazed down at the body. "You're late."

Ben felt his heart pounding with anger and jammed his fists into his pockets to keep them still. "You haven't even asked me what Tawil called me about."

"I expect you will put it in your full report, if you ever get around to writing another one."

Shaath turned away and moved back toward the body. Ben followed him. Tawil lay facedown in the street, his blood staining the pavement. The receiver of a phone mounted on the outside of a shop door, the one he must have used to call Ben, dangled over him. Dozens of red splotches showed through his uniform, and Ben recalled the sound of automatic gunfire that had come over his answering machine. A window adjacent to the phone had been shattered by bullets. Tawil's own pistol lay on the pavement just out of his reach.

Ben knelt down to study the angle the bullets had come from, then turned his gaze down the street in that direction, anxious to fix the scene in his mind.

"Leave now," he heard Shaath say from over him. "Or I will have you escorted away from here."

"Go ahead."

"This was preventable," Shaath said, still looming. "With all the recent unrest, I gave orders that no man should be out patrolling alone at night. Too easy a target for anyone with a gun."

"Not just anyone," said Ben, returning to his feet to look the big man in the eye. "Someone who came to kill him."

Shaath's ears perked up and he glowered at Ben. "What do you think you're saying?"

"This wasn't random. He wasn't executed because he was a cop on patrol. Tawil was murdered because he had found something out he was trying to tell me."

"I told the mayor a more senior officer would have been a much better choice when he forwarded your request."

"I chose Tawil because he had initiative, too much apparently. He had already made . . . certain discoveries. I should have discouraged his enthusiasm, should have insisted that he keep me more up to date." Ben felt himself stiffen, not able to hold back the thoughts flooding forward. "And I will not stand here now and listen to anyone belittle the dedication to his duty that ultimately got him killed."

"Did you file reports outlining Officer Tawil's discoveries?"

"They only surfaced today."

"Then you will not mind confining yourself to a desk tomorrow until you have filed your reports. Consider that an order, Inspector."

Ben headed back in the direction the bullets had been fired from, moving slowly in order to look for signs of Tawil's presence near any of the buildings along this section of the street. The night breeze had blown a thin trace of fresh dirt and dust over the sidewalk, impossible to discern individual footprints in most cases. But Tawil's standard police-issue heavy-soled boots made a distinctive impression wherever a print was visible. Also, since the young officer's pair was relatively new, they were still shedding black from their treads.

Ben found enough black smudges and recognizeable

imprints to follow a trail heading down the street toward the phone booth. The trail disappeared at a building that housed a small gift shop, located a mere block from the alley where the man who called himself Harvey Fayles had met up with al-Diib.

Ben pulled a small flashlight from his pocket and crouched low. The one set of footprints that continued on clearly matched Tawil's shoes. He must have been retracing the path he believed the victim had taken that night. The street where Fayles had parked his Mercedes was in this direction as well, another few blocks beyond the alley.

Something dawned on Ben, something he should have realized earlier and had somehow missed. Fayles had left the car in the nearby driveway just after midnight. Since the earliest possible time of his death, according to al-Shaer, was at least an hour after that, he must have been killed *after* whatever meeting he had come here for had been completed. That was what Tawil had realized. They had been looking in the wrong areas for the person he had come to meet, asking about the wrong times. And what if the person wasn't as important as the location? What if the victim's meeting had taken place right here on this very street in this building where Tawil had seen something that had led to his excited phone call to Ben?

But someone must have seen Tawil, someone from inside the building perhaps, who had then tailed the young officer to the phone booth and cut his message to Ben short in a barrage of bullets.

Ben switched off his penlight and rose, hand reaching for the doorknob of the building in question, when he heard footsteps behind him. He looked up to find a police officer he didn't recognize standing defiantly over him.

"Commander Shaath insists that you leave the crime scene."

"I didn't know this was part of it."

"I have orders to escort you back to him if you refuse."

"Then let's go."

He let the officer lead him toward the lighted area where Commander Shaath was making a show of assigning men to search for witnesses, sending them off to do a door-by-door, canvass the neighborhood. Talk to a bunch of people who weren't about to talk back.

He made Ben wait several minutes before acknowledging his presence. "You would be better off working on your past-due reports, Inspector, instead of interfering in matters which do not concern you."

"This is *my* case. I think that means it concerns me."

Shaath took one step forward. "Officer Tawil's murder is *not* your case. I do not accept your theories, and Mayor Sumaya is not here to overrule me this time. I'll want all your reports on my desk by noon tomorrow. Failure to have them there will mean your ass. No excuses. We at headquarters would like to know what you and your Israeli friend have been doing. That includes Major al-Asi. And the mayor."

"I think I'll wait to hear all this from the mayor, if you don't mind."

"I *do* mind. I mind that you are an American just passing through our world. Free to leave it, to walk away anytime you choose."

Ben understood Shaath's mentality all too well. Having grown up during the *hakba,* the loss of Palestine, he was a hard-liner who would accept nothing short of a complete and unilateral Israeli withdrawal from the West Bank, Gaza, and Jerusalem—settlements included. He loathed the peace process for its concessions and compromise. And he loathed anyone who would accept anything less than what he believed the Palestinian people rightfully deserved. To Shaath, Ben's presence here represented a compromise in the name of peace that he could never accept.

"If I really had that kind of choice," Ben said, "I'd have been long gone. I stayed because of men like you, what you represent: the old fears, the old hopelessness, the refusal to believe that change is really possible, because you don't want change. So I stay to help make sure that change happens, and sweeps you away with it."

"But where were you when the real battles were being fought?" Shaath shot back at him. "What do you know about the pain we suffered during the whole of the occupation years? The sight of settlements springing up on fields the Israeli government confiscated from us. The arrest of children for carrying books home from school. Men detained for months because they misplaced their identification cards. They tried to break our spirit, and when that failed they agreed to give us land that was ours already. Peace at the expense of self-respect. They got everything they wanted, and we got nothing."

"Spoken like a true enemy of the peace process. Maybe I should add you to my list of suspects, Commander."

Shaath glared at him. "Only if they find you among the dead."

CHAPTER 32

WHEN HE RETURNED to his apartment, Ben lingered outside walking up and down the street in a fog, feeling despondent and listless. Though exhausted, he found himself alert and aware of every motion, every breath. He ached but couldn't identify where the pain originated. Tawil never should have been following up leads or theories alone. But as his direct superior, it had been up to Ben to keep in better touch. If he had known what the young officer had been up to, Tawil would very likely be alive tonight.

Another death added to the list. First his family, then Dalia, now Tawil . . .

And Ben had no idea what the young officer had uncovered at that building in the moments preceding his murder. Tomorrow morning he would return to the Hisbe and inspect its interior. His hope was that Tawil's killers had fled before their work inside had been completed. If nothing else, the presence of police through the rest of the night would keep them from returning, so Ben would be able to see the building in virtually the same state Tawil had.

Ben finally entered his building, climbed the stairs wearily to his apartment, and unlocked the door. The light was on. A warning pang of alarm snapped him instantly alert.

"Bang," said Frank Brickland, before Ben even had a chance to go for his gun. He was seated in the ancient easy chair, feet up on the hassock.

"Make yourself right at home, Colonel," Ben said, feeling strangely glad to find Brickland waiting for him.

"Thanks."

"What's on your mind?"

"I'm on a roll, hoss, and you should be on a plane; it's time for you to use that American passport of yours and hightail it outta here." Ben noticed the framed picture in Brickland's lap just before the colonel returned it to the end table. "This your family?"

"Used to be."

"You wouldn't have come back here if it still was."

"No, I wouldn't."

"Means you're here for all the wrong reasons, hoss. Doesn't mean you can't leave for the right ones. Listen to someone who's been there. Pack up and go home."

"I am home."

"Bullshit you are. Home is where you know what the fuck is going on. Walls of this fucking town are tumbling again, Benny. Get out before they crush you." Brickland laced his fingers behind his head. "You're better than I thought you were. I underestimated you. You find the kid you were looking for?"

"Don't you know? You know everything else."

"That information hasn't caught up with me yet. Thought I'd save myself some hassle."

"And what if I have?"

Brickland's voice was stone cold. "What did he see, Benny?"

"He claims he didn't see anything."

"You believe him?"

"No."

"Smart kid. Probably the only way he might live another couple days, 'way things are going."

"You didn't ask me about Officer Tawil."

"Didn't know you were expecting me to."

"Someone killed him tonight. They got Shanzi, they tried for the boy in Jerusalem, and they killed Tawil."

"They," Brickland echoed. "The Wolf you're after have cubs or something?"

Ben sighed. "I don't know what's going on anymore."

"My point exactly. Now tell me about the woman they found this morning."

"This morning . . . It seems a lot longer ago than that."

"I heard you knew her. I'm sorry . . ."

"Thank you."

"You didn't let me finish. I'm sorry because it's become personal for you now, hoss. You had a better chance of solving this when you didn't give a shit."

"Maybe I have solved it, Colonel: *you* could have sent those gunmen in Jerusalem."

"You still alive?"

"For the most part."

"Then I didn't send them." Brickland took a deep

breath. "God, this part of the world is a fucking mess. . . ."

"Should I ask my Israeli friends about your son, Colonel?"

"Goddamn, just when I was starting to have some faith in you . . . Shit, Benny, you really think they'd tell you? You really think they'd even know?"

"If he worked for them? I should think so."

"Don't bother. Israel's compartmentalized for a reason. Kept secrets don't travel. Israelis learned that because they're always fighting to survive. You think your Israeli girlfriend can punch a question into a computer and come up with an answer, you're in the wrong business. Go home, hoss. Go home before it eats you up."

"I couldn't bear the thought of leaving you on your own, your own mission incomplete."

"Maybe I'm getting close too. See, I didn't come here empty-handed." Brickland reached into his pocket and drew out a white envelope. "Beware of fellow Americans bearing gifts. Maybe you forgot about those fingerprints you gave me last night. Got a positive ID for you on the corpse from the alley. Gives a whole new meaning to the den your wolf comes from. I assume your channels have come up with diddly so far, and I wouldn't expect that to change if I were you."

Ben made no motion for the envelope.

"When I got this, I figured I'd better come by in person, make sure you didn't get killed before I had a chance to give it to you," he continued. "I'd miss your company. I love our little talks."

"And because you were here, they didn't bother coming, or didn't stay long if they did."

"That's the idea," the colonel told him. "I think you're even ready to get the number where I can be reached now."

"I'm honored."

"I figure you might need me 'fore this is over."

"Why?"

Brickland thrust the envelope at him like a dull blade. "Good news is that body ain't my son's. The bad news . . . Well, I think you can figure that out for yourself."

DAY FOUR

CHAPTER 33

I THOUGHT WE were supposed to meet at your office," Danielle said after entering the store to which Ben had traced Officer Tawil's last movements the night before.

"A change in plans. I apologize for not notifying you."

"They told me at the detective branch you were here," she said.

The popular knickknack shop had closed inexplicably on Monday, Ben had learned, not long after the body of the victim calling himself Harvey Fayles was found. Ben had returned first thing today to see if there were any contents that might yield a clue. Danielle had arrived when he was rechecking the main area fruitlessly for a third time.

"I am careful to keep my log updated now, Pakad. The price I have to pay if I want the mayor to keep siding with me in my feud with Commander Shaath."

"I'm sorry."

"Don't be. You're the only reason I'm still on the case. The PNA would never dare offend the Israelis."

"You're on the case because you're the only one who can solve it."

"And you think that's what your side wants?"

"I think that's what both sides want," Danielle replied, trying to sound like she meant it.

"You're wrong," Ben said flatly.

He opened a storage closet and shone his flashlight through it, hoping for some paper, some trash left behind. Anything.

"What's that supposed to mean, Inspector?" Danielle asked when he turned back toward her and turned off his flashlight.

"Are you as dumb as I am, Pakad, or are you just a good actress?"

"I heard about the young officer," Danielle said, drawing closer. "I'm sorry."

"So am I. He was talking to my answering machine from a public phone just down the street when he was shot. I heard the whole thing happening. And the worst thing is, Tawil died because he figured out something I should have."

"And what's that?"

Ben swept his eyes about the shop's single, partitioned room. "That this was the place where the man we know as Harvey Fayles came before he was murdered."

"*Before?*"

"Absolutely. The meeting was already completed when the killer struck Sunday night. It had to be that way, you see."

Danielle shook her head, confused. "What meeting? What are you talking about?"

"You really don't know, do you?"

"No."

"No one's said a word . . ."

"No."

"Kept you in the dark. Used you as much as they used me."

The words stung Danielle, her father's warning flashing through her mind.

He had said the same thing!

"What is this about?" she managed.

"The real Harvey Fayles has been identified by his fingerprints. His real name, *real* identity, was Mohammed Abdul Fasil. Name ring a bell?"

Danielle went cold. "Oh my God . . . Are you sure?"

"My American friend Colonel Brickland is sure, and that's good enough for me. Fasil was one of the most radical leaders of Hamas, as I'm sure you're aware, known primarily for organizing the string of suicide bombings in Israel that almost paralyzed the peace movement several years back. If he came here for a meeting, it isn't hard to figure out what the participants were talking about, is it?"

"Then we should be glad the Wolf happened to choose him as a victim."

"There was no coincidence about it," Ben said, kneeling near a strangely clean spot on the floor. He stopped and looked up at her. "And it wasn't the work of al-Diib."

"I don't like what you're getting at."

"Neither do I, but that doesn't make it any less obvious." Ben stood up when he saw the suspicion swimming in her eyes. "This is your work."

"*Mine?*"

"*Israel's.* Excuse me for lumping you in. I know you had nothing to do with it personally, and it wouldn't surprise me if all of Shin Bet was in the dark. But someone in your intelligence community saw al-Diib as a magnificent opportunity: execute Mohammed Fasil and make it look like the work of a madman who's already killed eight other Palestinians."

Danielle shook her head defiantly. "That's ridiculous. When we hit someone, we *want* the world to know."

"In years past, yes. Now even Israel can ill afford the political repercussions. The world's changed, Pakad." Ben smiled thinly. "Even the walls of Jericho have come down. Your intelligence people are now held accountable for their actions. But, when temptation to get Fasil must have proven too great, they came up with a plan that wouldn't require any accounting. They replicated the attacks of the serial killer, figuring the world would blame al-Diib—"

"Which it would have, if not for you."

"*Us,* Pakad. We're a team, joined together by the fact that both of us are being manipulated."

"What do you have to prove all this?"

"I have a dead terrorist and a murdered cop who had the misfortune of uncovering this part of the truth while someone was cleaning this place out last night."

"You think they saw him . . ."

"And then they killed him."

"Are you accusing us of killing your young officer as well?"

"No, that was clearly the work of whatever terrorist cell brought Fasil to Jericho. Shanzi is another matter.'' Ben paused, just long enough for his words to sink in. ''So is the attempt made on the boy's life in Jerusalem last night.''

''That's ridiculous!'' Danielle tried to chuckle and failed. ''You're giving us too much credit, Inspector.''

''I am giving you credit for having infiltrated Palestinian refugee camps like Jalazon and Einissultan. Right or wrong, Pakad?''

''Before—yes. Now—I don't know.''

''Let's assume Israeli intelligence still has people inside the camps. Then the people behind Fasil's murder would have learned about *both* potential witnesses. Shanzi, because very likely she couldn't keep her mouth shut . . .''

''And Radji?'' Danielle asked when Ben's voice tailed off.

''Because I came looking for him. In the camps, word travels fast.'' He stopped. ''But that can't explain how they happened to show up in the Slave Market at the same time we did.'' He looked her straight in the eyes. ''Did you report your intentions to your superiors, Pakad?''

''Of course. I was required to.''

''So they knew where we were going and why.''

''I haven't reported what I uncovered before coming out here this morning.''

In spite of himself, Ben looked at her expectantly.

''According to what I've been able to learn,'' Danielle continued, ''Sunday night wasn't the first time the man we knew as Harvey Fayles entered the West Bank from Israel. He made an almost identical trip thirteen days ago.''

That struck a chord in Ben he couldn't identify.

''What is it?'' Danielle probed, searching his face.

"I don't know, just something about the date of that first trip," Ben said, and then he let it go.

"I can't say for sure he came to Jericho. But he was staying in Tel Aviv at another hotel and followed the same pattern he did on Sunday night: rented a car and drove legally into the West Bank, with all his papers in order."

"That strengthens my theory that Fasil's murderer was an Israeli copying al-Diib's MO."

"How so?"

"It would have given the killer more time to set up the murder. Maybe he could even have found out when and where Fasil would be returning to Jericho so he could be waiting for him."

Danielle fumed at another unsubstantiated implication. "Are you saying one of our deep-cover moles *killed* Fasil?"

"No, only supplied the information that got him killed, just like somebody else supplied those case files that allowed the killer to copy al-Diib's work exactly."

Danielle remembered something. "But our case files didn't mention everything yours did. The oil your Doctor al-Shaer uncovered in the wounds of the first Jericho victim, for example."

"And that makes it impossible for the second killer to have copied that part of the pattern. So, if I'm right, al-Shaer won't find any of the oil in the blood samples he took from Fasil's wounds. Everything hinges on that."

Danielle was right with him. "Then what are we waiting for?"

CHAPTER 34

DOCTOR BASSIM AL-SHAER lumbered away from the dual-lensed microscope and invited Ben to take his place.

"See for yourself."

Ben moved stiffly toward the stool that creaked as he dragged it forward from the strain of having held al-Shaer's weight. He focused on the left-hand lens first.

"The first Jericho victim," the medical examiner said from behind him. "Leila Khalil."

Ben knew he was looking at a blood sample corrupted by some foreign matter, though the specifics were beyond him. He studied the slide briefly and then shifted his eye over to the right-hand lens.

"The second Jericho victim," al-Shaer narrated. "Unidentified male."

Ben tightened his stare, finished his inspection, and returned his eye to the first lens. He shifted back and forth, doing his best to discern a difference in the two slides. But the tissue sample on the second slide had been corrupted as well.

"Now look at this one," the medical examiner said, replacing one of the slides with another. "This is from the woman killed two nights ago, Dalia Mikhail."

Ben reluctantly forced his eye back against the lens. Once again there was no discernible difference.

"All three are virtually identical," al-Shaer confirmed. "Whatever that oil is, I can say without question that it was present in the wounds of all three victims found in Jericho."

Ben raised his head, realized his eye was sore from pressing against the lenses too hard. His head began to throb at the temples, the ache extending deep into the skull itself. He'd thought he had everything figured out, but al-Shaer had destroyed his theory with a trio of laboratory slides.

"I thought you'd be happy," the fat man said, when Ben just sat there dumbly. "Once I identify this oil, it might be the clue that helps us catch him."

"You've done excellent work," Ben responded, his eyes on Danielle. She wasn't gloating, maybe even looked a little disappointed herself. "Now tell me about the knives."

Al-Shaer snickered and pulled a cigarette from a rumpled pack in his back pocket. He lit it, inhaling deeply. "Your damn knives . . . We are dealing with microscopic readings here. First, I stab the side of beef, then I have to cut the section with the wound off and study it under a microscope to get the precise measurements. Officer Tawil brought me over fifty different knives. It's taking forever."

"How many so far?"

"Almost twenty. A few have been close, but nothing that's call for excitement."

Ben lifted himself stiffly off the stool. Exhaustion was catching up with him, quickened by his feeling of disheartenment. He was trying to refocus on the matter at hand, shove his theories aside in the face of al-Shaer's revelations.

"I need some air," Ben heard himself saying.

Danielle trailed him through al-Shaer's office and out into the street, keeping her distance until Ben was ready to talk.

"One killer, then," he said, yet his tone suggested he still wasn't convinced.

"I'm sorry."

"Are you?"

"I know how strongly you believed there were two."

He looked at her. "And did you?"

"What you said made very good sense."

"Shanzi's death could have been an unconnected accident, but not the attack on the boy in Jerusalem last night. They came looking for him, just as we did."

"Maybe not."

Ben stopped and faced her. Before them, drivers on the narrow side street battled pedestrians for control of the road. This part of the old city was not equipped with sidewalks.

"I seem to recall you being there last night and getting shot at just like me." Ben directed his eyes toward the bulky bandage on her arm, clearly pushing against the sleeve of her blouse. "Unless I'm mistaken."

"We *were* both shot at. But do we know for sure that Radji was? Think back now. They shot up that

BMW and then we started shooting at them. They fired back.''

"They went after the boy!" Ben persisted.

"Maybe because *we* did and they had turned their attention upon us after we disrupted the attack on their *true* target."

"The driver of the BMW . . ." It hurt as much for Ben to think it as say it.

"Something we never considered. Simply a different interpretation of the same events. We were in the wrong place at the wrong time, just as the boy was. And what if the boy had nothing to do with it? What if they had been sent to kill us?"

"By who, Pakad?"

"The same party that kidnapped you Monday night."

"Hamas? What would they have to gain from killing us at this point?"

"What did they have to gain by kidnapping you?"

Ben knew he was grasping now. "And Officer Tawil?"

"Hamas again, because they didn't like him snooping around."

"He only had time to tell me there was something I needed to see."

She moved a step closer to him, remaining silent as if her point had been made.

"You wanted me to be wrong. You're glad I was wrong."

"Because I would hate to consider the ramifications of your being right."

As Ben stood there looking at her, a white van darted through a stop sign and slammed into a car just up the street. The van's rear doors flew open as it spun out of control, spewing buckets of fresh iced fish into the street. Bouncing and sliding as though they were still alive, the fish ended up atop hoods, lodged against windows, and upon the pavement along with masses of crushed ice. The whole section of the street seemed covered, as the van's driver pried open his door and climbed out to confront the driver of the car he had hit.

The rest was predictable, the two men screaming, each blaming the other for the accident. The van driver wore a rubber apron that flapped in the wind as he spoke, gesturing furiously at the fresh catch that was spoiling on the pavement.

"All I'm saying," Danielle started, "is we—"

Ben stiffened and grabbed her arm before she could continue.

"What's wrong?" she asked.

"My God . . ."

"What *is* it?"

"Our killer," he replied flatly.

CHAPTER 35

THANK YOU FOR coming, Inspector,'' Ghazi Sumaya greeted forty minutes later.

Upon his return to the police headquarters, Ben had found an urgent message that the mayor needed to see him. Commander Shaath sat in his customary chair, leering at Ben with a confident sneer.

Sumaya's eyes fell briefly on Shaath before he continued. ''The commander has briefed me on the events of last night.'' His voice was low, almost sorrowful. ''Your involvement in this case has become something of a problem for us. . . .''

''Chief Inspector Barnea is just outside,'' Ben broke in. ''Would you mind if I invited her in?''

Sumaya was taken aback by the question. ''Inspector Kamal, do you understand the reason for me summoning you here?''

Ben ignored him. ''We wanted to give you an update on the investigation. There are some new developments, a major breakthrough.''

The mayor gazed at Shaath briefly before responding. He looked relieved when he swung back toward Ben. ''Show her in.''

Ben obliged, and Commander Shaath made a show of turning away from both of them as Danielle entered. The two moved to face the mayor, who beckoned them to be seated in the chairs set immediately before his desk.

''Very well,'' the mayor said when they were settled. ''What are these new developments? What breakthrough?''

Ben accepted the evidence envelope from Danielle and held it tightly in his hand.

''Although at present Chief Inspector Barnea and I don't know who the killer is, we believe we know where he can be found.''

''You . . . *do*?'' the mayor posed.

''I'll start with the two major pieces of evidence the Jericho murders have yielded for us. Credit for that must go to Doctor al-Shaer.''

''Yes, yes. Go on, please.''

''The first piece of evidence was an oily substance Doctor al-Shaer found coating the wounds on all three Jericho victims. The second piece was the size of the entry wounds themselves, clearly indicative of an effective, but uncommon double-edged weapon.''

''Go on,'' Sumaya urged eagerly.

''The other problem Pakad Barnea and I faced was reconciling certain facts not consistent with the events as they must have occurred. Most importantly, how did al-Diib come and go unobtrusively in each instance, *in spite of* the fact that these killings must have left him splattered with blood?''

The mayor looked at Shaath, who sat in his chair stone-faced, letting Ben continue.

''Answer: he was someone whose presence was so common at odd hours that witnesses failed to even remember him, just as the presence of blood on his person wouldn't have stood out, even if it were evident.''

Shaath leaned forward. ''Perhaps you are suggesting he was able to bathe after each killing.''

''No. He wore an apron.''

Shaath swallowed hard. The mayor's mouth dropped.

''A fish merchant, *sidi*,'' Ben finished, not about to explain the fortuitous accident that had led him to that conclusion. ''Al-Diib is a fish merchant, a sight so common on the streets at odd hours that they simply blend into the scenery.''

''They are in the streets at all times, *all* hours,'' the mayor affirmed.

''Doctor al-Shaer has identified the substance found in the wounds of all three Jericho victims as some sort of fish oil—actually, different sorts but from the same general family as the catch brought into the West Bank from Gaza every day. He has also positively identified the murder weapon as a scaling knife, used in both the filleting and skinning processes. One of these . . .''

Ben removed a plastic zip-lock bag from the evidence envelope Danielle had handed him and held it up so the mayor could see the squat-handled, double-edged knife inside. It looked like an ugly, thick stiletto.

The mayor rose slowly out of his chair and accepted the bag from Ben. He could scarcely contain his excitement, as he fingered the knife through the plastic. He held it out to Shaath, who made no motion to grab it.

"This isn't the murder weapon, of course," Ben explained, "but we believe it's a reasonable facsimile."

"Would it be possible for us to generate a list of such fish merchants, Inspector?" the mayor asked.

"As you know, sir, these peddlers are required to be licensed now for tax purposes, but the law has not been strictly enough enforced to rely solely on such a list. However, the only merchants allowed passage between Gaza and the West Bank are based on the docks of the Gaza seaport. Our man will almost certainly be among them."

"*Hundreds* of potential suspects," Shaath chimed in derisively.

"We may be able to narrow it down some by studying passport applications."

"Why?"

"Because since he travels between Gaza and the West Bank, he would probably want to be able to enter Jordan."

"Even if you are fortunate, you'll never be able to positively identify him."

"I think we can," Ben said, and looked over at Danielle. "You see, we have a witness in custody."

CHAPTER 36

"WHY DIDN'T YOU tell your superiors the identity of the second Jericho victim?" Danielle asked as soon as they were outside the mayor's office.

"I sent the fingerprint card through the proper channels. We'll wait until it yields the answer for them."

"Only you don't think it will."

"No more than you do, or Brickland." Ben paused, uncomfortable. "I was wrong about there being two killers. I accept that, and now I just want to wrap things up."

"The boy says he *can't* identify the killer."

"I'm hoping something jars his memory."

"You think it's worth placing him in such danger while we wait for that to happen?"

"No," Ben told her, "and that's where you come in. . . ."

*   *   *

THERE WAS A message for him when Ben returned to his office at police headquarters. Lieutenant Jack Tourcot from the NYPD had called and for a moment Ben wondered why, until he remembered the name and address he had asked Tourcot to check out for him:

> Max Peacock
> 1100 AMsterdam Avenue
> New York, NY 93097

Ben had met Jack Tourcot during the Sandman investigation when an ad hoc task force was assembled, comprising specialists in the lore of serial killers. Tourcot had been point man on New York City's Son of Sam investigation and had ultimately nailed the killer with the help of parking tickets. The capture of serial killers was almost always due to such dronelike, methodical police work, such as Ben's uncovering the fact that the Sandman was a locksmith.

Ben forgot about the time difference and only realized how early in New York it was when a groggy voice answered the phone.

"Your case is getting major play on the news over here, Benny," the New York City detective said. "A historical first, and all that sort of shit. Is it true? Are you really partnered with an Israeli? And a woman at that?"

"It's true."

"I'll be damned. And I thought I'd heard everything. You got the third page of the *Times* yesterday. The reporter called it a 'joint press release.' They spelled your name wrong."

"It figures."

"Any luck, Benny?"

"We may have a lead," Ben said unenthusiastically.

"Good thing, because I struck out on all counts. First off, there's no such address on Amsterdam Avenue, and nobody by the name of Max Peacock in the whole city directory. The really weird thing is, you might be looking on the wrong coast."

"What do you mean?"

"Didn't you notice the zip code? Nine-three-zero-nine-seven. That's California, I think."

With everything else that was going on, Ben had missed what should have been a very obvious clue. Not that it mattered at this point.

"Want me to look it up for you?" Tourcot asked him.

"Don't bother. It must be a dead end. Go back to sleep."

WHAT IS IT I'm supposed to do?" Radji asked suspiciously from the other side of Yousef Shifa's kitchen table.

"Come with me to the docks in Gaza and see if you spot the man you saw from the alley."

"I told you, I *didn't* see anything!"

"I know, but we have to do this anyway."

"Who says?"

Ben gazed around him. "You happy here?"

"What of it, cop?"

"When was the last time you slept with a roof over your head?"

"Do abandoned buildings count?"

"No."

Radji frowned and stretched his arms out over the table. "Long time."

He looked different with his hair washed and pulled back from his face. He was wearing the clothes of one of Yousef Shifa's sons—still not a great fit, but far better than the rags he had learned to accept.

"So what?" the boy snapped.

"So we go to the docks every day starting tomorrow, and as long as we keep going, you keep the roof."

Ben could see Radji's eyes flashing like the lights of a computer. "I want to see my sister."

"Bad idea for you to return to the camp."

"Then I want you to bring her to see me."

"An even worse idea, considering the condition she's in. She shouldn't be moved without medical attention."

His head popped up. "Get it for her!"

"That would mean transferring her to the clinic here in Jericho."

"Do it!"

Ben shrugged. "Difficult to arrange, maybe impossible."

"Then it's impossible for me to go to Gaza and find your killer."

"I'll see what I can do." He paused and made sure the boy could see him take a deep breath. "Of course . . ."

"What?"

"Well, once word gets around the camp of why she left, what her brother's doing to help the police, it won't be safe for her to return. Maybe we should just leave her there, maybe sneak you in for a visit."

"Bullshit, cop! You get her out and make sure she doesn't have to go back!"

"What happens when she gets out of the hospital? She needs a place to live."

"Get her one!"

"We do have some subsidized apartments, but the waiting list—"

"Fuck the waiting list!" Radji blared as he stood up dramatically. "You want your killer, you get my sister a place to live!"

Ben leaned forward. "Can you identify him?"

Radji nodded demonstratively. "If my sister gets a place to live, yes."

"You drive a hard bargain."

CHAPTER 37

OUT OF THE question!'' Commander Shaath roared, springing from his chair in the mayor's office.

Sumaya calmed the big man with an open palm raised toward him, studying Ben the way a teacher might his prize student. "Let him finish, Commander."

Ben cleared his throat. "My point is that an operation of this magnitude requires a lot of personnel and equipment. The equipment we plainly don't have, and the personnel available have not been properly trained in surveillance techniques. That will make them easily recognizable on the docks in Gaza, even in plain clothes. Our only alternative is to make use of Israeli teams to provide surveillance and back-up."

"Armed?" Shaath badgered.

"Considering the man we are going up against, yes."

"And what would we tell our own men? That they are not good enough, not skilled enough, to handle such a complex operation?"

Ben fixed his attention on the mayor. "This entire operation was supposed to be about the benefits of mutual cooperation. I would say that accepting the offer of additional Israeli manpower toward making a *joint* arrest is not only the most effective approach, it also promises to generate tremendous positive publicity."

The mayor's eyes flickered at that. He straightened in his chair, seeming to ignore Shaath's presence in the room. "A very persuasive argument, I must admit, Inspector. How would the logistics work?"

"The Israeli teams will be under Pakad Barnea's direct command and control, while I remain with the boy at all times in constant communication with these teams."

The mayor nodded. "I'll have to call the President for final approval, of course. I'm assuming he'll want us to move a few select teams of our people in as well to handle the task of arresting the suspect, if it comes to that."

"I think the Israelis would prefer that, too, sir."

"And you also think Pakad Barnea will have no trouble getting her superiors to go along with this, obviously."

"Why not? We're both on the same side this time, aren't we?"

MOSHE BARUCH AND Hershel Giott listened attentively to Danielle's request, waiting until she was finished to express their reservations.

"I would prefer, Pakad," Giott argued, "that we not act until there is stronger indication that the man we're after can actually be found at the seaport. You're talking about tying up considerable manpower, and we must have some degree of certainty that it will not be wasted."

"Because of the ramifications of failure, you understand," Baruch added, agreeing.

"If we're going in there, you don't want us to look bad," Danielle interpreted.

"It is a concern," Giott acknowledged.

"The possibility of failure always is," from Baruch.

"And on the other hand, it's important we catch this killer before the peace talks reconvene in six days," said Danielle. "I agree that the pendulum of public opinion has swung our way, taking attention away from the murders. But if the Wolf kills *again* while we are on the job, we stand to lose everything we have gained. Can we take that chance when we are so close to catching him?"

The leaders of Shin Bet and the National Police grudgingly agreed to allow Israeli surveillance teams to participate in the operation. An hour later, Danielle arrived at the records department to pick up a stack of laser-printed checkpoint logs for the last year, hoping the name of a fisherman would appear on at least most of the days murders had been committed in the West Bank. She was paging through the stack when another thought suddenly occurred to her.

"Where's the second batch of materials I requested?" she asked the technician on a whim. She couldn't get Ben's claims of a second killer "manufactured" by Israeli intelligence out of her head. Even though all the evidence seemed to dispel that theory, she too remained troubled by the evidence that supported it. There was only one way to satisfy herself once and for all.

"Second batch?" he replied, befuddled.

"Copies of the files of the cases that occurred before the withdrawal of our troops from the West Bank."

The technician hit a few keys. "Those were already requisitioned."

"Yes, for the Palestinians. Now I need copies for myself." She hesitated briefly, eyes angling for the phone. "Call upstairs, if you like, for authorization."

"That won't be necessary for such a simple request."

Danielle hoped the man didn't notice how she had gradually repositioned herself in order to follow his hands across the keyboard. They moved fast, but she was able to commit to memory the log-on and access codes he plugged in.

When he was finished, Danielle politely accepted the files and tucked them under the same arm holding the checkpoint logs. Rav Nitzav Giott had arranged for her to use an empty office to collate and study her material, one with a computer that was a virtual twin of the machine the technician used.

Danielle closed the door to the small, windowless office and sat down at the desk. Then she turned the machine on, keyed in the technician's access code to get into the file bank, and typed in the log-on he had used to open the file containing the case reports she had left on the other side of the desk. With the file open, she clicked on the View window and asked to see the entire contents listed by name. They appeared instantly in alphabetical order, followed by the data history of each: that is, she reminded herself, when each had been updated, complete with notations of specific memory computations before and after.

The two complete and two partial case reports compiled by Shin Bet before jurisdiction was passed on to the Palestinian authorities were not next to each other alphabetically, so she pulled them out in order to study their data histories together. The most recent "update," of course, had been just minutes before, when the technician printed them for her. Before that there was an identical notation from Monday, accounting for the copies she had handed over to Ben in Jericho. As expected, the Data columns were identical in terms of disk memory used in both occasions.

The case reports hadn't enjoyed a particularly active history, especially since adoption of the second phase of self-rule and the subsequent Israeli pullout from most of the West Bank had left investigation of the murders wholly in Palestinian hands. In fact, there shouldn't have been any activity between the time Shin Bet withdrew from the case and the beginnings of the cooperative effort just days before.

But there was one.

The entire scroll of information didn't fit on a single screen, so Danielle jotted down the columns she was interested in for comparison purposes. The updates had all taken place on the same day, which in itself was hardly surprising. What had happened to the case reports was something else.

Danielle wrote it all down and then double-checked her work to be sure she was correct, feeling her breath shorten slightly. The numbers didn't lie:

	BEFORE	AFTER
CASE 1:	25,621	21,395
CASE 2:	21,433	17,657
CASE 3:	32,907	29,350
CASE 4:	31,650	28,657

Danielle didn't need to be a computer expert to understand that some of the data had been purged from each file when they were accessed several months before. The computer couldn't tell her who had done it or why. Nor could it give her any inkling of what had been deleted. Only one fact was certain:

Someone had tampered with all four case reports well before she had passed them on to the Palestinian authorities in Jericho.

And *something* was missing.

DAY FIVE

CHAPTER 38

THIS IS FUN !'' Radji said a few hours into their first day at the Gaza seaport overlooking the Mediterranean. He had been excited about the adventure from the very start when a pair of Israeli security cars had met their vehicle at the final checkpoint and ushered them across Israel into Gaza.

Ben shrugged, only wished he could have agreed. The heat was sweltering this time of year and the breeze provided little respite. The only saving grace was that the assignment allowed him to dress out of uniform, in comfortable clothes that made him blend into the scene on the docks.

As for their ''cover,'' Ben had little hope it would hold up under close scrutiny. For safety, they remained in each section of the docks only long enough for Radji to get a close look at all the men working the area in search of the man he had described to Ben the day before:

*"He was very big, tall and broad. He had a scar
on the left side of his face and he moved like a ghost.
I know he didn't see me, but I saw him in the moonlight when he cut across the street. I'll recognize his
face when I see it. . . ."*

So far the only things that had grabbed Radji's attention were a huge fish being displayed or a boat
coming in with an especially large catch.

Even in these early hours of their partnership, Ben
knew he was getting much closer to the boy than he
had intended, responding to his vast need for companionship and love. When Radji's hand began to fall too
easily upon his shoulder, Ben's first impulse was to
shrug it off. But the fact was, he liked it there, liked
the feeling of being needed by someone emotionally
again. It seemed like another lifetime since he had felt
that last.

He stopped with Radji at a filleting station where a
long line of knife-wielding men stripped the bones
from the carcasses rapidly and piled them in steel pans
set before them. When the pan was full, another
worker took it away and replaced it with an empty
one.

"Nope . . . Nope . . . Nope . . ."

Radji's intonation came softly as he passed by each
one. His words were being picked up by the transis-
torized microphone Danielle had provided for Ben. He
had seen her early in their rounds and not once since,
even though he knew she was never out of plain view
of him. So, too, no matter how much he tried, he could
not spot any of the Israeli undercover personnel shad-
owing their every move, ready to pounce on a suspect
at a second's notice.

It was to Danielle, though, that his mind kept returning. He had been attracted to her from the first time they'd met in Mayor Sumaya's office. It was impossible not to be taken with her beauty, perhaps even the allure of a relationship forbidden by culture. But it had become much more than that now.

Danielle and his dead wife, Jenny, had become intertwined in his psyche, especially in the haunting dreams where Jenny kept *becoming* Danielle. He felt when he was with her the same joyous sense that he remembered feeling around Jenny, the same pangs that came whenever they had to part. He wasn't sure whether he had forgotten that feeling or merely repressed it. Either way, suddenly, he couldn't think of one without the other popping into his head. More than just the bond this case had forged between them was responsible. Surviving that gun battle in Jerusalem's Slave Market had clarified his feelings for her, but instead of feeling relieved he felt frightened. After all, was this case *all* they really had between them? When it ended, would they go their separate ways as if they never had met?

Worse than that, Ben felt as though he had something to lose again. His own life had meant little to him since he had found the Sandman in his home. Now he was struck by the uncanny feeling that the first woman he had felt anything for since then would find herself in similar jeopardy because of al-Diib. Thinking of it that way made Ben shiver, left him wondering if these monsters were destined to haunt him forever.

"Nope . . . Nope . . . Nope . . ." Radji was still saying as they came to the end of the table. "Where do we try next?"

"We start from the beginning of the dock again.

The people keep changing, the boats too.''

"And tomorrow?" he asked, disappointed.

"We start even earlier. Plenty of peddlers are here and gone by seven a.m. They have to be early to have their daily supplies ready when the people want to shop.''

Ben watched as iced tubs of the freshly filleted fish were placed in the back of vans, deals having been closed and the merchants eager to be on their way. What they could not sell would be lost, especially in this heat. Time lost was money wasted. Everyone hurried.

Ben led Radji further down the sprawling complex of piers connected to the long dock toward another brigade of Palestinians hoisting fresh catches from boats to dock.

"Inspector Kamal, can you hear me?" Danielle's voice called.

Ben pressed the concealed transmitter tighter against his ear and spoke into the mouthpiece. "I can hear you.''

"Meet me at the front of the quay right away. Something's happened.''

CHAPTER 39

DANIELLE HADN'T MENTIONED anything to Ben yet about the case files having been altered. She decided there was no point in bringing that up until she knew what had been deleted. It could have been superfluous or redundant information purged routinely. Since she had violated the rules by logging on, she was in no position to bring it to anyone's attention anyway.

Nor, though, was she willing to forget it. She knew how Israeli intelligence operated well enough to believe that *nothing* was beyond them. If they were behind the existence of a second killer, as Ben had believed, they were sure to have left nothing that might implicate them.

But how could they have pulled this off?

She waited for Ben at the head of the quay, a long narrow outdoor market located beneath a pair of docks, its location shifting every day depending on the

Mediterranean's tides. Here, residents could buy their fish direct at bottom-line prices. But on the quay, merchants were considerably less discriminating about the quality of the fish they sold; virtually anything that swam was for sale. A novice buyer might end up losing money by saving it.

She watched as Ben approached anxiously, Radji right by his side.

"What is it?" he asked her.

"Some of the locals are on to the presence of undercover Israelis here. Word is spreading through the crowd fast."

"Dammit! How?"

"You tell me."

"Shaath," Ben guessed.

"Why would he want to sabotage our work?"

"So we would have to replace your teams with Palestinian police who'd be spotted in a minute. Or . . ."

"Or what?"

"He wants us to fail—wants *me* to fail." Ben gazed about the quay, half expecting to find Shaath glowering at him. "Can you come back tomorrow with new personnel?"

"Yes."

"I'll speak with the mayor about this, let him handle Commander Shaath."

"Will he?"

"Unlike Shaath, he has not forgotten the larger ramifications of what we're doing here."

"It'll be even easier to forget us if we fail."

"Then we'll have to make sure we don't, won't we, Pakad?"

*   *   *

THE FIRST DAY of surveillance ended just like that, and Danielle was glad for it. She was uncomfortable with the way they were following through on their pursuit of the Wolf. The need for a rapid solution to this case had taken them away from accepted, more methodical procedures. They should have come down here with a picture of the killer instead of a boy who might recognize him. They should have a name to question regulars on the dock about.

Danielle had not bothered to make a formal request to check the records of Israel's Ansar 3 detention camp, because she knew her superiors would never approve it. So too, she had not made the trip down to the camp's Negev Desert site, because she was certain the authorities at the camp would not be cooperative. But she was growing equally certain that the Wolf had been born amid the squalor and torture of the camp's confines. His name and background lay somewhere inside. But how to find it?

Dedicating herself to that task, she made a brief stop in Jerusalem and then drove out to the camp to pursue an apparently legitimate course of action: a visit to Ahmed Fatuk, the terrorist whose arrest in Jerusalem had led to her promotion to Shin Bet.

"What, no candy?" Ahmed Fatuk greeted her, after he had been escorted into one of Ansar 3's many interrogation rooms. It was square and windowless, the walls heavy and dark. A steel table and pair of folding chairs made for the only furniture. In spite of the desert heat beyond, the room had a dank, chilly feel to it that made Danielle long for a sweater.

Her chair made a screech across the floor as she shifted it inward. "I left the box in the car."

"You come here to gloat?"

"I checked on your family."

Fatuk's features froze. His lower lip trembled.

"They're doing fine," Danielle continued. "They've sent many letters. I'm sure you'd like to see them."

"And what do I have to do for you in return?" he asked suspiciously.

"Answer a few questions."

Fatuk pushed his chair away from the table. "They've been through this already with me."

"For their questions—not mine. Mine have nothing to do with you or anyone you've worked with in the past."

"And if I answer them?"

"You get your letters."

"I want to see my children."

"You know I can't do that."

"Then you leave here disappointed."

"And you *stay* here disappointed." Danielle slipped an envelope from out of her pocket and slid it across the table. "From your wife. I'm sorry it's not longer, but I couldn't wait around for her to write more."

Fatuk's eyes widened. He picked up the letter as though it might shatter at his touch. His hands quivered as he read it. Fatuk claimed he had renounced his past life after marrying his present wife, who was a Christian. Up until now Danielle thought it was just another elaborate cover. But watching Fatuk savor the few short sentences his wife had jotted down for him made her realize he was telling the truth. He would never have stayed in Jerusalem if he'd had anything to do with the crimes that made him one of the most wanted terrorists in Israel. She had arrested an innocent man, at least innocent of perpetrating the acts that had served as the basis for his incarceration.

"The letters from your children are downstairs," Danielle said after he looked at her again.

"Let me see my children and I will help you."

"I can help you see them sooner; that's the best I can do."

"Sooner?"

"I can make sure you are given a firm trial date, do everything I can to guarantee the truth comes out."

Fatuk gazed around him. "The truth doesn't seem to mean very much in here."

"All the more reason you should give yourself every opportunity to get out."

Fatuk's stare turned wary. "All right, what do you want?"

"I need to know the name of a Palestinian tortured here who was released, say, somewhere around a year ago, maybe eighteen months, and—"

Fatuk laughed out loud. "Just take the prison roster with you."

"Let me finish. This Palestinian would have suffered severe damage to his genital area, perhaps even mutilation."

"Oh," Fatuk said, and looked down.

Danielle studied him. "You know something," she prodded. "I can tell you know something."

"I know the man you're looking for is gone, all right, but his balls never left the camp."

ABU GARIB," FATUK continued as Danielle hurried to write everything down. "What happened to him is quite well known."

"Why did the Israelis do it?"

"It wasn't the Israelis, Pakad; it was Garib's fellow Palestinians who tortured him."

"He was a collaborator?"

"Of the worst kind. Cost many men their lives. I heard some who might eventually have joined his list of victims got a hold of him in the shower. It wasn't pretty."

"Describe him."

"I wasn't here at the time, but I understand he was a very big man and powerful. He didn't go easily."

"When was he released?"

"A few months before I arrived."

"A year, then?"

"A little more than that, I think. The Israelis knew he wasn't any good to them anymore. So they cut him loose."

"Bad choice of words," Danielle told him.

To CONFIRM THAT Abu Garib had been released from Ansar 3 just before the murders in the West Bank began, Danielle went to the camp's main office and requested his file. Her identification smoothed the process considerably and she had begun believing she had actually tracked down the Wolf when the clerk returned to the counter.

"I'm sorry, we have no prisoner by that name."

"Perhaps I didn't make myself clear. He *was* a prisoner, released perhaps twelve to fifteen months back."

"I'm saying we have no such name on any of our data bases, Chief Inspector. I don't know where you got your information, but Abu Garib was never a prisoner in this facility."

DAY SIX

CHAPTER 40

DANIELLE'S NEW SHIN Bet troops were in position by the time Ben and Radji arrived to pick up where they left off the next morning, or, more accurately, to repeat much of what they had done the day before. The boy looked bored and restless, disgruntled about having to go through the same routine for a second day in a row. At least he and Ben would be safe, enclosed by what Danielle termed a "movable bubble." Her men pretended to work at various legitimate tasks, so as not to draw attention while they shadowed Ben and Radji. Their disguises were so remarkable that in the dim early morning light, Danielle herself had trouble discerning them from the locals working on the docks.

After returning to Jerusalem from the detention camp in the Negev yesterday, she had busied herself with another painstaking review of the case files on the murder victims prior to the Israeli pullout from most of the West Bank, searching for a clue as to what might have been deleted. Whatever it was, no degree of scrutiny was going to yield it; the perpetrator had been too thorough in his work, the text of the files so complete that nothing at all appeared to be missing. But someone had gone to great lengths to delete something from them, just as someone had erased all trace of Abu Garib's internment at Ansar 3.

With no firm evidence to back up her suspicions, Danielle had said nothing to Ben about Garib's existence. Yet everything indicated that Israeli authorities might have accomplished far more in this investigation than they had ever let on. Why? The only answer seemed to lie in Ben's earlier assertion that two killers were at large, the second merely imitating the methods of the first so Fasil could be targeted without fear of recriminations. Danielle felt as if she and Ben had switched roles, so that she was now seriously considering what she had vehemently denounced just two days earlier.

Danielle watched Ben and Radji approaching one of the first boats to return with last night's catch. Even to her, the two looked like a father and son out for a leisurely stroll. The sight made it so easy for her to picture Ben in that role that it hurt. Despite how her own losses haunted her, she could not even contemplate what losing his family the way he had had done to him.

What she could contemplate was the growing attraction she felt for him. She had it passed it off at first to her own desperate longing for a relationship, perhaps *any* relationship, apart from the career that had so dominated her life. But she understood now it was much more than that. It was almost as though Ben was her emotional twin, that fate had thrust them together as the only two people who could save each other. Danielle found the irony in that striking, for finally it seemed that fate had conspired for, rather than against, her.

She couldn't squander this opportunity any more than he could, because it could be the last one either would get. The differences between them were nothing compared to what they held in common. But what would happen when this case was finished? Would she have the courage to tell him how she felt? Would they both have the courage to build a bridge strong enough to overcome the pressures of culture?

She was watching Ben, his arm tossed comfortably over Radji's shoulder, wondering if he felt at all the same way, when she saw the boy suddenly stiffen, his right hand starting upward.

B Y T H E S E C O N D day, Ben found himself becoming discouraged. There were a dozen piers, each packed with boats bringing in their catch or steering out to sea again, not to mention the various buyers, merchants, and packers scattered about.

He had returned to his office the previous afternoon to find the first batch of licenses permitting passage of select merchants between Gaza and the West Bank waiting for his attention. He intended to cross-match this list against another of all men treated at hospitals and clinics for genital mutilation or sexual disfunction. But, given the poor state of record keeping in the West Bank, he wasn't optimistic this would lead anywhere.

Moreover, there was something nagging at him he couldn't quite grasp, something Danielle had said, misty words Ben hadn't cleared up when they were right in front of him, and therefore had lost. He walked alongside Radji on the edge of the dock where it adjoined the many piers, distracted by trying to remember. He let the boy lead the way to help cheer him up, lift him from the funk he was experiencing ever since a disturbing visit to his sister, Zahira, yesterday.

"In there," Ben had said when they reached the hospital room in Jericho where she had been transferred.

The boy had swallowed hard and entered, while Ben lingered in the doorway.

Zahira looked much better than she had when Ben saw her in the refugee camp infirmary, but the bruises and swelling still made her a scary sight for a brother longing for the beautiful sister he remembered. Ben watched Radji's knees wobble as he neared the bed. Standing there, the boy could do nothing but stare in silence until she reached over and took his hand in hers.

Ben was waiting in the hall when Radji reemerged, shoulders hunched, sniffling from the tears he'd just shed. He noticed Ben watching and an angry snarl crept across his face.

"I'm going to get the man who did this."

"I already took care of it."

"You arrest him?"

"I beat the shit out of him."

The boy smiled at that. "You're a better cop than I thought."

"No, I'm not."

Ben looked at Radji and knew he wanted, *needed*, to break down like any child would. But he couldn't because he wasn't a child anymore and hadn't been for some time. Radji had learned to turn every emotional scar into a callus, and one was already forming over his latest wound as Ben stood there beside him. Ben wanted to take the boy in his arms and comfort him, looked down again and nearly gagged.

It was his oldest son! Looking up, smiling at him as he said, "Daddy..."

Ben shook himself alert, trembling. First Danielle had turned into Jenny and now this boy was turning into his son. Was he losing his mind? Or was it gone already?

"You should have killed him," Radji had said then, and started off alone.

But today, here on the docks of Gaza he was, however briefly, a typical boy again, with an adult he could trust and depend on by his side. Secure in the knowledge that he would have a roof over his head that night.

Perhaps the Wolf had done some good, after all.

Ben's thinking veered suddenly in another direction. How many days ago had al-Diib first struck in Jericho? And, according to Danielle, when had Fasil made his first visit in the guise of Harvey Fayles?

He recalled the answers, examined them in his mind.

Of course!

The answer had been so obvious that he'd—

Ben realized Radji had suddenly stopped and stiffened. He watched as the boy pointed a finger at a hulking figure lugging a basin of fish down the pier directly before them.

"That's him," Radji said.

CHAPTER 41

BEN'S EYES FOLLOWED the line of Radji's finger. The huge man the boy indicated had stopped dead in his tracks and lowered his basin of fish slightly. Their eyes met and in the frozen moment that followed, Ben *knew*.

My God, it's al-Diib!

For an instant it seemed the man would simply turn away and continue about his business. But instead of moving on, he backpedaled and let the basin drop to the dock, holding Ben's hate-filled stare the whole time. Al-Diib knew who Ben was, had killed Dalia Mikhail because this was some kind of game for him, a game Ben was determined to win.

The basin clamored against the concrete pier, dumping fish in all directions.

Ben already had the microphone at his mouth. "I've got him! Danielle, I've got him!"

The Wolf had turned his back and was retreating

along the pier past the boats moored there. Ben took a step forward, felt for the pistol concealed beneath his baggy shirt, didn't rush. Al-Diib wasn't going anywhere.

"He's getting away!" Radji screeched, and lurched forward into a dash before Ben could grab him.

"Shit!" Ben exclaimed, and bolted too, his feet hitting the cold wetness of the dock seconds after Radji's.

He tried to hurdle the spilled basin of fish, but slipped and fell, precious moments lost as the boy gained ground on the killer he had recognized.

"Stop! *Killer!* . . . *Stop!*" Radji wailed.

Ben gave chase down the dock, as the Wolf lunged suddenly onto the deck of a fishing boat with Radji close behind.

I'VE GOT HIM! *Danielle, I've got him!*"

Danielle, astonished as she was at the identification, responded instantly nonetheless.

"All teams, converge on Batman and Robin!" she ordered, using the code names she had pinned on Ben and Radji. "Suspect is fleeing down pier number seven and, oh God, they are in pursuit!"

From her position as shadow well back of the piers, she saw her teams respond instantly, their intricate covers abandoned in a breath's length. Pistols and submachine guns, hidden until a moment ago, appeared in their hands. A few toting larger sniper rifles in canvas sacks rushed *away* from the action in search of the best vantage points from which to take aim. The rest bolted toward the pier in Ben's wake, making no effort to conceal or disguise their intentions.

"*Police! Police! Police!*" they screamed, to clear

the crowd before them, and Danielle realized with inane embarrassment that a few of the cries had been shouted reflexively in Hebrew instead of Arabic.

''Ben! Ben, can you hear me?'' she roared into her microphone, lurching through the mounting crowds toward the dock.

He didn't answer. She saw him racing down the pier after the boy, who was charging after the suspect. She watched the Wolf jump onto the deck of a fishing boat and disappear from view. Radji hurdled over the gunwale with Ben right on his heels, just before the boat tore away from its mooring.

BEN FELT HIS feet ripped from under him when the boat sped off. He fell backward and his head rammed the gunwale. Stars exploded before his eyes and he realized he had lost his pistol. Dimly, he flapped his hand around the deck in search of it, coming up empty.

The fishing boat roared on into the Mediterranean, the dock shrinking behind it.

Radji appeared a yard before him, terrified. He looked away from Ben for the deck. Ben followed his gaze, saw the pistol lying at the boy's feet half buried in the murky water coating the deck.

The roar of the engine softened, and the boat slowed. Ben shook his head to clear it and started to rise, as Radji reached down for the gun.

Al-Diib pounced on the boy and yanked him upward, razor-sharp scaling knife pressed against his throat.

* * *

SNIPERS, TALK TO me!" Danielle ordered, as she charged onto the dock and then down the pier, joining the eight members of her contingent already there. "Does anyone have a shot?"

"Negative."

"Negative."

"The boy's too close to him."

"Knife pressed against his throat."

"They'll be out of range soon unless we can find a higher vantage point."

"Damn!" Danielle longed for a pair of binoculars to determine exactly what was happening on that boat.

"We've got to get a boat!" she said to the men clustered about her, their weapons still drawn with no-where to aim. "There!" And she bolted for one that was just preparing to moor, a sleek craft that would suit her purpose nicely.

Suddenly a flood of Palestinian police in dark green uniforms stormed the dock in the Israelis' wake, their guns drawn too. In the confused moment that followed, the two parties had turned their weapons on each other, locked stiffly in place.

"Don't shoot!" Danielle screamed, waving her arms desperately. "Nobody shoot!"

BEN'S HEAD CLEARED instantly, and he leaped back to his feet.

"Stay where you are!" al-Diib ordered, drawing Radji's head violently toward him.

The boy arched his back, trying not to move. The boat's forward motion slowed so much that it was lost to the whim of the currents, bobbing aimlessly.

"You can't escape," Ben said, not raising his voice, holding his ground like a statue.

"I'll kill him!"

"You still won't escape."

Al-Diib tightened his grip on the blade, panic and madness intermixing on his features.

"I'll do it!"

Ben advanced a step, hands raised into the air. "Calm down."

"You," al-Diib ordered Ben, twisting Radji sideways, "you drive the boat."

Ben nodded his acceptance, keeping his hands up as he slid toward the controls. Nothing else he could do at this point, not without a gun anyway.

The gun!

Radji had been reaching down for it and now Ben's eyes turned to the deck casually, searching. He saw the pistol lying there in the water, exactly where he remembered it. But his eyes must have given too much away, because al-Diib followed his gaze downward, lighting up when they encountered the weapon almost at his feet. He started to crouch, holding fast to Radji in the process.

When al-Diib stooped awkwardly to retrieve the pistol, the boy sank his teeth deep into the wrist wrapped under his chin. The Wolf wailed in agony and slashed sideways with his knife a mere instant after Radji had torn from his grasp.

The boy lost his balance and and went sliding along the deck, Ben lunging past him for the gun.

DROP YOUR WEAPONS!'' one of the Palestinian police officers shouted.

"We can take them all out!" the voice of Danielle's lead sniper reported in her ear. "Firm shots on all ten. Just give us the word."

Danielle wondered if she had a choice. An honest mistake or calculated move by Commander Shaath had placed her men in a deadly stalemate promising peril. Time had slowed to a crawl, letting her visualize the coming moments as they might be if she gave the order to fire:

Israeli police and their Palestinian counterparts shooting it out on the docks of Gaza. The first cooperative effort by the respective peoples ending in a terrible, and preventable, tragedy while a killer got away.

With Ben.

She risked a glance at the water. The fishing boat seemed to have stopped well beyond the harbor, providing hope she might be able to reach Ben in time.

"We are members of the Israeli National Police force here on a joint mission with the Palestinian Authority!" Danielle shouted. "My men and I are going to climb onto this boat now. Shoot us if you want."

And, holding her breath, she leaped onto the deck of the fishing boat and motioned her men to follow.

CHAPTER 42

BEN DOVE FOR the gun. Unable to reach it, he managed to knock it skidding across the wet deck out of al-Diib's reach.

Flat out on the deck now, Ben was caught by a vicious kick to the head. The blow from al-Diib's heavy rubber boot caught him along the lower skull and jaw, rattling his entire face. The pain exploded through him as he tried to roll away, and a second kick smashed him in the kidney. He reached the gunwale and used it for leverage to hoist himself up.

The Wolf lunged for him, the scaling knife poised in his hand, looking dark and dull under the sun. With no space to backpedal, Ben sidestepped as the killer slashed the blade at him. It sliced through his shirt and drew a wet burst of agony across his chest. He could feel the blood soaking through the cotton. Ben recoiled in pain and shock, stumbling. It probably would have ended there had not al-Diib slipped on the wet dock when he tried a second thrust with the fish knife.

Ben recovered enough to sidestep again, but knew he couldn't beat the killer at this game.

A weapon, I've got to find a weapon . . .

His pistol was too far away to even consider, so Ben was sweeping his eyes across the deck in search of something else when he saw Radji charging at al-Diib from the port side of the boat. The boy grabbed the killer's arm with both hands and yanked the blade downward with all his strength.

Ben rushed al-Diib in that instant, halfway there when the killer yanked his arm from Radji's thin grasp and lashed out with the blade.

Ben saw the knife slicing up and back, Radji still trying to strip it away.

"No!" Ben screamed as the blade sank into the boy's stomach.

ONCE ABOARD THE Palestinian fishing boat with her team, Danielle directed its captain to head out of the harbor at full throttle. The man was too scared to argue. He took his place behind the controls and steered the boat out into the open waters of the Mediterranean after the still-drifting craft the Wolf had fled upon.

From this distance she could see nothing but shifting figures on the deck and took that as a sign that, if nothing else, Ben must still be alive.

"Faster!" Danielle ordered the captain, as her men steadied their weapons on the starboard side of the boat facing the stalled craft.

*   *   *

BEN HEARD THE boy gasp, a sound like air escaping from a tire as he stumbled backward and collapsed, hands clutching for the knife centered in a widening splotch of blood across his shirt. His eyes swam with fear, which quickly gave way to glazed shock as Ben threw himself upon al-Diib.

"Bastard!"

Did he scream or merely think it? He would never know, just as he never felt the impact of his body crashing into the bigger man's, staggering him. In close, Ben felt better able to neutralize the Wolf's superior size, strength, and reach. He pummeled *al-Diib* with a series of wildly savage blows, the rage in him spilling over. This was the Sandman all over again, only this time there was a life he could *still* save.

The Wolf regained control of himself and rammed Ben into the cabin door. Ben felt his feet dangling off the deck as the killer yanked him forward and then slammed him into the door again. His spine stung, but Ben still managed to crack his forearms against the big man's ears and then dig a thumb into one of his eyes.

Al-Diib wailed in agony. He dropped Ben and jerked both hands upward to comfort his injured eye. Ben lunged and aimed a kick for the Wolf's groin. The Wolf started to double over but managed to lash out a vicious roundhouse blow that caught Ben in the side of the head. His teeth smacked against each other and his face whiplashed to the side.

Al-Diib pounced again, hands closing on Ben's shirt before he flung him hard to the deck, and Ben looked up to see the Wolf tear a long baling hook from the outer cabin wall.

* * *

SHOOT!'' DANIELLE ORDERED, when she saw the large shape lift the baling hook over his head. *"Shoot!"*

But there had not been time to wait for her marksmen to join them on the boat and three hundred yards was still too much distance for submachine guns and pistols to manage effectively. The result was a barrage of bullets hopelessly off the mark. A lucky shot was the best she could hope for until her boat closed the gap by at least another hundred yards or so.

That was still seconds from happening.

And she could see the baling hook starting down toward Ben.

BEN WAS DIMLY aware of the distant gunfire clacking over the boat. He kicked out with a leg as al-Diib put all his weight into his planned killing strike. The blow buckled the man's right knee and threw his blow well off to the side, where the hook ripped shards of wood from the cockpit.

Ben skittered across the deck, no time to rise, and saw his pistol propped up on its butt against a bench seat just out of reach.

The Wolf started to raise the baling hook to position it for another wicked slash, having to rotate his weight to keep it off his ruined knee, his back to the water now. Ben watched the hook rise ominously overhead. He was still groping for the pistol when it began its deadly journey downward.

* * *

CROUCHED ON THE fishing boat's deck, Danielle steadied her pistol with both hands, sighting down its barrel. Less than two hundred yards separated the two boats now, an acceptable distance though complicated by the expected rocking which turned all aim to shit. Fire, keep firing, and hope for the best was all she could do.

She exhaled deeply and squeezed the trigger, pulling it again and again without bothering to adjust her aim.

A BURST OF BLOOD erupted from the Wolf's shoulder and he twisted violently sideways, giving Ben time to close his hand on the wet butt of his pistol. Ben drew the gun upward and fired in the same instant the Wolf was angling the baling hook yet again.

His first shots took the Wolf in the chest and punched him backward. Ben didn't try to better his position or angle; he just kept firing. Enough of his bullets ripped into the Wolf's midsection to stagger him toward the gunwale. Ben adjusted his aim so that his last shots caught the killer in the throat and face, spilling him over the side of the boat into the water below.

CHAPTER 43

BEN CRAWLED ACROSS the deck and cradled Radji against him, pressing a trembling hand atop the boy's blood-soaked fingers to help stanch the bleeding.

How small his hands were. How terrified and childlike he looked now as he lay near death.

The scaling knife was still in the wound, a blessing since it would help reduce the blood loss. Its short blade, meanwhile, might have kept damage to the internal organs to a minimum.

He cradled the boy to him, trying to keep him alive by sheer force of will, and grateful for the chance. He had never gotten such a chance to save his own sons. A few minutes earlier, if he had gotten home a few minutes earlier, he could have raced up the stairs and shot the Sandman before he went to work on them while they lay in their beds. That, Ben realized now, was what had been most unfair, what he had never been able to accept or rationalize. He had killed the Sandman when nothing but his own life was at stake, which wasn't very much at all. Five minutes could have made all the difference, yet they were minutes he would never get back.

His eyes closed briefly to shut out the ache, and when he opened them al-Diib was climbing over the gunwale back onto the boat's deck, his flesh chewed away in patches by fish and one eyeball hanging by a single strand down his cheek.

Ben came alert with a start, having been out for only a few seconds, the victim of a concussion-induced nightmare or hallucination. The world wavered, spun. He clutched the boy tighter to keep himself from sliding off.

He heard another boat approaching off the stern and felt his craft waver as Danielle led some of her team aboard.

"Ari!" she ordered.

Ben saw a man hurrying across the deck to him with a first-aid kit tucked under his arm. The man leaned over, placed it down and popped it open, then tried to pry the boy from Ben's grasp.

Ben wouldn't let go.

A shape knelt next to him. Ben felt soft hands on his shoulders, stroking him gently.

"It's all right," Danielle said softly. "Ari's a trained medic. Let go of the boy, Ben. Let go."

Ben looked up at her and released his grasp. Ari slid between them and went instantly to work.

"Will he live?" Danielle asked after Ari had inspected the wound.

"I've seen worse," the medic replied tersely.

"That's not what I asked you."

"They lived."

B EN REMEMBERED ONLY scattered bits and pieces of what followed. His body felt mercifully numb and he couldn't seem to keep his eyes from closing. He was aware of a blanket being wrapped around him and someone holding on to him tightly:

Danielle. He knew her by the soft, lovely smell he had come to know so well these past few days.

A crowd had gathered by the time they returned to the docks. Two ambulances were waiting. If this had been America, Ben reflected in insane counterpoint, there would be media hounds about too. Here in Gaza, though, only the crowd greeted them, parting to allow the stretchers carried by the Israelis to pass through and held back at the fringes by the Palestinian police officers they had almost done battle with.

Danielle squeezed into Ben's ambulance, keeping herself out of the way against the door. His eyes sought her out as the paramedics hooked him up to an IV. He began to feel better, more lucid anyway, almost instantly. His mind cleared and the memories flooded back like fresh blows from al-Diib himself. He cataloged his own wounds and figured, everything considered, he had come out all right. Nothing felt broken, and the slash across his chest qualified as little more than a laceration. The strikes to his head left him feeling like a watermelon was riding his neck, and the inside of his mouth tasted as though someone had stuffed it with cotton, but all that would pass.

Danielle was stroking his forehead. "It's over, Ben. It's over." Her voice was relaxed, relieved.

But not sounding like she meant it.

CHAPTER 44

THEY GAVE BEN a Demerol drip at the hospital and the world turned to a drifting fog that soothed all the pain away. Hours meshed together, becoming practically indistinguishable. Ben was almost lucid when someone was in the room with him—a doctor, nurse, or visitor. But when alone, his mind tended to wander and he surrendered himself to it.

Early reports on Radji were positive. The Israeli medic had managed to get the blood loss slowed enough for him to reach the hospital alive.

Mayor Sumaya was Ben's first official visitor and, not surprisingly, he was beaming.

"Congratulations," he told Ben, triumphant and yet restrained. "Calls from the international press are typing up our phone lines. We've scheduled a joint press conference with the Israelis tomorrow to explain what transpired. The President is coming in personally to participate. He's looking forward to meeting you."

"I'll have to send someone for a fresh uniform. . . ."

Sumaya smiled thinly. "The Wolf's name was Abu Garib. Apparently your theory about genital mutilation was correct, inflicted by other Palestinian prisoners when they learned he was trying to buy his way out of Ansar 3 by informing."

"How did you learn that?"

"The Israelis were most forthcoming with the information."

"They wouldn't have been if they'd done the inflicting."

"I've heard from Doctor al-Shaer, as well. He confirms that the knife recovered from the scene matches the wounds in all three of the Jericho victims. Not an exact match, of course, but it's safe to assume Garib didn't use a single knife for all his killings." Sumaya looked at Ben struggling futilely for comfort in his hospital bed. "The press is desperate to talk to you, you know, once you're up to it."

Ben tried to look pleased, neglecting to inform the mayor that Zaid Jabral was going to get an exclusive once he felt up to telling the story.

"You made history today, Ben. Thanks to you, the walls of Jericho may have come down for good, and the world is looking in."

"Let's hope they like what they see," Ben replied.

BEN DRIFTED OFF and didn't come around again until Danielle shook his shoulder. His eyes opened groggily and once more he breathed in her soft scent.

"I thought you'd like to know Radji's asking for you."

"I'd give him some blood, but I'm afraid he'd get to like the Demerol too much."

"Amazing the resiliency of the young."

"Fortunately the young of most cultures don't have to deal with knives in their stomachs."

"No, in some cultures it's car bombs." She ended the retort with a forced smile. "It's good to see you're feeling better."

Ben propped himself up on his elbows. "What's wrong?"

"It can wait."

"Not from the look on your face, it can't."

Danielle took a deep breath. "I think you were right. I think there were two killers."

Ben sat up a little more.

"Ansar 3 conveniently had no record of Abu Garib being detained there until you killed him. All at once, the records of his incarceration were suddenly available."

"You *went* there?"

Danielle nodded.

"What else?"

"The case reports on the murders Shin Bet investigated before the pullout have been tampered with. Something's missing."

"Any idea what?"

"Not yet. But it's clear we knew far more than we ever let on to the world."

"Enough to create a copycat killer?"

"That depends on what was deleted from the files."

This time it was Ben who looked less than convinced. "Radji identified Garib as the killer. That's good enough for me."

He tried to look away, but Danielle's voice wouldn't let him. "You're scared again. I'm sorry."

"I never stopped being scared, Danielle."

"What happened on the boat brought it all back to you."

"At least this time only the monster died."

"And you saved a boy's life."

"Who knows? If he's really lucky, they might take him back at the refugee camp."

BEN VISITED RADJI after sundown. The boy still looked groggy and pale. A thick bandage covered his entire midsection. But his liquidy dark eyes found Ben and followed him across the room.

"No fucking television," the boy said softly between dried-out lips. "In the hospital there should be television."

"I'll speak with the mayor."

"They wouldn't let me see my sister."

"She's in the hospital in Jericho. We're in Jerusalem."

"Does she have television?"

"I don't think so."

Radji shifted painfully. "Speak with the mayor about that, too."

Ben laid his hand on the boy's shoulder. "Anything else?"

"I got stabbed. It hurt. And it was a fucking waste."

"Why?"

"I didn't realize until I was very close to him."

"Realize what?"

Radji's eyes locked open. "The man on the boat wasn't the one I saw from the alley."

DAY SEVEN

C H A P T E R   4 5

I T   W A S   T H E   pungent scent of cigar smoke
that woke Ben up the next time. He surfaced disoriented in the darkness broken only by the light from
the dim outdoor lamps sneaking in through his window. He had lost the rest of the night, hours swimming
by somewhere in the Demerol-powered cloud. He
fumbled for the bedside clock and it slipped off the
table, hitting the floor with a crash.

"Just after two in the A.M., hoss," Colonel Frank
Brickland greeted him.

"You shouldn't smoke in here," Ben told him.

"I know, bad for my health."

"I was thinking of mine."

"That what the guards are for?"

"Mostly to keep unauthorized individuals out."

"I showed them my pass."

Ben laced his hands behind his head. As with everything else right now, it took considerable effort.

"I guess you'll be going back home now, Colonel."

"Pissed off I didn't send you flowers?"

"I was talking about going back to America."

"Haven't found my son yet, Benny."

"At least you know he's still alive."

"He wasn't the victim you found Sunday, but that doesn't mean he's not dead."

"You'd know if he was."

"What makes you say that?"

It wasn't easy for Ben to put into words. "On the boat, when I was holding the boy, I knew he was going to live."

"And you're not even related."

"My point exactly."

Brickland's attitude toward Ben had clearly changed since their initial encounters. Ben's mind pushed the fog far enough aside to understand the colonel considered them equals now. Ben had passed the test that morning on the boat, and had the bandages and bruises to prove it. To Brickland, they were trophies.

"You know it's not over, don't you?" he asked the colonel.

Brickland smiled like his teeth were ready to chew steel. "What'd the kid tell you?"

"How do you know I've been to see him?"

"Because I would."

"He says the man I killed wasn't the one he saw kill Fasil. He claimed that man had a scar. The Wolf—Garib—didn't."

"You're still a hero."

"That's not good enough."

"Welcome to the club. Don't tell me any of this surprises you, hoss."

"I was surprised when all the indications pointed to a single killer."

"That's because you're up against clever opponents who aren't about to leave anything to chance."

"You're talking about the Israelis."

"I wouldn't put it past them; hell, I'd *expect* it of them. They don't want to do anything that might fuck up the peace process, but the terrorists are determined to do just that and they've got to be stopped somehow."

"My thinking, too."

"Then think about this, hoss: you and your Israeli girlfriend keep pushing the envelope and people on both sides are gonna get plenty pissed off. They like closure, and you gave it to them today when you saved the state the bother of an execution. Now you want to take it away, walk out of here and tell them there's a *second* killer still out there nobody's caught yet. I can see their faces now. . . ."

"It's not just the killer: it's Fasil."

"You lost me."

"He came to Jericho from Tel Aviv twice in the last two weeks, both times to attend meetings. Hamas kidnapped me because they couldn't find something in his personal effects they were looking for after he was killed. That makes me think Fasil was in the middle of planning something big."

"And maybe that 'something' didn't die with him, that it?"

"Maybe."

"You think he was targeting the peace talks?"

"You read his file, Colonel. He was one of the best and most deadly Hamas had. I wouldn't put anything past him."

Brickland pulled the cigar from his mouth and let the smoke drift toward the ceiling. "La, la, la, hoss. You're humming a tune that ain't gonna play well for either side. Dredge all this shit up and you'll do Fasil's work on the peace talks for him. Nobody's going to want to listen no matter how tightly you tie things up."

"Got any advice?"

"Same as before: walk away. Far as you can."

"You know I can't."

"Then turn your back. Have your cake and eat it, hoss. Stay a hero and tell yourself that whatever Fasil was working on died with him. Call up your Israeli girlfriend and take her out on a date."

"Dates," Ben said suddenly, sitting straight up in bed.

"What about them, hoss?"

"Something I just remembered . . ."

Y O U   W E R E   R I G H T ," Ben said, after waking Danielle up with a phone call. "There is a second killer."

"You were right, too," she returned, chasing the sleep from her voice. "But can we prove it?"

"Radji says Abu Garib wasn't the man he saw kill Fasil."

"That won't be enough."

"There's more. What if Fasil wasn't the only terrorist the copycat killer was responsible for? What if he had targeted Fasil's entire cell? You told me Fasil had been to the West Bank passing himself off as Harvey Fayles once before."

"Around two weeks ago."

"Fifteen days now, to be precise." Ben paused. "The very same night Leila Khalil was killed in Jericho."

CHAPTER 46

YOU ARE TO be commended for your outstanding work in this matter,'' Raz Nitzav Hershell Giott said to Danielle early Sunday morning.

"As well as your discretion," added Moshe Baruch. "This investigation is certain to quicken your advancement through our ranks."

Giott spoke again. "I was actually thinking that you might perhaps want to return to the National Police as an assistant commissioner."

"As an undercover operative, you will of course be spared the press conferences and resulting publicity." Baruch turned to Giott, perhaps doubting himself. "But God knows we could use some favorable press, and if she is to accept your offer . . .''

"Pakad Barnea would be best advised to take some time off at this point," Giott suggested in a fatherly tone. He turned to Danielle. "Visit one of the resorts at Elat."

Danielle found it incredibly ironic. Just one week before she had been *looking* for a way out, and now it was hers, on wondrous terms to boot, and she wanted no part of it. She couldn't leave this case now, couldn't leave Ben.

"A good idea," she said anyway. "I think I will."

More talk was exchanged, but none of it meaningful; all meaning in the room had ceased for Danielle with the lie she was nurturing. She could not tell these men about the possible existence of a second murderer and altered case files. If her and Ben's suspicions turned out to be accurate, then the trail would lead, inevitably, back to Israel and maybe even to them. Her life would be on the line. She would have to tread very lightly while following that trail, wondering where it might take her.

"Enjoy your time off, Pakad," Giott said at the door, squeezing her shoulders warmly. "And think about my offer."

"Thank you," she replied with a smile. "I will."

BEN LEFT THE hospital without being formally discharged, and took a cab back to Jericho. He entered the old police building through a side door just as the press conference with Arafat and the Israeli Defense Minister was scheduled to begin in Jerusalem. He was almost at his office on the first floor when he heard a voice from the other end of the hall.

"I thought I would find you here, Inspector."

Ben turned and found himself face-to-face with Major Nabril al-Asi, dressed today in an elegant olive-taupe suit that bagged fashionably over his sinewy frame.

"I see your Armani came in, Major."

"I should give you the name of my tailor," al-Asi said, drawing a little closer. "I understand congratulations are in order."

"Thank you."

Al-Asi made a show out of checking his watch. "As a matter of fact, I believe you are supposed to be elsewhere right now."

"I've had my fill of hospitals."

"A lesson you'd be wise to remember for future reference." Al-Asi's stare narrowed, sharpened. "You have done your job exceedingly well, and for that I applaud you. You should consider that job done now and celebrate with everyone else."

"I intend to."

"That's my hope. You see, Inspector, I would never get in the way of a man doing his job here, even if it happened to contradict my own interests. But if a man were to contradict my own interests while doing something other than his job, I would have to involve myself."

Ben stood his ground. "Is that all?"

"Unless you'd like me to have one of my men drive you back to Jerusalem."

"That won't be necessary."

"I think it is."

"Why don't you call Sumaya, tell him you found me?"

Al-Asi scoffed at the remark. "If I called anyone, it would be Arafat. But Arafat does not like to be bothered until I have something to report. What would that be now, Inspector?"

"That I'm sorry I didn't get to meet him," Ben said, and continued on to his office.

Once inside, with the door closed behind him, Ben turned his attention to the complete case file on the first victim murdered in Jericho, Leila Khalil. After his previous experience at their home, he knew there would be no cooperation coming from the family. That left one other interested party, who had been questioned several times, but only cursorily: her boyfriend, an eighteen-year-old young man named Siyad Hijjawi, who had been among those in the car that had dropped Leila Khalil off.

Muslim tradition dictated that children go out in groups, rather than couples. Everything about Hijjawi's statement was consistent with that, except for a single line Ben had failed to take heed of until now:

I went straight home afterward. Left the car in the street and went to bed.

Then how had the others who said they had been in the car when Leila Khalil was dropped off gotten home? Hijjawi had stumbled over his words a bit because he must have been alone when he dropped the victim off. Ben never would have noticed the anomaly if a potential link between Leila Khalil and the infamous terrorist Mohammed Fasil had not cast Hijjawi in a potential new light.

He had an idea what was going on here now, and it terrified him.

DANIELLE WENT STRAIGHT from her meeting at National Police headquarters to East Jerusalem, where Lieutenant Yori Resnick was supervising a security zone. According to Danielle's case report, Resnick, then a sergeant, had initially been in charge of the investigation into the first murder eventually attributed to the Wolf in the Muslim Quarter of Jerusalem.

"Of course, I remember the case," he told her in his office. "Seeing a body in that condition, well, it's not something you easily forget."

"The report was vague on how you proceeded."

Resnick looked at her quizzically. "That's strange, because I was quite specific, I'm sure I was. The victim was killed late at night, so we weren't expecting much. But there were two other couples in the area, hidden from plain view, *schtupping* maybe, we never found out one way or the other."

"The report said the victim was going to meet her boyfriend."

"A coincidence. The other couples did not know her or each other. We weren't even sure if their descriptions of the man they saw right around the time of the murder meant anything until we realized both descriptions of him were virtually the same."

Danielle's eyes narrowed. "Wait a minute, you're saying you had a *description* of the killer?"

"Better than that, we put each couple separately with the same sketch artist and the portraits that emerged were almost identical."

Danielle could not believe what she'd just heard. "There was a *drawing* of the suspect?"

"Passed along to Shin Bet as soon as they assumed control of the investigation. You seem surprised."

Danielle didn't respond. Someone had not only removed the details of Resnick's report from the case file, but also the composite sketch arrived at by *four witnesses* to the East Jerusalem murder, the Wolf's first strike!

"We're just trying to tie up all the loose ends." Danielle tried to cover her agitation so that the young lieutenant would not suspect her true intentions. "Would you happen to remember the name of the sketch artist?" she asked him.

SIYAD HIJJAWI LIVED in Musa 'Alfami, a town just to the south of Jericho. He was not home when Ben got to the white stone house he still shared with his family, one of a long row of virtually identical structures separated by alley-wide spaces. Ben was happy just to sit in his car and wait for the young man's return for as long as it would take. Doctors in Jerusalem had told him rest was the best medicine right now to help him heal. Whether he rested here seated in his car or back in the hospital couldn't much matter.

It was three hours into a sparkling late afternoon before the gaunt, boyish-looking figure of a young man approached the front door with a key in his hand.

Siyad Hijjawi had just opened the door when Ben stepped up behind him and spoke his name in as intimidating a fashion as he could manage. Startled, Hijjawi turned and viewed Ben's police uniform with a mixture of concern and amazement. The young man was well groomed, wore his dark hair cut short, and had the shadowy beginnings of a beard.

"We need to talk," Ben said.

CHAPTER 47

THE YOUNG MAN reluctantly agreed to accompany Ben on a walk. The pain medication had worn off, and Ben could feel every ache and pain from the battering his body had suffered the day before. Each step was an effort.

"I already told you everything I know," Hijjawi protested.

"Others. Not me."

Hijjawi looked at him more closely and his eyes widened suddenly. "You're the one who killed al-Diib yesterday! I saw your picture in the paper!"

Ben didn't bother denying it.

"I thought you were in the hospital."

"I was. I left to see you."

Hijjawi's entire demeanor had changed, grown much more respectful, almost reverent. "I should be thanking you. I am grateful for this opportunity. After what the animal did to my girlfriend—"

"She wasn't your girlfriend, Siyad, and both of us know it."

A series of changing expressions followed one another across Hijjawi's face. Ben noted the changes and slowed his pace.

"Please spare me the denials, Siyad. We both have better things to do with our time."

Hijjawi shrugged. "You killed her murderer all the same."

"No, I didn't, and both of us know that, too. I killed a man her murderer was imitating so no one would notice the difference."

Hijjawi was trying very hard not to look scared.

Ben turned into the next alley they came to and stopped. It was deserted, leaving the two men entirely alone. "I'm going to tell you what I think, Siyad, and then I'm going to tell you how you can help me. I think Leila Khalil was a terrorist. I think she was part of Hamas, and I think you are too. That's why the two of you were alone when you dropped her off, not in a group as you claimed."

"The other statements—"

"Fabricated. There was no one else in the car. You were the only one with Leila Khalil before she was murdered." Hijjawi started to protest again, but Ben steamrolled his words. "Now, your particular politics are of no concern to me, but catching the man who actually killed her is. To do that, I need the truth."

"You are talking madness!"

Ben clamped a hand on Hijjawi's shoulder. "Listen to what I'm going to do for you, Siyad, in exchange for your cooperation. I am going to forget that you are Hamas too. I am going to leave it out of my report, on the condition that you tell me about the meeting the two of you were coming from just before Leila Khalil was killed.''

''What meeting?''

''Mohammed Fasil was there,'' Ben continued, convincing even himself with his words. ''And when he returned for another meeting in Jericho two weeks later, he was killed too.'' Ben softened his tone. ''But you know that, of course. All of you must know there's a killer out there who's marked terrorists for his victims. And you know what, Siyad? He's still out there. Maybe you'll be next.''

''I don't know what you're talking about!'' Hijjawi's eyes flicked rapidly about, as if searching for the best way to flee from the alley.

Ben tightened his grip on the young man's shoulder. ''Let's see, judging by your age and naïveté I'd say you'd be an ideal candidate for Hamas's armed wing, the Qassam Brigades. Suicide bombings are their specialty. Is that what they had planned for you, Siyad?''

''No! No! It wasn't like that!''

Ben steered the boy to a stop. ''Then what was it like? Leila Khalil recruited you, stroked your libido to trap you in the fervor of the terrorist movement, make you give up your life in exchange for getting your dick wet? I don't blame you. I saw her picture. A truly beautiful girl. That probably explains why Hamas wanted her.''

''No! Not *her*!''

''Then who brought you in?''

''Her father.''

T H E   S K E T C H   A R T I S T   was an older man who looked as though he belonged behind an easel instead of a computer. Better fit for elegant tapestries than carefully drawn composites of criminals. He worked out of his house just outside of Jerusalem, instead of National Police headquarters, ready whenever he was called upon to breathe life into the often disconnected and contradictory words of witnesses.

"Copies?" Moshe Goldblatt asked unsurely, looking up at her from the wheelchair he had lived in since taking a bullet in the spine in one of Israel's more recent wars.

"Of your past works," Danielle elaborated. "There is a sketch missing from a file on a case I'm working on. This was the only way I could think of to replace it."

"I scan them into the computer, include the sketches in the disk when I submit my report."

That accounted for more of the missing bits of information she was seeking, Danielle reflected. "I'm afraid that portion was inadvertently deleted during a recent purging of the system."

"What's going on there at the National Police building?" he asked, switching on his computer.

"I wish I knew," Danielle replied.

YOU'RE TELLING ME Leila Khalil's father is Hamas?" Ben managed, trying to keep his thoughts collected.

"I grew up with Leila. We were friends. There was never anything like . . . what you suggest. And *I* went to *him*," Hijjawi continued, almost boasting. "I wanted to be part of the movement, help change our hopeless way of life."

"And now, as a result, you have as many enemies among Palestinians as Israelis."

"They will see we are right, that ours is the only way. It will take time, but they will see. Peace changes *nothing*!"

"Spare me the rhetoric. I care only about the meeting that occurred the night Leila was murdered. Was Fasil there?"

"Why should I tell you anything?" the young man challenged bitterly. "You're one of *them*."

Ben smiled warmly and released his grasp on Hijjawi's shoulder. "You know, Siyad, my most recent assignment has left me with a number of very close Israeli friends. They're not bad people once you get to know them, more like us than different. I think they'd be interested in accumulating names of Hamas members, especially those of the Qassam Brigades."

"Bastard!"

"You'll find them infinitely less patient than I am, Siyad."

The boy's eyes had stopped roving; it was perfectly clear there would be nowhere for him to run to now. "What do you want?"

"The meeting. Was Fasil there?"

"Yes."

"What was discussed?"

"I don't know. I drove Leila, guarded the villa's front door—that's all." Hajjawi's expression turned almost sad, dejected. "It was my first real assignment and I couldn't even keep her alive."

"Did her father know what the meeting was about?"

"I don't know. It was a Qassam Brigade cell— you're right. We are not his domain. But . . ."

"But what?"

"I can't tell you any more," Hijjawi said fearfully. "They'll kill me, you know they will."

"They won't find out."

"They always *find out*."

"It's not them I'm after. I'm after the real killer of Fasil and Leila." Ben paused and looked squarely at Hijjawi, hoping his eyes did a passable job of disguising the half-truth. "Help me find him."

"Leila's father is very high in the movement, but he stays away from anything that might incriminate him. He believes in his work, but there is his family to consider."

"I understand."

"He must have known what the meeting was about. Why else would everything have been coordinated through Leila?"

"Go home," Ben said suddenly. But then something else occurred to him, something that had been lurking in the back of his mind until the boy's words had pushed it forward. "Wait!"

Hijjawi turned stiffly.

"A woman named Dalia Mikhail. Think very hard now. Was she one of you? Was she part of the cell?"

Hijjawi looked at him for what seemed like a long time before speaking. "The night Leila was killed, the meeting was held in Dalia Mikhail's villa."

DANIELLE HELD THE black-and-white portrait in her hand as Goldblatt's laser printer hummed softly in the background.

"Do you recognize him?" the artist asked her.

Danielle moved toward the window into the light.

Goldblatt truly deserved his reputation as a brilliant artist. The suspect's face, even sketched in black strokes further enhanced by the computer, was as particular as a photograph and more; after all, a photo could not capture the fiery intent of a subject's expression as Goldblatt apparently could, and that was more than enough to help Danielle recognize the face of Abu Garib.

The Wolf.

The Palestinian who'd been mutilated by his fellow inmates at Ansar 3 was a perfect match for the man Radji had described, except he was indeed missing the scar the boy had been adamant about seeing on the face of Mohammed Fasil's murderer.

"Pakad?" Goldblatt prodded.

Garib's composite sketch had been deleted from the case files, just as his very presence, and motive, had been deleted at Ansar 3. That meant Israeli authorities not only had known a serial killer was operating from the beginning, they had determined exactly who it was and had still failed to act. Instead, they had used this information to *create* a second killer, dispatched to kill terrorist targets with impunity. And under normal circumstances the murders of Mohammed Fasil and Leila Khalil would have simply been attributed to the Wolf. But whoever had run this masterful ruse had neglected to factor one variable into the equation: Ben Kamal. And now a second variable had been added: herself.

"He's the one who was killed yesterday in Gaza, isn't he, Pakad?" the artist asked curiously.

"Yes, this man is dead," she acknowledged, leaving it at that.

*   *   *

IT WAS ALMOST dark by the time Ben reached Akram Khalil's home. No backup accompanied him. He had not stopped off at the Palestinian Authority building to brief Mayor Sumaya on his progress or to ask for reinforcements before he paid a visit to Khalil. He thought he had a very strong reason to believe the terrorist would cooperate willingly and fully with him. And by this time he was indifferent to the possibility that instead, Khalil might simply have him killed.

Dalia Mikhail was one of them!

He could no longer deny the fact; the meeting on the night Leila Khalil was murdered had been held in her villa, of all places, amid the priceless treasures Ben had thought were her only companions. How wrong he had been. No wonder Nabril al-Asi's Protective Security Service had been investigating her. Al-Asi's interest in Dalia had nothing to do with her infamous editorials. He must have suspected she was leading a double life, allowing Ben to see only a small part. Had it been the same for his father? Had she snared him using a different kind of bait?

He should have figured it out before; it had been obvious for some time. Once he formulated the theory that Leila Khalil was Hamas, then Dalia had to be as well, since the Jericho pattern had been clearly established.

But the reality nonetheless numbed him, the lie grating. A lie even though it was unspoken, and because he was certain his father had been no wiser than he. Ben recalled the sketchy details of the ambush that had claimed his father's life, electricity surging through him now, the tips of his fingers going numb.

He could almost hear it this time, the blood in his veins replaced by current. If Danielle was right about the Israelis not being responsible for his father's death, then the true perpetrators could only be Palestinian. Why not? Jafir Kamal had made his share of enemies when he left for America. When he returned to the West Bank in the wake of the Six-Day War, the resentment would have been further compounded even before he advocated a dialogue with the Israelis, negotiations with those who had *stolen* their land. He saw the futility of continued violence, but it was a picture other Palestinian leaders opted not to see. So he had to be silenced, and who better to arrange it than the woman whose terrorist roots dated all the way back to the birth of the Fatah movement itself?

The logic of it sickened him. The fact that he didn't doubt she had really loved his father made the whole scenario even harder to stomach.

At their last meeting she must have known she was in danger. Yet Ben hadn't been paying enough attention to her to recognize it because he was too busy spilling out his own problems to her.

My God, I told her everything!

He felt violated. Brickland had it right all along: he was out of his element. This world was meant for men like the colonel and al-Asi. Ben should have run while he still could. But now it was too late. He had to finish what he had started.

Ben made no attempt to be subtle. He approached the door to the Khalil home in full uniform and in view of any of the few neighbors who might have been watching. He did not believe for an instant that Sayed Hijjawi would have dared alert Akram Khalil to his coming and the reason for it. To do so would be to admit that he had talked, and for that the young man would suffer the same punishment all collaborators did.

He knocked on the door and a boy of eleven or so answered this time. Before Ben had finished his greeting, a hand eased the boy away and his older sister Amal, whom Ben had met on his previous visit here, took his place.

"I told you we had nothing to say, cop."

"I'm here to see your father."

"And you're a fool for it," she snapped.

Ben was still forming his response when he felt a thud against his skull. The pain exploded through him as he crumpled, actually conscious until his body hit the ground half inside the house and half out.

CHAPTER 48

JUST PAST DUSK on Sunday, Danielle stepped out of the elevator on the second sublevel, which contained the forensics offices of the National Police. She entered one of the labs and located a pathologist she knew had worked on at least two of the murders investigated prior to the Israeli pullout. The man recognized her and rose from his stool.

"Pakad, what a pleasant surprise. I didn't expect to see you—I mean with your transfer and all."

"I need you to conduct a very simple test."

"Now?"

"We would like to wrap up a certain matter to everyone's satisfaction."

"A matter concluded yesterday?"

She nodded.

He smiled at her, coming up just short of a wink. "No one officially knows it was you in Jericho, of course. So please accept my unofficial congratulations, and let me know what I can unofficially do for you." ·

From her handbag she removed a small laboratory vial, a third full of a thick, murky substance. She held up the vial before the pathologist.

"I want to know if this oil matches up with the oil found in the wounds of the Wolf's victims while the West Bank was still under occupation."

The pathologist took the vial, tipped it sideways and back again, then headed for a microscope and refrigerator.

"That shouldn't take long."

"Then you're saying you previously identified some kind of oil to be present in the wounds of the early victims."

The pathologist looked at her befuddled. "Of course. My report was in the file."

Until it, too, had been deleted, Danielle thought, along with the drawing, Ansar 3, and everything else that had proven the existence and revealed the identity of the Wolf to Israeli authorities months before.

BEN AWOKE TO an intense pain throbbing in his head, an all too familiar sensation of late. He tried to raise a hand to comfort the stinging lump he felt and only then realized his hands were tied to the back of the chair.

"He's coming around," a voice said.

Ben opened his eyes slowly, trying to take in as much as he could before being accosted once more. He was in a large square room with lots of chairs and little light. There were enough cracks in the drawn blinds to show that night had fallen outside. He couldn't see his watch to determine how much time had passed since he had stepped up to the door of the Khalil home.

"Who are you?" the same angry voice demanded, as a tall man appeared from behind the chair, hovering over him.

"I've come to see Akram Khalil," Ben stated simply.

"What do you want with him?"

"I speak to no one but Akram Khalil."

"He does not wish to speak with you."

"He should. I'm here about his daughter. I'm here about the man who killed her."

"The man who killed her is dead!"

"No. Someone else killed her. I should know; I shot the man you think murdered her."

"Liar!"

"Read the newspapers. They printed my picture today next to the story on the front page of both Palestinian dailies. Not a very good likeness, mind you."

"Enough!" a voice boomed from somewhere behind him, and Ben heard steps approaching. The voice sounded somehow familiar, authoritative but very nasal now.

Ben saw the man from the side first and then the front. Dark and thick-framed, seething in his intensity, with very dark eyes that had turned black and blue over a bandaged nose. Ben recognized the voice now, remembered breaking the nose of a Hamas leader with a head butt in the back of a van six nights before, when he had been kidnapped.

"You wanted me." Akram Khalil greeted him coldly, his nose encased in gauze. "Here I am."

"It's good to see you finally," Ben said to him. "I'm sorry about your nose."

"You should be dead now, American."

"You'll be glad I'm not after you hear what I've got to say."

Khalil's nose was running, and he dabbed at his nostrils with his sleeve, careful not to disturb the bandage. "You're not surprised."

"That you are a Hamas leader—no. That you were the man who kidnapped me Monday night—yes."

"And you still came here?"

"Because we need to talk—"

"Do we?"

"—and help each other."

"How?"

"The real murderer of your daughter must be caught."

"And you know who he is, I suppose," Khalil said, sneering.

"I will," Ben assured. "I caught the first. I'll catch this second butcher, too. That's what I came here tonight for, to propose a trade: your daughter's killer in exchange for information."

Khalil had stopped directly in front of him. Ben could see he was short and stocky, lots of muscle gone to fat and as much gray hair as black.

"Information about Mohammed Fasil," Ben continued. "What he came to Jericho twice for, as well as the subject of the meeting your daughter attended before her death."

"Then I'm afraid I cannot live up to my side of the bargain you propose. You see, I can't tell you the subject of the meetings that brought him to Jericho."

"Then your daughter's killer remains free and more of you will die."

"You misunderstand, American. I *can't* because I *don't know*. Not the specifics, anyway."

"I'm not a fool, Khalil. I know how important you are to the movement. Fasil wouldn't have been in Jericho unless you set it up, approved it."

"Helped to organize—yes; approved—yes; but as for the specific agenda—no. The Israelis tried to infiltrate our ranks for years with little success. Then with the *peace*—" He uttered the word with contempt. "—came the pressure on our own people to crack down on us. Suddenly our large-scale missions were betrayed from the inside, our soldiers turned in by our *own*! Arafat's secret police, men like you." He fixed his gaze on Ben, eyes as contemptuous as his voice had been. "You don't know how much damage you've done. Collaborators all!"

"We were talking about your daughter, Khalil. Do you want her killer caught or not?" Ben asked quietly.

"I would have killed you by now if I didn't, American. I know Fasil was putting something big together that he needed lots of people for."

"Manpower drawn from the Qassam Brigades?"

"Coordinated by my daughter. The mission was a very complicated one, required lots of travel back and forth to the United States. Fasil was making arrangements to pick something up there. In New York."

Ben remembered the name and address Jack Tourcot had been unable to identify in New York City.

"I don't know what, where, or when," Khalil resumed. "No one did, except Fasil. The recent wave of betrayals had turned him dangerously secretive. He trusted *no one*."

"You only knew he had set up a second meeting."

"And we learned he'd been killed right after that

second meeting on Jaffa Street. We were hoping he might have had some clue on his person about what he was plotting.''

''And when you couldn't find anything at the medical examiner's, that's when you kidnapped me.''

''In the hope you had found it first,'' Khalil explained disdainfully.

''I may have,'' Ben told him. ''In Fasil's Tel Aviv hotel room there was a name and an address in New York City.''

''If you know that much, why did you bother coming to me?''

''Because the name and address I found don't exist.''

''They must be written in some kind of code. Fasil was too cautious to leave anything so important where anyone could find it.''

''What about the other members of the Qassam Brigade cell your daughter was part of? They have to know *something*.''

''They were all to be given assignments independent of each other. Fasil never met with all of them at once. Small groups instead, a few at a time. We know their assignments hadn't all been issued prior to his death.'' Khalil paused painfully. ''That was to be my daughter's job. What else can we do to find her killer?''

''For starters,'' Ben told him, ''you can untie me.''

''That's a good idea,'' Danielle Barnea said from the open doorway, a nine-millimeter pistol held threateningly in her hand.

C H A P T E R 4 9

PLACE YOUR WEAPONS on the floor and put your hands in the air,'' she ordered the gunmen surrounding Ben. ''Slowly,'' she added.

Her approach to the door had been so silent and the attention focused on Ben so intent that none of them had heard her. Danielle turned to Khalil.

''Untie him.''

Khalil sneered at her and then looked at Ben unsurely before starting to unlace the knots.

''This isn't necessary, Pakad,'' Ben said, feeling his wrists come free. ''Mr. Khalil and I were just having a friendly little chat. He is, in fact, most interested in helping us bring the real killer of his daughter to justice.''

Danielle made no motion to lower her gun, eyes fixed on the other Hamas soldiers. ''How noble.''

''How did you find me?''

She looked at Ben quizzically. "I got your message to meet you here."

Ben rose, suddenly wary. "I didn't leave one."

Danielle turned her eyes on Khalil. "Then I incapacitated your two outside guards for nothing."

Now it was Khalil who looked suddenly uncertain. "I had no guards posted outside."

"Then who—"

Khalil swung toward a few of his men. "Check the windows!" he ordered.

They stooped to retrieve their weapons before moving to obey. Danielle reached one of the dark drawn blinds ahead of them. She lifted a corner to gaze down into the street and saw a pair of jeeplike vehicles parked directly in front of Khalil's home. Two figures crept across the lawn, bringing long cylindrical tubes up to their shoulders.

Rocket launchers!

"Down!" Danielle screamed, and dove to the floor just before a huge section of the wall exploded behind the dual impact.

Halfway to the window, three of Khalil's men were blown backward through the air, lost to the flaming debris that crashed against the opposite wall. Ben and Khalil dove, too, Ben covering his head and looking up after the initial blast to hear a fresh sound whizzing their way. He thought he actually *saw* the rocket spinning through the newly created chasm, then buried his head again before it tore out a huge chunk of the far wall, spewing fragments of stone in all directions.

"My family!" Khalil was wailing, pushing shards of it off him. *"My family!"*

The terrorist tried to rise, screamed, and collapsed

anew, clutching his leg. Ben crawled to his side and saw the jagged splinter of stone sticking out just above his knee.

"How many?" Ben asked him.

Khalil was breathing very hard. "My wife, son, and daughter—Amal."

"Where?"

"Downstairs."

Ben looked at Danielle as the last of Khalil's soldiers rushed across the debris-strewn floor to the chasm facing the house's front. He had barely gotten his gun leveled when a sharp burst of automatic fire snapped him backward to the floor. Danielle used the distraction to crouch low and move fast for the doorway.

Khalil screamed in pain and rage, trying to rise again. Ben tried to restrain him, but he tore away briefly as Danielle disappeared into the hall.

"No!" Khalil raged. *"Not my family!"*

Ben wouldn't let go, dragged him back down to the floor.

Khalil smashed a hand into his face. "You did this! You brought them here! *A trap!*"

"No!" Ben insisted, holding on tight and accepting the wild blows. "They came to kill me!"

Khalil's struggle lost some of its fire. His eyes met Ben's and saw the truth.

"I'm going to get you out of here," Ben promised.

"My family . . ."

"We'll save them, I swear to you. Whatever hap—"

The rest of his words were drowned out by a piercing explosion from downstairs.

*   *   *

DANIELLE HAD JUST reached the top of the staircase when the front door and frame simply disintegrated beneath her. She thought she had seen two or three figures scampering past the door just before it disappeared, but wasn't sure. She shook the debris off and started to climb back to her feet. Below, what had been the front door was a dark, smoke-shrouded chasm.

A shrill sound stung her ears and Danielle hit the floor again an instant before another rocket sliced through the smoke left by the first and ripped into the stairway, blowing fragments in all directions. She felt the landing start to go, heard the entire structure groan as the floor gave way beneath her. She felt herself plunging downward, trying to brace for the coming impact.

THE BLISTERING BLASTS downstairs showered pieces of the ceiling on Ben and Khalil just after they reached the hallway. The whole house seemed to yaw. Khalil was muttering something, prayers it sounded like, but Ben dragged him on.

A jagged breach lay where the second floor landing had been. Ben grabbed a pistol wedged through Khalil's belt and tried to peer downward through the smoke, clutter of debris, and smoldering flames.

Where was Danielle?

The utter blackness of the house, together with the blast-ruined air, made a clear view of anything impossible. Ben was trying to figure out the simplest way down when he saw the three men enter through the jagged chasm encompassing the front door, sharp blue beams of light sweeping the area before them.

DANIELLE HAD LANDED like a cat, stunned but not badly hurt by the plunge. She found herself lying on her side staring straight up at the ceiling when she heard moans.

A child's moans.

What had Khalil said upstairs? A wife, daughter, and son, that was it. Three more down here amid the shattered remnants of the house, then, but only one set of moans.

Danielle shifted toward the moans and began to crawl through the debris. The fall from the second floor had left her with no weapon, but instinct drove her on nevertheless. Palestinians or not, the three victims down here were innocent bystanders caught in a firestorm meant for her and Ben.

Her body wasn't cooperating, slowed and aching from the impact she'd suffered from the fall. Still, she was drawing closer to the moaning, thought she saw a young terrified face, and reached out for it.

Suddenly a pair of hands latched onto her, fingernails raking her back.

"Noooooo!" Khalil's daughter Amal cried madly, as the trio of lights poured through the remains of the house.

BEN STEADIED HIS pistol just as Amal Khalil grabbed Danielle from behind. He sighted as best he could through the billows of smoke, fired, and kept firing at the figures lurking behind the sweeping lights.

He knew he'd succeeded when he saw the shafts of blue spiral upward and dance madly on what was left of the first floor ceiling before being stilled.

"You got them!" Khalil wheezed thankfully, removing a second clip from his pants pocket.

Ben accepted the clip and jammed it home. Looking downward again he saw more shapes advancing toward the house, briefly visible through the steady blue beams.

THE GUNFIRE FROM above echoing in her ears, Danielle twisted fast and knocked the girl's hands aside. She swept the girl's legs out, landing hard atop her amid the remnants of a wall and ceiling. A thumb pressed deep into the enraged girl's windpipe stilled her instantly.

Danielle left her in the rubble and crawled for the nearest body downed by the gunfire from the second floor. The dead man's automatic rifle was propped upward, pinned between the corpse and a thick pile of charred debris. The corpse's face was semitic, whether Israeli or Palestinian she could not tell. As she grabbed the rifle and doused the light affixed to its barrel, she glimpsed a second grouping of shapes approaching the house across the lawn.

Danielle moved back to the young figure she had found covered in debris before being attacked by Khalil's daughter. Closer inspection revealed a young boy lying semiconscious across the legs of a woman who must have been Khalil's wife. Danielle reached down to feel for a pulse, found it weak but steady, as the new wave of gunmen stepped into the house.

* * *

BEN FELT KHALIL grasp his shoulder when the gunmen began to fan out. Though a number were clear in his sights, he elected to hold off firing. With only this single clip remaining, he had to make every one of the sixteen shots count. That meant holding off until as many of the enemy's number as possible were contained downstairs.

He heard Khalil gasp and followed his gaze to find Amal rising with a severed plank in her hand. She cracked it across the back of a gunman's head, continuing to pummel him with it as the other killers swung toward her.

"Get dow—"

A burst of automatic fire spun her around before Khalil could finish the desperate warning to his daughter. Ben could feel the air gush out of him as if he too had been shot.

In the same moment, Danielle lurched into the line of fire between the falling girl and the gunmen. The muzzle of the automatic rifle she was wielding blazed angry orange. But the sound of the reports was lost to Ben, who was deafened by the noise of his own. He was conscious of bodies tumbling below, both to his bullets and to Danielle's. Others fled through the rear, escaping their barrages. Hot spent shells danced at his feet, and the bitter stench of gunsmoke rose above all the others that had filled the house.

He couldn't take his finger off the trigger even after the slide locked open, only vaguely conscious that Danielle had appeared beneath him with a fresh rifle salvaged from another of the corpses.

*   *   *

DANIELLE SLUNG THE rifle's strap around her shoulder and dragged a reasonably whole stone beam sideways so that it rested against the sagging second floor landing near Ben and Khalil's perch.

"Come on!" she called, rifle back in hand, sweeping the room in all directions as she backpedaled in search of Amal.

Ben helped Khalil onto the beam first. The terrorist's wounded leg dragging like a lead weight didn't stop him from negotiating the drop quickly and then limping off in search of his fallen family. Ben followed him down a bit more cautiously in the darkness, pausing at the bottom only long enough to retrieve a still hot enemy rifle Danielle had left for him.

He found Khalil hunched over the body of the dead Amal, the second daughter he had lost to violence in barely two weeks. Ben turned to find Danielle tending to Khalil's wife and son. It was difficult to continue thinking of Khalil as a terrorist, although Ben knew he had lived by violence and murder for the better part of his life. Right now he was just a tragic figure grieving over another senseless loss.

"Check the front," Danielle said.

Finding a vantage point from which he could view most of the house's front, Ben pressed his shoulders tight against the remnant of a casement window and peered out. One of the Jeeps was just tearing away in a screech of rubber. He turned around again and saw Khalil cradling his daughter Amal closely against him, his sobs rising above the cracking and creaking sounds of the house. Ben grabbed hold of him and hoisted.

"I won't leave her!" he insisted, trying to pull free.

The stone wall behind Khalil was crumbling, the entire rear portion of the house ready to collapse. Ben grabbed hold of Khalil with one arm while he lifted Amal in the other, dragging both of them through an obstacle course of teetering beams and raining chunks of stucco stone. Danielle had carried Khalil's wife and son outside just before him and had already laid them down on the lawn when Ben emerged.

"You did this! You brought them here! YOU!"

Khalil lunged, and Ben felt the terrorist's hands close on his windpipe. Khalil was too weak and drained to do any damage with his grip, and his wounded leg gave out almost instantly. Ben sat down next to the man on the lawn and lay a hand across his shoulder.

"And I promise I'll make them pay. Whoever they are, I'll make them pay."

CHAPTER 50

THE JEEP THE attackers had left behind easily accommodated all of them. Danielle rode in the passenger seat next to Ben, Khalil in the rear squeezed between his wife and son, the dead Amal still clutched against him. All were silent and fearfully tense, expecting the second Jeep to come flying at them any moment.

"Which clinic should we take you to?" Ben asked, as he put the Jeep into gear.

"No clinic, no hospital," Khalil replied softly. "There's a doctor who takes care of us at his house. I'll give you his address."

Khalil recited it and Ben swung right at the next block, needing to backtrack a bit. Danielle couldn't help thinking what this would have meant a few years ago: a top-ranking Hamas member her virtual prisoner en route to a doctor who would be able to identify the entire network. Tonight that didn't matter. Tonight they were on the same side.

The doctor's house was dark. Ben and Danielle helped get Khalil's wife and son out. Khalil stopped them before they could proceed with him up the walk, holding Amal in both arms now.

"The doctor doesn't like strangers. It's best if you leave me on my own from here."

"I'm sorry," Ben said.

Khalil gave him a long look. "I know who you are. I know you know how this feels." He swallowed hard. "Just remember your promise."

Ben nodded and waited until Khalil and his family disappeared inside before retreating the short distance back down the walk with Danielle.

"What now?" she asked.

"We find somewhere to hide for the night."

INSPECTOR! COME IN, come in," Yousef Shifa beamed after opening his front door. "You keep very strange hours." He peered behind them. "Is the boy with you?"

"Not tonight."

He shrugged. "He's a good boy. Can't help that life treated him like shit."

The big man stood aside and beckoned them forward. "Speaking of shit, that's what both of you look like."

"It could have been a lot worse," Ben told Shifa, and turned to Danielle once the door was closed behind them. "This is . . . my partner."

Shifa nodded. "You look very good together."

*   *   *

HE INSISTED ON giving up his own room for Ben, and herded his three oldest children from theirs for Danielle. Ben accepted reluctantly, feeling the man had already paid the debt owed him. His presence and Danielle's was an imposition, and a dangerous one at that.

He had been lying on his back atop the covers, unable to sleep or even close his eyes, for nearly an hour when the door creaked open and Danielle entered. She padded across the floor in the darkness and lay down next to him in silence. Ben liked the feeling of having her this close next to him, enjoyed the brush of her shoulder against his as they lay there.

They should have been exhausted, totally drained. Craving sleep, both knew it would not come. They had each faced death up close before, and the result was often an exhilaration, a catharsis, a feeling as close to invincibility as can be known.

They were alive, goddammit! They were alive . . .

Maybe it was the adrenaline still kicking in. Or the curious scent of fear mixing with the chalky dust that covered their clothes. Or the "fight or flight" syndrome that reduces civilized man to his most base instincts. Or maybe it was just surviving *together*, lying there with all the defenses, petty politics, and cultural distinctions reduced to a big fat nothing in the face of looking at death and living to tell.

Alive!

And what they felt, what they *wanted*, spilled over, neither able to restrain it any longer. Their lips came together before either knew what was happening and, once together, didn't part. Seconds drew into minutes as they rolled onto their sides and swallowed each other in an embrace that stretched into heedless passion. These were two people who had both wanted this, needed it, from their first meeting in Mayor Sumaya's office. Trained to suppress their feelings, their emotions at last broke through and raged all the more fiercely.

And when the kissing moved on to more, each rhythm flowed so naturally and mutually that neither would remember which had done the initiating. What they would remember was a stubborn squeak in the bedsprings that adversely brought to mind the Khalil house cracking as it broke apart around them. Instead of disturbing their passion, though, this merely increased it, placed their love in the context of the lives they lived. Where it belonged, yes, yet leaving each wondering how long it might stay.

Were they extending this case only to postpone their own parting? Had they constructed a convenient scenario that would provide their passion a context in which to continue?

Neither posed these questions during the rhythmic pacing that accompanied the squeaks and groans of the bedsprings. But later, when their passion was spent and Ben lay with his face against Danielle's neck, when the grasp of sleep continued to elude them, they needed to speak as much as they had needed to make love.

"The attack tonight," Ben started. "It must have been your people. Wanting to silence us, keep us from the truth."

"What if it was Fasil's people, trying to keep us from destroying whatever it is they're planning?"

"Would such people know where to leave you the

message that drew you to Khalil's house?''

He felt her go tense alongside him, then heard her sigh. "No. Not very likely."

"It doesn't matter which set of enemies was responsible for what happened tonight. I only brought it up because I wanted you to understand that I know how you feel. The woman who was killed three nights ago,'' Ben continued more softly, ''my father's mistress, she was one of them—Hamas. We've both been betrayed, you see. I should have known, of course. I should have listened. She tried to tell me but . . .''

"But what?"

"She was all I had left of my father. I was seven when he left us. I never saw him again. It never seemed fair.''

"Is that why you came back?"

"I don't know. Maybe. I looked for Dalia, in any case, and I found her. She made me feel less cheated. But it was a lie. *She* was a lie, to me and to him. She had us both fooled, the father and the son. I can live having been left nothing. It's realizing you never had anything to begin with that's hard.''

She pulled slightly away from him. "Losing what you've always believed in is just as bad. I spent my day confirming how someone in Israeli intelligence 'created' the second killer. They knew exactly what they were doing. . . ." And she proceeded to explain how the deleted portions of the case file had led her to a sketch artist and then the forensics lab with a vial of fish oil. She told him that the sketch was of Abu Garib, the man Ben had killed on the boat, and confirmed he had no scar.

"They recruited someone who looked like Garib

and sent him after Fasil and the other members of his cell.''

''Then, all of a sudden, my government offers to help catch him.''

''The real Wolf, Pakad, not the imposter someone else created.''

''A rogue faction?''

''It's the only thing that makes any sense.''

''So my superiors knew what was going on and sent me to stop it, making as little fuss as possible. Save the peace process, become a hero, but most of all, end this radical faction's renegade operation.''

''Because once the real killer was caught, the copy-cat could no longer function with impunity.'' Ben seemed to tense. ''But it's not over, Pakad, because now we've got to deal with whatever Fasil's group was planning. If it didn't die with him, then the threat is still out there.''

''What can we do?''

''Go back to our respective superiors tomorrow and explain our suspicions. We keep it simple, the truth, at least as we know—believe—it to be: a second killer is still at large, responsible for at least three terrorist deaths. About the cover-ups and complicities, well, we play dumb.''

''And Fasil's plan?''

''That's the kicker, because only by continuing our investigation can we uncover what he was up to and stop it.''

''If his death hasn't ruined it already.''

''A man like Fasil would have had a backup, you can bet on that. I think even Dalia was starting to have doubts. I think it was because of whatever operation Fasil was planning.''

"But our superiors are more likely to gamble on it dying with him than we are; they think they have more to lose if this blows up in their faces."

"They'll listen to us because they have to now."

"And why is that?"

Ben smiled sardonically as he reached for her again. "Because we're heroes."

DAY EIGHT

CHAPTER 51

COMMANDER SHAATH LUMBERED over to the door in a rage, eyes fixed hatefully on Ben the whole time.

"I'll brief you as soon as Inspector Kamal and I are finished," Mayor Sumaya promised, keeping his small frame between the two men.

He heaved a sigh once Shaath was through the door, and fixed a gaze of grave concern on Ben.

"Requesting that a superior officer leave the room shows severe disrespect. I trust you have good reason."

"I'm afraid I don't respect him, sir, nor do I trust him. He didn't want me getting this case to begin with, and then did everything in his power to see that I failed."

Sumaya stopped directly in front of Ben. "Actually, he approved of your being given the assignment."

Ben was taken aback, but only briefly. "Of course,

because it took the heat off him. The blame for failure, when it came, would be mine to bear. He never considered I might actually succeed.''

''I may have been alone in that regard. You proved me right. Don't do anything to prove me wrong now.'' Sumaya slid back behind his desk, remained standing. ''I understand you checked yourself out of the hospital yesterday. Left no word where you could be reached. There were matters that needed attending, loose ends. And you missed the press conference. The President was disappointed. He had hoped to meet you.''

''I will be glad to meet him,'' Ben told him, ''once this case is really over.''

''I don't understand.''

''There are two killers, sir, and one of them's still out there.''

DANIELLE WAS PLANNING to set up a meeting with Herschel Giott and Moshe Baruch, but they beat her to the punch with a phone call early Monday morning. She dressed quickly and hurried straight to the National Police building.

Upstairs in Giott's office, the rav nitzav and Baruch had been joined by a leisurely dressed nondescript man with a cigarette dangling from his fingers. Neither Baruch nor Giott introduced her, acting as though he wasn't there. The stranger hung back in the room's shadows, smoke rising toward the ceiling.

Giott's and Baruch's grim faces were in stark contrast to the triumphant expressions they had worn yesterday.

''Sit down, Pakad.''

Danielle took her customary seat. Giott stole a glance at Baruch before resuming.

"A number of disturbing reports have crossed my desk over the past twelve hours. I expect you can explain them."

"I'll try."

"Indications," began Moshe Baruch, "are that you are continuing an investigation that is considered closed."

"This behavior is not befitting a hero to the state, Pakad," Giott added. "I'm sure you have a perfectly logical explanation for your actions."

"I would like to continue working on this investigation."

"And why is that?" Baruch asked her.

"Too many inconsistencies, things that don't fit."

"The Palestinian's ideas?" from Giott.

"His name is Kamal. And the ideas were mine as well. We were working together, remember?"

"A caustic attitude is not an endearing feature on a woman or an officer of Shin Bet," Baruch cautioned.

Danielle felt the eyes of the third man in the room upon her. "I'm sorry. I didn't get much sleep last night."

"You look like you've been injured," Giott said suspiciously.

"Just a fall. Clumsy and stupid of me."

"You should have listened to me and taken your vacation." The rav nitzav's voice was the sternest she could ever recall. "As it is now, you have caused this office considerable embarrassment."

"But I'm about to save you from even more," she said in a firm voice. "Both of you."

"And how will you do that, Pakad?"

"We thought this case was closed. We were wrong."

BEN HAD METHODICALLY presented his evidence to Sumaya. He had told him of the initial trip the terrorist Mohammed Fasil had made to the West Bank on the very night Leila Khalil had been murdered. He explained Danielle's discovering the doctoring of the original case files in order that the killer's MO could be copied without fear of recrimination. And, finally, he related the deadly plot Fasil had been hatching in the days before he too was murdered.

"This second killer has concerned himself only with killing *terrorists*. That's what you're saying, isn't it?"

"Three that we know of," Ben nodded, swallowing hard, "all linked to Hamas."

"The Khalil girl first, then the unidentified victim . . ."

"Mohammed Fasil," Ben reminded.

"And the third?"

"The victim found the night before last: Dalia Mikhail."

Sumaya's stare tightened. "The commander was kind enough to brief me on that."

"He told you she was my father's whore. Is that a problem?"

"It seems to me this case is getting rather personal for you, Ben. I wouldn't want to see you reading more into a scenario that is complicated enough already."

"Whether it's personal or not does not change the facts, sir. You can speak with Major al-Asi about Dalia Mikhail; I believe he is well acquainted with her case."

The mayor bristled at mention of al-Asi's name. "You believe this second killer is an Israeli."

"All indications point to that."

"Indications that are, at best, vague. And we know some of your conclusions are based on information gathered by breaking rules we have set forth for our officers and investigators. We take a very dim view of such things, you should know that."

Ben knew Sumaya was referring to his unauthorized visit to Akram Khalil after learning he was a Hamas leader. Such contact was expressly forbidden without formal authorization. That was why Ben had asked Commander Shaath to leave before he told his tale. Shaath might yet claim his head over this, but at least it would be on Ben's terms.

"There wasn't time to file a formal request," Ben explained, trying to sound reasonable. "Khalil could have been next, for all I knew. And, as it turned out, he was."

"He and his family seem to have disappeared."

"I don't blame them."

"It would help if we could question him, obtain corroboration for your story."

"I think he'll be staying underground for a while."

"Unfortunate."

Disheartened, Sumaya shook his head as he rose and walked away from the desk. He moved to the window and cranked the blinds open. The mayor clasped his hands behind his back and continued gazing up the street.

"You have done wonderful work this past week," he said without turning. "You are a hero now, and rightfully so. For that reason I'm going to do you a favor." With that he swung around deliberately and faced Ben, silhouetted by the sun's rays. "I'm going to forget this conversation ever took place, but only if you leave this office now."

Ben stayed in his chair.

DANIELLE HAD TOLD her story to Giott and Baruch, leery of the stranger looming in the room's shadows who smoked throughout her tale.

"You realize what you are suggesting?" Giott asked her plainly when she was finished.

"Yes, sir, I do."

"Then do you also realize the implications should such a story escape the confines of this room?" Baruch challenged.

"Yes, again."

"A plot hatched by us to murder members of a certain Hamas cell using the guise of a serial killer."

"Not *you*."

"Don't be naive, Pakad," sighed a sullen Giott. "Israel *is* us, *all* of us. That includes you."

"I understand."

"No," Baruch snapped, "I don't think you do. What the rav nitzav is saying is that depending on how such a revelation, or accusation, is interpreted, it could destroy the peace talks."

"The peace talks are precisely what I'm concerned about. That's why I wanted to bring it to your attention immediately."

"The preservation of the peace talks is your primary concern, then?" Baruch demanded, staring at her with his piercing eyes.

"That, and finding out whether the plot by Fasil's Hamas cell is still operational," Danielle told him.

"Which," Giott assumed, "would mean continuing with this . . . investigation."

"Perhaps even expanding it," Danielle conceded.

Giott and Baruch looked at each other somberly, then turned questioningly to the figure haloed by cigarette smoke in the office's darkened corner. That was all the prodding the man needed to rise and step into the light, still puffing away.

"I think it's time we talked," he said.

CHAPTER 52

FOR A LONG moment the ceiling fan's lazy spin composed the only sound in the mayor's office. Then Sumaya spoke again, softer, his voice as devoid of emotion as his office was of color.

"There is much at stake here, Inspector."

"That's what you said last week when you convinced me to take the case."

"And we're both out on a limb now as a result."

"If Fasil's plot goes forth, far more than us will fall."

Sumaya turned back to the window and jerked the blinds upward. They rattled against each other and flapped against the glass as light washed into the room, illuminating the blank starkness of the walls.

Ben watched the mayor gesture toward the window. "Look outside. There's no protest anywhere to be seen today. I'm told a march in *support* of the peace process has been organized for this afternoon. You caught al-

Diib, Ben. You made it possible." Sumaya's voice sank again, his tone growing incredulous. "And now you want to *squander that*?"

"Fasil's plot is something big, the biggest Hamas has ever taken on."

"So the Israelis had him executed, along with the cell he was working with."

"We don't know if that stopped it."

"You would have me *accuse* them of killing individuals we would just as soon see dead ourselves?"

Ben thought of Dalia and felt the familiar dull ache rising through him.

"These individuals committed themselves to destroying all chances for peace," Sumaya said, "and, now that we are rid of them, you would risk accomplishing *the very same thing*?"

"Just keep the investigation open. I'll only need a few men at most. We can keep it quiet."

"It will blow up in your face."

"My face was almost blown up last night."

"Because you had the misfortune to be in the wrong place at the wrong time, and without any formal authority at that. Hamas must have grown suspicious of Khalil, felt it was time to cut their losses. You would be well advised to accept that scenario."

"I can't. Pakad Barnea got a message to meet me that I never sent. Whoever did send it knew this was a *cooperative effort*, so they wanted to be fair and kill both of us."

"That's enough, Inspector."

"It will only be enough when we are sure Fasil's plot died with him."

"It did; accept that."

"I can't. Let me continue on the case alone if necessary. I'll take full responsibility."

The mayor was nodding as if Ben had made his point for him. "And will you also take responsibility for your people, Ben? You claim to be Palestinian. Now act like one! You think autonomy, independence, even the founding of a Palestinian state is the end of the process? It's only the beginning. With peace comes the opportunity for us to open our doors to tourists *as well as* Israelis. The towns that have enjoyed peaceful coexistence for years will become the model for the entire West Bank. Don't you see?"

Ben remained silent.

"And it doesn't stop there," Sumaya continued. "We're also looking at the lowering of trade barriers, the end to embargoes. Israel will be able to export freely into Syria, Jordan, Saudi Arabia, all the countries she has been pariah to these many long years. I am talking about goods that will cost a fraction of what they do when imported from Europe or the United States. I am talking about the new Israel's manufacturing base increasing fivefold, even tenfold. Do you understand what I'm saying?"

"No."

"Who will do the work, Ben? Who will do the manufacturing? I'm talking about jobs, jobs for the Palestinian people in Gaza and here in the West Bank. I'm talking about Israel needing the labor we can cheaply and conveniently supply. I am talking about manufacturing and distribution centers constructed on Palestinian land with *Israeli* capital. It doesn't stop there, either. Even now, already, Arab consortiums are negotiating with Israeli interests on joint investment projects. A sixty-million-dollar Marriott hotel in Gaza. A hundred-million-dollar investment bank in Ramallah. And that's just the beginning. With the opening of trade will come investment opportunities for the world in a great untapped market, and that means unprecedented opportunities for our people.''

Sumaya grabbed his desk and leaned over it passionately.

''This is what your father would have wanted. But without a final and lasting peace it will never happen. We have a window of opportunity here. If we let it close, given the political climate in Israel, it will be years before it opens again.'' Sumaya settled slowly back into his chair. ''The peace process may not survive this plot you allege of Fasil's. But it definitely *won't* survive the allegations you are lodging against the Israelis.''

''What would you have me do, then?''

Sumaya thought about that briefly. ''Maybe you should go home for a while . . .''

C HIEF I N S P E C T O R B A R N E A , '' the man with the cigarette continued, purposely not introducing himself, ''first let me offer my commendation for the brilliant career you have enjoyed thus far in the service of Israel.''

God, Danielle thought, *he sounds like my father— like he used to, anyway. . . .*

''This meeting today is about several things,'' the man continued, ''but mostly it is about that career. It would be a shame to waste it, to throw it away for nothing. Agreed?''

''Agreed.''

The man nodded, satisfied. ''I am here today out of

respect not only for you, but also your family, especially your father. I am here to tell you there have been no murders since your Palestinian counterpart shot the killer known as the Wolf, and there won't be any more. Am I making myself clear?"

"Yes."

"Now, as to the business about a plot hatched by the murdered Mohammed Fasil, I agree this is a threat we must take seriously since we cannot rule out that it is to be aimed at Israel. We will be moving the venue of the peace talks to an undisclosed location. I want you to know that. We will also be conducting a full-scale investigation into the possible existence of this plot, which you are free to participate in once the talks have concluded. Are those terms acceptable to you, Pakad?"

Danielle knew she was not being given a choice here. They were stonewalling her investigation out of fear of the scathing media backlash that might accompany it. She had to assume Ben was facing the same response in Jericho, albeit with far more dire repercussions if he failed to heed the warnings of his superiors.

"We're waiting, Danielle," Giott urged, speaking out of turn.

"They are acceptable," she made herself say.

"I know you still have many concerns," the stranger continued. "I am not in a position to address them all, but I want to assure you that everything is under control. Do you understand? *Everything* is under control. I ask you to trust me on that. I ask that you accept the fact that your participation in this matter is no longer required. Is that clear?"

"Very."

* * *

I AM SPEAKING of the United States," the mayor of Jericho elaborated.

"I understand what you're speaking of."

"I'm not talking long term here, you know; you're a hero now, after all. I'm talking about a short visit, a well-deserved vacation to celebrate your solving a case that had baffled everyone associated with it for nearly a year. Your leave would be only a few weeks, three at the outside."

"I'll be able to follow the peace talks on CNN."

"It will be a different world if these talks accomplish what many expect them to. I'm told to expect surprises." He made sure to beam a warm smile at Ben. "Thanks in large part to you. You have made your point. You have proven yourself. Go to the United States and relax for a while. Is that such a bad thing?"

"It depends what I find when I get back."

I T WAS AS *if he was waiting for her, knew not only that she would be coming but also the subject of her visit.*

Danielle arrived at the convalescent home at noon to find her father as sharp as she had seen him since the stroke. The notebook computer was already on his lap, and this time the newspaper that had dropped to his chest was rightside up.

"I've been to see them."

His eyes urged her on.

"The investigation is finished. They are satisfied with the results."

He started typing. ARE YOU SATISFIED?

"No, not at all. They know I'm telling the truth. But that's not the issue."

WHAT IS THE ISSUE?

"Embarrassment, humiliation—this is what they are trying to avoid at all costs now. They can't afford another setback to the peace process." She hesitated, moved slightly sideways, and watched his eyes follow her. "There was another . . . man there today, someone I'd never met before, never seen in the building."

MOSSAD?

"Maybe. Who knows? You'd know him, though. He's one like you. The old guard."

DEFINITELY FROM INTELLIGENCE.

"They're turning their backs on the truth. I've been ordered to give up the investigation."

Her father thrust a trembling finger at her again and again, then typed: AND WILL YOU?

Danielle shrugged. "Israel has much to lose from this truth. That's one of the points they harped on."

EVERYBODY LOSES, INCLUDING YOU.

"They raised that point, too."

NO!, her father insisted on the screen, fighting to summon his last reserves for the day. THEY'RE NOT FINISHED WITH YOU YET. YOU'RE TOO GREAT A RISK NOW.

Danielle thought back to the meeting, the cleverly veiled insinuations all three men had made.

A LIABILITY, her father typed when she remained silent. YOU KNOW HOW THEY TREAT LIABILITIES.

Danielle swallowed hard. Her father's eyes were glazing over now, losing the little vitality they some-times exhibited. He fought to retain control of his fin-

gers, rebelling against him as he typed one final line:
THE TRUTH IS THE ONLY THING THAT CAN SAVE YOU.

BEN SAT SLUMPED in his office back at police
headquarters, staring at the map stuck with pushpins,
trying to determine what he should do next. The mayor
wasn't wrong in his claim that continued investigation
on Ben's part could destroy the peace process. But he
was underestimating the devastating potential of
Fasil's plot. Still, his offer was clear: keep his mouth
shut and Ben could remain a hero.

A hero . . .

He had hunted two monsters in his life now, killed
them both. And both pursuits had left him beaten and
empty. The Sandman had killed his family and sent
him here, and now al-Diib was sending him back to
the States. Like a ping-pong ball.

His instinct told him to stand his ground, but without stronger proof of what Fasil was planning, could
he take such a responsibility on himself? If he was
wrong, he could destroy his father's dream forever. He
wished Dalia Mikhail was still alive, wondered what
advice she would give him . . .

She must have found herself in a similar position in
the end, must have known that she was in grave danger after the murders of Leila Khalil and Mohammed
Fasil. Ben wondered if she'd been trying to tell him
at their last meeting. All that talk about secrets, wispy
allusions to his father. In retrospect, it sounded more
like an apology than anything, sounded like a woman
trying to make peace with herself. She had often told
Ben he was the closest thing she ever had to a son.

Could she leave a son with nothing, just as his father had done?

Ben straightened in his chair, feeling suddenly cold and clammy. Of course she'd left him with *something*! She had told him as much, come right out and *said* it!

Secrets . . .

And the proof he needed.

CHAPTER 53

DANIELLE DROVE TOWARD the West Bank queasy with anxiety after her attempts to reach Ben by phone had failed.

The checkpoint to enter the West Bank was just ahead, and Danielle readied her identification and pass. The line for those with passes was thin compared to the snarl of cars and supply trucks awaiting clearance. She quickly reached the front and handed her badge and pass over to the soldier.

"One moment please, Pakad," he said, instead of simply waving her through.

She watched him disappear into the guard house and tapped the steering wheel impatiently. The soldier returned with a captain by his side.

"I'm sorry, Pakad, your pass has been canceled," the captain informed her stiffly.

Danielle stiffened. "That's impossible. There must be some mistake."

"Even so, we cannot let you through until it is straightened out. I'm sorry," he repeated, and backed away.

There was no sense in arguing the issue, because Danielle knew there was no mistake at all. Giott and Baruch were shutting her down, making sure she did not continue this pursuit on her own. The officials of this checkpoint would undoubtedly inform them of her appearance here, if they hadn't already, impelling her superiors to take even more drastic measures to control her.

Danielle swung her car around, facing Israel again. But her mind was racing. She had come too far now to go back. There were other ways into the West Bank and she would try them all, if that's what it took.

As BEN HOPED, Shaath had left no guard at Dalia Mikhail's villa. He had simply secured the front door with a police padlock that took the standard key many officers had in their possession. Ben unlocked the door and stepped inside. He expected the townhouse would already have been looted of its many treasures. To his surprise, the interior looked undisturbed other than for the footprints left behind by the parade of cops on the night of the murder. Ben remembered Major al-Asi's interest and figured his men had kept watch over the villa until al-Asi had determined there was nothing inside he needed.

Ben made his way through the first floor slowly, recalling his many past visits, still feeling the presence of his father's mistress inside and half expecting to be greeted by her ever-present, reassuring smile. There was so much of her in the treasures she had spent a lifetime collecting, so much of her personality present in these pieces that fit each space as though they'd been made for it.

Ben stopped in front of the armoire and paused briefly before opening it. He would soon know if his hunch was correct, if he stood any chance at all of proving Mohammed Fasil's plot might still be active. The door opened easily and he felt his heart hammering against his ribcage as he reached inside to grasp the Chinese Buddha chest Dalia had insisted he hold in his hand just one week before.

Secrets . . .

He set the chest on a table before closing the doors to the armoire. Settling into the nearest chair, he eased the chest's thin ebony doors open. Hands trembling, he reached in for a computer disk and what looked like a note folded around it.

DANIELLE HAD PULLED over and parked her car back a few thousand yards from the checkpoint amid a tangle of other vehicles, hoping the authorities were too busy to notice. To drive miles to another entry point would cost her time Ben might not have. He needed her now—they needed each other—and every minute made a difference.

Her eyes fell on the line of Palestinian vehicles creeping forward. The papers of each driver were being carefully checked out and the vehicle inspected. She could see a number of cars stacked up on the shoulder, their owners removing the tires one by one so their insides could be carefully examined. The soldiers overseeing the process seemed to be enjoying themselves.

"Need to get through?"

Danielle turned toward a woman who had suddenly appeared alongside her.

"There is no shame in being turned away," the woman continued. "It depends what kind of mood they're in." She was about Danielle's age, a Palestinian woman of natural beauty and features quite similar to hers. "Maybe I can help."

She must think I'm Palestinian too, Danielle realized.

"How?" Danielle asked her.

"See the produce truck ten from the front? It's coming from Gaza. There's room for you in the back."

Danielle walked over to the truck the woman had indicated to take a closer look. It was crammed with bushels of fruits and vegetables that were already poking out through the sides and spilling over the top.

"You said there's *room*?" she asked the woman.

The woman shrugged. "I'm not saying it's comfortable, but at least you'll get where you want to go."

CHAPTER 54

BEN UNFOLDED THE note, tense with anticipation. He realized he'd been holding his breath and now released it in a melancholy sigh as he saw his own name at the top and began to read.

Ben—

There's so much I want to tell you, but let's start with the obvious: if you're reading this, it means I'm gone and you've proven yourself to be the great detective I know you are. I couldn't tell you about this in advance because I couldn't stomach your even suspecting the truth about me so long as I was alive.

To begin with, I had nothing to do with your father's death. He came back to me because he knew the Fatah group I was a part of was the only hope of lending leadership during the occupation. But his proposed methods differed from theirs. They did not share his breadth of vision and he did not share their desire for violent resistance. He was making things very difficult for them, so they opted for what they saw as their only option. I was not part of the decision, and made myself believe the Israelis were responsible until years later when I learned the truth.

History has proven your father right, I suppose. All these years later, our methods have changed little and accomplished even less. In any event, the computer disk in this chest will tell you everything I know about the operation Mohammed Fasil was running. It details my part in it. I know no more than certain details. Strange, but it was Fasil who brought me the Buddha chest. He asked me to hold it for him and when he was no longer in a position to come back for it, I appropriated the chest for my collection.

It has obviously come in handy, hasn't it? I knew you would know where to look, you and no one else. You are so much like your father. I can't tell you how much I miss him. He loved his family, Ben, and he wasn't happy being over here away from you. I don't think he was planning to stay much longer. He would have probably left earlier if it wasn't for me, because he didn't know how to say good-bye. Not just to me, but also to this world he loved much more than me.

Welcome to that world, Ben, and do with the disk whatever you must.

Allah Yunsrak
Dalia

Allah yunsrak—May Allah grant you victory—instead of a more traditional closing. Dalia was giving him another signal, knowing that if Ben ever read this he would be in the midst of the biggest struggle of his life.

Ben held the letter in his hand for a very long time before moving. The disk visible inside the Buddha chest resting on his lap didn't seem as important as her words. Those words had brought clarity to his life, but in the clarity there was pain. Why should he be surprised? There was pain in everything, but the most pain lay in surprise, and Ben had suffered a life full of them. Stability was something he had seldom known and, ironically, had sought upon his return to this world, just as his father before him.

And, like his father, he had become a hero, only to find that alone wasn't enough. There was always more to do, more that had to be done.

Ben removed the disk from the chest and brought it to Dalia's computer. He turned the machine on and slid the disk into the slot.

A single icon appeared on the screen. Ben clicked on the icon and the computer whirred to life. He waited expectantly and anxiously until the screen glowed alive with long columns of figures in what looked like some kind of balance sheet.

Ben scrolled through the disk's contents, studying them carefully. The balance sheet was actually a list of expenditures detailing huge amounts of funds and the paper trail of their transfers all across the globe. The money, millions of dollars in select foreign currencies and gold certificates, had originated in Iran and been distributed into a number of bank accounts through New York City and . . .

Ben's heart skipped a beat.

... *Moscow!*

The nonexistent name and address in New York City he and Danielle had found in Fasil's Tel Aviv hotel room flashed through his mind. But Moscow? What was the connection to *Moscow*?

He paused to sort out the facts. Dalia had obviously been in charge of keeping track of large amounts of money transfers. She had moved funds from Iranian accounts which must have been subsequently used by Fasil to purchase *something*. Significant deposits into Moscow banks indicated Russian involvement. And New York City, he knew from his life in the States, was a hotbed of Russian underworld activity. An infinite number of black market goods were brokered, including *weapons-grade nuclear materials*! The collapse of the Soviet Union had led to the worst fears of the world being realized. The vast Cold War arsenal they had amassed was being broken up, destroyed for the most part, but distributed in amounts significant enough to empower fringe groups with an efficacy only modern weapons could provide them.

The thought terrified Ben. What else would have cost Fasil so many millions of dollars? What else would give the murder brokers of Iran their money's worth? And, in all probability without realizing *any* of this, the Israelis had destroyed Fasil's cell. Sheer good fortune had left the operation in limbo, assuming Fasil did not have a contingency plan in effect. Ben believed his return to Jericho for the second meeting immediately before his murder meant he had not taken delivery of the goods yet. But they would be waiting for him—or someone else—in New York City.

How was Fasil to have picked those goods up? And why had he opted to stay in Israel under an alias instead of somewhere in the West Bank?

Ben did not have those answers, but this disk was the proof he needed to give to Mayor Sumaya. No one would be able to deny the existence of a horrifying plot any longer. They would have to take action and risk the consequences.

Ben ejected the disk, replaced the plastic sleeve, and tucked it carefully in his pocket. Halfway to the door, he remembered the Buddha chest and retraced his steps in order to return it to the armoire. To do otherwise seemed a disrespect to Dalia, especially since this was the final piece she had added to her collection.

Added because its real owner had died. And now, as a result, the evidence was in the hands of the authorities. The irony of that was chilling; Ben left to ponder it on the drive back to the Palestinian Authority building.

BEN ENTERED THE mayor's office without waiting to be announced.

"Mr. Mayor," he started, and paused expectantly as the big desk chair swung around from the wall on which hung Arafat's portrait.

Ben found himself staring into the one cold eye of Commander Omar Shaath.

"Where is the mayor?" he posed lamely.

"Called to Gaza by Arafat," Shaath replied, "to help plan the upcoming the peace talks. He won't be back for some time." Something between a snicker and a smile crossed the commander's lips. "I have taken over all official duties in his absence."

"I need to talk to the mayor," Ben said.

"And I need to talk to you, Inspector, because as my first official act I am ordering your arrest."

With that, a pair of Palestinian police officers stepped through the door behind Ben, guns in their hands.

"You're a damn fool."

"Please raise your hands in the air, Inspector."

Ben did as he was told. "I insist upon speaking to the mayor!"

"He doesn't want to speak to you." Shaath rose to his menacing height, as the officers yanked Ben's arms behind him and clamped on a set of handcuffs. "You will like our detainment camps, Inspector," he said, coming around the desk. "They're modeled after the Israelis'."

DANIELLE COULD NEVER recall a time when she'd been more uncomfortable. Though the truck had been only ten vehicles from the checkpoint when the woman had helped her climb into its rear, the maddening stops and starts, combined with the cramped quarters and the stifling darkness, made the hour it took to reach the front seem more like a day.

At the checkpoint, the rear door of the truck was opened and light streamed through her confines. But its contents were so tightly packed that the guards' inspection was merely cursory. The door banged shut and Danielle again found herself in darkness.

Once the truck got rolling, the slightest bump in the road sent what felt like prickers digging into her back.

She wrapped her arms around her face to protect it from the shifting contents and weaving branches.

The truck rumbled and bucked, rattled and jittered, each bad stretch of road threatening to shake it to pieces. As time went on, the road improved and the trip became easier until the truck creaked to a halt and she felt the emergency brake being applied just before the engine was shut off.

We're here, she thought, waiting patiently for the bushels about her to be hoisted away before trying to exit. Those last minutes were the worst, the toughest to bear. She could hear voices issuing instructions, men heaving the supplies from the bed.

As the fruit boxes layered above Danielle were removed, the light from the sun blinded her for a moment. She stumbled to the rear. A hand helped her up atop the truck's rickety rail, and then she jumped down into the waiting arms of two men standing beneath her.

"Thank you," she said, her vision clearing to the sight of a circle of men each of whom held a gun trained on her.

I know this place, she thought as her eyes focused. *This isn't the West Bank, it's Israel!*

"Hands up! Hands up now!" a voice commanded in Hebrew from behind Danielle, while an armed figure glided toward her from the front.

It was a figure she recognized, or thought she did anyway. Everything was falling together, making the worst kind of sense.

"Your gun please, Pakad," ordered a man with a jagged scar down his face, a man who looked like a double of Abu Garib, the Wolf.

* * *

SHAATH LED THE way downstairs, his officers holding Ben by either arm. Ben imagined a car would already be waiting outside to take him away.

They reached the first floor and Shaath started to turn toward Ben gloatingly, when Major Nabril al-Asi appeared before him. Four of his Protective Security Service plainclothesmen stood between al-Asi and the door.

"I am assuming jurisdiction in this matter, Commander," al-Asi demanded.

Shaath stiffened, clearly unsure how to proceed. He drifted back toward Ben almost protectively.

"It would not be wise to question my authority, Commander, not if you wish to enjoy a long career. I need not remind you that the Security Service takes precedence over all local concerns."

When Shaath didn't respond, al-Asi advanced and pulled Ben away from his escorts.

"Thank you, Commander. You may return to your office."

Shaath remained motionless.

"*Thank you,* Commander."

This time Shaath turned and, with his men, retraced his steps up the stairs.

"Get those off him," al-Asi ordered as soon as they were gone.

One of the major's men unfastened his handcuffs and, dumbfounded, Ben stretched his arms before him.

"I told you I never get in the way of a man doing his job, Inspector," al-Asi explained, as he led Ben toward the front door. "And, clearly, yours is not finished."

Ben wondered if he'd found a willing audience and was about to speak when al-Asi continued.

"I'm afraid I can do nothing further to assist you."

Ben continued outside alone, turning back toward al-Asi when he was halfway down the steps leading into the Palestinian Authority building.

"But you can tell me who really killed my father."

Al-Asi regarded him tentatively from the doorway. "Is that something you really want to know?"

"I wouldn't have asked if I didn't."

"You deserve that much," al-Asi nodded. "Unofficially, of course."

"Whatever you say."

"A young Fatah recruit was given the job. His name was Omar Shaath."

Ben felt himself quiver, understanding quite clearly now why his relationship with the commander had been doomed from the start.

"Thank you," he managed.

Al-Asi straightened his tie. "Save your thanks. Just send me a suit when you return to the States."

Ben drove back to the old police building and sat down at his desk, intending to find a way to contact Mayor Sumaya. Suddenly the phone rang. He snatched up the receiver, expecting Shaath to be on the other end.

"Hello."

But the voice that responded was not Shaath's at all. Ben started to feel queasy as he listened without comment, sinking into his chair. He was still holding the receiver against his ear well after the click signaled the connection had been broken.

The people behind all of this had Danielle!

His instructions were to proceed to a rendezvous point in Israel or she would be killed . . . and if he showed up, he would be killed too. He was out of his league here; they knew it and he knew it.

Ben gazed down the hall, ready to call desperately for al-Asi. But the major was gone and, in any event, had done everything he could do. Ben needed to find someone who could do more.

He pounded the switchhook until the dial tone returned, then dialed a number he had committed to memory just three days before.

"Yeah?" a craggy voice answered.

"I need your help, Colonel," said Ben.

CHAPTER 55

COLONEL FRANK BRICKLAND approached the checkpoint casually, as if the Israeli soldier glaring through the windshield was his own private guard.

"Keep cool, hoss. This is gonna be the easiest part of the day. Fun don't start until later."

In the backseat, Yousef Shifa shifted his huge bulk uneasily.

"And tell King Kong back there to relax."

"I speak English," the big man reminded him.

"Just making sure."

Their car snailed on, the soldier's outstretched hand signaling it to stop.

"They want to talk," Ben had told Brickland nearly two hours earlier when the colonel had picked him up outside the old police building. "They gave me a time and place to meet."

"And if you don't show, they'll kill her. I recognize

the scenario. No points for originality here.''

''Any suggestions?''

''Where's the rendezvous set?''

''The amphitheater in Caesarea.''

''Wise choice, one I might've made myself. Closed on three sides, the Mediterranean not too far off on the fourth. You must have earned their respect.''

''I don't find that very comforting.''

''Then try this: it's your lucky day, hoss. It's a good thing I stayed in town, after all.''

''What are you really doing here, Colonel?''

''Right now, saving your girlfriend's ass.''

''And what about for the last week?''

''Story about my son starting to wear a little thin, hoss?'' Brickland had asked with a smile.

''As tissue paper.''

''Surprised you bought it for as long as you did.''

''That was the gullible side of me.''

''And what's this?''

''The pissed-off side.''

''At me?''

''Depends on what brought you to Jericho.''

''A job,'' Brickland said succinctly, leaving it at that.

''You're after the second killer and whoever's behind him. Something like this is what you were hoping for all along. You used me—and Danielle—to flush them out for you, because you couldn't do it on your own.''

''Ouch.''

''Who are you working for on this, Colonel? Who's signing your checks?''

''Cash only in my business, hoss, and right now you'd be best off concerning yourself with what I can do for you at the same time I complete my assignment. You want your girlfriend back; I want who's got her. I'd say we got more going for us than most marriages.''

"You make it sound easy."

"Thing is, I'm the wild card in all this. We've got no reason to think they even know I'm here, never mind on your side."

"You're going to *help* me?"

"Been doing that all along, 'case you forgot. I'm the one came up with Fasil's fingerprints for you, started this whole game rolling. Looks like using you wasn't such a bad idea, after all."

"What are we going to do?"

"Everything I tell you, hoss, just like it was in a script. Third person would help the odds, if he's good."

"I've got someone in mind."

BRICKLAND HAD INDEED been impressed upon meeting Yousef Shifa, nodding his satisfaction at Shifa's size and obvious power.

"This is going to be dangerous," Ben warned, holding nothing back from the big man.

"That is not a problem."

"We may have to hurt some people," Brickland added tersely, without missing a beat.

Shifa's reply had been a smile stretched across his thick face. "That is not a problem either."

WHEN BRICKLAND'S CAR reached the checkpoint, the guard waved him through after only a cursory look at his papers and paid not even a second glance to his passengers.

"You're an amazing man, Colonel," Ben complimented.

"Well, hoss, shit travels a long way, but wherever it lands it smells the same. Now, let's go over your instructions again."

"Enter the amphitheater, keeping my hands in plain view, and wait for them to approach."

Brickland digested the information. "I figure there'll be two, maybe three snipers zeroed in on you the whole time. Another reason why they chose the amphitheater for a meet."

"That a problem?"

Brickland smirked. "Sure, for the snipers." He glanced in the backseat at Shifa. "So how'd the two of you meet up, hoss?"

"You wouldn't believe me if I told you."

"Try me."

Ben was halfway into the story of how he had found Shifa in the process of breaking up a restaurant, when Brickland began to chuckle and then laugh.

"What's so funny?" Ben wondered.

"You just gave me an idea."

CHAPTER 56

BEN ENTERED THE amphitheater in Caesarea as instructed, his hands in plain view. He checked his watch casually: fifteen minutes had passed since Brickland and Shifa had exited the car at the entrance to the parking lot on the chance that Danielle's captors had placed spotters in the area.

"Should I give you time to get into position?" Ben had asked the colonel.

"You won't have to. They'll keep you waiting, make you sweat a little, hope you get nervous."

"How will you know when—"

"Leave that to me and King Kong here," Brickland interrupted.

And this time Shifa smiled at the use of his new nickname.

Ben looked at the big man one last time. "You don't have to do this if you don't want to."

"Why not?" Shifa had said, smiling. "I've done it before."

"And when it's over, do you remember what to do?"

"Call the editor Jabral. Explain you've got a story to tell him if he helps me."

"Very good."

Ben replayed that exchange in his head and began pacing about the front of the amphitheater's circular stone floor. Black folding chairs had been laid out in neat rows before the stage, looking oddly out of place when compared to the ancient tiered seating that rimmed the theater in a semicircle. Especially considering that floor had once been the site of gladiator battles and lion fights.

The amphitheater was one of the showplaces of Caesarea, itself one of Israel's greatest archaelogical treasures. Comprised of wondrously restored ruins of the Crusader City, an aqueduct, and the remains of an ancient Jewish settlement, Caesarea sits on the shore of the Mediterranean. Ben could hear the waves from where he was standing, though view of the sea was partially blocked off by fortified walls that had once protected the residents.

He checked his watch again. Ten more minutes had passed. Ben couldn't resist gazing up at the stone seats that climbed toward light towers utilized for nighttime events, wondering where the snipers Brickland was expecting were posted. A quartet of exit portals were strategically placed amid the seating, leading down into the labyrinthine underbelly of the amphitheater. He couldn't see the touristy Via Maris restaurant from here, but knew Yousef Shifa would already be inside, waiting for Brickland's unspoken signal: a bullet through an out-of-the-way window, once the colonel had incapacitated the snipers.

Ben swung back toward the front at the sound of footsteps crunching gravel. Two groups of men approached from opposite sides of the theater, three in each. The group on the right was led by a big man who was holding Danielle leisurely at the elbow, like an old friend.

A chill passed through Ben, as the big man drew closer. He felt as if he were watching the ghost of al-Diib coming for him, then noticed the scar that looked like an exclamation point on the left side of the man's face when he stopped ten feet away, shoving Danielle even with the center of the stage between them.

"Pull your shirt out, hold it up, and turn around with your hands in the air," the big man who looked like the Wolf ordered. And Ben realized a number of the others were holding pistols now, low by their hips, concealed from any tourist who might happen by.

"What's it going to take for you to let the woman go?" Ben asked as he complied with his instructions.

"My orders are to deliver you both."

"To whom?"

"You'll see soon enough."

Danielle spoke, eyes darting between the big man and Ben. "Someone from the Israeli right wing, no doubt, who cares nothing for peace."

"It would be difficult to maintain the peace if you don't eliminate the butchers who are against it."

"I'm glad you believe in what you've done," Danielle snapped back sarcastically.

"We all believe."

"Pity Pakad Barnea and I cut your work short," Ben told him.

"We eliminated one of our primary targets and two members of his cell. We put a stop to Mohammed Fasil's reign of terror."

"Then why bother with us now?" Danielle wondered.

"Because you wouldn't drop it, neither of you."

"We've got our reasons. You may have stopped Fasil, but that doesn't mean you've stopped the operation he kept coming to Jericho to implement."

"That is not our concern."

"It should be," Ben said, knowing Brickland wasn't in position yet. "I think terrorists are about to purchase part of Russia's Cold War stockpile. We're not talking about rifles and bullets here; we're talking about *nuclear materials*. Huge sums of money have already been transferred. It's a done deal. All that's left is for Fasil to take delivery or arrange a pickup. I can prove it."

The big man didn't respond right away, which gave Ben time to study Danielle's response to his revelation. Initially it seemed she thought he was bluffing, but now a clear look of shock covered her features.

"You'll have to prove it to my superiors," the big man said suddenly.

"Bullshit!" Danielle blared. "You think I'm a fool? You think I don't know how operations like this work? We'll be killed as soon as you get us where we're going, maybe even en route. There aren't any 'superiors' waiting."

"Would you prefer we just kill you here?"

"It's as good as anyplace."

Ben watched the big man tense and realized his attention had strayed to a sudden rush of Israeli security personnel toward the Via Maris restaurant. Brickland must have given Yousef Shifa the signal! Ben could almost picture the big man inside breaking the place up, just as he had done on the morning Ben had first met him. Brickland's strategy was having precisely the effect the colonel had been counting on by drawing Israeli forces away from the amphitheater.

"Drop your weapons," Ben said suddenly.

The big man looked ready to laugh.

"This is your last chance," Ben added.

The big man was about to say something when the man on his immediate left collapsed, followed by the man on his right. Ben barreled into Danielle and took her to the rubble-strewn ground, aware now of the soft spits echoing faintly in the wind

The spits increased in frequency as the men twisted in toward the stone seating enclosing them, firing wildly. The Wolf's near twin had hit the ground and was crawling amid the black chairs, barking orders into a walkie-talkie, to his snipers no doubt. Ben could hear the fear creep into his voice when there was no reply, the snipers having been dispatched by Frank Brickland.

The other figures had scattered now, pistols clacking wildly and inefficiently, carving harmless chunks from the structure of the stone amphitheater.

"Let's go!" Ben said to Danielle, Brickland's covering fire slackening slightly as the colonel stayed on the move to keep the enemy from getting a fix on his position.

Ben and Danielle reached the stone seating and bounded up the tiers as bullets coughed stone and rubble around them. They darted into a portal poised over the lower section of seats, ducking when a shower of debris exploded just over their heads. Then they plunged into the cool darkness that made up the guts of the amphitheater and followed a spiraling ramplike path that wound downward. The floor leveled off and the feeling of being trapped in a maze struck them. The light dimmed, precious little able to sneak through the air holes and cracks in the structure.

They slowed at the sound of echoing footsteps. The confines made it impossible to tell where they were coming from. All they could do was continue along and hope they belonged to Brickland.

Danielle passed under the threshold leading into an inner lobby just ahead of Ben. She registered a flash of motion before something got hold of her head and slammed her against the wall. She felt like a rag doll, splayed against it, her grasp on the world lost as Abu Garib's near twin steadied his gun on Ben.

"It wasn't supposed to be this hard," the killer snarled, hesitating long enough to decide which of them to shoot first.

"I'll say," Ben heard a familiar voice say from behind him.

The big man spun, swinging his gun around.

God, he's fast, Ben thought.

But Frank Brickland was faster. He squeezed off six shots to a single one the big man fired errantly skyward. The bullets drove the Israeli backward and tumbled him onto the gravel floor, a cloud of yellow dirt and dust rising in his wake.

Brickland wedged the pistol back into his belt and looked from Danielle to Ben, shaking his head.

"What was that boy thinking . . ."

CHAPTER 57

THEY REACHED THE parking lot together, sprinting. Brickland took point, a fresh clip snapped into his rifle, switch turned to automatic now. Israeli troops, distracted for a time by Shifa's antics in the restaurant, converged upon them.

"Go! Go! Go!" Brickland ordered, swinging around to open fire on the troops as they reached the car.

His bullets were fired errantly, meant only to hold them back long enough to facilitate their escape.

Danielle lunged into the backseat, while Ben and the colonel hurled themselves into the front through a hail of bullets that dug pockmarks in the car's frame.

"*Stay down!*" Brickland ordered, the windows exploding around him.

He gunned the engine and screeched off, just as reinforcements tore into the parking lot. Brickland tore right past them, doing sixty by the time he hit the road and ninety just seconds after that. He didn't use the brakes until they hurtled into the parking lot of the Dan Caesarea Hotel several miles down the road.

Three minutes later they were on their way again in a stolen minivan, Brickland more relaxed now, at peace with the accelerator.

"You're working for Israel too, aren't you?" Danielle asked suddenly, her voice icily calm.

"I was until ten minutes ago, ma'am, tracking down some people who were out of control."

His final word made Danielle snap forward. Control . . . The unnamed man in Herschel Giott's office had used the same word, told her everything was under *control*, that she didn't have to worry. *Brickland* must have been what he was referring to.

"Who were those men back there working for?" Danielle asked.

"I don't know exactly, and I don't care. I doubt your government does either. They wanted things handled quietly. If they didn't mind noise, they could have hired someone else."

"What exactly *did* they know?"

"Not much more than you do now, ma'am. That's why I needed the two of you. If I had played this out in the open, it would have been a different game altogether. So I had hoss here front for me. Fed him just enough information to keep him where I wanted."

"Thanks," said Ben.

"Your girlfriend's bosses knew what was going on, but they didn't know all the principals involved or how to stop them. Didn't even know who they could trust, how deep it went."

"So they brought in someone from the outside," Danielle concluded. "A contractor."

"If I got paid by the body, I'd be a rich man by now, ma'am," Brickland told her, his eyes twinkling. "Thing is, hoss, if they couldn't find this group that went bad, I figured what chance did I have? So I came up with a plan."

"The investigation," from Ben.

"The two of us working together," Danielle picked up. "The joint effort."

"*Your* idea?"

"Mostly, hoss. They didn't pick you, I did." His eyes flicked a glance at Danielle. "And I picked the lady too. Last-minute decision."

"After what happened in Old Jaffa."

"Showed me you were my type of gal, ma'am, someone I could rely upon. What the hell, I figured the two of you together just might be able to pin bull's-eyes on my targets for me."

"In other words, you used us as bait."

"I was always watching your back, hoss, remember? Gave you a little boost, when I could, to keep you moving. Then, lo and behold, the two of you went and did it. Forced them out into the open, where I'd get my shots."

"So your assignment didn't include the ones who actually did the planning," Danielle concluded.

"People who hired me just wanted the whole mess stopped and everyone who was in the know removed from the scene."

Ben and Danielle looked at each other.

Brickland laughed. "Relax, people; if I wanted the two of you dead you'd be back in the amphitheater with the rest of them. I can still think for myself and the truth is, shit, I like you. Another goddamn American who doesn't belong in this fucked-up part of the world any more than I do. I did my job.'' He cocked a brief gaze at Danielle. ''Your bosses ain't happy; maybe I'll just go after them instead.'' A chilling smile crossed his features. ''I don't think they'd be happy about that.''

''What about us now?'' Danielle asked.

''I kept you alive. That's the best I can do. Benny, here, being the smart man that he is, should head on home. You, getting along with him like you do, should go with him.''

''It's not over,'' Ben said stridently. ''Listen to me! Fasil had *closed* a deal with the Russians. They'd already been paid and he was waiting for delivery.''

''Delivery of what, hoss?''

Ben gazed at Danielle and swallowed hard before answering. ''Nuclear weapons: what else could it be? Tens of millions of dollars had changed hands, the transactions completed those two nights, two weeks apart, that Fasil had spent in Israel—the same times he visited Jericho.''

''Russians,'' Danielle echoed, remembering the gun fight in Old Jaffa in what felt like another lifetime, realizing. ''He stayed in Israel because he had to meet his Russian contacts. . . .''

''But Fasil was also making lots of trips to New York City,'' Ben reminded.

''His stays in Israel are still the key,'' she insisted.

''Key to what, ma'am?'' asked Brickland.

''How we can find out when he planned on picking up his merchandise.''

DANIELLE EXPLAINED HERSELF as Brickland drove on toward Tel Aviv.

"The day I received this assignment, there was a gun fight in Old Jaffa."

"We got to work on your aim a little, ma'am," the colonel said lightly.

"An Arab-Israeli smuggler was about to send his latest shipment into the West Bank and Shin Bet was finally ready to nail him," Danielle continued. "Trouble is, somebody beat us to it: Russians. How do I know? Because one of them called me *suka*, a bitch in that language."

"I'll kill him," promised Brickland.

"I already did. Now Ismael Atturi—the smuggler— was mostly small-time, but this shipment turned out to be machine guns, lots of them. He was trying to move up a notch, and somebody took offense at that."

"The Russians," Ben concluded.

"Because they must see guns as their territory. This is the Russian underworld we're talking about, and apparently they've set up shop in Israel, specifically Old Jaffa."

"They're Fasil's contacts!"

"The middlemen between him and the Russians he was dealing with in New York City."

"And that means they *must* know what Fasil had purchased, Pakad."

"Along with when and where he was going to pick it up."

They both looked to Brickland at the same time.

"Are you with us, Colonel?" Ben asked.

Brickland's stare remained noncommittal, the road ahead all that mattered. "I'll drive you to Jaffa and watch your backs. What the hell, it's on the way to the airport anyway."

CHAPTER 58

BRICKLAND PARKED OUTSIDE the flea market and Danielle led the way in, following her nose. The area never seemed to change, the same merchants from last week assaulting her again with claims of bargains and one-of-a-kind items.

She led Ben and Frank Brickland into the heart of the market and walked casually toward the row of warehouse shops across from its busiest section. The deadly street battle from seven days before had led to the posting of more soldiers, and she did her best to avoid them on the chance they had been warned to expect her.

Ben and Brickland made sure to walk on either side of Danielle, offering as much cover as they could while she tried to identify all the shops they passed that were operated by Russian immigrants. One of these shops, she was certain, would be owned by the middleman between Fasil and the Russian criminals in

New York City he had been dealing with.

Danielle was able to rule some of the shops out by the appearance of the proprietors, others by the merchandise available, and still more by the clear intonations of native Hebrew. It took several passes up and down the street before she positively identified a cluster of three warehouse-style shops as being Russian-operated.

"It's one of those, but I can't tell which one," she reported to Ben and Brickland, after signaling them to follow her further up Jaffa Street.

"That shop selling stoves one of the three you're talking about?" Brickland asked her.

She looked at him, surprised. "Yes. How did you know?"

"Only shop with a pair of guards in the upstairs windows keeping a very keen eye on potential patrons. Where I come from, not very good for business." Brickland's eyes stayed rooted on Danielle. "You think you and your boyfriend can handle things downstairs?"

"Just fine," she replied.

"Give me a few minutes," Brickland told them. "Say about five. Then head in." He paused. "I'll make sure you're not disturbed."

BEN AND DANIELLE waited five minutes, wandering around like distracted tourists, then entered the warehouse that was packed with ancient, rusting stoves. Their entry coincided with a lull in business, and they found themselves the only potential customers inside the shop. The sharp scents of fresh fish and falafel grilling sifted in from the outside

"May I help you?" a man with a flabby stomach asked them.

"We're looking for a stove, but a newer one, something in better condition, anyway," Danielle said to him.

"You mean one that works," the man smiled and flapped a hand at them. "This way. My private stock."

He steered them through a thick curtain into a smaller room in the rear. At first glance the merchandise didn't look any newer or better than the stoves showcased in the front.

"Ah, but these are powered by propane," he boasted, sensing their reaction. "Less to break down. Much longer lifespan. And it's been a lousy week, so I'll make you a good deal."

"A friend recommended you to us," Danielle told him.

"Really? Who?"

"Mohammed Fasil."

The man's eyes wavered and he started to backpedal for the curtain. Ben blocked his path.

"I would advise against this," the Russian threatened. "I'm not alone here."

"Yes, you are," Danielle said coldly. "We gave your men upstairs the rest of the afternoon off."

"Are you from the police? The army? Because if you are, I am used to dealing with your kind. You forget I'm from Russia. I came here to escape people like you."

"We're not from the police or the army," said Danielle, "but you may wish we were before this is finished." She advanced toward the man. "You see, we are not accountable for what we do. There are people who want us dead and we have already killed to stay alive. It wouldn't bother us terribly to kill again."

The man had backed up as far as he could, his lower back pressed up against one of his propane stoves. Danielle's advance mirrored his every step, threatening in its deliberateness.

"I know Fasil! All right? I know him! He came here looking to be set up with some contacts I have in America. I put him together with them and that is all. I *swear,* that is *all*!"

"You're a salesman, of course."

"Yes."

"I'll bet you're very good."

The man nodded, no idea obviously where Danielle was going with this. "In Russia, I was known as—"

"A salesman knows his customers better than that, no matter what product he is brokering. I'm sure you know more about Fasil than you're telling us now. But you will tell us. Believe me, you will."

Danielle smiled almost seductively and eased an arm around his shoulder. Faster than Ben's eyes could record, she thrust him downward and slammed a knee into his stomach. The man gasped, slumping, halfway to the floor when Danielle grabbed his hand and jerked it over one of the burners.

Ben heard a hissing sound and then saw the flames shoot up with a soft *poooooof*, as she worked one of the propane stove's control knobs.

"You're right," Danielle said, holding the man's hand just a few inches above the flames. "This one does work."

"Please," the man rasped.

"Tell me about Mohammed Fasil." She turned the

knob ever so slightly, just enough to make the tips of the flames lick the Russian's palm.

"All right! All right!"

She brought his hand up a little and waited for him to continue.

"The men I set Fasil up with . . . horrible bastards. They'd kill their mothers if it was good for business. Hell, they *have* killed their mothers."

"Get to the point!"

"They deal in major contraband, like guns."

"What about strategic weapons?"

"You mean . . ."

"*Nuclear* weapons."

The Russian nodded slowly, eyes glued to his hand. "If anyone does, it is them."

Danielle stole a glance back at Ben. "You're saying you don't know what he purchased from them."

"No, I swear I don't! My hand, please, it's starting to hurt."

"Get used to it."

"New York City! It was all handled on their end. I made the initial contact, played middleman when the payments were collected. That's all!"

"It didn't bother you, *a Jew*, that you were helping a terrorist?"

"I spent the better part of my life choosing sides, trying to do the right thing; I came here to do business."

Danielle's fingers tightened over the knob. "I think I'm going to burn your hand now."

"No! I told you what you wanted to know!"

"Tell me everything else. Now."

"There's not much more to say. Fasil was going to return to New York to make the pickup."

"Himself?"

"Unless something went wrong."

"In which case . . ."

"A surrogate would take his place."

"Then how did he handle the arrangements?"

"A meeting was set—I don't know where, just that it was in New York City. Fasil—or whoever came in his place—would be bringing something that would identify him as the buyer so the transfer could go forth."

"*What* would he be bringing?" Ben asked suddenly, bursting forward from the curtained entryway.

"I never knew, never asked. Something unusual and unmistakable, that's for sure. Something unique."

"Simple as that?" Danielle resumed, as Ben backed off again.

"My countrymen in America already had their money. What did they care?"

"Then what kept them from keeping the money and just not showing? It seems too easy."

"That's a question I never asked. I don't know the answer."

"And you don't know when this delivery was supposed to take place."

"Only that it was going to be soon. Very soon."

"Before the peace talks reconvene?" Danielle demanded. "Before Wednesday?"

When the Russian refused to answer, she twisted the knob and the flames shot upward, singeing his palm. He screamed and she turned it down again, as Ben caught the stench of burned flesh in the air.

"*Answer me!*"

"Yes, yes!" the Russian managed between winces. "That's *two days* from now!"

"I'm telling you the truth!"

Danielle let go of him and turned off the burner. The Russian sank to the floor with his back against the stove, cradling his burned hand against his stomach and whimpering. She started back through the curtain, but Ben followed slowly, distracted.

"What is it?" she asked when they were again in the main body of the warehouse.

Ben waited until they passed a pair of browsing customers. "What's the date tomorrow?"

"September 30."

"1997."

"Why?"

He fished through his pockets and brought out the crinkled piece of paper Danielle recognized as having come from Mohammed Fasil's hotel room at the Tel Aviv Hilton:

>Max Peacock
>1100 AMsterdam Avenue
>New York, NY 93097

"Look at the zip code. The cop in New York I asked to check out the address told me to look in California. Now I see. It's not a zip code; it's *a date*. Tomorrow's date."

"Then the rest of it . . ."

"He also told me that there's no number eleven hundred Amsterdam Avenue. But notice how the A and M are capitalized?"

"AM . . . as in *morning*?"

"*Eleven o'clock* in the morning," Ben continued, nodding.

"So Fasil was going to meet someone named Max

Peacock at eleven o'clock in the morning tomorrow in New York City.''

"No," Ben corrected her, "*someone* was going to meet Max Peacock. Either Fasil or a surrogate.''

"Carrying something that would identify them.''

"Exactly.''

"Then if we can find this Max Peacock, we can be there waiting.''

"Problem there. My detective friend also informed me there is no such person in New York City.''

"There's got to be.''

"But if my friend couldn't find him, what chance do we stand of faring any better in the next twenty-four hours?''

"Even if we get lucky," Danielle said, "we don't have whatever the courier was supposed to bring to identify himself to the Russians.''

"Not yet," Ben told her.

CHAPTER 59

I HAD IT in my hands, right in my hands. . . .
Ben had been torturing himself with that thought
ever since the shopkeeper's revelation of how the Russian conduits were to identify Fasil or his surrogate.
Dalia had told him as much in her letter, given him
all the clues he needed without coming out and telling
him. It was just like her.

The Buddha chest!

To have explained the truth about the chest in detail
would have been to invite Ben to take Fasil's place at
the meeting with Max Peacock in New York City. She
would never have endangered him so directly; instead,
she chose to give him the information he needed only
if he came looking for it specifically.

*It was Fasil who brought me the Buddha chest. He
asked me to hold it for him and when he was no longer*

in a position to come back for it, I appropriated the chest for my collection.

The intent of the words, so thinly veiled, seemed obvious now.

"You're going *where*?" Brickland asked incredulously when the three of them rendezvoused back on the street.

"Back to Jericho," Ben told him.

"*Both* of you?"

"I know the ways terrorists and smugglers have managed to enter Israel through the West Bank," said Danielle. "He needs me to show him."

"You're both frigging nuts, you know that?"

"We aren't asking you to come," said Danielle.

"You've done more than enough already," added Ben.

"What chance you think you got to pull this off?" Brickland challenged them.

"What chance will this region have, if Fasil's people take delivery from the Russians of the means to destroy Israel?" Ben shot right back.

Brickland smirked, then chuckled. "We're two of a kind, hoss. Know why? 'Cause neither of us knows when to quit. Let's get ourselves a new car," he told them both, "and hit the road."

TRUE TO DANIELLE'S word, the roundabout, time-consuming route got them into the West Bank without incident. Ben was more worried about the area around Dalia Mikhail townhouse. Would Shaath have ordered a stakeout surrounding it on the chance he'd return there? It was possible, but Ben's lesson plan had never gotten to stakeouts and he sincerely doubted Shaath was capable of executing a proper one.

Still, he warned Brickland to be wary as they crossed through Jericho. The colonel navigated the streets slowly and parked a block away from Dalia's villa, insisting that he check the area himself on foot before letting them proceed.

Brickland climbed back into the driver's seat ten minutes later. "No cops. Nobody waiting in the apartment or outside it."

Ben and Danielle breathed twin signs of relief. They walked back to the villa accompanied by Brickland, Ben planning to use his police key on the padlock as he had before.

But the padlock was gone, the hasp half torn off and the door shattered in the area of the latch. Ben's heart sank. He had feared a break-in when he visited Dalia's earlier that day. Now that fear had been realized.

"You two go on inside," Brickland instructed. "I'll hang here in case any visitors show up."

Ben nodded and led Danielle through the door.

Inside, the villa was a shambles, the contents of drawers and cases strewn all over the floor. Some of the smaller pieces of furniture were missing. The walls had been stripped bare of their artwork and Dalia's pedestals stood with nothing atop them. Her computer was gone and her big-screen television lay on its back halfway across the living room floor, as if the thieves had abandoned the effort after realizing how heavy it was.

The armoire, though, stood miraculously untouched, by good fortune the last piece the crooks would have reached. Feeling more confident, Ben popped the latch and eased the double doors open.

The Buddha chest was gone.

HE STOOD THERE staring for what seemed a very long time, hoping he had returned it to a different shelf and that he just wasn't looking in the right place. But the chest didn't reappear.

"The thieves?" Danielle asked, suddenly by his side.

Ben shook his head. "It wasn't even that valuable. And why would they take it and ignore the rest of the valuables inside? No, one of Fasil's people came here and took it. They messed up the rest to throw off the police, or anyone else who came looking."

Frank Brickland entered the townhouse, leaving the door open behind him. "We've been here too long, hoss."

But Ben wasn't quite ready to leave. "Fasil's replacement will take the chest to New York, to the meeting," he told Danielle. "Take delivery from the Russians of whatever Fasil purchased. I guess we should be grateful."

"Why, for God's sake?" Danielle wondered.

Ben resealed the doors and popped the latch back into place as Brickland began to shift about impatiently. "Because if it had been thieves we'd be totally out of luck. Now at least we know where it's going."

"To a man who doesn't exist," Danielle reminded.

"I'm going to New York," Ben insisted staunchly. "And, whatever it takes, I'm going to find Max Peacock."

The colonel stopped and burst out laughing. "Max

Peacock? *That's* the guy you've been talking about?
The guy your cop friend in New York *can't find*?''

"Yes," Ben said, befuddled.

"Ever been to New York City, Benny?"

"Yes."

"Obviously you didn't see all the sights."

"What do you mean?"

"Max Peacock isn't a *person,* it's a *place!*"

S TRIP BAR OFF Forty-second Street I've
dropped my share of Franklins in,'' Brickland continued after the shock had worn off. "But you'd better
get moving if you expect to get there by eleven a.m.
tomorrow.''

Neither of them moved.

"We need you, Colonel," said Danielle.

He shook his head. "Sorry, ma'am. I've done too
much already, mixed in where I didn't belong. I *in-
terfered.* In my business, that's the only thing you
don't do.''

"Then let us hire you," Ben proposed.

Brickland shot a scathing frown his way. "*Hire* me?
Put both your next year's salaries together and it
wouldn't touch my price.'' He looked at the two of
them standing there utterly crestfallen, and shrugged.
"Oh what the hell, I was gonna fly home through New
York anyway. . . .''

DAY NINE

CHAPTER 60

Max Peacock's was located on Eighth Avenue just around the corner from Forty-second Street. Ben and Danielle had the cab driver leave them off slightly down the block just after ten o'clock Tuesday morning. Brickland had promised he'd be there to meet them before the eleven a.m. meeting time, and take things from there.

Gaining seven hours in the flight west was the only thing that saved them after a grueling eighteen-hour journey that began outside Dalia Mikhail's villa the day before. They drove to Haifa, where Danielle secured passage for the three of them on board a Turkish freighter en route to Egypt's port city of Alexandria. From there, a taxi brought them to Cairo, where one of Brickland's contacts was waiting with passports and tickets on a plane bound for Kennedy Airport in New York.

"I'll put it on your bill," the colonel had quipped.

Once they had landed and made it through Customs, the colonel sent them on to Max Peacock's alone while he went to round up some reinforcements, promising to be at Max Peacock's no later than 10:45. Ben and Danielle could do nothing but wait for him, keeping the strip bar in sight as best they could while walking up and down the street to avoid attracting attention.

When 10:45 came, fifteen minutes to go before the scheduled delivery of whatever Mohammed Fasil had paid twenty million dollars of Iranian money for, there was still no sign of Brickland.

"Something's wrong," Ben said suddenly as they stood directly across the street from Max Peacock's. "He's not coming."

"Then we'll have to follow his plan on our own."

Before Ben could respond, a bearded man wearing aviator sunglasses approached the entrance to Max Peacock's. He stopped to study the street carefully, then headed through the door.

"That's Fasil's surrogate," Ben said, recognizing the man not so much from his appearance as from the bulky tote bag he carried in his hand, easily large enough to accommodate Dalia's Buddha chest.

Danielle could see Ben's mind working as he scrutinized the area around Max Peacock's, then checked his watch.

"I'm going in," he said suddenly.

"You're *what*?"

Ben's eyes were still on the door. "That man must be the one taking Fasil's place. I'm going to take *his* place."

*   *   *

IT WAS 10:50 when Ben entered Max Peacock's in search of the man who had preceded him through the smoky, artificial air. The room was comfortably cool, thanks to an air conditioner he could hear rattling through the ductwork. A trio of theatrical stages featured dancers at various stages of disrobing. And in the center of it all, a breakfast buffet had been set up. Above the table, hanging from the ceiling, he saw the sign:

LEGS and EGGS!

A novel idea, Ben thought, making his way past the first stage where a dancer in cowboy garb, leather chaps glued to her thighs and buttocks had looped a lariat around the neck of a patron flashing a twenty-dollar bill, trying to reel him in. The second and third stages were on opposite sides of the room, the third very near the larger of Max Peacock's two bars. Beyond the second stage were tables featuring dancers giving performances for individual patrons. The man who had just entered sat alone back by the wall, the tote bag that Ben surmised held Dalia's Buddha chest tucked into his lap.

Ben's watch read 10:52. He steadied himself, took a deep breath, and weaved his way through the naked table dancers, who paid no attention to him whatsoever.

Approaching the man's table, he noted his strong Arabic features and felt somewhat reassured. Ben reached the table and watched the man bring the tote bag from the floor into his lap.

"There's been a change in plans," Ben said.

The Arab looked unsure. "Who are you? I don't know you!"

"But I know *you*. And I don't sound like a Russian, do I? What does that make me? Come on! If I knew where to find you, what does that tell you about me? Stand up and walk out of here with me." When the man continued to hesitate, Ben threw just enough desperation into his voice. "Hurry! Before it's too late!"

The man rose, tote bag in hand, and fell in behind Ben, his eyes darting nervously in all directions. No one paid any attention to them, the eyes of all those in Max Peacock's having other sights to hold their attention.

Instead of retracing his steps through the main body of the bar, Ben led the Arab through a nearby exit door that spilled out into an alley.

"Now what is this—"

Ben grabbed the man's head and shoved it against the building's brick exterior. Dazed, the Arab nonetheless managed to lash a quick backhand across Ben's face. Ben still had firm hold of the man's hair and jerked his head sideways. It cracked into the brick again, stunning him, and when he tried to pull free, Ben slammed him against the wall face-first this time. He was certain he heard something crunch, but the man continued to resist, so Ben jammed his face forward a fourth time. This time the man went limp and crumpled. Ben dragged the inert form behind the Dumpster, then grabbed the tote bag off the ground where it had fallen and rushed back through the side door.

* * *

WHEN BEN UNZIPPED the tote bag, he saw instantly that his hunch was correct: Dalia's Chinese Buddha chest was inside. He rested it on the same table at which the Arab had been sitting. He tried to scan the room for his potential contact, but the presence of naked dancers churning about at nearly all the tables in front of him blocked his view.

Suddenly he made out a quartet of beefy figures approaching through the washed-out, smoky haze. They curled around the tables featuring the dancers, moving with the cocky swagger of men used to getting their own way.

Ben's watch read 11:00 exactly.

The burly one in the center, built like a barrel, caught sight of the heirloom in front of Ben and steered the other hulks toward him. The four men reached his table and enclosed it in a semicircle. Ben could see nothing over them but the smoke rising.

"You're right on time," greeted the one in the center, his English burdened by a thick Russian accent.

"So are you."

"Haven't I been reliable from the start?" The Russian's voice took on a dangerous edge. "But you wouldn't know, would you?, because we've never met. Where is my friend Fasil?"

Ben realized the man was quite short, more stocky than muscular. His self-confidence came from the three hulking, muscular bodyguards who watched Ben's every move.

He stroked the top of the Buddha chest. "You were told someone would come to take delivery of the merchandise, not necessarily Fasil."

"My friend Fasil say he come himself, unless something go wrong."

"It did: he's dead."

The thick-bodied Russian looked genuinely shocked. "No."

"And you knew it. Please don't play stupid with me. It might make me think you intend to break our arrangement."

"I break *nothing!*" the Russian raged. "I keep terms. I am *honorable!*"

"Prove it."

"I have your deposit already. You think I would cheat you, cut out on a deal promising a rich future for *both of us*? What would I gain? I need you, you need me. We *partners!*"

Partners? Ben thought. *What was going on here?*

"You were partners with Fasil, not me. Everything's changed."

The Russian's eyes narrowed. Ben thought he might be growling under his breath. "You want new deal? You want money back? That it?"

"Not at all. I only want what we paid for."

The Russian settled his bulk into the chair immediately across from Ben's. It creaked under the strain. "Then what's changed? Deal the same. Terms the same." He threw a wink across the table. "Future the same for both of us and our people. We make a lot of people rich, eh, my new friend? Make enough for you to buy whatever you want for your people. Buy them power, whatever."

Ben tried to keep his thoughts collected and his demeanor calm, but his mind was racing. He had come to Max Peacock's expecting to pick up the merchandise Fasil had purchased. Obviously, though, the deal the terrorist had struck with the Russian underworld was considerably more complicated than that. He had

o keep probing, find out exactly what was going on
here.

"Time is a factor," he tried.

"We keep to schedule already agreed upon," the
Russian told him. "Ship loaded. Leave port today as
promised. You have goods in three weeks." He smiled
reverently. "What a sight, my new friend. I take you
there now. You must see."

"Of course."

The Russian's gaze moved toward the Buddha
chest, which apparently hid more secrets than even
Dalia Mikhail had realized. "Can I see?"

Ben slid it absently his way. The Russian inspected
it lovingly, opened and closed its thin doors several
times. "I keep?"

"Consider it a gift."

The Russian thanked him profusely, then said, "For
my wife. My wife will love it. You know, we going
to make history together, my new friend." And he
stuck out a beefy hand warmly. "I am Krechensky,
Vladimir Krechensky. Call me Vlad. Is good doing
business with you."

"Kamal. Call me Ben."

"An American name . . ."

"I lived here for a while before going back home,"
Ben said.

"Is good country. I find I don't miss home at all."

"You're lucky."

"In my old country you can only go so far. I hear
the stories of us taking over, making billions, trying
to run things. Ha! There's *nothing* to run. So I come
here. Don't have to run something to have power. Here
a man can be anything he wants. You agree?"

"If I didn't, I probably wouldn't be here."

Krechensky sat back, the chair creaking again, and uttered a contented sigh. "This is wonderful country, I tell you that much." He stood up. "What do you say, my new friend? Let's go down and see the ship off."

DANIELLE HAD TO keep fighting back the fierce temptation to enter Max Peacock's when Ben had not reemerged by 11:20. All sorts of terrible scenarios entered her mind. What if the surrogate he went in to replace had gotten the better of him? What if the four men she had watched enter—the Russians he was expecting, certainly—had uncovered Ben's true identity? There were unquestionably more exits and very likely private rooms inside the bar where they could be interrogating Ben now, torturing or even killing him.

Only the awareness of what an anomaly a fully clothed woman in such a bar would be had kept her from entering so far; that and the sure knowledge Ben would need her when and if he emerged. Her patience had nearly reached its limit when the front door burst open and Ben exited in the company of the four huge Russians she had watched go inside just a few minutes before. He and the stockiest of the four trailed slightly behind the human wall formed by the other three. The stocky Russian was smiling and laughing, slapping Ben on the back as they moved toward a black Lincoln Town Car. Ben was laughing too. But Danielle could tell the gesture was forced. He looked very uncomfortable, not gazing her way even once as the group led him to the Town Car.

She felt certain he wasn't a prisoner. Clearly,

though, they were taking him somewhere, perhaps to where the real delivery was to take place.

Danielle watched the three hulks squeeze into the backseat. She could see their shoulders pressed right up against each other even through the window. Ben climbed into the front seat between the driver and the stocky Russian.

She stepped out to hail a cab as soon as the black car pulled away from the curb. An agonizing minute followed in which there were none to be had, and she began to fear the Town Car and Ben would both be lost to her.

Finally Danielle saw a taxi come to a halt just before her. She had started toward it when the back door was thrust open and a familiar face peered up at her.

"Get in," said Frank Brickland. "We got problems."

CHAPTER 61

"YOU ARE PREPARED to handle distribution?" the Russian asked as the Town Car threaded its way west along Forty-second Street.

Ben hesitated before answering. He didn't dare say too much or too little.

"Everything is in place," he ventured noncommittally.

That seemed enough for the Russian. "There will be problems at first, kinks to work out—there always are. You are new at this sort of game, you must remember."

Ben waited, as the Town Car turned onto the West Side Highway. "We're fast learners."

"Just make sure you learn how to count money, because it will be coming in faster than you can imagine."

*   *   *

SEEMS LIKE YOUR Israeli friends didn't like me voiding the terms of my contract,'' Brickland said after their taxi turned onto the West Side Highway after the Town Car. "I go looking for some people to help us finish this mess and—wouldn't you know it?—I find people are looking for *me*. I'm shut out.''

"What's that mean?"

"In the short term, it means we got no backup and two whole pistols for firepower. In the long term, it means, even if the three of us can pull this off by ourselves, home for you won't exist anymore. You went against them. You broke the rules, maybe the only rule.''

Danielle had tried not to think of that before, but she knew Brickland was right: she had gone too far, stepped over a line that would cause her to face the consequences if she was lucky to live that long.

Suddenly the winding road ahead seemed like a tunnel in which she was trapped. Her entire life, everything she had worked for, might well be gone, stripped from her. Her father had sensed the risks from the beginning, had warned her in the broken language of his keyboard.

DON'T TRUST THEM.

The sadness had been so profound in his eyes during her last visit, she thought because he feared the imminence of his own death. Now she realized the sadness he felt came from the fear that he would never see her again.

"Jesus Christ," Brickland said suddenly, when the Town Car turned east, heading toward the Brooklyn Bridge.

*   *   *

THE TOWN CAR surged into Brooklyn with a thump that jostled Ben against Krechensky and the driver. The driver muttered something in Russian and continued onto the Brooklyn-Queens Expressway. He stayed in the right-hand lane and kept his speed down, a signal to Ben that they were getting close to wherever they were going. He gazed to his right at the East River and then the Buttermilk Channel, which ran between Brooklyn and Governors Island, past a succession of piers. Freighters waited patiently against the concrete berths, either on- or off-loading their cargos.

Ben felt his heart begin to hammer even faster against his ribs, sensing they were almost at their destination. The Town Car slowed to a crawl at a sign reading "Port of New York Authority Piers," and eased off the expressway where the Hudson River joined with Upper Gravesend Bay. He could see the piers more clearly now, as well as the freighters rising over the scene with their sterns facing him.

The Town Car pulled to a halt between the pair of concrete storage sheds outfitted with what looked a dozen garage-style doors on their left sides closest to the mooring slips.

"Here we are," Krechensky said, thrusting a meaty arm across Ben's chest to indicate a massive freighter moored diagonally across from them. "See it?"

Ben could see only its stern bobbing slightly atop the water. "Yes."

"Come. We go inside," Krechensky said, urging Ben out excitedly.

Ben climbed from the front seat of the car at the same time the three hulks emerged from the back.

"I will show you a sight you remember forever,

h?'' the bearlike Krechensky promised, and led the
way through the shed's open front end.

It was like stepping into a huge, tunnel-like bunker.
Lamps dangling from the ceiling did little to break the
darkness splintered by shafts of light spraying in
through the open bay doors. The shed held heat like
an oven and the result was stifling temperatures even
though the hottest part of the day was yet to come.
Krechensky led Ben on a weaving trail through neatly
stacked, innocuous-looking cargo, until they reached
the final third of the structure, where another pair of
his men stood guard ominously.

The men smiled as Krechensky's entourage swept
past them into the light cast through four open garage-
type doors. The section of the shed beyond was two-
thirds empty, drawing loud echoes from their heels
clacking against the cement floor. Outside, the moored
freighter was taking on what must have been the last
of its shipment. Forklifts and loaders adroitly negotiated the narrow confines of the cluttered loading shed,
handling sharp turns and narrow-miss collisions without a loss of speed or cargo.

The cargo . . .

Bags and bags of what looked to Ben like lawn
fertilizer were being packed into one of those trailer-
sized containers prior to each container's being lowered into one of the freighter's cargo holds.

"We reserve second ship to handle the overflow
still in shed," Krechensky explained to him, referring
to the bags remaining in neatly stacked rows. "Second
freighter has same name, same Algerian registry as
first, same serial numbers. No one know any different.
It set sail in five days. Once at sea, no one ever know
your freighter existed."

My freighter, Ben thought, meaning Fasil' freighter—*Hamas*'s freighter.

They headed along the length of the berth past the open doors. Krechensky swung left at the last one, into the sunshine, where the rusted ship was taking on it cargo. Ben could see crewmen frantic with final preparations to make the freighter ready to sail. Departure looked to be only minutes away.

Still, a pair of heavy cargo forklifts carrying the last bags of the load slid forward toward the ship. They stopped just outside the door next to a tall, thin man holding a clipboard. Krechensky left Ben long enough to move toward him, listened briefly, then issued some instructions.

"The freighter is packed solid," he said, returning to Ben's side. "No sense wasting another container or such a small amount, eh? We will load these bags somewhere safe on the second freighter."

Krechensky had stopped between the two packed forklifts and stroked one of the remaining fertilizer bags almost lovingly.

"A wonderful sight," he said, starting to tear into the bag with a beefy hand. "It is good to make history, eh, my new friend?"

The bag gave way in a jagged tear, allowing Krechensky to plunge his hand inside, emerging with a palmful of a fine white powder Ben recognized instantly. He tried not to show any surprise.

It was pure, uncut cocaine!

"The biggest shipment of drugs the world has ever seen," the Russian continued, smiling broadly and tapping his chest with his free hand. "And it is ours."

CHAPTER 62

HOW MUCH EXACTLY?'' Ben dared to ask.

''Fifty tons, mostly cocaine, like this,'' Krechensky said, spooning it through his palm. ''The rest heroin.'' Then, with a twinkle in his eyes, he added, ''I got a good buy.''

Ben tried his best to smile back at the Russian, wasn't sure if he managed it. His head grew light and he felt almost dreamy. The huge freighter undulated against the pier and blew its horn mightily to announce its coming departure, assaulting Ben's ears and snapping him alert.

He was looking at the unthinkable! Palestinian terrorists entering into a drug distribution deal with a Russian underworld that was already allied with powerful drug cartels out of Colombia. An unholy trinity if ever there was one, in an arrangement that made a twisted kind of sense from the terrorists' perspective.

After all, with the gradual progress of peace through the Middle East, most of the primary sources of funding for militant groups had evaporated. Without money, they could not adequately train their guerrillas, could not equip them properly, and, even more, could not expand their numbers through campaigns of propaganda and intimidation. To succeed took considerable funds.

The marketing of drugs through the region would ensure a steady stream of those funds, guaranteeing a perpetuation of terror for generations to come. The contents of this freighter could keep real peace away forever. The violence would be incredible, unprecedented.

Hamas would have what they wanted.

"What's it mean," Krechensky wondered, *"Muna Zarifa?"*

Ben followed the Russian's gaze to the freighter's name printed in tall, peeling letters across its bow. *"Muna* is a woman's name. *Zarifa* means beautiful."

"Oh," from Krechensky. "What you say we go on board and see something *really* beautiful?"

BRICKLAND HAD THE cab drop Danielle and him off just past the spot between the twin piers where the Town Car had parked illegally. They loitered, pretending to watch the sea, until all six figures, including the driver and Ben, had disappeared inside the concrete loading shed.

Brickland moved out ahead of Danielle, slid past the Town Car, and then stopped casually at its trunk.

"The release is just under the steering wheel. Pop it for me," he directed.

The door and windows had all been left open. She simply reached in and pressed the button. Danielle heard a soft click and turned to see Brickland raising the lid. When she joined him at the rear, he was already yanking the black carpet lining away to expose a hidden compartment.

"Just like I figured," he said, reaching in to make his choice from the cache of weapons revealed. "Fucking Russian scum think they own this city, do anything they please." He slid a submachine gun, a twelve-gauge shotgun, and a nine-millimeter pistol up to the trunk's sill, concealed for the time being. "Good thing for us."

He moved aside, turning his back to the car so he could keep watch.

"Your turn," he told Danielle. "Take your pick."

THE TUGBOAT THAT would guide the *Muna Zarifa* south out into the open waters had just squeezed against its starboard side when Krechensky began Ben's tour of the freighter, dodging a massive crane at the outset. He seemed especially proud of the fact that the cargo holds containing the drugs were actually hidden discreetly behind false walls in the legitimate holds, brilliantly camouflaged to look like the inner hull right down to the proper angle. On the chance the *Muna Zarifa* was boarded at sea or subjected to a surprise inspection in port, the secret bays would survive even the closest scrutiny.

Ben had never been on board a ship this large before; the slippery decks seeming to stretch forever. The freighter boasted not only an Algierian charter but also a crew composed almost entirely of Arabs. He wondered if these crew members had any idea how much the contents of their ship could change their world, perhaps even eventually destroy it. Not only would these drugs provide an infinite supply of funds to promote murder, mayhem, and destruction, but also they would be a means by which the terrorist leaders could better control the people they claimed to represent. They no doubt intended to turn them into *addicts*, dependent on the Hamas network for their drugs. As a man, Ben was sickened. As a Palestinian, he was enraged.

He was careful to hang on Krechensky's every word, wanting to be able to provide as complete a description as possible to the Coast Guard. He had no plans to do anything foolish or rash, considering himself lucky indeed to have made it this far without incident.

The *Muna Zarifa*'s horn blew loudly again, three quick blasts signaling the crew to make ready for the tow.

"I guess we'd better be going," Ben said to Krechensky as they reached the entrance to one of the hidden holds.

"No rush. Still plenty of time," the Russian replied, feeling the wall for the secret door. One of his behemoths had to come forward with a flashlight to help him find it. "You must see this first."

He located the door and pushed. The steel parted effortlessly, and Krechensky led the way in, ducking through. Ben followed.

"We should have done business before," the Russian said happily. "We may have different agendas, but together we can accomplish far more than alone. A few more deals like this, we bring more like us ogether, we could run the world, eh? Think about it!''

Ben was trying very hard not to when a pair of men
e recognized from the cargo hangar appeared at the
ecret doorway.

"You'd better come out here," one of them said.

"Can't you see I'm busy?"

"There is something—"

"Bring it in here. Now."

The two men looked at each other and shrugged.
One turned back around as if to reach for something
while the other ducked through the doorway and
waited. Ben watched as a figure was dragged through,
between the two men now as they faced Krechensky.

"We found this woman in the hangar," the man
said.

It was Danielle.

READY?'' BRICKLAND HAD asked her
minutes earlier after she had selected a pistol and submachine gun from the secret cache in the Town Car's
trunk.

Danielle wasn't looking forward to the battle she
suspected was in store, but she nodded anyway. She
knew Brickland was enjoying this because she understood the man well. Oh, not him specifically, but others in Israel who were no different. Men like this, who
were lucky enough to survive their youth, grew to understand the narrow line between life and death and
how to walk it. They weren't as fast or strong as they
used to be, and they couldn't splash blood with every
shot. But what they lacked in speed they made up for
in experience and cunning.

They had entered the loading shed together, slicing

a path through the clutter of cargo and continuing unti the pair of men guarding the final section of the shec came into view. Brickland stopped and checked hi weapons: the twelve-gauge short-handled pump in one hand, the submachine gun with double clip in the other, pistol jammed through the front of his belt.

Brickland signaled her to stay behind cover and wai while he pressed on. His confident gaze assured he he'd be back, but on the chance he failed she knew i would be up to her to finish this.

Only seconds passed before he returned, but time had slowed to a crawl. Danielle knew Brickland hac eliminated the two posted guards, but he was barely even breathing hard.

He gestured for her to follow him on.

They reached the spot where the guards had beer and crept into the mostly empty remainder of the shed Brickland signaled Danielle to move to the right while he shifted to the left in search of Ben. If neither founc him here in the shed, then they knew he would be or board the *Muna Zarifa*.

Brickland spun away, Danielle following almost in stantly. She curled around a line of empty cargo con tainers and pressed her back against one for cover. She was continuing her wide sweep of the shed around tc the dock when a pair of the garage-style doors rattlec closed, stealing a measure of the shed's light. She turned that way and glided into the newfound darkness until gunfire froze her: shotgun blasts interspersed with rapid bursts of automatic fire.

Brickland!

She whirled into the open and sprinted toward the source of the shots, cutting across the darkness anc dodging the light. More fire came from a different an-

gle, followed by screams this time, and she veered that
way down a narrow aisle between two long rows of
weather-beaten cargo containers that looked like
rusted hulks splashed bright by the sun. She swung
left and saw a huge forklift piled high with individual
brown bags coming straight for her. She turned to run,
but the driver stopped short, hurling the bags from
their perch. They crashed into her and she fell, scram-
bling free quickly and scampering to her feet.

She stooped to retrieve the submachine gun she'd
dropped when two men with rifles appeared amid the
spilled bags, barrels angling straight for her.

Danielle stood back up slowly with her hands in the
air, and one of the men slammed her against the nearest container. A harsh search followed, netting them
only the pistol she had jammed through her belt. The
second man slapped her hard in the face and she felt
blood trickling from her nose. Then he dragged her
through an open bay door beneath a huge dangling
crane toward the gangway leading up to the *Muna
Zarifa,* while the other held his distance with a submachine gun trained on her back.

Danielle moved stiffly, expecting Brickland to come
to her rescue at any moment. She figured he was waiting until she was on the gangway, where the narrow
confines would help swing the odds in his favor. Then
they would rush the ship together, in a hail of fire,
after Ben.

To her dismay there was no sign of him as she
reached the gangway's midpoint, or even when she
neared its close.

Once on deck, she saw the freighter's smoke stack
blow out huge plumes of smoke, horn blasting to signal her intention to get underway. Where was Brick-

land? Had he been ambushed, killed? Had the Russians inside the cargo hangar been lying in wait for both of them?

Danielle's escorts kept shoving, pushing, and prodding her down into one of the freighter's massive cargo holds, stopping only when they reached a hidden door impossibly built into the hull itself. Danielle shook the illusion off and realized she was looking at a secret compartment.

A brief exchange followed and then they forced her inside, where she came face to face with Ben and the stocky Russian standing next to him.

WE FOUND HER snooping around the hangar," Ben heard one of Danielle's escorts tell Krechensky "With these," the Russian added, and produced a pistol and submachine gun.

"She was alone?"

"No. There was another man."

"One?"

The Russian nodded. "He killed two of our men. Then I think we shot him."

"You're not sure?"

"We haven't found the body."

Krechensky turned to one of his massive bodyguards. "Tell the captain he is to get underway *immediately.*"

The hulk grunted his acknowledgment and hurried out of the secret hold. Krechensky turned to Ben.

"Others will be coming. We must put distance between them."

"With us still on board?" Ben posed, trying not to let his eyes linger on Danielle.

"I call for helicopter once we're at sea. Fun machine to ride. Just bought it last month." Krechensky turned toward Danielle. "That way we can dump her body." He looked at his two remaining hulks. "But first we have talk with her, see what enemies out there we don't know we have."

The two giants took a pair of twin steps forward, mirror images of each other. Ben watched as Danielle remained stock still, not giving an inch. He was calculating distances and his chances of grabbing a weapon, when gunfire from the foredeck echoed through the *Muna Zarifa*.

CHAPTER 63

IN THE MOMENT of confusion that followed, Danielle and Ben found each other's eyes and silently acknowledged what they had both realized:

Frank Brickland was on board!

Ben thought he saw Danielle nod, all but imperceptibly, and knew she was giving him a signal.

Ben lunged. Krechensky didn't even see him until the moment of impact that spun both of them against the bulkhead. Before the Russian could respond, Ben smashed an elbow into his throat and tore the big pistol from under his jacket. Krechensky gagged and grabbed his damaged windpipe with both hands as he fell to the floor.

The Russian's pistol was a forty-five caliber, old U.S. Army issue. Ben had never fired one before and when he started pulling the trigger it showed. He jerked the first shots hopelessly high, his ears numbed from the echo. But his eyes caught the two remaining hulks whirling to draw their weapons and the two workers who'd brought Danielle down here bringing theirs up. Instinct focused his aim on the hulking bodyguards and he began squeezing the trigger again.

He saw the throat of one of them explode in a burst of red, that man's gun lost before he found his trigger. The other looked as though he was being jerked backward by a rope, the big bullets punching into him before Ben dropped to a squat and turned to face the other gunmen.

One of them was writhing on the floor, clawing at his eyes where Danielle had no doubt focused her attack, his submachine gun forgotten on the other side of the door. She was still struggling with the second, pummeling him with blows as he too kept trying to steady his pistol on Ben. The barrel flashed orange and a shot clanged through the steel hold.

Then another bullet zipped by Ben's head, fired from somewhere else. He felt its heat and swung back toward the second hulking bodyguard he had shot. The big man's stomach had taken a forty-five round dead center, the shirt over it shredded and smoking from the heat of the round and escaping blood. Tattered material mixed with his ruptured innards, a wail of agony like a baby's cry piercing from him as he slumped down the wall but bringing his pistol up again nonetheless.

No, he couldn't be!

Ben resteadied Krechensky's forty-five and pulled the trigger.

Click.

Eight bullets, and he'd used them all. Not fourteen or more, as in a nine-millimeter.

How could I be so stupid!

He was staring helplessly down the barrel of the dying hulk's gun when the man's head snapped sideways, blood pouring from his temple as he finally sprawled lifeless. Ben swung to his right and saw Danielle ten feet away with her finger on her assailant's trigger, the smoking gun still grasped in his hand while they continued to struggle.

"AHHHHHHHHHHHHHHHH!"

Ben heard a guttural wail an instant before Krechenksy slammed into him. The Russian's hands dug into his scalp and cracked his head into the steel container packed with drugs. Spittle ran from both corners of Krechensky's mouth and his breath came in short wheezes thanks to the damage Ben had done to his windpipe. Krechensky pounded him against the container again and again to return the favor.

Danielle was so focused on the gun locked between her and her assailant that she only dimly recorded Ben's struggle. The man made the mistake of trying to slam her into the bulkhead, opening up his face for an elbow that shattered his nose. The pain made him relinquish enough grip on the pistol for Danielle to tear it free and fire three shots into him. She was turning toward Ben when she saw the other man she'd temporarily blinded groping for a submachine gun that dangled over the doorjamb.

It took two shots to drop him before he reached it and Danielle again swung toward Ben. She had sighted down her barrel on the stocky Russian when his third hulking bodyguard exploded back through the doorway and smashed into her.

Danielle's breath fled her like it had been sucked right out. She gasped for air, lost her bearings, and felt the hulk's thumbs close on her windpipe. She heard herself gasping, bulging eyes recording everything before her in eerie surreal motion. The hulk drew his clenched hands upward, sneering, and Danielle was dimly aware of her feet dangling in the air.

Across the compartment, something like a warm blanket had spread over Ben by the sixth impact against the steel container. His hands sought grasp on something, *anything*, to deaden the impact, and closed on a latch already weakened by the blows from his own body. It gave as soon as he grabbed it and he tore the loosened panel free with his fingers. It came away bent and jagged at the rear. He tightened both hands upon it. Then, when Krechensky jerked him backward yet again, Ben added his own momentum to the move and jammed the jagged side of the panel toward the Russian's eyes.

He felt the makeshift weapon dig home, Krechensky's screech ringing in his ears. The Russian's hands groped for his face as he stumbled away, wailing in agony, bouncing off the walls as he shook his head in all directions, fingers held as if to catch the blood running through them. Ben staggered and threw down his makeshift weapon, watching Krechensky slide to the floor writhing, head held between his knees.

Ben swiped a sleeve across his face, clearing away enough of the blood leaking from his head wound to see Danielle kicking her dangling feet desperately. The hulk holding tight to her neck was shaking her, making her look like a rag doll as her features purpled toward death.

Ben rushed him and pounded the man with a vicious series of wild blows. When they seemed to have no effect whatsoever, Ben swung toward the door and saw the discarded submachine gun propped up against the jamb.

He scampered for the gun and was aiming even as he drew it to him. By the time he opened fire, Danielle's hands hung useless by her sides. The switch must have been set on Semi, because the best the submachine gun would give him was single shots as quick as he could fire them. Ben started forward pulling the trigger, but the hulk seemed not to feel the bullets tear into him, refusing to let go his grasp on Danielle.

Finally, in desperation, Ben pressed the barrel right against the man's spine and fired again and again. The hulk's whole body jerked as though he'd been shocked each time. But his hands still clutched Danielle's throat, refusing to let go. Ben could smell the stench of burning fabric and could see the neat black charred holes in the hulk's suit jacket that quickly reddened for each pull of the trigger.

At last the hulk sank to his knees. Danielle collapsed to the floor, his hands still locked on her throat until Ben pried them free. She was unconscious and breathing shallowly. Ben felt the pulse in her neck as he lifted her to him. Her weight buckled his knees and they dropped together, Danielle ending up in his lap, her face still deeply discolored. Ben just sat there holding her, unable to move, when he felt a sudden shift of motion. He tensed, feeling the floor was being separated from him. Then his shoulders came to rest again against the bulkhead as the entire hold yawed.

The *Muna Zarifa* had gotten underway.

CHAPTER 64

It was the sound of Danielle's breathing against him that snapped Ben alert. He looked at her and realized only one of his eyes was working.

He probed a hand up fearfully, expecting to touch an empty socket where the eyeball used to be. But what he found was merely blood left over from the cracks Krechensky had given his skull.

Krechensky!

He remembered him just before an angry wail preceded the stocky Russian's charge across the hold. Ben thrust Danielle from him and jammed a hand under the final hulk's smoldering jacket for the pistol he'd glimpsed there.

By the time he found it, Krechensky was reaching for him. Ben's first bullet blew the Russian's knee apart. Momentum carried him sideways and he crumpled near Danielle. He had swallowed her face in his huge hands, intending to slam her head into the bulkhead, when Ben wheeled and stuck the pistol against his skull. He pulled the trigger and the muffled *splat* of the gunshot was followed by a sound like mud hitting a wall. Ben felt a back-blast of skull fragments bite into his cheek and jaw and turned away from the spray of gore sliding down the steel bulkhead toward Krechensky's near-headless corpse.

The sounds of gunfire brought Danielle back to consciousness. She willed the strength back into her legs and tried to hoist herself to her feet, rasping out dry heaving coughs as if something was stuck deep in her throat. She couldn't speak yet and was desperately mouthing words when Ben moved along the bulkhead to join her.

They embraced and the slight sway reminded them the ship was in motion, reminded them they, too, had better move. The stench of bitter gunsmoke, pungent blood, and death itself assaulted them relentlessly as they started back for the door and the outer hold beyond. They were almost there when a shape rushed through it.

Krechensky's *driver,* a pistol rising in his hand. Ben threw himself in front of Danielle, heard the shot, felt something thud into him.

Opened his eyes.

The driver lay facedown at his feet, a blotch of red spreading across his back.

Colonel Frank Brickland stood in the doorway to the secret hold, smoking pistol in hand. He stepped inside, looked around, and shook his head.

''What a fucking mess.''

* * *

LEAVE YOU ALONE for a few minutes and
ook what happens. . . .''

Ben had pressed part of his jacket against his skull
o stanch the flow of blood. Danielle tried to take a
step, stumbled, and fell over into Brickland's arms.

"Come on, ma'am, come on. I'm gonna need you.
'm gonna need both of you.'' His breath smelled like
stale cigars.

Ben lowered his jacket and looked at him.

"We ain't waiting for the Coast Guard,'' Brickland
old them.

BACK IN THE outer cargo hold, Brickland read-
ed a submachine gun in one hand and a shotgun in
he other.

For Ben, the next few minutes became a blur of
bodies and bullets. Brickland led the way down a nar-
ow corridor atop a floor formed by a steel grate before
starting the trek upward for the deck. Each step, it
eemed, brought more gun-wielding crew members
nto their path. Brickland dealt with them impassively,
barely slowing his pace as he rotated his fire between
he submachine gun and the shotgun, turning the *Muna
Zarifa* into a labyrinth of blood-splattered death.

Brickland started up a steep, almost ladderlike staircase just before a pair of crew members' footsteps
clamored downward. The reverberations from the
quick shotgun blasts in such narrow confines deafened
both Ben and Danielle. Brickland waited to cover
hem, as they climbed over the corpses.

They had reached the last sublevel before the main
deck and had swung into the shaft of another narrow
stairwell when a barrage of fire sprayed down at them.

Ben brought Danielle to him, watching the colonel bound up the stairs firing his submachine gun in a constant scream. Bullets clanged everywhere around Ben, the dull screeches peppering his already weakened eardrums. A chorus of screams punctuated the end of the gunfire and then Brickland poked his head down into the shaft.

"Coast's clear," he called. "Let's go."

Ben could see daylight now and climbed anxiously toward it, Danielle slumped against him again. Brickland reached the main deck first and had squatted to help Ben hoist her up, when a bullet caught the colonel in the thigh. He spun away and fired with both weapons as he toppled backward down through the hatchway. Ben caught him, cushioning his plunge, then eased Brickland carefully to the floor.

"Shit," Brickland rasped, his leg giving out under him. "And to think I was gonna push you two overboard, finish this myself."

"We weren't paying you enough for that."

"That's why I wasn't bothering with life jackets." He grimaced badly. "Fuck, that hurts." He squeezed his leg until he could get a tourniquet in place. "Well hoss, I guess that leaves the rest up to you. You go and get it done, while your missus and I guard the door."

"Get *what* done?"

"Blow the freighter." He balled up a section of his shirt he'd torn off and winced as he tightened it around the bullet wound. "Gonna turn these fucking drugs into a giant Alka-Seltzer tablet in a glass of Hudson River water."

*   *   *

BRICKLAND EXPLAINED HOW to reach the engine room and mapped out for Ben what to do when he got there. Amazing how simple it was to set fire to an old freighter like the *Muna Zarifa*. The ancient diesel-burning lines and nonfireproof material made it scarcely a challenge. The challenge would come when Ben reached the engine room, depending on the level of resistance he encountered. With only the nine-millimeter pistol the colonel had given him for firepower, there had better not be much.

Brickland's route took him the back way through the cavernous layers of the old ship, into the deep lower bowels. Taking it meant retracing his steps down the same ladder-like stairs they had used to reach the main deck. Ben felt the heat increase as he dropped ever lower, the unventilated hull acting like an oven.

Encountering no resistance, he reached a complex of catwalks that rose twenty feet above the hull's black bottom. Thirty feet over those catwalks was the engine room. Part of its floor had been finished in a grate to help drain the enormous volume of heat that would otherwise make working within it intolerable. Ben ducked through a hatchway that reminded him somewhat of a submarine, and reviewed the rest of Brickland's plan in his mind.

Cross the catwalk through this section to a ladder where he would—

The sound of many footsteps rapidly coming his way from the left made him stop. He charged back to the hatch he had passed through to reach this cavernous pipe room and grabbed hold of the rounded steel door. The thing was monstrously heavy and probably hadn't been closed for years, its joints rusted through.

It took all his strength just to budge it, but Ben managed to get it sealed an instant before the sailors came down a nearby ladder. He slammed a bolt lock into the rusted slots tailored for it and moved on, satisfied the approaching party would be kept out.

He then sped down a catwalk for the ladder Brickland had described, only to hear another flood of footsteps converging from the right side of the cavern. The door to this hatch gave with less resistance and clanked shut just as he heard the first party trying to bang their way through directly across the floor.

Ben backed off, heart hammering against his chest, intending to enact the rest of Brickland's scheme. He headed for a steel ladder that rose from a pumping station to the engine room above, at once realizing the folly of trying to commandeer the entire facility with a single pistol.

Then his eyes fell on the network of pipes rising from the pumping station, locking on a warning in faded paint printed just above a turn wheel and spigot:

WARNING: DO NOT OPEN TO PURGE SYSTEM
UNTIL ENGINES ARE SHUT DOWN

Those engines now, of course, were running. Ben could hear them cranking noisily in the engine room above. Heavy diesel fuel crawled like blood through the *Muna Zarifa*'s rusted network of steel veins. The nearby spigot was intended to bleed the pipes of excess air bubbles which could severely curtail engine performance. So if he opened it now . . .

Deviating slightly from Brickland's instructions, he leaned over, joined both his hands on the wheel, and

turned. He felt a rumbling after the first spin, followed
by a heavy wisp of air. Halfway through the second
turn, a jet of air burst from the nozzle beneath the
spigot, followed by a series of what sounded like rasping coughs. Ben had backed off by the time the black
fuel began to ooze out, the stream slow at first, then
steady, and finally gushing out in torrents that carried
it across the length of the catwalk, staining the rusted
grating an even darker color.

Ben tore a strip of fabric from his shirt and then
soaked it with some diesel oil. He climbed ten rungs
of the ladder leading to the engine room and stopped
to remove Brickland's lighter from his pocket. Wedg-
ing an arm through the rung even with his chest, Ben
touched the flame to the scrap of his oil-soaked shirt
and watched the fuel catch instantly. He held it out
over the catwalk, now engulfed in huge rivulets of oil
spewing down through its grated layers to the very
bottom of the ship, and dropped it.

The flaming rag fluttered through the air, settling
over the catwalk. It touched oil and Ben saw a cloud
of black smoke before the first flame peeked out and
quickly spread in both directions down the catwalk.
Ben began climbing as fast as he could, glancing once
or twice at the fire intensifying below. By the time he
reached a hatch that led into the engine room, the oil
dripping beneath the catwalk had caught too, making
it seem as though the air itself was on fire.

Ben slammed his way through the hatch, before the
befuddled stares of the nearby workers.

"Naar!" he screamed in Arabic. "Fire! Get out!"

A huge fuel tank against the far wall exploded to
punctuate his warning. In the next moment, men were
rushing in all directions as the flames spread through

the engine room. No sprinklers switched on to fight it. An old-fashioned bell alarm began to clang, covering the workers' desperate screams as they ran, the flames starting to appear on all sides now, with Ben caught in the middle.

THE FIRE ALARM had just started wailing when Brickland and Danielle returned to the main deck. The sharp, gritty smell of an oil fire assaulted their nostrils even before the black smoke belched up from below, followed by the sound of explosion after explosion, each shaking the freighter more violently. They watched as the crew topside frantically began lowering lifeboats down the length of the *Muna Zarifa*'s hull to the water. Others unfolded rope ladders and dangled them over the starboard side to provide access. The order to abandon ship must have already been given.

"Ben," Danielle murmered.

"Boy's got a knack for overdoing things, don't he?" Brickland said, still wincing in pain. "I think I'll get us one of those lifeboats. You stay here, wait for your boyfriend."

He left her the shotgun and hoisted himself over the rail onto a ladder that descended all the way to the water. Danielle turned back to stare at the stairwell Ben had disappeared down, willing him to appear. But all she saw was more of the black smoke that was quickly overtaking the entire ship. Any man trapped down there . . .

The thought terrified her. Ben couldn't die after all this. She couldn't bear another life to be stripped from her! Both brothers, her mother, her father wasting away. Not Ben. *Not Ben!*

Danielle took a deep breath and plunged into the blackness.

BEN KEPT CLIMBING. The black smoke choked off most of his breath and stole his vision, leaving him only ladders and stairs to feel for and take without thought of direction. He could feel the heat nipping closer at him with each frantic step.

He grew lightheaded, had no idea where he was, realized suddenly his hands weren't working anymore. He could smell clean air somewhere close, knew the main deck and the outside world were in reach, but he couldn't find them. Felt himself starting to slump, his lungs begging for air that was denied, when a pair of hands closed blindly upon him.

Ben felt himself jerked back to his feet and yanked upward, his feet thumping over steel steps. His lungs grabbed thirstily for the fresher air. His eyes found some light. He grasped the railing with both hands and helped pull himself upward. At last he emerged into the bright sun with Danielle still holding fast, pulling him toward the railing.

"Come on!" the voice of Frank Brickland screamed from below, where he was balancing himself painfully in a lifeboat.

Danielle helped Ben drag his legs and torso over the rail, holding on while he stretched out for the ladder and grabbed the top rung.

"I'll be right above you. Just keep going."

Ben negotiated the rungs with surprising ease. He kept focusing on one at a time and staring straight ahead at the ship's hull. He heard Brickland calling to him just before he thumped down to the lifeboat, taking the colonel to the deck when Brickland tried to reach up and guide him in.

"You're a real pain in the ass, Benny, you know that?"

Danielle dropped behind them and took control of the oars. With powerful strokes, she rowed the lifeboat away from the tanker, enshrouded now in a blackened haze. The smoke continued to bellow from it, the first of the flames appearing when they were a hundred feet away. The explosions followed rapidly in a series of poofs that coughed miniature fireballs into the air, temporarily lighting the blackness of the deck.

By the time a cabin cruiser fished the three of them from the water, the *Muna Zarifa* was nothing more than a floating coffin, charred barbecue-black, its load of cargo lost forever.

DAY TEN

CHAPTER 65

THE FLIGHT FROM New York City to Amman was about to land right on schedule early Wednesday afternoon. Ben lifted a nervous eye from his watch and gently rousted Danielle, who had slept for virtually the entire twelve-hour duration of their trip. They were due to land just a few hours before the official reconvening of the peace talks.

"We're back," he told her.

She didn't smile.

"You know we can never go home," Danielle had said as they huddled together on the cabin cruiser's deck the day before, watching the *Muna Zarifa*'s slow death continue, the smoke and flames visible for miles.

"We can if we're willing to face what's waiting for us."

"We're pariahs. We turned against our own people, disobeyed. We're traitors, Ben. That's the way they'll see it."

Ben's face tightened. "I left once. I'm not leaving again."

"What's the alternative?"

"Show the world who the real traitors are. Tell the truth both sides wanted so much to hide."

"And you think we can survive *that*?"

"Can we survive a life on the run? Because, Danielle, that's our only other choice. Keeping everything quiet only makes this a race to see which side can kill us first."

Frank Brickland swung toward them from the rigid post he had held at the gunwale. He dragged his wounded leg forward and leaned against the cabin for support.

"Only one way you can handle this, hoss, and that's to get them before they get you."

"We can't get them all, Colonel."

"You get enough, you won't have to get them all. I can help you with the groundwork, show you how to get it done without dirtying your own pistols. Your part of the world's got lots of hate. Makes things easy to manipulate."

Ben shook his head. "Not this time."

"It's the way of the world, Benny."

"*Your* world maybe. Not ours."

"Can I ask you a question, Colonel?" from Danielle.

"My calendar's open right now," Brickland replied, a smile rising through his next grimace.

"In the cargo hangar, when I heard you shooting—"

"Yeah," he interrupted. "I did it to draw you over there, make you think I needed help."

"Why?"

"Because I needed a distraction to help me get on board."

"You could have mentioned your intentions in advance."

"Sorry, ma'am, but the fact was, I never worked with you before and all the discussion in the world wouldn't change the fact that I didn't know how you were going to perform." He cocked his gaze toward the smoke-shrouded freighter. "My priority was getting on that boat."

"There had to be another way then and there's got to be another way now," Danielle insisted.

"There wasn't and there isn't, ma'am."

"No," said Ben, eyes widening in realization, "I think there might be."

Now, as the jet taxied for the gate, Ben ignored the flight attendant's warning not to move until the seatbelt sign was turned off, and fished a small tote bag from his overhead compartment. He kept it close to him as they disembarked.

Danielle was right at his elbow when they approached the end of the jetway to find Commander Omar Shaath waiting, flanked by Jordanian police officers armed with machine guns. The machine guns stayed at their sides, their presence enough to make the point.

"Inspector," Shaath greeted Ben ebulliently when they reached him, "how good of you to return yet again. I see you haven't learned anything from your mistakes."

"It runs in the family," Ben said. Even though he held back his rage, he looked into Shaath's eyes and had the feeling the commander knew exactly what he was referring to.

Shaath stuck a hand forward. "I'll take that case."

Ben held it out to him stiffly. "You can let the woman go," he said, sneaking a glance at Danielle.

"I could, but I won't. We'll see how badly the Israelis want her back. They're still holding three thousand Palestinians prisoner, you know." He smirked. "You should have learned from your first mistake."

Shaath didn't open the tote bag until they were inside a police van. Handcuffed now, Ben watched him from two seats back fumbling with the double zipper, finally getting it open and withdrawing an opaque ziplock bag. He fingered its contents through the plastic, testing its weight.

"How'd you sneak your little souvenir on the plane?" Shaath wondered.

"You have better sources than I gave you credit for, Commander," Ben told him.

"Just answer the question, Inspector."

"The bag is coated with lead. Gives the X-ray machine a false reading."

Shaath held the bag up for Ben to see. "You expected this to save you, no doubt. Use it so the two of you could prove your twisted story to your respective superiors. I would think exposing *the whole truth* of what transpired to the entire world would be a better approach. Let everyone learn how the Israelis dispatched an assassin to mimic the killings of al-Diib."

"You can't prove that."

"You left me all the information I need to prove it. And what little you didn't was easy to piece together." He held the opaque bag up for Ben to see. "Now you've given me the final bit of proof I need: a sample of Fasil's drugs. Distributed and sold with the express purpose of endowing Hamas's terrorist actions until

the Palestinians regain what is rightfully ours. Yes,
Inspector, the world *needs* to know.''

"You'll destroy the peace talks, our chance for
statehood.''

"I'll destroy a sham, a display of kowtowing that
sickens any Palestinian who remembers a time when
we weren't held hostage on our own land. Let the
terror continue. Let the fighting continue. Anything is
better than watching Arafat kiss Israeli ass, just as your
father wanted us to do.''

Again Ben bit down his rage. "You'll set the process back *years*. The damage will be irreparable!''

"My people will be better off.'' Then, after a brief
pause, he added, "You and the woman will accompany me, Inspector. It's the least I can do.'' A cruel,
thin smile crossed the big man's lips. "After all, I
couldn't have done this without you.''

T HE VENUE OF the peace talks had been
changed, incredibly, to Jerusalem, forcing a last-
minute scramble among the participating diplomats
and media officials who needed to book rooms and
transportation. The King David had been chosen as the
meeting site, ironically fitting since this very hotel had
been the setting for an Israeli raid back when Israel
was fighting for its own independence.

The King David had remained generally unchanged
in the many years since it had been rebuilt. Its ele-
gance lay in its tradition, although Ben could tell the
magnificent marble floor and plush leather seating in
the lobby were relatively new, along with the beautiful
arrangements of fresh flowers from one end to the
other.

He and Danielle entered the hotel, their handcuffs removed, but both protectively enclosed by Shaath's security troops. The commander's pass got him through the entrance and into the hubbub of the lobby, where no one seemed to notice him.

He hustled the group toward a private meeting room where a press conference featuring the Palestinian delegates was already underway. He carried the Zip-loc bag Ben had brought with him from America in a zippered briefcase pressed tightly under his arm.

He signaled his men to hold Ben and Danielle in the rear of the conference room while he squeezed through the crowd of reporters toward the front. From his vantage point, Ben could see a large wooden table with the Palestinian flag suspended from its front and draped toward the floor. A podium had been set up alongside the table, but the delegates, including Arafat in the center and Mayor Ghazi Sumaya on the far right of the seven participants, had thus far elected not to make use of it.

"President Arafat," one of the reporters called, "please comment on the continued refusal of the Israelis to discuss the partition of Jerusalem."

"The issue on the table," Arafat began humbly, "is not partition, but the creation of a mutual capital our two peoples can share in name."

Reporters scribbled furiously across their pads. Cameras whirred. Flashbulbs popped. Video cameras zoomed in for closeups, as a buzz spread through the room. It stopped when the room's occupants saw Commander Omar Shaath take his spot behind the podium. Ben watched Arafat turn to Mayor Sumaya, who whispered something that obviously didn't please the Palestinian leader.

Shaath was opening the zipper of his attaché case. "I apologize for my tardiness, Mr. President and other onored delegates. Ladies and gentlemen," he said to he gathered media which had turned its collective eye pon him, "the leaders of our proud people entrusted he with a mission I have only just completed, uncovring something they have insisted I make known to ou without any further delay."

Arafat had risen to his feet, fuming, stabbing the air vith his hand as he addressed the delegates nearest im. He had even started to move toward the podium imself when Shaath opened the zip-lock bag and tarted to tip it upside down, releasing the contents for ll to see.

"I give you the source of my reason for coming ere."

Ben watched Shaath gaze down in befuddlement vhen the assembled crowd of reporters remained silent xcept for the exchange of a few murmurs and scat-ered chuckles.

Sand was running out of the bag, spilling off a pile t had made on the podium all the way to the floor elow.

"Sand," someone said.

"Sand from the Sinai Desert," Ben elaborated oudly from the back of the room as he burst past the 'alestinian police guards with Danielle at his side.

All eyes in the room swung toward the two of them, ncluding Arafat's and Sumaya's. But it was Shaath's ate-filled gaze that Ben locked onto, watching the ommander's confident expression turn to shock as he ealized he'd been had.

That was for my father, you bastard, Ben thought, wishing Shaath could read his mind.

"Chief Inspector Barnea of the Israeli National Police and I bring it here today as a symbol of peace already established."

"And who are you?" a reporter asked, but some of them recognized him and were feverishly writing on their notepads again.

"Inspector Bayan Kamal of the Palestinian police force."

A murmur spread through the crowd. Photographers squeezed forward to snap pictures.

"Are you the detective who captured and killed the serial killer known as the Wolf?"

Ben eased Danielle up alongside him. "The two of us did it together, an Israeli and a Palestinian. Perpetuating that kind of relationship is what this conference is about." Ben turned back toward the delegates in the front of the room. "That is why our esteemed President and Mayor Sumaya of Jericho from the Palestinian Council asked the two of us to come. And we brought with us this talisman that . . ." Ben paused here and stared Shaath right in the eye. ". . . Commander Shaath was kind enough to display."

Arafat smiled and seemed to nod toward someone in the back of the room.

Sumaya glared at Shaath, who lumbered away from the podium.

The pack of reporters thrust more questions at Ben and Danielle, but they shrugged all of them off, deferring the answers to the distinguished panel better suited to answer them. Ben caught a glimpse of Major Nabril al-Asi hovering at the pack's rear, smiling at him, his expression coming up just short of a wink. The major exchanged a few words with an older Israeli man, casually dressed in a sports shirt and smoking a

igarette, before moving off to intercept Commander
haath.

"I *know* that man," Danielle said softly, watching
he Israeli slide discreetly from the room.

"What do you mean?"

She hesitated, looked as though she didn't trust her
yes. "Never mind."

Ben and Danielle slipped out of the room minutes
ater and quickly extricated themselves from even the
most stubborn reporters, en route to a deserted, book-
ined library just off the King David's lobby.

They embraced as soon as they had gotten inside,
he door closed behind them.

"You did it," Danielle said, after they finally parted
o catch their breaths. "They can't treat us like pariahs
ow. We'll be heroes with our pictures plastered in
very major newspaper in the world."

"I hope they got my good side."

"So what happens now? Would you like to be
round here when history is made?"

"Let's stay. . . . No, on second thought, let's get out
of here. I can think of plenty of better places to spend
he rest of the week."

"So can I," said a new voice.

Ben turned and saw a figure seated in a chair across
he room, his back to them. Ben thought for an instant
t might be Frank Brickland, until he saw a hand grasp
cane and lean upon it for support.

"You did very well at the press conference," Zaid
abral complimented, rising. "I thank you for saving
he entire story for the exclusive you promised me."

"I'll tell you the whole story. Then you can decide
how much of it they'll let you print."

"I think, more than anything this time, I just want to hear it. Then someday . . ."

"Always someday."

"Your friend Yousef Shifa called me," Jabral told Ben. "The Israelis held him overnight but will be releasing him this afternoon. I told them he worked for me, agreed to pay for all the damages."

"Thank you."

"I'll send you the bill." Jabral limped toward them. "How does it feel to be a hero again, Inspector?"

Ben looked at Danielle. "I don't think I make a very good one, to tell you the truth."

"Oh, by the way. I ran a story on that boy Radji and his sister in yesterday's edition. The Israeli press picked it up and printed it today. I'm told the hospitals treating them have been flooded with donations, adoption requests, even a film offer from Hollywood."

"They won't be going back to the camp, then."

"Not unless it's in the script." Jabral stopped a few feet from them. "And what about you, Inspector?"

"Home suits me just fine." Ben looped an arm around Danielle's shoulder. "Suits *us* just fine."

"And just where might that be?" Jabral wondered.

"It doesn't matter," Danielle replied.

"Just leave a number with me for when Hollywood calls. They're bound to, you know. I'd get working on the sequel now if I were you."

Ben drew Danielle against him, smiling. "We'll see what we can do."